CONFUSED ROARING

CONFUSED ROARING

Evelyn Waugh and
the Modernist Tradition

GEORGE McCARTNEY

INDIANA UNIVERSITY PRESS
Bloomington and Indianapolis

Manufactured in the United States of America

Library of Congress Cataloging-in-Publication Data

McCartney, George.
Confused roaring.

Bibliography: p.
Includes Index.
1. Waugh, Evelyn, 1903–1966—Criticism and interpretation. 2. Modernism (Literature) I. Title.
PR6045.A97Z735   1987   823'.912   86–46166
ISBN 0–253–31411–9

1 2 3 4 5 91 90 89 88 87

For Anne-Marie

CONTENTS

ACKNOWLEDGMENTS   xi

Introduction   2
    I. Confused Roaring   8
   II. Desire, Doubt, and the Superb Mean   21
  III. An Unguided and Half-Comprehended Study
      of Metaphysics   36
   IV. A Pure Aesthete   51
    V. Smashing and Crashing: Waugh on the
      Modernist Esthetic   66
   VI. Becoming Characters: The Shameless Blonde and
      the Mysteriously Disappearing Self   75
  VII. Film: The Glaring Lens of Satire   99
 VIII. The Satirist of the Film World   110
   IX. Chromium Plating and Natural Sheepskin:
      The New Barbarians   136
    X. The Wisdom of the Eye   155
   XI. Fanatical Existence vs. Aesthetic Education   169

NOTES   175
SELECTED BIBLIOGRAPHY   181
INDEX   186

In Memory of Frank Brady

This book would have remained an unrealized aspiration were it not for Frank Brady, who patiently helped me understand that I could do it if only I made up my mind to put in the effort required. In the year before his unexpected death, he generously assisted me as I struggled with my manuscript. He read the draft in installments, offering invaluable advice for improving it. I can't say I always welcomed his comments. They too often revealed my shortcomings and negligence, and, besides, I was impatient to get the manuscript off my hands. But my haste never deterred Frank. When I suggested he was being overly fastidious, he gently reminded me that, however laudable my desire for dispatch, the project would go nowhere unless I spent the time necessary to make it readable. "Of course, you want to go on to your next book," he graciously allowed, "but you've got a few more things to do here if you're to have a first." I'd grumble, carry off the manuscript, and wring the offending passages through another rewrite. Frustrating as it was, I know now that Frank was doing his best to prevent me from boring people with my partially considered enthusiasms. To do so, he was kind enough to endure them himself. For this and so much more, I will always remember him. He was an uncompromising professional, a consummate teacher, and a fiercely loyal friend. I was privileged to know him.

Shortly after Frank completed the major work of his career, *James Boswell, The Later Years,* he told me that he no longer worried much about the prospect of death. It was not that he had any particular reason to think his end near. He just wanted his friends to know that should it come he would not object strenuously. Hadn't he been given the time he needed to achieve his goals? Although I believe he meant what he said and rejoice that his last three years were among his happiest and most contented, this knowledge does not make his passing any easier to accept.

Frank Brady, Distinguished Professor of the Graduate School and University Center of the City University of New York, Chairman of the Editorial Committee in charge of the Yale Boswell Editions, died September 2, 1986.

There is no remedy for our loss.

ACKNOWLEDGMENTS

I would like to express my gratitude to the people and institutions who made it possible for me to write the book that follows. There is first my mentor, David Gordon of the Graduate School and University Center of the City University of New York, who assisted me in writing the dissertation from which this study grew. His editorial advice and patient encouragement were invaluable. Without them, I would not have been able to complete the first phase of my project.

Robert Day, Irving Howe, Alfred Kazin, and Michael Timko also read the dissertation, contributing important insights, which I hope I have been able to incorporate successfully into the book.

I owe debts of gratitude to the American Council of Learned Societies and the National Endowment for the Humanities for the financial assistance that permitted me to take fifteen months leave from my teaching duties and put the manuscript into its final shape. It was during this time that I had the pleasure of visiting the Humanities Research Center at the University of Texas in Austin. While there I was graciously assisted by Cathy Henderson and her staff in my research of the center's Evelyn Waugh holdings. Later the same year, I traveled to London, where I was able to draw upon the resources of the British Museum; I also had the honor of meeting Auberon Waugh, who was good enough to clarify a number of issues regarding his father's life and career.

I also wish to thank the people at my school, St. John's University, who assisted me. Dorothy Canner's word processing staff typed my drafts with care and dispatch. My chairman, Jack Franzetti, listened, sympathized, and gave of his time to write letters and memoranda on my behalf. And, finally, I owe a special debt of gratitude to Dean Catherine Ruggieri of St. Vincent's College on whose faculty I teach. Her unfailing support and generous vision have opened more than a few doors for me.

Portions of the first three chapters appeared in *The American Spectator* 18 (January 1985). I thank Wladyslaw Pleszczynski, the *Spectator*'s managing editor, for permitting me to reprint this material.

CONFUSED ROARING

TEXT CITATIONS

Quotations from Waugh's works generally come from the Little, Brown edition (see Selected Bibliography). The works are identified in the text by title and the quotations are cited by page numbers in parentheses. Wherever a reference might be ambiguous, I have included a title abbreviation with the page reference as follows:

CRSD *Charles Ryder's Schooldays and Other Stories*
LO *The Loved One*
MAA *Men at Arms*

INTRODUCTION

Although Evelyn Waugh rarely missed an opportunity to flaunt his traditionalism, he was not a traditional satirist. If conventional satire seeks to correct morals and manners, then his work clearly does not conform to the genre. What can the moralist make of the world Paul Pennyfeather and Margot Metroland inhabit, a world in which decent people are invariably boring and the wicked consistently charming? When critics try to evaluate Waugh's novels in terms of moral satire, they either give up the effort, deciding there is no coherent purpose to be discovered, or reduce the works to a formula that inevitably fails to account for their anarchic vitality.[1] As for Waugh himself, he flatly denied he was writing satire at all. The genre, he argued, "flourishes in a stable society and presupposes homogeneous moral standards. . . . It exposes polite cruelty and folly by exaggerating them. It seeks to produce shame. All this has no place in the Century of the Common Man where vice no longer pays lip service to virtue."[2]

Of course, this disclaimer is probably best understood as Waugh's consummate satiric ploy. Whether or not it was meant as such, it does reveal his primary concern: the bankruptcy of a civilization unable or unwilling to sustain its commitment to the metaphysical principles that had made moral distinctions possible in the first place. If Waugh is to be considered within the genre at all, it must first be said that his satiric objective was not moral but metaphysical and it is on this ground that his work achieves its consistency of purpose. Lapses in conduct, however outrageous, were never his preoccupation, though frequently his delight. He fully expected people would behave badly with or without moral standards and had no hesitation in admitting his own failings. Nor did he think his century any less moral than those that had preceded it. In his view, the real issue was the general disillusionment with the notion of absolutes, whether moral or metaphysical. After the tragic wastefulness of the Great War, "the standards of civilization" had come into question. Their legitimacy, he complained, no longer seemed self-evident. Instead of submitting to their "rigid discipline," people were inclined to cultivate "a jolly tolerance of everything that seemed modern."[3] For Waugh, this amounted to a profoundly dispiriting dereliction that could only serve to undermine the intellectual resolve necessary to maintain civilized order. "It is better to be narrow-minded," he reasoned, "than to have no mind, to hold limited and rigid principles than none at all."[4]

Waugh's first novel loudly demonstrates the consequences of tolerating a mindless lack of principles. It opens and closes with the "confused roaring" raised by the sons of England's ruling families "baying for broken glass" as they carouse through Oxford's colleges destroying every symbol of art and learning they come upon.[5] Their behavior goes conspicuously unchecked by the university's authorities who have chosen instead to hide in their darkened rooms. Such is the modern world, Waugh implies, where willful energy, lacking the discipline of a self-assured moral intelligence founded upon inarguable principles, expresses itself resentfully in random acts of destruction.

The one constant in Waugh's fiction is his portrayal of what happens to a society that disregards the metaphysical coordinates which had once given it a sense of purpose. This was a condition he thought especially apparent in the contemporary enthusiasms for experimental art and technological innovation. He read both as symptoms of a general decline into an aimless pursuit of the new. The prospect might be enticing, but it was nonetheless futile. It only excited a boundless appetite for fashion that deserved the ridicule he was glad to heap on it.

For all his disapproval, however, Waugh's response to the modern was marked by certain fruitful ambivalence. In his official pose he was the curmudgeon who despised innovation, but the anarchic artist in him frequently delighted in its formal and thematic possibilities. He was never quite the scourge of the new he pretended to be, though he did work on the role.

Writing of himself in the third person in his autobiographical novel, *The Ordeal of Gilbert Pinfold*, he announced that his "strongest tastes were negative. He abhorred plastics, Picasso, sunbathing and jazz—everything in fact that had happened in his own lifetime" (p. 11).[6] He went to a good deal of effort and expense to remove himself from the world that featured these abominations. At the age of thirty-four, this once intensely urban socialite set up house in the West Country far from London where he could ostentatiously turn his back on modernity in all its guises. When he began to lose his hearing in later life, he was pleased to transform his affliction into an emblem of his chosen isolation. Instead of an efficient battery-run hearing aid, he carried about a comically oversized Victorian ear trumpet, wielding it with blatant buffoonery as if he wanted to visually dramatize his inability to hear what the world had to say to him. But, for all his advertised disgust with contemporary developments, he kept remarkably informed about them. Throughout his writing career we find him addressing modern art, functional architecture, photography, and film—"everything in fact that had happened in his own lifetime." As a young man he rode motorcycles, flew with a stunt pilot, produced a film in which he co-starred with Elsa Lanchester, and commuted to Paris by plane. During the war, he volunteered for commando service, reporting later that his parachute training was particularly exhilarating even if he did break his leg on his first jump. For all his country-squire affectations, Waugh was very much a man of his century.

It has too often been assumed that Waugh was a sharper-tongued Wodehouse, a more substantial Firbank, or, to borrow Sean O'Faolain's formula, "a purely brainless genius, with a gift for satire," who created his own idiosyncratic world redolent of Edwardian nostalgia.[7] A closer reading suggests he had far more in common with modernists like Wyndham Lewis and T.S. Eliot. Like them he was keenly interested in the peculiarities of life in the twentieth century. True, he was never comfortable in this century. But it is hard to imagine him at home in any other. He certainly had little love for the nineteenth. In novel after novel, he ridicules those of his characters who try to go on living as though the Great War had never happened, as though the achievement of true happiness were only a matter of perpetuating the attitudes and values of the previous age. He portrays their world to be as laughably fraudulent as Llanabba Castle in *Decline and Fall,* an ordinary enough nineteenth-century country house the front of which has been made over to give it the appearance of venerable antiquity. This was the work of an enterprising mill owner who could not abide his workers' enforced idleness during the "cotton famine" caused by the American Civil War. Believing in enlightened self-interest and having nothing better to do with his employees, he had them build a "formidably feudal" facade for his home enhanced by "at least a mile of machicolated wall" and gates that are "towered and turreted and decorated with heraldic animals and a workable portcullis" (p. 18). Under the circumstances, the labor was cheap and the results charmingly Gothic. It was just this sort of blend of pragmatism and sentimentality for which the nineteenth century stood indicted in Waugh's mind. It was guilty of exploiting a cultural past for its purely decorative value, while neglecting its moral and metaphysical implications.

When this kind of travesty of tradition provoked Waugh to satiric attack, he often found his appropriate weapon among the artifacts peculiar to the twentieth century he professed to despise. He was vividly instructed in this strategy while at Oxford, if not earlier. In his travel book *Labels* (1930), he recalls how stunt flying could unsettle secular assumptions to salutary effect.

During what proved to be my last term at Oxford, an ex-officer of the R.A.F.

appeared in Port Meadow with a very dissolute-looking Avro biplane, and advertised passenger flights for seven and six-pence or fifteen shillings for "stunting." On a very serene summer evening I went for a "stunt flight." It was a memorable experience. Some of the movements merely make one feel dizzy, but "looping the loop" develops in the mind clearly articulated intellectual doubts of all preconceived habits of mind about matter and movement. . . . In "looping," the aeroplane shoots steeply upwards until the sensation becomes unendurable and one knows that in another moment it will turn completely over. One looks down into an unfathomable abyss of sky, while over one's head a great umbrella of fields and houses have suddenly opened. Then one shuts one's eyes. My companion on this occasion was a large-hearted and reckless man; he was President of the Union, logical, matter-of-fact in disposition, inclined towards beer and Ye Olde Merrie Englande, with a marked suspicion and hostility towards modern invention. He had come with me in order to assure himself that it was really all nonsense about things heavier than air being able to fly. He sat behind me throughout, muttering, "Oh, my God, oh, Christ, oh, my God." On the way back he scarcely spoke, and two days later, without a word to anyone, he was received into the Roman Church. It is interesting to note that, during this aeroplane's brief visit to Oxford, three cases of conversion occurred in precisely similar circumstances. I will not say that this aeronaut was directly employed by Campion House, but certainly, when a little later, he came down in flames, the Jesuits lost a good ally, and to some people it seemed as if the Protestant God had asserted supremacy in a fine Old Testament manner.[8]

Despite the cool irony of his tone, Waugh cannot conceal the enthusiasm he takes in reporting this innovative approach to evangelizing. He clearly approves. After all, this is no world in which to be comfortable. We should be reminded of its fundamental strangeness, its endless capacity for betraying human expectations. If an improbable feat of aeronautical daring accomplished this purpose, there was every reason to commend it. The airplane became an important element in Waugh's imagination, appearing time and again in his fiction usually as an adjunct to some abrupt revelation or disaster. Often both at once. Nothing served so well to dramatize modernity's assault on conventional attitudes. In 1951, according to Christopher Sykes, Waugh commissioned a painting by Richard Eurich depicting the interior of a plane's passenger cabin. The occupants are portrayed in a way that makes it unmistakably clear the plane is about to crash. "Every possible detail contributing to horror and irony was included at Evelyn's insistence." When Sykes wondered if visitors were shocked by it, Waugh replied, "I hope so."[9]

Waugh took a perverse delight in discomfiting the complacent. This was modernism's special value to him. Like stunt flying, it turned the ordinary world upside down, giving one a glimpse of the abyss guaranteed to unsettle everything one had taken for granted. Although he seems to have become increasingly reluctant to admit it as he grew older, the young Waugh found in modern art the kind of derisive but liberating iconoclasm Ortega y Gasset had applauded for its power to clear away the conventional esthetic pieties that only served to obscure one's view of the world as it was after 1914. Waugh might not have liked what was revealed—the metaphysical emptiness, the abdication of reason, the aimless pursuit of sensation—but he preferred to look at the disease rather than hide behind a facade of nineteenth-century reasonableness pretending nothing had changed.

It was more than fashionable cleverness that led him to make a functional architect of the Bauhaus school the cranky moral center of his first novel. Otto Silenus announces a specifically modernist critique of the nineteenth-century humanism Waugh detested for its deluding sentimentality. Silenus is convinced that "all ill comes from man" and, consequently, "the problem of all art [is] the elimination of the human element from the consideration of form" (p. 159). When he is commissioned to replace an aristocrat's sixteenth-century home with "something clean and square" (p. 156), he constructs a new residence in ferro concrete and aluminum to achieve an industrial look, explaining that "the only perfect building must be the factory, because that is built to house machines, not men" (p. 159). Besides, man "is never happy except when he becomes the channel for the distribution of mechanical forces" (p. 159). Like D. H. Lawrence's futurist artist, Loerke, in *Women in Love*, Silenus gladly subordinates his art to the contemporary spirit of commercial expedience. Yet he is not a hack; he has not sold out in any usual sense. In fact, he displays a certain perverse integrity in his determination to express the ruling passion of his age honestly, regardless of its dehumanizing consequences. Whatever else it accomplished, Waugh suggests, modernism unapologetically confronted its audience with the sour truth of the twentieth century's streamlined transience in which traditions are swept away as soon as they prove inconvenient and present arrangements sustained only as long as they are profitably functional.

Late in his career, Waugh testified to his involvement with contemporary experimental art. Writing of his vocation, he stated that "the artist, however aloof he holds himself, is always and specially the creature of the Zeitgeist."[10] It was his complicated response to modernism, the Zeitgeist of his formative years, that imparted a distinctive shape and energy to his fiction. At every turn, his writing pays parodic tribute to modernist art and literature. Although he deplored many of the movement's aims, he nevertheless admired its methods, borrowing them freely whenever it suited his purpose to do so. Like Wyndham Lewis, he developed an alternate modernism. Whether it was his playful handling of Nietzschean and Bergsonian themes, his ironic reworking of Bauhaus and Futurist theories, or his borrowings from film technique, Waugh gave every evidence that he was consciously taking his place in what he called "the advance guard" despite his notoriously "antique" tastes.[11]

Waugh's ambivalent reaction to modern art and thought was part of a larger pattern. He was one of those artists who thrive on contradiction. Although he declared himself committed to the "standards of civilization," he was unmistakably intrigued by savagery.[12] He prized rationality, but could never entirely resist the lure of anarchy. This is why he was at once fascinated and repelled by modernism's assault on conventional expectations. It spoke to him of the anarchic impulse he alternately indulged and resisted in himself. Much of his work sprang from his sustained and animated argument with what he perceived to be the excesses of the avant-garde. It was through this argument that he confronted what was at best an uneasy truce and at worst a volatile standoff between his orthodox and wayward selves, transfiguring his private struggles so that they represented the characteristic tensions of his time. Accordingly, our consideration of Waugh's interest in modernism begins with this uneasy truce, expressed in his fiction as a comically disabling severance of intellect from will.

I

CONFUSED ROARING

Evelyn Waugh's first novel, *Decline and Fall*, begins with a lopsided struggle between order and energy. Paul Pennyfeather, a thoroughly civilized theology student who has spent his first twenty years living within the "preconceived bounds of order and propriety," finds himself suddenly overwhelmed by the "confused roaring" of the tumultuous Bollinger Club, an improbable gathering of unruly aristocrats whose only organizational purpose is to celebrate their annual dinner as drunkenly and destructively as they possibly can. Their revelry has become fully frenzied when Paul chances to meet them on the college quad. It is a fateful encounter that will alter radically the reasonable course of his prudently managed life. Waugh anticipates their meeting by juxtaposing two carefully constructed scenes: in one the revelers rave wantonly through the night; in the other Paul carries on in his meticulously disciplined fashion.

> A shriller note could now be heard rising from Sir Alastair's rooms; any who have heard that sound will shrink at the recollection of it; it is the sound of the English county families baying for broken glass. Soon they would all be tumbling out into the quad, crimson and roaring in their bottle-green evening coats, for the real romp of the evening. . . . It was a lovely evening. They broke up Mr. Austen's grand piano, and stamped Lord Rending's cigars into his carpet, and smashed his china, and tore up Mr. Partridge's sheets, and threw the Matisse into his water jug; Mr. Sanders had nothing to break except his windows, but they found the manuscript at which he had been working for the Newdigate Prize Poem, and had great fun with that.

As the Bollingers proceed with their ceremonies of destruction, Paul approaches the quad unawares.

> Paul Pennyfeather was reading for the Church. It was his third year of uneventful residence at Scone. He had come there after a creditable career at a small public school of ecclesiastical temper on the South Downs, where he had edited the magazine, been President of the Debating Society, and had, as his report said, "exercised a wholesome influence for good" in the House of which he was head boy. At home he lived in Onslow Square with his guardian, a prosperous solicitor who was proud of his progress and abys-

mally bored by his company. Both his parents had died in India at the time
when he won the essay prize at his preparatory school. For two years he had
lived within his allowance, aided by two valuable scholarships. He smoked
three ounces of tobacco a week—John Cotton, Medium—and drank a pint
and a half of beer a day, the half at luncheon and the pint at dinner, a meal
he invariably ate in Hall. He had four friends, three of whom had been at
school with him. None of the Bollinger Club had ever heard of Paul Pennyfeather, and he, oddly enough, had not heard of them. Little suspecting the
incalculable consequences that the evening was to have for him, he bicycled
happily back from a meeting of the League of Nations Union. There had
been a most interesting paper about plebiscites in Poland. He thought of
smoking a pipe and reading another chapter of the *Forsyte Saga* before going
to bed. (pp. 2–5)[1]

With the confrontation that follows, Waugh announced what was to be his
major theme. All his subsequent work grows out of an irreconcilable opposition between energetic willfulness and effete reasonableness, here
represented by the barbarous Bollingers and the overly civilized Paul Pennyfeather respectively.

Despite their aristocratic pedigrees, the Bollingers both in appearance
and behavior are a rabble of yahoos. The language describing them has
been chosen carefully to suggest their degenerate natures. They number in
their ranks "epileptic royalty from their villas of exile; uncouth peers from
crumbling country seats; smooth young men of uncertain tastes from em-
bassies and legations; illiterate lairds from wet granite hovels in the High-
lands; ambitious young barristers and Conservative candidates torn from
the London season and the indelicate advances of debutantes." The "sono-
rous of name and title" are epileptic, uncouth, illiterate, uncertain, and
torn; they come from crumbling homes and squalid hovels. Together they
comprise the force of primitive disorder let loose once more upon an un-
suspecting world.

The ruling class may have turned against civilization, but Paul Pennyfeather has not noticed their treason. Until he crosses their path, his own
commitment to civilized values remains unshaken, although, like many another of Waugh's well-intentioned, well-bred young men of the middle
class, he has only the dimmest notion of the principles on which these values have been built, principles that have been carelessly set aside by those
in power. Reading Galsworthy's *Forsyte Saga* in measured installments,
Paul is absorbed in the Edwardian dream of an ordered, benevolently progressive world achieved and maintained by prudence and industry. His
carefully managed life of hard, steady work relieved by precisely measured
indulgences—three ounces of tobacco a week, a pint and a half of beer
each day—testifies to his nineteenth-century middle class faith that moderation is the way to a better life. Because he is a man convinced that the

course of events is amenable to reason, he attends the League of Nations
Union and takes serious interest in Polish plebiscites. But when he runs
afoul of the Bollingers, the irrational invades his measured life, changing it
"incalculably." He finds himself thrust from his predictable existence into
boundless possibility. From a world established on a set of reasonable assumptions, he tumbles into a state of unmanageable turbulence. Among
the Bollingers he discovers that the civilized distinctions he has always
taken for granted suddenly and unaccountably lose their power to organize experience.

> Out of the night Lumsden of Strathdrummond swayed across his path like a
> druidical rocking stone. Paul tried to pass. Now it so happened that the tie of
> Paul's old school bore a marked resemblance to the pale blue and white of
> the Bollinger Club. The difference of a quarter of an inch in the width of the
> stripes was not one that Lumsden of Strathdrummond was likely to appreci-
> ate. "Here's an awful man wearing the Boller tie," said the Laird. It is not for
> nothing that since pre-Christian times his family has exercised chieftainship
> over uncharted miles of barren moorland. (p. 5)

Acting as chief over uncharted wasteland is not likely to encourage an ap-
titude for fine discriminations. Civilized distinctions—that quarter-inch
difference in the tie's stripe—can no longer defend against the muddled
barbarians. And rightly so, we are made to feel. Those who make the distinctions appear pallid when put up against the robust revelry of those
drunk with the vitality of experience unmediated and therefore uncontaminated by conventional preconceptions.

Set upon by the Bollingers, Paul is promptly engulfed in their "kaleidoscope of dimly discernible faces" (p. 2). The individual committed to standards of social and esthetic order is submerged by the anonymous horde
intent upon destroying form and harmony. The Bollingers are natural enemies of disciplined order, as demonstrated by their destruction of the
grand piano, the Matisse, and the manuscript. The uniqueness of his identity already compromised by Lumsden's confusion about his tie, Paul then
suffers the removal of his trousers and is sent scurrying across the college
quad, his common humanity clearly exposed. For this "flagrantly indecent"
(p. 7) behavior, he is sent down while the Bollingers are merely fined.
Paul's "guilt" in this matter is compounded by his inability to meet the stiff
fines the college authorities expect men of character to pay for their esca-
pades. Once Paul's limited financial means have been ascertained, the college's Master lets it be known that his is "*not* the conduct we expect of a
scholar. . . . That sort of young man does the College no good" (p. 7). Expelled from his scholarly retreat, Paul must confront the "real world" for
the first time. There he is whirled from one outrage to the next, first be-

coming a marginal schoolmaster at a wildly negligent institution for demonstrably ineducable boys, then nearly marrying an aristocratic white slaver, next going to jail for unwittingly assisting her criminal schemes, and finally escaping his imprisonment by feigning death so that he can return to his theological studies at Scone College disguised as his own cousin. Paul's movements establish a circular pattern Waugh returns to in many of his novels.[2] It might be described as a decline from the decorum of a genteel life into the "confused roaring" of modern primitivism, a fall from the vantage point of orderly perception into a welter of promiscuous sensations that finally sends naive victims such as Paul scrambling to regain the protection of their earlier cloister.

The ease with which savagery supplants civilization in Waugh's twentieth century is largely due to a general abdication of authority. It seems those putatively in charge lack the will to impose the order they represent. Paul's brief encounter with the Bollingers is witnessed by Mr. Sniggs, the college's Junior Dean, and Mr. Postlethwaite, the Domestic Bursar, who prudently remain in their rooms throughout the evening's commotion with their lights off, the better to avoid any possible confrontation with the revelers. When Mr. Sniggs notices Paul approaching the host of celebrants, he mistakes him for Lord Rending and anxiously wonders whether they should do something to protect the young nobleman from injury. But Mr. Postlethwaite will have none of it.

> "No, Sniggs," said Mr. Postlethwaite, laying a hand on his impetuous colleague's arm. "No, no, no. It would be unwise. We have the prestige of the senior common room to consider. In their present state they might not prove amenable to discipline. We must at all costs avoid an *outrage*." (p. 6)

Both officials are greatly relieved when they discover the Bollingers' victim is only Paul Pennyfeather, an untitled individual of no account. In a lawless world there is little profit in defending the weak.

Having abandoned their commitment to civility, the administrators only concern themselves with their own protection and enrichment. The world has turned barbarous again, Waugh suggests, because the delegated custodians of civilized values have neither the courage nor the conviction necessary to their task. But the problem of authority goes much further than a cowardly bureaucracy. Sniggs and Postlethwaite are only the symptoms of the general failure of society to sustain a convincing rational order. The Bollingers overwhelm Paul not so much because these officials refuse to intervene on his behalf, but rather because, without any genuine conviction to support it, his dreary reasonableness cannot stand up to their drunken enthusiasm. "Paul had no particular objection to drunkenness—he had

read rather a daring paper to the Thomas More Society on the subject—
but he was consumedly shy of drunkards" (p. 5). Paul can entertain the
idea of drunkenness, but he has no stomach for the breathing, brawling
drunkard. It is precisely this disjunction between idea and experience that
fascinated Waugh. In his novels, actuality always proves too slippery and
upsetting for the intellectual categories that had once seemed to make
sense of it. Until meeting the Bollingers, Paul had been protected by the
intellectual environment of his college, an environment that seemed to respect the importance of ideas. But once actuality invades, these ideas
prove ineffectual either because they are bankrupt in themselves or because the people who officially subscribe to them do so without conviction.

Waugh's is a polarized world in which thought and desire have gone
their separate ways; with few exceptions, everyone ignores what once was
thought to be the civilizing struggle between reason and feeling. As a result, people have become either hopelessly prudent or heedlessly impulsive. Some retreat into nostalgic cloisters of intellectual order untested by
worldly events, while others plunge into the flux of immediate experience
unconcerned with tiresome metaphysical questions about meaning and
purpose. Neither group is quite human.

To explain this rift between intellect and will, Waugh introduces Otto
Silenus, the wonderfully gloomy German architect whose avant-garde design theories parody those of the 1920s Bauhaus movement. A philosopher
of sorts, Silenus carries the mock argument of the narrative on his unlikely
shoulders.and in so doing introduces a wild pastiche of popular intellectu-
alizing that serves Waugh's purposes as both parody and illumination.

Silenus has discovered a difference in human nature more fundamental
than gender: "Instead of this absurd division into sexes they ought to class
people as static and dynamic. There's a real distinction there, though I
can't tell you how it comes. I think we're probably two quite different species spiritually" (pp. 283–84). Life, according to Silenus, is "like the big
wheel at Luna Park" (p. 282).

> You pay five francs and go into a room with tiers of seats all round, and in the
> centre the floor is made of a great disc of polished wood that revolves
> quickly. At first you sit down and watch the others. They are all trying to sit
> in the wheel, and they keep getting flung off, and that makes them laugh,
> and you laugh too. It's great fun. . . . The nearer you can get to the hub of
> the wheel the slower it is moving and the easier it is to stay on. There's gen-
> erally some one in the centre who stands up and sometimes does a sort of
> dance. Often he's paid by the management, though, or, at any rate, he's al-
> lowed in free. Of course at the very centre there's a point completely at rest,
> if one could only find it. I'm not sure I am not very near that point myself. Of
> course the professional men get in the way. Lots of people just enjoy scram-
> bling on and being whisked off and scrambling on again. How they all shriek

and giggle! Then there are others, like Margot, who sit as far out as they can and hold on for dear life and enjoy that. But the whole point about the wheel is that you needn't get on it at all, if you don't want to. People get hold of ideas about life, and that makes them think they've got to join in the game, even if they don't enjoy it. It doesn't suit every one. (pp. 282–83)

Silenus's parable illustrates the rupture between thinking and doing. At life's game, one is either an impotent spectator or a mindless participant. There's no middle ground.

The name Silenus is full of suggestion. The Silenus of classical myth was the mentor of Dionysus, whom he encouraged to follow the promptings of instinct and will regardless of consequence. Otto Silenus's divided world seems remarkably similar to the one announced by the mythical Silenus, especially as imagined by Friedrich Nietzsche. Consider the following passage from *The Birth of Tragedy* concerning the natural antagonism between Apollonian and Dionysian imaginations. Nietzsche's distinction parallels both Otto Silenus's division of the human species and the collision between the static Paul Pennyfeather and the dynamic Bollingers.

And now let us imagine how the ecstatic sounds of the Dionysiac rites penetrated ever more enticingly into that artificially restrained and discreet world of illusion, how this clamor expressed the whole outrageous gamut of nature—delight, grief, knowledge—even to the most piercing cry; and then let us imagine how the Apollonian artist with his thin, monotonous harp music must have sounded beside the demoniac chant of the multitude! The muses presiding over the illusory arts paled before an art which enthusiastically told the truth, and the wisdom of Silenus cried "Woe!" against the serene Olympians. The individual, with his limits and moderations, forgot himself in the Dionysiac vortex and became oblivious to the laws of Apollo. Indiscreet extravagance revealed itself as truth, and contradiction, a delight born of pain, spoke out of the bosom of nature. Wherever the Dionysiac voice was heard, the Apollonian norm seemed suspended or destroyed.[3]

Was Waugh parodying Nietzsche? There is nothing that confirms he read Nietzsche other than some general remarks he made concerning his interest in philosophy at this time in his life.[4] But the parallels seem strong enough on their own without recourse to external proofs of influence. No less seriously and certainly no less playfully than Nietzsche's treatise, Waugh's first novel explores the antagonism between Apollonian order and Dionysian energy. Paul Pennyfeather is "the individual with his limits and moderations." The "demoniac chant of the multitude" is taken up in the "confused roaring" of the Bollingers. Paul lives in a world of settled arrangements; his sense of himself and his world depends upon his unexamined assumption that reality or being is inherently stable. According to Nietzsche, this is an illusion that beguiles most civilized people. Becoming is the only fundamental reality; human thought, however, requires that it be translated into the supposed categories of Being.[5] Running with the flux of Becoming, the Bollingers overwhelm the trivial artifice of Paul's measured world. Described as "a kaleidoscope of dimly discernible faces," the Bollingers comprise an undifferentiated Dionysian force intent upon annihilating the individual. In Nietzsche's vision of the Dionysian principle in its esthetic guise, "each single instance of such annihilation will clarify for us the abiding phenomenon of Dionysiac art, which expresses the omnipotent will behind individuation, eternal life continuing beyond all appearances and in spite of destruction. The metaphysical delight in tragedy is a translation of instinctive Dionysiac wisdom into images. The hero, the highest manifestation of the will, is destroyed, and we assent, since he too is merely a phenomenon, and the eternal life of the will remains unaffected."[6] The willful Bollingers engulf Paul and obliterate his rationally constructed individuality. They strip his pants from him in a parodic ritual that sacrifices reason to the will. This is why the narrator must later interrupt his story to tell us in an ironically self-conscious aside that "the whole of this book is really an account of the mysterious disappearance of Paul Pennyfeather, so that readers must not complain if the shadow which took his name does not amply fill the important part of hero for which he was originally cast" (p. 163). In a world in which reason has lost its struggle with the will, "Paul Pennyfeather would never have made a hero, and the only interest about him arises from the unusual series of events of which his shadow was witness" (p. 164). This also explains why Paul can so readily "die" and be reborn as his own cousin. Paul's death and rebirth parody Nietzsche's doctrine of the Dionysian will with its belief in an eternal return which guarantees that everything eventually comes full circle, the undifferentiated life force endlessly reproducing the same individuals and events through an eternity of time.

Paul's allegiance to Apollo is far too faint to stand up to Dionysian turbulence when it erupts in his life. He exemplifies one of Waugh's recurring themes: decency without force. Without strong convictions, educated people like Paul may continue to observe codes of morality and manners handed down to them from previous ages but generally think it embarrassing to have to examine the theological and metaphysical principles upon which their behavior rests. Tony Last in A Handful of Dust provides the perfect example. A decent, devoted family man, he glories in his nineteenth-century estate of pseudo-Gothic design, fulfills all the conventional obligations of a gentlemen, attends chapel on Sundays, and generally reveres the tradition into which he was born. But he does not bother himself about the metaphysics that originally gave his way of life its purpose. When the local parson tries to console him in his grief over the death of his son, he gets rid of the man at the earliest possible moment and then remarks, "after all the last thing one wants to talk about at a time like this is religion" (p. 158). Religion for Tony is a cultural ornament, a museum piece to be preserved with the same sort of care he expends on his pseudo-Gothic house. Beyond its esthetic value, however, it has little more to offer than a few ethical precepts founded upon an uplifting fiction. It was precisely this tendency to reduce religion to a cultural artifact that Waugh came to abhor. When he converted to Roman Catholicism in 1930, he wrote of modern sophisticated religious thinking that hesitated to commit itself to any definite beliefs: "If its own mind is not made up, it can hardly hope to withstand disorder from outside."7 He thought it futile to use religion as a sort of picturesque inducement with which to cultivate decency and social feeling. Stronger fortification was needed to withstand the savagery that had always besieged civilization.

Paul Pennyfeather, we are told, could "be expected to acquit himself with decision and decorum in all the emergencies of civilized life" (p. 163). His problem is that so very little civilized life remains and its polite emergencies seem exceedingly insignificant in the hurly-burly of modern times. This is the truth Paul discovers when his commitment to a reasonable ethic of moderation proves to be the flimsiest of defenses against the wild excesses of the Bollingers. This encounter parodically inverts Nietzsche's mocking reference to Anaxagoras, the ancient philosopher who had argued that "in the beginning all things were mixed together; then reason came and introduced order." Anaxagoras, Nietzsche observes, "with his concept of reason, seems like the first sober philosopher in a company of drunkards."8 What better describes Paul among the Bollingers? Only in this case, reason does not prevail. Instead, the Bollingers put Paul through a regressive rite of passage that reintroduces him to the original chaotic mixture of things, a primitive stew which reason's puny distinctions cannot reduce to order.

Paul is awakened from his Victorian dream of an ordered, purposeful life enshrined in a "code of ready-made honour that is the still small voice, trained to command, of the Englishman all the world over" (p. 252). His eyes open on a new reality. Now he is encouraged to go his way "careless of consequence" (p. 133) and advised to "temper discretion with deceit" (p. 24). Nineteenth-century decorum has given way to what Edmund Wilson describes as Waugh's twentieth century, a world of "perverse, unregenerate self-will" that gives "rise to confusion and impudence."9 Here Paul is taken up by Margot Beste-Chetwynde (pronounced beast-cheating), an amoral charmer who has climbed into the aristocracy by means of a strategic marriage and then, so it is rumored, hastened her widowing. She is a creature of undisguised self-assertion who supports herself by running a chain of brothels in South America. Unaccountably, she chooses Paul to be her next husband. Their marriage, however, is called off at the last minute when he is arrested for having unwittingly taken part in her white slave trade. It is then that Paul fully realizes there is "something radically inapplicable about this whole code" of "ready-made honour" (p. 252) by which he lives. It does not fit the age of Margot. At his trial on charges of procuring, he must decide whether to give evidence against her or allow himself to be convicted for her crimes. Paul does the honorable thing: he sacrifices himself. He cannot help but concede the "undeniable cogency" of her son's remark: "You can't see Mamma in prison, can you?" As the narrator explains, the more Paul considered this rhetorical question, "the more he perceived it to be the statement of a natural law. He appreciated the assumption of comprehension with which Peter had delivered it. As he studied Margot's photograph . . . he was strengthened in his belief that there was, in fact, and should be, one law for her and another for himself" (pp. 252–53).

> He *saw* the *impossibility* of Margot in prison; the bare connection of vocables associating the ideas was obscene. . . . if the preposterous processes of law had condemned her, then the woman that they actually caught and pinned down would not have been Margot, but some quite other person of the same name and somewhat similar appearance. It was impossible to imprison the Margot who had committed the crime. (p. 253)

If Margot could actually be "caught and pinned down," she would no longer fulfill her role; she would become merely a mortal, subject like everyone else to the usual constraints of humankind. But Margot is not mortal; she is a goddess of Becoming, a pure Dionysian principle quite beyond the censure of a spiritless morality. To expect her, then, to be responsible for her deeds is to ask her to be someone other than who she is. Margot's vital energy knows no restraint. Paul, on the other hand, for all the powers of discrimination bequeathed him by an Oxford education, is shadowy and effete; he has neither the conviction nor the energy to act decisively. There is one law for those who reside in the static world of fixed principles and another for those who live in the dynamic world of unprincipled self-assertion. Not only is this the reason he cannot testify against her; it is also the reason he cannot marry her. As Silenus points out, they are "two quite different species spiritually."

This division of characters into irreconcilable extremes has been frequently taken as a symptom of Waugh's moral confusion. James F. Carens, for instance, argues that

> the satirist seems to imply that amoralism may be justified by the very nature of things, that there are those such as Paul, who live within the law and are

judged by it, while there are others, such as Peter and his mother, who, by virtue of their dynamism and, perhaps, their position, are outside the "whole code of ready-made honour," inherited by Paul but "inapplicable" to them.[10]

This is true enough on moral grounds. But these are not the grounds upon which Waugh chose to work. The characters and situations in his novels—certainly his early novels—dramatize epistemological concerns anterior to moral considerations. They are frankly abstractions deployed in his analysis of the modern world. Even by the standards of satire, these characters are too flatly one-sided to be seriously considered as moral agents. This is the point, of course. Paul and Margot have been effectively removed from any known moral arena. They exist as polar remnants of a disintegrated humanity: one forever imprisoned by the bankrupt categories of a failed order, the other boundlessly self-assertive because she is untrammeled by any consideration of moral consequences. For Paul to testify against Margot would be as supererogatory as if one were to indict the will for having appetites. There is not much point in arraigning the given. For his part, Paul is prevented from exerting his temperate influence because the "code of ready-made honour" with which he has been brought up has become "radically inapplicable" in a society that has forfeited its belief in the possibility of moral absolutes. Reason can exert no force without a fixed fulcrum. The chapter in which Paul goes to jail, "Stone Walls Do Not a Prison Make," takes its title from Richard Lovelace's "To Althea from Prison," but Waugh ironically tweaks the original meaning. In Paul's case there is no need for walls; he is already imprisoned by the values of a tradition that people like Margot simply ignore. He might as well complain against his temperament as protest his prison sentence. Either grievance would be futile.

In its title, *Decline and Fall* suggests first the most famous of historical descriptions of barbarian assaults on an enfeebled civilization, Gibbon's *Decline and Fall of the Roman Empire*. But when Professor Silenus declares that Margot and Paul are of different species spiritually, his finding echoes that of his countryman Oswald Spengler. In *The Decline of the West*, a work that can be read as a continuation of Gibbon's, Spengler argued that the human race is divided into geographical groups, each manifesting a unique soul that distinguishes it from all the rest. Spengler's book appeared in an English translation in 1926, so it does not seem unreasonable to suppose Waugh had it in mind when writing *Decline and Fall* in 1928. Presumably he had at least a superficial knowledge of it some time earlier or he would not have referred to it as one of "two or three very solemn" works he packed for his 1929 trip abroad.[11] Although he recorded nothing else about it, there can be little doubt that Spengler's apocalyptic pessimism

would have appealed to the young Waugh, one of whose poses required
that he adopt a sardonic knowingness. Certainly Spengler's argument
would have provided Waugh with another explanation of the world in
which his little lost characters find themselves, and it would have had the
virtue of being an explanation that coordinated neatly enough with
Nietzsche's polarization of human nature.

Spengler isolates eight distinct world cultures and then outlines the ha-
bitual, one might say reflexive, perception of the world characteristic of
each. Working in the tradition that passes from Kant through Nietzsche, he
naturally assumes that a culture is best understood in terms of its own special epistemology. Whether in the arts or sciences, a culture's thought reflects the largely unconscious assumptions of its peculiar world view. The
static-dynamic polarity so dear to Professor Silenus appears in *The Decline
of the West* as the opposition that distinguishes the essential differences between the classical Greek and the Faustian European cultures. (As Spengler uses these terms, they parallel Nietzsche's contrast of the Apollonian
and Dionysian.) These labels are not meant to be applied to historical periods exclusively. They serve as well to make the familiar distinction
between classical and romantic sensibilities that is not limited to any particular time. Historical conditions in a given age tend to favor one of
several competing sensibilities. The favored one becomes dominant and
characterizes the period. This does not mean other predilections disappear; they simply become less visible because the individual finds it less advantageous to express them. Used here, Spengler's categories will refer to
sensibilities rather than specific ages.

Comparing the classical sensibility with the Faustian romantic, Spengler
wrote that

> the "Nature" of Classical man found its highest artistic emblem in the nude
> statue, and out of it logically there grew a static of bodies, a physics of the
> near. . . . Faustian man's Nature-idea was a dynamic of unlimited space, a
> physics of the distant. . . . Apollinian theory is a quiet meditation. . . . The
> Faustian is from the very outset a working hypothesis.

For the classical sensibility ideas are timeless Platonic forms; they are fixed
coordinates which we use to make the world intelligible. We can rely on
them to shape our understanding of the flow of experience. In contrast,
Faustian or romantic man values ideas not as ends in themselves but rather
as means with which to exert his will over his surroundings; he maintains
no absolute truths, only hypotheses devised as momentary expedients.
Spengler's descriptions of the Classical and Faustian sensibilities find their
way into Waugh's novels in various guises, most notably in the recurring
motif of the anachronistic naïf bedazzled by one of modernity's goddesses,

roles first filled by Paul Pennyfeather and Margot Beste-Chetwynde. Classical epistemology is capable of supporting Paul Pennyfeather's ready-made code of honor. The romantic sensibility with its provisional categories suits Margot, whose precarious career demands infinite adaptability. The classical attitude cautions us to live within the limits of the possible; the romantic urges us to transcend all boundaries. It is this binary opposition that Waugh parodies with Silenus's static-dynamic polarity. As Nietzsche seems to have done, so Spengler also served his abiding theme.[12]

Spengler's thesis further explains why the narrator of *Decline and Fall* insists upon Paul's inability to play the heroic role for which he had originally been cast. The traditional hero finds his strength in his cultural identity. Convinced of the values with which he has been raised, he stands ready to project them into the world around him. Once he is deprived of this type of unreflective conviction, Paul can only retreat from the barbarous shock of Waugh's twentieth century. The supposed custodians of tradition no longer believe in their ability to make a difference in such a world. Like Silenus's gallery of static spectators they must content themselves with watching impotently from the sidelines.

According to Spengler's analysis, Paul is a natural victim of his age. Spengler argues that the West had developed beyond the stage of societal cohesion by the modern period and was in the twentieth century loosely held together by the fading memory of a once vital and compelling body of convictions. Using a cyclical schema applicable to the growth and decay of societies in general, he observes that in the early cultural periods of a society's development individuals, singly and collectively, feel themselves bound up with the fate of their community. The meaning of their lives flows from the shared beliefs and traditions that have served them in their common struggle for survival. But once a society succeeds and flourishes as a civilization, its defensive cohesion begins to dissolve as it takes on an aura of skeptical cosmopolitanism. The populace tends to cluster in cities in search of economic opportunity. Wealth becomes a measure of value more important than honor, tradition, or property. (In *Decline and Fall* the Junior Dean and Domestic Bursar gauge the Bollinger infractions not in terms of moral but rather financial value. As they sit idly by, their only concern is how much they will be able to fine the celebrants for their drunkenly destructive behavior. They even pray that the revelers might attack the chapel so that the maximum in punitive damages can be levied against them.) With growing affluence and security, the cities swell with self-interested *déracinés* who have little sense of common destiny with their neighbors. The resulting ethos encourages the society Waugh portrays, a society in which it is every man for himself. *Sauve qui peut* serves as the ironic refrain of his last novel, *Unconditional Surrender*. It is clearly meant to reflect the final wisdom of Western decadence at mid-century, a world virulent with untempered self-regard.

There are a number of ways to express Waugh's central theme, some more complicated than others. Perhaps the best formulation is the simplest and oldest: the perennial human failure to behave reasonably. As themes go, there is certainly nothing new here, nor was there meant to be. The Western tradition begins with the fundamental conflict between knowing and doing. The gears of intellect and will are meant to mesh, but more often grind. This is the stuff of all human drama, but it seemed to Waugh that this failure had become especially acute in the twentieth century. In earlier ages the inevitable discord between reason and impulse was explained as a result of willful selfishness. One was capable of knowing how to act but chose to do otherwise. This was called sin. There was general agreement that the morality of individual acts could be assessed according to objective standards. What disturbed Waugh was that in our relativistic age morality had become disputable not only in specific cases, but also in principle. This is why Waugh disclaimed the title of satirist in 1946, arguing that satire is not possible in an unstable society that does not subscribe to "homogeneous moral standards." The satirist "seeks to produce shame" and this, he contended, was clearly impossible in a world in which "vice no longer pays lip service to virtue."[13] Another way of putting this is to say that without conviction in a transcendent purpose to life, it becomes impossible to discriminate among ethical systems; one will seem no more metaphysically compelling than another. At any given juncture, then, the will is left to choose from competing rationales. For Waugh this amounted to an abdication of reason's authority, which was bound to result in the mindless self-assertion he thought characteristic of modern life. It was this supposed decline of the traditional intellectual and moral order that so fascinated him, compelling his satiric response.

II

DESIRE, DOUBT, AND THE SUPERB MEAN

Polarization and counterpoint are constant features in Waugh's fiction. They were the structural analogues to the divisive tensions he sensed both within and outside himself. His first published story, "The Balance," turns on the counterpoise between sentimental narrative and comic commentary. It unfolds as though it were a silent film about young, affluent worldings, caught in the toils of romance. We "watch" the narrative at a movie house with two serving women on their night off who, for our edification, provide a noisy but very sensible assessment of the "soft" proceedings.[1] By juxtaposing party scenes in *Vile Bodies,* Waugh satirizes the generational division that afflicts his society. While the elders settle into Anchorage House, a revered family seat, for an evening during which they will reassure themselves that all is right with their world, some miles away their offspring stumble about in a tethered dirigible that floats a few feet above the ground. These Bright Young People, eager martyrs to modernity, are quite willing to suffer the nausea that inevitably results under the combined influence of drink and the uncertain footing of their swaying quarters. *Black Mischief* alternates between scenes of shiftless Londoners and feckless Africans. In *Work Suspended* and *Sword of Honour* protagonists meet their unseemly doubles from whom they belatedly discover unwelcome truths about themselves.

All these examples are permutations of Waugh's original preoccupation with the uneasy balance between rational order and willful energy. This said, it must be emphasized that he focused precisely on the dividing fulcrum, not one side or the other. Divergent critical opinion has tended to place him in one scale or the other, reductively labeling him a compulsive conservative or an unprincipled anarchist. In truth, he was a bit of both. Harold Acton put it best when he described Waugh as a "prancing faun, thinly disguised by conventional apparel. His wide-apart eyes, always ready to be startled under raised eyebrows. . . . The gentleness of his manner could not deceive me . . . so demure and yet so wild! A faun half-tamed

21

by the Middle Ages, who would hide himself for months in some suburban retreat, and then burst upon the town with capricious caperings."[2] Waugh's personality was a battle zone of contending forces. He was by turns reflective and impulsive, traditional and anarchic, reclusive and cosmopolitan. In *Decline and Fall* he projected these tensions into Paul Pennyfeather's diametrically opposed colleagues, Mr. Prendergast and Captain Grimes, who, taken together, vividly illustrate the consequences of living in a world in which reason has lost touch with impulse. Standing at allegorical extremes from one another, Prendergast personifies intellect immobilized by doubt while Grimes expresses will unhindered by reflection.

Captain Grimes is the incorrigible rascal who flouts morals and manners so cheerfully that no one would ever want him brought to account. He may be a bisexual bigamist who leaves schoolmastering in Wales for pimping in South America, but these faults cannot be held against a man who so genially admits, "I can stand most sorts of misfortune, old boy, but I can't stand repression" (p. 264). Following the dictates of his impulses wherever they lead, he repeatedly lands "in the soup" (p. 31), as he puts it. His casual treatment of complaisant women together with his excessive interest in adolescent boys has made it necessary for him to cultivate the wiles of a confidence man and the skills of a quick-change artist to merely survive as he keeps one small step ahead of the authorities. And survive he does with splendid resilience. While in the armed service, he is given the choice between a dignified suicide and a squalid court-martial for disgraceful— probably homosexual—behavior. Left alone with a revolver to do the decent thing, he gets drunk instead. Grimes is not one to be cowed by somebody else's conception of honor. Intuitively he knows the world to be a much dicier place than any code of ethics can explain. He also knows his luck. It is a fellow Harrovian who discovers him in the stupor of his double infamy. Recognizing Grimes as a public-school man, this loyal advocate of the old-boy tradition soon has him shipped to Ireland to work in the postal service for the war's duration. Later, when Grimes's erratic, not to say erotic, teaching career takes him to Paul's school, Llanabba Castle, he finds himself forced into marriage with the headmaster's daughter. To escape this odious involvement, he pretends suicide by swimming out to sea. Shortly after this adventure, he appears at Margot's to apply for a managerial position in one of her brothels. Sometime later, when Paul goes to prison, there is Grimes again. Having decided that three years is too long to serve for bigamy, however, he soon escapes under the cover of fog during a work detail. When he is not located in the countryside surrounding the prison, the guards confidently agree that he has drowned in the bogs of

Egdon Mire, a Hardyesque fate that long experience has taught them no mortal can evade. But Paul knows better.

> Grimes, Paul at last realized, was one of the immortals. He was a life force. Sentenced to death in Flanders, he popped up in Wales; drowned in Wales, he emerged in South America; engulfed in the dark mystery of Egdon Mire, he would rise again somewhere at some time, shaking from his limbs the musty integuments of the tomb. Surely he had followed in the Bacchic train of distant Arcady, and played on the reeds of myth by forgotten streams, and taught the childish satyrs the art of love? Had he not suffered unscathed the fearful dooms of all the offended gods of all the histories, fire, brimstone and yawning earthquakes, plague and pestilence? Had he not stood, like the Pompeian sentry, while the Citadels of the Plain fell to ruin about his ears? Had he not, like some grease-caked Channel swimmer, breasted the waves of the Deluge? Had he not moved unseen when darkness covered the waters? (pp. 269–70)

Grimes is another character who approaches the condition of pure Dionysian becoming—formless, protean, infinitely adaptable. That echo of Genesis in the last sentence of this passage—"Had he not moved unseen when darkness covered the waters?"—mockingly suggests that Grimes is like the clay of brute matter before the form of being has imparted shape and destiny to its unconditioned potency. Indeed, his name further supports this reading: he is the original grime of the world always ready to subvert the tidy housekeeping of civilization by letting in the primal messiness once more. Like Margot, Grimes is one of Waugh's willful gods going his way "careless of consequence" (p. 133), slipping society's restraining nets with an ease as astonishing as it is comical. He is an untamable life force, pure energy; disruptive of good manners, certainly, but quite beyond moral censure.

Grimes's opposite is Mr. Prendergast, the agnostic parson who has given up his ecclesiastical living and stooped to schoolmastering, a profession notoriously open to rascals such as Grimes and failures such as himself. An abysmally incompetent teacher, Prendergast has spent the last ten years as the butt of schoolboy pranks, most of which he fecklessly calls down upon himself. He wears a cheap and obvious wig that naturally becomes the irresistible target of his students' cruelest jokes. As he explains to Paul, once he put the wig on he felt he could not go back. Removing it might cause increased mischief, a risk he is unwilling to run. Prendergast does not have the will to expose himself honestly, and without this power of will he is ineffectual in all his efforts. At their first meeting, Prendergast offers Paul some port. Having had a glimpse of conditions at Llanabba, Paul eagerly accepts. But they find there is only one glass in the commons room, the one from which Prendergast is drinking. Prendergast makes a feeble attempt to locate another, but quickly gives it up. The failed clergyman possesses the wine but he cannot produce communion; there is promise but no delivery. He does not have the power to give anyone, including himself, what is needed.

On their second meeting, Prendergast tells Paul his story. "I should be a rector with my own house and bathroom . . . only I had *Doubts*" (p. 36), he confides. It was not "the ordinary sort of doubt about Cain's wife or the Old Testament miracles" that had unnerved him.

> I'd been taught how to explain all those while I was at college. No, it was something deeper than all that. I *couldn't understand why God had made the world at all.* . . . You see how fundamental that is. Once granted the first step, I can see that everything else follows—Tower of Babel, Babylonian captivity, Incarnation, Church, bishops, incense, everything—but what I couldn't see, and what I can't see now, is *why* did it all begin? I asked my bishop; he didn't know. He said that he didn't think the point really arose as far as my practical duties as a parish priest were concerned. (pp. 36–39)

Prendergast raises the fundamental issue but hasn't the will to resolve it. Instead, he foolishly jumps at the chance to return to the cloth as a prison chaplain when he discovers the post does not require him to subscribe to any particular creed at all. Of course, such agnostic felicity cannot last. Among his caged flock there is a religious lunatic unhindered by any doubts at all. His beliefs are as unswerving as they are unexamined. Convinced that the angel of the Lord has commissioned him to murder the faithless, this self-styled "lion of the Lord's elect" (p. 240) decides—with some cause—that Chaplain Prendergast is not a Christian and so murders him by sawing his head from his body with tools conveniently provided him by the prison's enlightened arts and crafts program, which stresses the criminal's need for emotional release through artistic self-expression.

Prendergast's inability to sustain a coherent religious vision is one of the many instances in which Waugh satirized the modern abdication of intellectual authority that calls forth the fanatic. Whether religious or political, these zealots are led by the inner light of untutored emotion alone. Surrounded by an ostensibly sane citizenry whose lives lack a rationally defined purpose, their peculiarly mindless dedication gives them devastating strength. Prendergast's grisly end provides Waugh with a metaphor of his central theme: twentieth century man decapitated, his intellect severed from his will. When reason neglects its reign, impulse usurps its place with predictable results.

Reported casually, Prendergast's fate seems neither all that shocking nor particularly lamentable. Instead, we are made to feel he got no more than he deserved. He is one of Waugh's well-meaning humanists, personally inoffensive but culturally lethal. Without convictions of any kind, these characters wander through the novels vaguely unnerved by the chaos that surrounds them. Their failure to sustain the tradition of which they are the immediate beneficiaries has emptied their world of purpose and left those who are more willful and less scrupulous either to drift into aimless dissipation or to channel their otherwise undirected energy into one of the many perverse ideologies that plague the day. This was Waugh's assessment of a culture that has lost confidence in itself and its ability to make sense of the world. It explains the frequent appearance of fanaticism in his fiction. In *Vile Bodies* Lady Melrose Ape, the stalwart, lightly bearded evangelist modeled on Aimee Semple McPherson, wows London with her feel-good religiosity and her troupe of nubile singing angels, while Colonel Blount rents his ancestral estate to serve as the location for an "all-talkie super-religious film" (p. 202) about the eighteenth-century religious enthusiast John Wesley. In *Black Mischief* a young Oxford-educated African emperor is convinced that he is the apostle of Progress "at [whose] stirrups run woman's suffrage, vaccination and vivisection." He confidently declares, "I am the New Age; I am the Future" (p. 22), as he builds railroads that go nowhere and equips his barefoot, spear-carrying army with a tank. Aimée Thanatogenos in *The Loved One* unreservedly devotes herself to Dr. Kenworthy's euphemistic mortuary and its denial of death. These and other true-believing lunatics like them are desperate symptoms of a society that has lost its way.

The early novels are populated by half-human characters who are either dynamically willful or statically reflective. The world of Captain Grimes and Mr. Prendergast has given up the dialectical struggle between classic restraint and romantic striving. There is, however, one remarkable exception: Imogen Quest in *Vile Bodies.* She is one who has "achieved a superb mean between those two poles of savagery Lady Circumstance and Lady Metroland" (p. 158), Lady Circumstance being all purblind allegiance to an otiose nineteenth-century ethic and Lady Metroland (Margot Beste-Chetwynde in a later incarnation) seething with insatiable modernity. Imogen, unlike almost every other young person in Waugh's novels, is happily married and content with her lot in life. "From the first she exhibited signs of a marked personality . . . her character . . . a lovely harmony of contending virtues—she was witty and tender-hearted; passionate and serene, sensual and temperate, impulsive and discreet" (p. 158). Imogen, in other words, is a whole, self-sufficient individual capable of balancing the claims of reason and impulse in her life. In fact, she is too blessedly sane to be true. She is, of course, imaginary, a joke of sorts. Her "lovely harmony" of romantic impulse and classic poise turns out to be a fiction made up by

Adam Fenwick-Symes, the novel's protagonist. As a gossip columnist for a paper appropriately named the *Daily Excess,* Adam finds himself strapped for material and so, in the dishonorable tradition of his trade, he resorts to invention. Imogen becomes his most successful creation. In fact, she positively captivates his readers, inspiring them with her benevolent normality. "And this knowledge of the intangible Quest set, moving among them in uncontrolled dignity of life, seemed to leaven and sweeten the lives of [his] readers" (p. 159). Soon Adam's readers, including his employer, Lord Monomark, are clamoring to meet Imogen. But Adam goes too far, and disaster falls. In detailing Imogen's social activities, he makes a serious mistake when he announces her plans to give a party and, for the sake of verisimilitude, includes an address in his report. "On the following day Adam found his table deep in letters of complaint from gate-crashers who had found the house in Seamore Place untenanted" (p. 159). When soon after Lord Monomark approaches him requesting an introduction, Adam has no other recourse but to improvise a hastily arranged Jamaican holiday for the Quests, their stay indefinite.

Modern England is clearly no place for civilized men and women. Imogen's "superb mean" has become the stuff of whimsical nostalgia; her balanced life is no more than an attractive fiction and even at that it cannot survive the gate-crashing barbarism of the twentieth century. Imogen's leavening power fades from the world, leaving people bereft and bewildered. Certainly what we overhear in Adam's desultory conversation with his fiancée, Nina, reflects a profoundly irresolute mind that Imogen would find intolerably alien.

> "Nina, do you ever feel that things simply can't go on much longer?"
> "What d'you mean by things—us or everything?"
> "Everything."
> "No—I wish I did."
> "I dare say you're right. . . . I'd give anything in the world for something different."
> "Different from me or different from everything?"
> "Different from everything . . . only I've got nothing. . . . what's the good of talking?"
> "Oh, Adam, my dearest . . . "
> "Yes?"
> "Nothing." (p. 273)

Neither Adam nor Nina has the strength of Imogen's "marked personality" and without it they have little chance to direct their lives purposefully. Instead, they allow themselves to be carried away by the sweep of sensational but pointless events, including an endless series of parties— "Masked parties, savage parties, Victorian parties, Greek parties, Wild

West parties . . . almost naked parties . . . parties in flats and studios and houses and ships and hotels and night clubs, in windmills and swimming baths," sickening boat and plane trips, grotesque evangelists, suicidal auto races, "all that succession and repetition of massed humanity . . . those vile bodies" (pp. 170–71). The surfeit of excitement finally reduces them to listless passivity. In these early novels, the impoverished mind typically founders in a vertiginous swirl of sensation. None of the characters has the poise to manage his experience of a wildly fragmented culture.

The world divided between a fading vision of classical order and the lively anarchy of romantic excess—this was Waugh's concern from the hectic humor of his early satires to the elegiac ironies of the *Sword of Honour* trilogy. His treatment of the issue was all the more effective because he resisted facile moralizing. Nor, despite what some have said, did he merely champion past order over present disorder.[3] Even when Waugh donned his conservative cap the better to advocate a stern application of traditional restraints to modern behavior, he always made allowance for the healthy play of impulse. The latitude of his position can be demonstrated by comparing what he had to say about discipline and repression with the remarks of his friend Ronald Knox, whose thought Waugh greatly respected. There are two passages in particular that display these apparently like-minded men reaching tellingly different conclusions. The first comes from Knox's *God and the Atom*, a work exploring the theological and social consequences of living in the atomic age that Waugh urgently pressed on friends and acquaintances as necessary reading.

> I take it that we do not exceed the bounds of legitimate metaphor, if we think of the human personality in this way. At the core of it, there is a bundle of instincts, impulses, prejudices, phobias and what not, each of them bound, and each, though often in a very slight degree, straining at its bonds. They are held together and held in by the elastic band of Repression; some of it conscious, much more of it unconscious, or half-conscious at the best. If the band snaps, the result is lunacy; all the hidden impulses of a man's nature regain their freedom, held in only by random, external checks. If the band slips, the result is that sudden brain-storm or black-out which the psychologists have christened schizophrenia; the subject "forgets himself," is untrue to his normal habits of behaviour; it may be, only for a short interval. But in the ordinary life, the elastic band holds, and the hidden impulses remain bound, only betraying themselves by casual mannerisms and fidgetings, by the images that haunt us in our dreams, and so on. What must be the strength, when you come to think about it, of this band which holds our psychic life in position, consisting in part, but only in part, of that free will which we consciously exercise![4]

The second passage comes from one of Waugh's characteristic essays, a piece of journalism Waugh was commissioned to write in 1929 concerning the impact of the Great War on the generation coming of age in the 1920s and 1930s. He finds it unsurprising that these young people should be "undiscriminating and ineffectual." The blame can be laid especially on the mood of tolerance that followed the war.

> The only thing which could have saved these unfortunate children was the imposition by rigid discipline, as soon as it became possible, of the standards of civilization. This was still possible in 1918 when the young schoolmasters came back to their work. Unfortunately, a very great number, probably the more influential and intelligent among them, came with their own faith sadly shaken in those very standards which, avowedly, they had fought to preserve. They returned with a jolly tolerance of everything that seemed "modern." Every effort was made to encourage the children at the Public Schools to "think for themselves." When they should have been whipped and taught Greek paradigms, they were set arguing about birth control and nationalization. Their crude little opinions were treated with respect. Preachers in the school chapel week after week entrusted the future to their hands. It is hardly surprising that they were Bolshevik at eighteen and bored at twenty.
>
> The muscles which encounter the most resistance in daily routine are those which become most highly developed and adapted. It is thus that the restraint of a traditional culture tempers and directs creative impulses. Freedom produces sterility. There was nothing left for the younger generation to rebel against, except the widest conceptions of mere decency. Accordingly it was against these that it turned. The result in many cases is the perverse and aimless dissipation chronicled daily by the gossip-writer of the Press.[5]

Examined closely, these two defenses of repression turn out to be quite different. At first Waugh seems to be saying much the same thing as Knox except for the curmudgeonly pose with which he calls for whipping the young and sneers at their "crude little opinions." But Waugh's emphasis differs sharply. For Knox repression is an elastic band that holds back dangerous impulses, a sort of moral girdle. For Waugh it provides the tension necessary to channel one's energy usefully. Repression in this view is basic to culture not merely for moral reasons but also, and perhaps just as importantly, for esthetic reasons. Repressive culture in the form of discipline and standards provides the means, not to hold back impulse, but rather to strengthen and direct it. One hesitates to say it, knowing Waugh's opinion of the good doctor, but this is pure Freud. Confronted with the constraints of the civilized order, libidinous and creative energies must find cleverer ways of expressing themselves than if they were allowed free, undirected play. Without Apollonian restraint, Dionysian impulse dissipates itself in futile, aimless expression. Conversely, and this is sometimes left unremarked in discussions of Waugh, without Dionysian ebullience, Apollonian order is lifeless.

On the evidence of his essays and reviews, Waugh clearly believed that in an ideally constituted society classic restraint and romantic energy would temper one another. Yet he seems to have taken inordinate delight in demonstrating their contemporary incompatibility. So much so that, even after allowing for the distortion of satire, we must stop to ask whether his fiction is giving us the peculiar world of his experience or his peculiar experience of the world. Do Waugh's novels reflect, in however exaggerated a manner, the world as it is, or do they represent his special way of seeing things? The answer must be yes to both questions. The truth is that Waugh, like many artists, throve on contradiction. Although he promulgated the redemptive virtues of traditional Western culture, he was, as Harold Acton put it, "always ready to be startled" by the spectacle of barbarism wherever it was to be found. He seems to have been quite determined to see his cherished values flouted. Certainly he spent enough time searching round the world for what he considered examples of man's inherent disregard for civilized order. Believing barbarism "was a dodo to be stalked with a pinch of salt," he went "to the wild lands where man had deserted his post and the jungle was creeping back to its old strongholds." It was in "distant and barbarous places," he reported, that his literary sense came alive, especially at "the borderlands of conflicting cultures and states of development, where ideas, uprooted from their traditions, became oddly changed in transplantation."[6] This is not surprising. The savagery and civilization he discovered flourishing promiscuously together in Abyssinia, Kenya, and Brazil were sure to intrigue one so divided between the appeals of order and anarchy within himself. This is why he found California so captivating. Here he stalked the lurid inanities of Forest Lawn cemetery. It was, in his words, "a first-class anthropological puzzle of our own period," a cemetery that welcomed suicides but refused burial to Fatty Arbuckle "because, although acquitted by three juries of the crime imputed to him by rumour, he had been found guilty, twenty years or so earlier, of giving a rowdy party."[7] Such a travesty of civilized protocol could not fail to quicken the imagination of one for whom outrage was a positive addiction. The payoff was his gloriously ghoulish novella, *The Loved One*.

All this is to say that Waugh's own unresolved tensions prepared him to satirize an age that professed allegiance to a code of behavior founded upon principles it had called into doubt. As one who must frequently have felt himself cramped by his chosen orthodoxy, he could not have failed to notice the lure of moral relativism. Why struggle, why suffer for a tradition with no more valid a claim on one's loyalty than another or than none at all, if such were imaginable? Much of Waugh's writing is about resisting the proposition implicit in this question.

Waugh's inner division also accounts for the practical decisions he made as a writer. His natural penchant for polarizing experience along the axes of reason and will provided him with extraordinarily effective means for satirizing his world. As a satirist, he did not want to use ambiguous shading and textured nuance. He was attempting to create fiction that would be as hard-edged and reductive as the schematic cartoons he drew to illustrate his early novels. These drawings serve as visual analogues to his writing. In both media he employed a firm, resolute stylization that portrays disorder without succumbing to it.

When Waugh's life is aligned with his writing, it becomes unmistakably clear that the divorce between reason and impulse dramatized in his novels began in himself. It is nothing less than his signature, to be read with equal clarity in his subject matter and his style. Although he entertained a life-long preoccupation with reason and decorum, he frequently behaved with gargantuan rudeness. He made a point of announcing that his conversion to Roman Catholicism was quite without emotion, a matter of cold, rational conviction, and yet, on other occasions, he could be brutishly unreasonable.[8] Having become exasperated with the fulsome praise *Brideshead Revisited* so often attracted, he put an abrupt end to one woman's fawning. "I thought it was good myself," he snapped, "but now that I know a vulgar, common American woman like yourself admires it, I am not so sure."[9] After reducing another admirer to tears, he was asked how he could behave so badly and profess to be a Catholic. His now famous rejoinder was, "You have no idea how much nastier I would be if I was not a Catholic. Without supernatural aid I would hardly be a human being."[10] There's no getting round the contradiction: Waugh was a man who declared himself committed to the "standards of civilization," yet conducted his life with legendary incivility.[11]

This contradiction seems to have produced in Waugh what might be called a polaristic imagination that strengthened his art while leading him to take political stands from which a more practical man would have prudently shied. This is apparent in both his fiction and his life. In *Sword of Honour* his protagonist, Guy Crouchback, rejoices when he receives news of the Hitler-Stalin Warsaw pact. The agreement may seriously threaten the Allies but it simplifies the ideological issues. Now, Guy thinks, he can go into battle with the clear conscience of a principled warrior fighting the dehumanizing collectivism of "the Modern Age in arms" (p. 8). If this is meant ironically—as I think it is in a partial and complicated way—then the irony is directed not only at the fictional character but also at Waugh's younger self. Waugh had recorded the following thoughts on the Hitler-Stalin agreement in his diary, 22 August 1939: "Russia and Germany have agreed to neutrality pact so there seems no reason why war should be delayed." Later, when it became clear that British policy favored working with the Russians, he wrote:

> The papers are all smugly jubilant at Russian conquests in Poland as though
> this were not a more terrible fate for the allies we are pledged to defend than
> conquest by Germany. The Italian argument, that we have forfeited our nar-
> row position by not declaring war on Russia, seems unanswerable.[12]

Better the risk of an ideologically pure fight against near impossible odds
than the contamination of a prudent but compromising alliance. Waugh
never wholly abandoned this position. His was always the wish for neat divisions, clear lines of allegiance, uncompromised efforts. How could such a
wish not decay into the embittered nostalgia that periodically darkened his
later years?

Waugh used a similar polarizing strategy to describe Ronald Knox some
thirty years after *Decline and Fall.* In his preface to Knox's *A Spiritual Aeneid* he borrowed his friend's own terms to portray his nature.

> He [Knox] liked the classic division of mankind into the "drastic"—the men
> of action and decision who know what they want and how to get it, who have
> little patience with the hesitation of others, who never shrink from "making
> a scene"—and the "pathetic" who take what is on the table when it is offered
> them, who suffer neglect rather than assert their rights, who hate to incon-
> venience anyone.
> In this sense he was eminently pathetic.[13]

By calling Knox pathetic, Waugh meant he was a man willing to suffer the
world in order to understand it. The drastic man, by contrast, is so driven
to dominate his surroundings that he plunges himself into the sweep of
events before he has time to assess their significance. These categories do
little more than make the familiar distinction between the man of action
and the intellectual, but, familiar as it is, Waugh's use of it is peculiarly
characteristic of him.

The drastic-pathetic polarity Waugh uses to place Knox is, of course, another version of Silenus's division of mankind into static and dynamic subspecies. Waugh's admiration for the "pathetic" Knox suggests there was an
aspect of himself that was drawn to Paul Pennyfeather's static soul, a part
that desired the intellectual order and steadfastness of Platonic categories
only fully available to those willing to remove themselves from the world's
seductions. This explains in part, but only in part, why he became a Catholic. As a seemingly timeless institution, the Church offered a retreat from
modernity's "confused roaring." But Waugh was too worldly for the kind
of cloister in which Knox, a priest and Oxford don, prospered. However reclusive he became in later life, he could never permanently resist the
temptation to behave drastically, not to say rudely, when opportunity
arose. His desire for metaphysical stability had as much to do with his apprehension of his own wayward inclinations as with the alarm he felt when

confronted by what seemed the dissolution of Western culture.

As an artist Waugh used his divided nature to construct a sort of knock-about allegory that satirized the troubled relations between reason and impulse in a world that had, so to speak, lost its head. Many have assumed he was on the side of reason in this issue. Certainly Waugh's essays support this reading. His comments on literature and art reveal a man generally more intrigued by intelligent craftsmanship than with esthetic passion. Intense feeling was pointless without artistic discipline. In 1946 he flatly declared that "the artist's only service to the disintegrated society of today is to create little independent systems of order of his own."[14] But this was Waugh's official self simplifying the issue he treated rather more complexly in his fiction. It is often assumed that despite his own flagrant indulgences, Waugh was committed to an ascetic, life-denying version of Christianity that secured order at the cost of vitality. But if this were the case, we must wonder why his willful rogues are so engaging and his Paul Pennyfeathers so lackluster. Even indisputably committed Catholics such as Bridey in *Brideshead Revisited* often come off as sententious bores, admirably devout, perhaps, but unquestionably limited. Contrary to some moralistic readings, Waugh's satire does not fasten on the will and instincts as though they were the exclusive source of the world's evil. Mockery was enough for the folly of his impulsive rogues. He reserved his scorn for his law-abiding bores, the decent, reasonable characters like Paul Penny-feather and Mr. Prendergast who conduct themselves prudently according to their inherited morality but either doubt or ignore the principles on which it was founded. This is true throughout his works and is expressed quite vividly in a surprisingly explicit passage from "Charles Ryder's Schooldays," the fragment of a novel that was to depict the youth of the character who narrates *Brideshead Revisited.* When young Charles willfully steps from the prescribed path of his public school's routine, his state of mind is described with a startling allusion.

> Today and all this term he was aware of a new voice in his inner counsels, a detached, critical Hyde who intruded his presence more and more often on the conventional, intolerant, subhuman, wholly respectable Dr. Jekyll; a voice, as it were, from a more civilized age, as from the chimney corner in mid-Victorian times there used to break sometimes the sardonic laughter of a grandmama, relic of Regency, a clear, outrageous, entirely self-assured disturber among the high and muddled thoughts of her whiskered descendants. (CRSD, p. 282)

It seems to me that the reversal in this passage expresses something of Waugh's essential vision. To see what this is, we must ask the obvious question it raises: in what sense could Jekyll be thought subhuman and Hyde civilized? This seems merely perverse until we reconsider Robert Louis Stevenson's late-Victorian parable and discover that by taking it out of the hands of the depth psychologists Waugh has conveyed the tale's real meaning in his seemingly casual allusion. Once suggested, it is obvious. Of course, Jekyll is the real monster of the story and Hyde his maddened victim. Jekyll is a monster of rationality and good intentions whose belief in man's perfectability requires that he brutally deny the Hyde in himself. As the story makes clear, Hyde is not the product of repression psychoanalytically understood. His appearance is not the result of unconscious denial. Long before Jekyll concocted his transforming potion, he had been acting quite consciously on his Hyde-nature in furtive nocturnal philandering. The purpose of his experiment is neither to repress nor subliminate his troublesome Hyde-self. Rather he wants to purge and ignore it so that he can get on with his ambitious program of scientific and social reform undistracted. Hyde, then, is the product of Jekyll's refusal to take responsibility for the flawed condition of his human nature. Undirected and unleavened by a morality that accepts sin as an inevitable, even salutary part of human experience, he splits in two. There is the noble, intellectual Jekyll, well-intentioned but ultimately irresponsible, and there is the bestial, impulsive Hyde, growing more uncontrollably powerful with each new outrage. Despite his anguished handwringing Jekyll must bear the moral if not the legal responsibility for the Hyde he has created by turning his back on his willful nature. Waugh's Jekyll is modern secular society whose professed moral relativism and progressive materialism require that it ignore a difficult truth: the energy that sometimes erupts as feral viciousness is the same that at other times springs forth as moral virtue.

Jonathan Swift had made the same point in Gulliver's fourth voyage to the Land of the Houyhnhnms, where Gulliver is so seduced by the dream of pure reason that he does everything in his power to deny his Yahoo humanity. Gulliver like Jekyll is a moral infant who desires nothing less than a shadowless life in which choice is invariably rendered uncomplicated. The point of both characters is that they reject the moral adventure implicit in being creatures endowed with free will. Each would rather forfeit his freedom than face the anguish of ambiguous moral decisions. They want blueprinted guides to behavior, foolproof and fully guaranteed. They long for a sunny world of childish irresponsibility in which their lives will be laid out, every wrinkle anticipated and smoothed in advance. Waugh directed his satire at just this sort of irresponsibility. Both in his fiction and in his journalism he attacked those of his contemporaries who relied on reasonableness and decency alone to face an increasingly uncivil world. Characters such as Paul Pennyfeather and Mr. Prendergast were muddle-headed Jekylls naive enough to behave as though good intentions alone could banish the Hyde both within and outside themselves. Waugh's argument is always that people who persist in the simpleminded belief that unaided decency will prevail in human affairs must continue to be at the mercy of the savagery they refuse to acknowledge.[15] By dividing human nature into Silenus's static and dynamic subspecies, Waugh in effect was bringing our attention to the delicate and often uneasy balance between Jekyll and Hyde, Houyhnhnm and Yahoo in us all. Put too much weight on Jekyll's side and you get Mr. Prendergast, a well-meaning but bumbling humanist who lacks the force of will to put his good intentions into effective action. Pile on with Hyde and you get Captain Grimes, the irrepressible rascal whose outrageous carelessness may seem jolly enough at first but has an unfortunate way of sliding irreversibly toward havoc.

This Jekyll and Hyde relationship between reason and will was, of course, a common theme in the late nineteenth and early twentieth centuries. We find the major novelists preoccupied by it. Their emphasis, however, differs markedly from Waugh's. Conrad, Mann, Lawrence, Woolf, and Joyce all portray European man as a victim of his overly intellectual culture. It was a disease that had enfeebled his will and left him devoid of healthy spontaneity. The generally prescribed cure called for turning off the intellect so that one could abandon oneself passionately to the flow of immediate experience. Health and wholeness could be regained by those who were able to mute the commands of convention and listen once more to their instincts.

Waugh was as aware as Mann and Joyce of the supposed enfeeblement of will that afflicted the thoughtful segment of the European population. In his own way he was no less attentive to the excesses of abstract thought than were Lawrence and Woolf. There is no doubt he agreed with Yeats that the best lacked all conviction, while the worst were filled with passionate intensity. His diagnosis of these familiar symptoms, however, was decidedly different. In his satires it is not the dominance of one faculty over the other but the failure to sustain a dialectic between them that has left contemporary society divided between mindless action and spineless reflection. Unhampered by conventional moral restraints, the doers of his fictional world go their way "careless of consequence" while the thoughtful find themselves chained by the forms of a tradition they observe but no longer believe in.

Perhaps the clearest statement of Waugh's position can be found in the work of Martin D'Arcy, the Jesuit who assisted him in his preparations for entering the Roman Catholic Church and with whose works he must have been thoroughly familiar. One of D'Arcy's principal arguments in *The Nature of Belief* (1931) may be read as Waugh's recurring thesis abstractly formulated. Taking the Thomistic view of the relation between thought and desire, D'Arcy argues that "they are both distinct and inseparable; the mind is a paralytic and the will is blind, and to meet concrete situations the two must help each other out." The will is naturally inclined toward truth, beauty, and goodness but can go astray unless reason guides it. Human nature, however, is fallible; it cannot be depended upon to behave reasonably in all situations. A man's mind is shaped by his experiences into a "pattern or complex" that "reinforces the native power of intellect." But if "the affective or desirous constituent of the complex usurp the authority of the main constituent, the mind," then "distortion comes about." According to D'Arcy, these "distinct but inseparable" faculties can only find their proper balance in subordination to God's design in which knowledge and power are not antagonistic but rather complementary. This follows the Thomistic conception of God. The essential simplicity of the divine nature does not admit any distinction between intellect and will. As a created being, then, man fulfills his nature to the degree that he approximates, at his own level, the divine unity of knowledge and deed. The solution to the perplexing conflict between thought and desire is faith in a divinity that bridges the distance between them. Only commitment to an absolute can strike a balance between the reflective intellect and the impulsive will.[16]

D'Arcy's work clearly explains what became Waugh's own view of the contemporary obstacle to living a purposeful, civilized life in the twentieth century and how Waugh proposed to overcome it. We can see him addressing himself to related theological issues in his nonfiction as early as 1930, the year of his conversion.[17] With few exceptions, however, he did not do so in his fiction until 1946 when he wrote his first avowedly "Catholic novel," *Brideshead Revisited.* In his earlier and some of his later works, he preferred to represent the crippling division between intellect and will with categories he adopted and parodied from modern philosophy and esthetics. To understand how and why this was so, it is necessary to explore the influences on his thought that preceded and, in some measure, prefaced his commitment to Catholicism.

III

AN UNGUIDED AND
HALF-COMPREHENDED
STUDY OF METAPHYSICS

As an undergraduate in the early 1920s, Waugh worked on the *Oxford Broom*, a publication founded and edited by his friend Harold Acton. Its first number included an unsigned manifesto, "A Modern Credo," which asserted in its opening paragraph that

> human nature requires an absolute. The exquisite chaos of modern thought offers this one incomparable opportunity—the creation of new absolute values. Recent intellectual sap has yet to vitalize any adequate forms of existence, and an imaginative apathy is still in vogue. But what sporadic imagination has survived is inevitably God-seeking.

The credo goes on to patronize Plato as one who had supplied a useful "life-concept" for earlier ages but can no longer be taken literally. There must be a quest for a modern "life-concept," one that "can scarcely come about merely through the cerebral or sensual irritations of our usual existence. Something slightly less primordial is required and more sufficient. . . . The ultimate requisite is always idealism incarnate."[1]

Whether or not Waugh had a hand in this piece of undergraduate self-importance, it certainly reflects the longing for certitude and wholeness evident in the novels he was to begin publishing a few years later. In fact, its argument is remarkably similar to the one Father Rothschild makes in *Vile Bodies.* Rothschild, the enigmatic Jesuit who becomes the unlikely moral spokesman of Waugh's second novel, seems to epitomize Western tradition. His name and vocation suggest antecedents in Judaism, Christianity, and European liberal capitalism. This background together with his extensive connections among the rich and powerful ideally situates Rothschild to assess his society—as he does whenever he can get someone to listen. But, oblige him as they occasionally will, none of his influential contacts pay serious attention when he explains that since the

Great War the Western world has been plagued by a "radical instability . . . a fatal lack of permanence" (p. 183), which has left the younger generation desperately disillusioned. Rothschild knows what the older, prewar generation refuses to believe: that while many of these heirs to Western civilization want nothing more than a sense of purpose, as many more have given up all hope of ever finding one among the fragmentary remnants of their cultural tradition. Without direction, both groups pursue an endless round of casual debauchery. As Rothschild tries to make clear, a hedonism as willfully improvident as theirs indicates something more than youthful irresponsibility. The Bright Young People have succumbed to a serious case of metaphysical despair. Waugh knew their world firsthand, and, while there is little doubt he was attracted to its energetic pursuit of pleasure, he came to be disenchanted with its emptiness. By 1930 he decided to satisfy his own longing for permanence by entering what he considered a rational faith that gave life a purpose beyond the enjoyment of the moment. But, as his letters and diaries testify, he sought explanations in secular thought well before his conversion.

Having lost his faith as a young man, Waugh turned to philosophy in search of some reliable principles with which to order his life. Instead he discovered "the exquisite chaos of modern thought." Writing of his early intellectual development, he once recalled how he had been deprived of the consolations of his boyhood faith. An Oxford theologian who came to teach at his public school during the First World War had unmoored him from his world of settled certainties and cast him adrift to discover for himself how best to satisfy his metaphysical longings. "This learned and devout man," he explains, "inadvertently made me an atheist" the day he informed Waugh's class that none of the Bible's books were written by their supposed authors and then invited his students "to speculate in the manner of the fourth century, on the nature of Christ." Once this worthy had "removed the inherited axioms" of his faith, Waugh found himself quite unable "to follow him in the higher flights of logic by which he reconciled his own scepticism with his position as a clergyman." And so, one supposes, the feckless Mr. Prendergast first entered Waugh's imagination.[2]

It was during this period of schoolboy doubt that Waugh read Pope's *Essay on Man*. The notes in his edition led him to Leibnitz, after which he began what he refers to as "an unguided and half-comprehended study of metaphysics," advancing only "far enough to be thoroughly muddled about the nature of cognition. It seemed simplest to abandon the quest and assume that man was incapable of knowing anything."[3] But, of course, he did not.

Seven years later (1925), his diary records that he was reading Henri Bergson. What did he make of the philosopher of Becoming? Typical of

Waugh, his entries include nothing in the way of evaluative comment. He only notes that he was "reading a little Bergson."[4] But a few years afterward, Bergsonian concepts appear in his fiction, most notably and comically in *Vile Bodies* in which he plays with the metaphysical differences between Being and Becoming. In this episodic novel, the one chapter that might be thought pivotal concerns an automobile race. As was his manner in this period of his career, Waugh has his narrator interrupt this story and, with apparently sublime indifference to his unfolding plot, indulge in what seems a digression but turns out to be in its own bizarre way absolutely pertinent to the novel. He pauses in the midst of describing the race preparations to meditate with Olympian aplomb on the fruitful comparison to be made between passenger and race cars.

> The truth is that motor cars offer a very happy illustration of the metaphysical distinction between "being" and "becoming." Some cars, mere vehicles with no purpose above bare locomotion, mechanical drudges such as Lady Metroland's Hispano Suiza, or Mrs. Mouse's Rolls-Royce, or Lady Circumference's 1912 Daimler, or the "general reader's" Austin Seven, these have definite "being" just as much as their occupants. They are bought all screwed up and numbered and painted, and there they stay through various declensions of ownership, brightened now and then with a lick of paint or temporarily rejuvenated by the addition of some minor organ, but still maintaining their essential identity to the scrap heap.
>
> Not so the *real* cars, that become masters of men; those vital creations of metal who exist solely for their own propulsion through space, for whom their drivers, clinging precariously at the steering-wheel, are as important as his stenographer to a stockbroker. These are in perpetual flux; a vortex of combining and disintegrating units; like the confluence of traffic at some spot where many roads meet, streams of mechanism come together, mingle and separate again. (pp. 227–28)

With this comic distinction between the cars of Being and Becoming, Waugh parodies the philosophical argument as to whether essence or existence should be granted ontological primacy. Traditional metaphysics, following Plato, used the term Being to refer to that which constituted the permanent essential core of things providing their identity and intelligibility. The accidental appearances of individual existents might change from one moment to the next, but their participation in Being guaranteed that underneath the shifting surfaces of daily experience there was an abiding stability. The more existential turn of modern thought, however, led many in philosophy to argue that this traditional assumption of Being's stabilizing priority in the order of things obscured and devalued the vitality of existence. Of the leading philosophers of this century who have concerned themselves with metaphysics at all, most have focused on change rather than permanence, relativity rather than identity, time rather than eternity.

Instead of a universe of definable beings and settled purposes, thinkers such as Bergson and Alfred North Whitehead had depicted an unfinished world evolving toward an unknown but vaguely beneficent end. Ceaselessly unfolding, the open-ended Becoming of their existential reality had been liberated from the fixity and closure of Being.

This struggle between essentialist and existentialist ontologies was much on Waugh's mind when he was writing *Decline and Fall* and *Vile Bodies.* It was a time when he seems not to have fully resolved the issue for himself. It is not surprising, then, to discover that, along with references to Bergson, he was also alluding to a critic and a theorist who were both affected by the philosopher's ideas. *Vile Bodies* includes a mock footnote to explain the provenance of some absurdly avant-garde party invitations. These, it turns out, were adapted from Wyndham Lewis's short-lived but influential Vorticist journal, *Blast,* and Filippo Tommaso Marinetti's *Futurist Manifesto.* The reason for Lewis's appearance is clear enough. His 1927 treatise, *Time and Western Man,* had attacked Bergson's thought at great length from a classical essentialist perspective. If Waugh was familiar with this work, as one must suppose he was, there is no doubt it appealed to his polaristic imagination. Lewis was the perfect counterweight to Bergson. Marinetti's role is not so immediately apparent, but Waugh seems to have associated his celebration of technological speed and efficiency with Bergson's concept of Becoming. Although he only mentions Marinetti once in a footnote, Waugh's choice of race cars as the embodiment of Becoming had to be more than coincidentally similar to the Futurist's paeans to the "intoxication of great speeds" in roaring cars.[5]

I want to consider first what Waugh found useful in Lewis and Bergson and then take up the Marinetti connection.

In 1930 Waugh paid tribute to Lewis, calling him the Samuel Butler of his age. Like Butler, he was a valuable "critic of contemporary scientific-philosophical systems" and, more than this, had "the finest controversial style of any living writer."[6] So impressed was Waugh, he seems to have set himself to imitation, telling his literary agent that he was ready to write more "Wyndham Lewis stuff" for the magazine editors he was cultivating at the time, a decision that may have been both literarily and economically motivated.[7] At this point in his career, Waugh was avidly courting notoriety. What would be more to his purpose than to become as controversial as Lewis? It would no doubt bring him more and better-paid assignments and he was never unduly delicate about writing occasional pieces to suit a paying market. But, economics aside, Waugh's intellectual preoccupations were such that he could hardly have failed to respond to Lewis's ideas.

For his part, Lewis wrote approvingly, if with some of his typical condescension, of Waugh's early novels.[8] While there is little danger of mistaking Lewis's writing for Waugh's, one cannot help but notice the similarities in their thought and temperament. Both had a highly developed visual sense: Lewis was a respected painter, Waugh an accomplished illustrator. Their training in the visual arts seems likely to have contributed to their dedication to an objective narrative style. Each in his own way composed his fiction with what Lewis called "the method of the external approach . . . the wisdom of the eye."[9] This was the strategy Lewis had suggested in *Satire and Fiction* (1930), a work Waugh reviewed enthusiastically, calling special attention to Lewis's "observations about the 'Outside and Inside' method of fiction," which, he declared, "no novelist and very few intelligent novel readers can afford to neglect."[10] Waugh was responding to something more than technical advice. Lewis had emphasized the importance of writing objectively from the outside as a strategy to hold psychological investigation to a minimum. It was imperative that the novelist resist the temptation of subjective sentimentality. Few counsels could have been as agreeable to a natural satirist such as Waugh, whose purpose was to depict the superficiality of modern life. Lewis and Waugh shared other predilections. Both were politically rightward. Each lamented the bankruptcy of traditional modes of order, and fastened upon this presumed cultural failure as an opportunity to create his own idiosyncratic vision. True, their novels have little in common. Lewis's lumbering narratives gain whatever crude energy they have from his unique brand of bullying animosity. Nothing could be further from Waugh's unlabored ironies and easy poise. His work exhibits none of Lewis's gnashing irascibility. Still, they shared common ground in their opposition to the modernist fashions that were taking hold in the art and thought of their day.

Although Waugh never referred to it directly, Lewis's argument in *Time and Western Man*, published a year before *Decline and Fall*, seems to have supplied him with a good deal of satiric ammunition. In this flagrantly unfashionable treatise, Lewis defends Western philosophy's traditional enthronement of the intellect. Reason, he argues, is in imminent danger of being subverted by modern philosophical trends which characteristically worship the will. When, to demonstrate his point, he exhibits Bergson's philosophy of Becoming as a prime source of contemporary metaphysical confusion, his influence on Waugh seems all but inarguable. As we have seen, Bergsonian Becoming plays a central role in *Vile Bodies*. There are other allusions to the issues Lewis raised with regard to Bergson. In *Decline and Fall*, for instance, the enigmatic Otto Silenus imparts something of the Lewis touch to a speech that parodies Hamlet's disgust with human nature as though its major fault was its tendency to illustrate so convincingly Bergson's concept of Becoming.

> What an immature, self-destructive, antiquated mischief is man! How obscure and gross his prancing and chattering on his little stage of evolution! How loathsome and beyond words boring all the thoughts and self-approval of this biological by-product! this half-formed, ill-conditioned body! this erratic, maladjusted mechanism of his soul: on one side the harmonious instincts and balanced responses of the animal, on the other the inflexible purpose of the engine, and between them man, equally alien from the *being* of Nature and the *doing* of the machine, the vile *becoming!* (p. 160)

Along with the Shakespearean cadences, Silenus seems to be echoing Lewis in one of his more misanthropic moods. He attacks the "vile becoming" in terms only slightly more vehement than those Lewis used to argue that Bergson's thought was a major threat to Western man's understanding of himself. In fact, here and elsewhere the affinities between Lewis and Waugh are such that a close examination of Lewis's criticism of Bergson can be used to excavate the unspoken assumptions on which Waugh's fiction stands.

Bergson presented Lewis and Waugh with a convenient target. His work distilled and popularized intellectual trends that traditionalists like themselves thought inimical to civilization. With his democratic assumption that all experiences—sensory and emotional as well as intellectual—were equally worthy of philosophic attention, he was sure to affront those who held to the classical notion that only a discriminating mind disciplined by the 2500-year tradition of Western thought could properly engage the rigors of metaphysical reasoning. His advocacy of intuition as a philosophical tool must have made it seem he was practicing a do-what-you-feel philosophy that located truth in the intensity of the unmediated moment rather than in the rationally demonstrable premises of classical philosophy. Today, Bergson seems rather less formidably subversive than Lewis liked to make him out, but he did call into question Western assumptions about knowledge and truth.

Bergson's thought turns on the opposition between Being and Becoming. His object was to examine the limitations of classical philosophy and find a way to overcome them. In its quest for the bedrock certainty of timeless Being, he argued, the essentialist metaphysics of the West had been chasing a will-o'-the-wisp. Reality was not to be discovered in static concepts, but in the relentless process of evolutionary growth he called Becoming. The reason this had not been understood previously was the Western tendency to trust only the analytical intellect when making metaphysical inquiries. Philosophers had come to assume that reality was only that which the intellect could objectify and communicate by means of representation in language and symbol. Other forms of knowledge—sensate and intuitive—were discounted. They were tainted by their immediate contact with the changeable and therefore unreliable world of material existence. Bergson questioned this evaluation, reminding his readers that the intellect's prized version of reality was, after all, an abstraction from immediate experience.

In Bergson's assessment, this emphasis on intellectual knowledge at the expense of other forms of apprehension exacts a serious toll. Maintained strictly, it manages to alienate us from the world of our immediate perception. Reality becomes an object out there that presents itself to our subjective awareness from across an epistemologically impassable gulf. Since the intellect traffics in representations, it is always and necessarily at one remove from concrete experience. It is as though the reasoning mind were only able to apprehend the visible shell that has just been discarded by the numinous principle within. In order to think or speak about experience at all, we enter into a collaborative fiction by which we pretend that this remnant fossilized by the intellect is the real thing so that we can attach stable, clearly identifiable qualities to it. The thing-in-itself, life itself, which is fundamentally a process of Becoming in time, always eludes our static categories. According to Bergson, this purely intellectual approach to experience cannot help but produce a sense of homelessness. By standing apart from its object of thought, the mind necessarily feels itself to be in an adversarial relation to it. There is a remedy, however. Bergson urges that we "install [ourselves] within change," that is, allow ourselves to experience the moment directly without the intervention of analytical judgment about its significance. In the moment of intuitive experience, there is no gap between the perceiving subject and perceived object; they join in direct, unreflective intuition. Only this total embrace of experience can give us that awareness of the irreducibly real that puts us into emotional and imaginative harmony with our world. This is the incommunicable, almost mystical experience of *durée* in which we unmistakably contact the numinous principle of existence: Becoming. Despite the quasi-sacramental character with which it is described, *durée* turns out to be within the bounds of ordinary experience. As Bergson emphasizes, it is commonly available in those moments of unreflective awareness when we are self-forgetfully engaged with the external world. The problem, Bergson argues, is that the Western philosophical tradition has not valued this experience properly.[11]

Bergson's thought is basically romantic and optimistic; it celebrates each coming moment as one more in "the perpetual climax of the now," to borrow the phrase of another romantic, Norman Mailer, and shares the egalitarian spirit found in Emerson and Whitman.[12] Every new moment collects and advances all previous moments. Time is democratized so that each instant fulfills itself in the universal Becoming. There are no declines, no falls from anterior ideals, only the sense of an ever-improving, gradual evolutionary development. Like Waugh's cars of Becoming, everything is in a "perpetual flux," always becoming but never being itself. It follows that there are no points of definition from which to measure improvement or deterioration. Each existent is no more nor no less than it can be in each successive moment. This, of course, is a vision guaranteed to provoke anyone who either believes in or longs for absolute standards.

Bergson's general argument in *Creative Evolution* was a prime exhibit of the romantic vision that Lewis thought so harmful. In *Time and Western Man* he argues that Bergson's philosophy is subversive to Western civilization because it threatens the privileged positions of reason and individualism in our culture.[13] It naively urges us to abandon the distinction between subject and object so that we can plunge into the temporal flow of experience. Lewis is at pains to warn us that however intense or rapturous this union of subject and object may be, it can only serve to blur our understanding of ourselves and our surroundings. To enter what Lewis calls Bergson's "time-world" requires that we surrender to the confusion of Becoming. It is a devolution into the amorphous world of primitive consciousness in which the self is so thoroughly involved in its experience that the intellect loses the leverage it needs to abstract itself from the immediate moment and thus becomes powerless to formulate the generally applicable distinctions necessary to establish civilized order.

Lewis recognizes, grudgingly it seems, that Bergson's intuitionism can be emotionally rewarding, but he is nonetheless cautionary, describing this reward as though it were a pleasurable but potentially addictive drug. Excessive use can result in passivity and loss of initiative with the fall of civilization to follow hard upon. If not a willful misreading, Lewis's version of Bergson might be considered a creative exaggeration. As no doubt he would have agreed, his argument has the tendentiousness useful for satire. He makes his point by overstating his case. Adopting something of a siege mentality, he warns that surrendering the intellect's spatial world of static forms will unavoidably undermine the fortifications of culture. The uncertainty of Becoming is a weak substitute for the stability of Being. In Bergson's philosophy, Lewis explains,

> pattern, with its temporal multiplicity, and its *chronologic* depth, is to be substituted for the *thing*, with its one time, and its *spatial* depth. A crowd of hurrying shapes, a temporal collectivity, is to be put in the place of the single object of what it hostilely indicates as the "spatializing" mind. The new dimension introduced is the variable mental dimension of time. So the notion of the transformed "object" offered us by this doctrine is plainly in the nature of a "futurist" picture, like a running dog with a hundred legs and a dozen backs and heads. In place of the characteristic static "form" of Greek

philosophy, you have a series, a group, or as Professor Whitehead says, a re-iteration. In place of a "form" you have a "formation."

In other words, Bergson replaces clear thinking with vague approximation. With this analysis of the consequences of Bergson's epistemology, Lewis seeks to prove that far from putting us in touch with reality, the philosophy of Becoming, for all its emphasis on the immediate, offers instead just another instance of the abstract posing as the concrete.

This has important consequences. Lewis reasons that an epistemology that favors ongoing formation over static form will naturally encourage a politics of passivity. Without definite starting and stopping points, it is difficult, if not impossible, to make firm judgments about one's experience. Individualism tends to get lost in the drift of mass opinion. Just as the rowdy Bollingers overwhelmed the orderly Paul Pennyfeather, so the Bergsonian "crowd of hurrying shapes" confounds "the single object" of the classical mind. Because the philosophy of Becoming deprives us of the intellectual tools with which to segment and arrange experience, we lose our purchase upon the terms of our existence. Unable to exercise the civilizing force of the intellect in balance with the will, we lapse into the amorphous world of primitive consciousness and allow our surroundings to shape us, especially the pressure of group thought. The resulting consciousness, for Lewis, is as tribal as it is modern.

> It is definitely our segregations that are to be broken up, our barriers to be broken down. The paradigmatic "objects" that are held up to us, as our mirrors or as pictures of *our* reality, are of that mixed, fluid and neutral character; so that, if we survey them long enough, and accept them as an *ultimate* —as a metaphysical, as well as scientific—truth, they will induce us, too, to liquefy and disintegrate, and to return to a more *primitive* condition.

Lewis finds Bergson's thought most disturbing in its apparent depreciation of the European philosophical tradition. For Lewis, classical metaphysics in the West was to be accounted a positive achievement of the moral will on behalf of intellectual sanity. By insisting that essence precedes and defines existence, Western thought had imposed boundaries on experience that made it manageable. It is this vision that Lewis wants to sustain. Rather than the dynamic flow of *durée*, he offers as his chosen reality the sculptural statics of Platonic forms glimpsed at just those moments when the object of perception most realizes its essence. In this epistemology, the mind is discriminating rather than passive in its pursuit of understanding. It actively seeks the essential nature of things by isolating what is humanly intelligible in them. Lewis approves of this deductive approach to knowing because he adheres to "classical science" in which an object realizes itself, working up to a climax, then it disintegrates. It is its apogee or perfection that is it, for classical science. It is the rounded thing of common sense. Eternity is, for classical science, registered in those moments, or in those things.

The purpose of Bergson's thought, according to Lewis, is to replace this essentialist epistemology of the clearly defined idea with a cloudy, quasimystical existentialism that claims to locate reality in the shapelessness of the passing moment. But Bergson's pursuit of truth in the flux was, Lewis argued, even more of a chase after the will-o'-the-wisp than Western philosophy's longing for Being. Worse, it threatened to undermine the stabilizing categories of the commonsense world of ordinary men that rested, however unconsciously, on the metaphysics of Being. Lewis does not make claims for the ontological reality of Platonic forms; he merely observes that life is more orderly and therefore more civilized when it is assumed that permanent principles underlie the flow of appearances. Lewis's point is that whatever reality is, Bergson's particular version of it is but one among many and to insist on its metaphysical preeminence is irresponsibly misleading. Of course, he involves himself in a difficulty here. Even as he argues for fixed principles, he confesses his own relativism. For all his emphasis on reason, Lewis was arguing for what he felt as much as what he thought. Waugh would try to resolve this contradiction through his faith in a transempirical reality.

Lewis was convinced Bergson was "more than any other single figure . . . responsible for the main intellectual characteristics of the world we live in." This included contemporary esthetic assumptions. He was particularly exercised that under Bergson's influence artists had come to assume that their appointed task was to develop strategies that would bypass the intellect. Modernist writers and artists were increasingly intent on capturing those moments of unreflective communion that put one in touch with reality unmediated by any preconceptions whatsoever. Lewis considered this at best sentimental nonsense, at worst potentially subversive of Western sanity. It could only serve to encourage the sort of decadent subjectivism he had detected in such writers as Virginia Woolf, Gertrude Stein, and James Joyce, writers who had turned away, so he thought, from the "Great Without" of the ordinary factual world to dawdle among the velleities of their pampered sensibilities. In Lewis's opinion, such suspension of rational thought was a failure to meet one's responsibility to impose human order on the world.[14]

Waugh's parody of Being and Becoming suggests he agreed with Lewis, even if he was not so militantly ferocious about it. Bergsonian philosophy, according to Lewis, is an "egalitarian science" which recognizes no "objects," that substitutes for them a cluster of "events" or of perspectives, which shade off into each other and into other objects, to infinity. Reality is where things run into each other, in that flux, not where they stand out in a discrete "concreteness."[15]

Waugh provides the appropriate image of this reality with his cars of Becoming in *Vile Bodies*. His description closely parallels Lewis's account of Becoming and even contains one of Lewis's favored words, vortex. These Bergsonian cars, "masters of men," are in a "perpetual flux; a vortex of combining and disintegrating units; like the confluence of traffic at some spot where many roads meet, streams of mechanism come together, mingle and separate again" (p. 228). As for Lewis, so for Waugh: Bergsonian Becoming is a metaphysics that threatens to dissolve the classical world view, submerging the individual in the flux of relativism. Traditional metaphysics was like the cars of Being which maintain "their identity to the scrap heap" (p. 227); it provided stability and continuity. In Waugh's vision, however, the cars of Being have been left behind. In their stead, the cars of Becoming have taken the field, "those vital creations of metal who exist solely for their own propulsion through space" (p. 227). But, vital and efficient as they are, these cars are liable to the same charge Lewis had leveled at Bergson's Becoming. They are more abstract than concrete, more romantic notion than sensible reality. They lack definition and purpose and are much too mercurial to be put to ordinary human ends. Always about to become themselves, they are never actually anything at all. This is the true Bergsonian élan vital: not to exist at any one time in any one place, but rather to be in a "perpetual flux." As the cars roar around the track, they make frequent pit stops to replace worn parts. Like the river of Heraclitus, they are never quite the same car from moment to moment. They are always in the process of becoming the car they will be in the next moment. Rather than an objective car tangibly continuing its existence in time, they present instead the abstract notion of car-ness. This is Waugh's figure of Bergsonian Becoming, then, a world of ceaseless change in which there are no befores or afters, but only a blurred now. This is the modern age in which the clear and distinct idea has surrendered to the shapeless smear of sensation. It was apparently important to both Lewis and Waugh as essentialists that they disprove Bergson's claim that intuition put one in direct contact with reality. Lewis's argument and Waugh's metaphors are meant to illustrate that, upon close analysis, Becoming is far more abstract than the intelligible forms of Being. Neither may bring us substantially closer to the ever-elusive thing-in-itself, but the cars of Being offer this advantage: they permit us to keep our heads and steer our own course, rather than be carried away by a vehicle whose only purpose is its own "propulsion through space" and for whom its driver "clinging precariously at the steering-wheel [is] as important as his stenographer to a stockbroker" (pp. 227–28).

Having examined Lewis's importance to Waugh, we can understand why Lewis is linked to Marinetti in *Vile Bodies.* If Lewis's critique of Bergson shaped Waugh's theme, then Marinetti seems to have supplied his image. Waugh's paean to the racing car closely resembles the kind of celebration of the new technological age found in the modern art manifestos of the early twentieth century, particularly Marinetti's Futurist proclamations. It seems safe to assume that Waugh intended the race episode to satirize not only Bergson's *Creative Evolution* but also the Futurist's worship of speed, mechanism, and inhuman efficiency, or what Lewis scornfully called the cult of "automobilism." Waugh's explicit mention of the *Futurist Manifesto* suggests that the cars of Becoming were a deliberate parody of Marinetti's penchant for saluting the automobile as the instrument which would liberate Europeans from their sentimental attachment to a dead cultural past. As Marinetti wrote:

> The intoxication of great speeds in cars is nothing but the joy of feeling oneself fused with the only *divinity.* Sportsmen are the first catechumens of this religion. Forthcoming destruction of houses and cities to make way for great meeting places for cars and planes.[16]

> We say that the world's magnificence has been enriched by a new beauty; the beauty of speed. A racing car whose hood is adorned with great pipes, like serpents of explosive breath—a roaring car that seems to ride on grapeshot—is more beautiful than the *Victory of Samothrace.*[17]

These passages seem a likely source for Waugh's mock tribute to "the real cars." As if to underscore the connection, the most formidable contestant in the race is named Marino, who is known as "a real artist" (p. 238) for his brutally competitive driving. His name, his reckless driving, and his designation as an artist all point to Marinetti as Waugh's model.

A figure such as Marinetti could not have failed to ignite Waugh's imagination. His wild disregard for the cultural past perfectly incarnated Waugh's worst fears about the age of the Common Man, as he liked to call the twentieth century.[18] But other than as a bogeyman, Marinetti must have struck Waugh as being no more than his time deserved. At least he spoke the truth others were too squeamish to admit. Who could deny the perverse justice in Marinetti's call for an unsentimental, dehumanized art that would deal honestly with the mechanism and speed that had helped to create a world of headlong change? Although Marinetti's practical objectives could have hardly been less congenial to Waugh, his esthetic provided the means with which the artist in Waugh could accurately portray the consequences that follow from an uncritical indulgence of the Bergsonian sensibility. In a racing car one could embrace Bergson's *durée* at its most intense; the heady acceleration of the twentieth century provides immediate kinetic gratification to those willing to abandon themselves to its participatory excitement. As handled by Waugh, Marinetti's Futurism and Bergson's Becoming are closely allied. They both turn their attention to the immediate sensate moment, neglecting questions about before and after, motives and consequences.

Futurist and abstract artists make appearances throughout Waugh's work. They are usually in the background, like the geometric abstractionist in "The Balance" and the Belgian Futurist in *Brideshead Revisited*, but their presence points to Waugh's continuing preoccupation with the significance of modern art. Futurism was particularly useful to him. It offered opportunities for portraying the inhuman consequences of Bergsonian existentialism. He seems to have found in Marinetti's "automobilism" a particularly apt figure for depicting the diminishment of the individual in this century. *Vile Bodies* creates a world in which people have become as replaceable as the standardized parts of their cars. The anonymous race-car drivers are especially expendable. These are the

> Speed Kings of all nationalities, unimposing men mostly with small moustaches and apprehensive eyes; they were reading the forecasts in the morning papers and eating what might (and in some cases did) prove to be their last meal on earth. (p. 223)

The Speed Kings have come to win the prize trophy, "a silver gilt figure of odious design, symbolizing Fame embracing Speed" (p. 230). In the modern world the prize goes to those who can best keep pace with Becoming; those who lag behind among the timeless categories of Being are not in the race at all. This, of course, is another version of Silenus's Big Wheel metaphor with which he separated the dynamic from the static as though they were distinct species. But here the dynamic participants enjoy no advantage over the static spectators. The cars of Becoming master those who drive them. These "unimposing men" lose their individuality to the race; as Paul Pennyfeather had faded into the background of "dimly discernible faces" when he fell from his spectator's position into the "confused roaring" of the Bollinger dinner, so these drivers become indistinguishable from one another as they hide behind their identical "small moustaches and apprehensive eyes." One of the characters exclaims, in a rare moment of insight, "How people are *disappearing*" (p. 266). Paul Pennyfeather had been the mysteriously disappearing hero of *Decline and Fall*. In *Vile Bodies* his disappearing act has become the general condition of society. Individuality is one of the casualties of the dehumanizing speed of a technological society.

Like the cars of Becoming, Waugh's characters lead foreshortened lives. They have little sense of continuity and purpose. Stripped of both their cultural and personal past, they are swept along in a "perpetual flux, a vortex of combining and disintegrating units." Impermanence is the one given in their existence. Waugh signals this by making disguise a prominent feature of his novels. In *Decline and Fall* a butler may be a gangster, a tavern keeper, or Arnold Bennett. In *Vile Bodies* a Jesuit, a rascal, and an aristocrat all affect false beards while titled gentlemen scurry from one party to the next working as gossip columnists. Colonel Blount writes Adam, his prospective son-in-law, a thousand-pound check, signing it Charlie Chaplin. Many improbable complications later, Adam returns to Blount's home disguised as the man his former fiancée has married instead of him. His imposture goes undetected. While one set of characters passes through a seemingly endless succession of disguises, another set responds to the resulting confusion by lapsing into the forgetfulness of cheerful senility. Lottie Crump in *Vile Bodies* is among the earliest of this type. Based on Rosa Lewis, the famous London hotelier, she has solved the problem of memory and identity in her busy world by reducing everyone she meets to namelessness: "You all know Lord Thingummy, don't you?" "There's Mr. What-d'you-call-him." "Your Honour Judge What's-your-name, how about a drink for the gentlemen?" (pp. 43–45) Her policy seems quite logical. Anonymity becomes the most salient characteristic of a world in which people and events so readily shift and slide from under their identifying labels. Like the race cars, no one is quite the same person from moment to moment. Continuity, identity, tradition have all disappeared in the blur of unordered experience.

Speaking on behalf of the Futurists, Marinetti jubilantly proclaimed that they had created "the new aesthetic of speed." "We," he went on, "have almost abolished the concept of space and notably diminished the concept of time. We are thus preparing for the ubiquity of multiplied man."[19] Waugh no doubt agreed with this assessment of the modern sensibility, although he hardly shared Marinetti's enthusiasm for it. To his mind, aimless speed and undiscriminating democracy were the specific symptoms of a general failure of the essentialist tradition to hold its ground against the growing existentialist mood, especially as it was expressed in Bergson's concept of Becoming. His esthetic problem was to find a way to register this mood without succumbing to it. He wanted nothing to do with the expressive fallacy implicit in stream-of-consciousness narration, nor was he attracted to the studied turmoil of literary surrealism. Instead, he devised a fiction of controlled chaos. To do this, he drew upon his knowledge of avant-garde art and, turning its assumptions to his own purposes, shaped an esthetic which might be thought of as an alternate modernism.

IV

A PURE AESTHETE

Interviewing Waugh in 1960, a television journalist rashly assumed he must have turned against the attitudes of "the aesthetic set" with whom he associated at Oxford. Waugh quickly corrected him. "I'm still a pure aesthete," he declared.[1] His nonfiction bears him out. From his first book, a study of Dante Gabriel Rossetti, through his journalism and travel writing, artistic values were his constant preoccupation—so much so that esthetics came to shape his social and political views. He assessed the world in terms of its art and, more often than not, charged it with the same incoherence he professed to find in experimental painting and functional architecture.

Like Wyndham Lewis, Waugh enjoyed posing as a scourge of the avant-garde, a man who stood for the "superb mean" of classicism, honoring the values of restraint and decorum in the arts. But, as in Lewis's case, a good deal of countervailing evidence indicates that Waugh was not immune to the tradition-breaking provocations of modern art, which is not surprising in one so divided between the orthodox and the wayward. This conflict seems to have been an important source of his fiction's characteristic energy. He may have been known as the bête noire of modernist art, but that never prevented him from pilfering its innovations when they served his purpose.

Waugh frequently addressed esthetic issues in general and modern art in particular, but his observations were usually made as glancing asides that interrupted the flow of his travel books, reviews, and occasional essays, the work he did quickly to gain income and notoriety. Of his few sustained arguments, only a handful deal with literature. The others develop his ideas on art and architecture. When taken together, however, his arguments and obiter dicta on both art and literature provide a revealing look at his working esthetic; it is one that seems to have prospered on contradiction. I want to consider both sides of this conflict in order to see what it meant for his work.

The familiar Waugh of unreservedly traditional values was never shy about making his orthodox esthetic preferences know. We meet an extreme version of him in his unfinished novel, *Work Suspended*. This is the

narrator's father, an accomplished painter who prides himself on being totally out of step with the avant-garde: "Only Philistines like my work and,
by God, I like only Philistines." As far as he is concerned, the public is
much better served with opportunities to view his copies of the old masters
than to make themselves "dizzy" by "goggling at genuine Picassos."[2]

This was a character with whom Waugh could identify. In his articles and
reviews he frequently took similar pleasure in ridiculing what he considered the excesses of modern art. In 1938 he satirized twentieth-century architecture as the excrescence of "the post-War Corbusier plague" during
which "horrible little architects crept about [Europe]—curly-headed,
horn-spectacled, volubly explaining their 'machines for living.' Villas like
sewage farms, mansions like half-submerged Channel steamers, offices like
vast bee-hives and cucumber farms sprang up round their feet, furnished
with electric fires that blistered the ankles, windows that blinded the
eyes."[3]

In 1956 he alluded to Paul Klee's work as "the acme of futility" and did
not hesitate to attack those who had been championing such experiments
since the turn of the century. These were the fashionable critics who liked
to argue that, given sufficient time to develop "new eyes," the public
would one day come to appreciate such artists. To explode this "humbug,"
Waugh derisively pointed out that "in the last fifty years we have seen the
drawings of savages, infants and idiots enjoying fashionable favour. The
[artistic] revolutionaries have grown old and died. No new eyes have
grown in new heads."[4]

This was Waugh's official line, put out for public consumption. With it he
was able to stage-manage his chosen role as a Tory debunker of sham fashions. But, as it was meant to do, this official front obscures his highly developed taste for esthetic experiment.

Although Waugh often affected a sneering attitude toward the representative works of twentieth-century art, he just as frequently found himself
fascinated by their esthetic innovations. In a very early essay, dated 1917,
he stoutly defended cubism against "deliberate misunderstanding of a
prejudiced public."[5] In later years he would come to think James Joyce a
madman, but in 1930 he was commending his development of narrative
technique as a model for young novelists.[6] As late as 1948, he was willing
to testify to his conviction that "the artist, however aloof he holds himself,
is always and specially the creature of the *Zeitgeist;* however formally antique his tastes, he is in spite of himself in the advance guard."[7] Waugh may
have enjoyed playing the unreconstructed Philistine singing the praises of
eighteenth-century architecture, Victorian furniture, and artistic verisimilitude, but a close appraisal of his essays and reviews tells a somewhat
more complicated story. His fiction also belies his pose. The abstract, sche-

matic composition of his early work has much more in common with the deliberate distortions of contemporary narrative experiments than it does with the traditional novel.

Waugh may have deplored the metaphysics of modern art but he was quick enough to recognize its esthetic usefulness. A telling example of the ambivalent response it evoked from him appears in his ironic appreciation of Antonio Gaudi i Cornet's buildings, which he chanced upon while passing through Barcelona in 1929. In Gaudi's works, he declares, "is apotheosised all the writhing, bubbling, convoluting, convulsing soul of the Art Nouveau," and he relishes its having broken "through all preconceived bounds of order and propriety, and coursed wantonly over the town, spattering its riches on all sides like mud." Then he goes on to explain in detail.

> But, indeed, in one's first brush with Gaudi's genius it is not so much propriety that is outraged as one's sense of probability. My interest in him began on the morning of my second and, unfortunately, my last day in Barcelona. I was walking alone and without any clear intention in my mind, down one of the boulevards when I saw what, at first, I took to be part of [an] advertising campaign. . . . On closer inspection I realized that it was a permanent building, which to my surprise turned out to be the offices of the Turkish Consulate. Trees were planted in front of it along the pavement, hiding the lower stories. It was the roof which chiefly attracted my attention since it was coloured peacock-blue and built in undulations, like a rough sea petrified; the chimneys, too, were of highly coloured glazed earthenware, and they were twisted and bent in all directions like very gnarled fruit-trees. The front of the building, down to the level of the second row of windows was made of [a] mosaic of broken china . . . , but thoughtfully planned so that the colours merged in delicate gradations from violet and blue to peacock-green and gold. The eaves overhung in irregular, amorphous waves, in places attenuated into stalactites of coloured porcelain; the effect was that of a clumsily iced cake. I cannot describe it more accurately than that because, dazzled and blinded by what I subsequently saw, my impression of this first experience, though deep, is somewhat indistinct.

Having caught his first glimpse of Gaudi's work, he tells us that he rushed off to see as many more examples as he possibly could before he had to leave Barcelona. Of some buildings on the grounds of a recreational park he writes that as he looked at them he

> could not help being struck by the kinship they bore to the settings of many of the later U.F.A. films. The dream scene in *Secrets of the Soul*, the Oriental passages in *Waxworks* particularly, seem to me to show just the same inarticulate fantasy.

He remarks of a church

> that Gaudi has employed two very distinct decorative methods in his sculp-

ture, the one so evanescent and amorphous, the other so minute and intricate, that in each case one finds a difficulty in realising that one is confronted
by cut stone, supposing instinctively that the first is some imperfectly
moulded clay and the second ivory or mahogany. . . . [Gaudi] is a great example, it seems to me, of what art-for-art's sake can become when it is
wholly untempered by considerations of tradition or good taste. Picabia in
Paris is another example; but I think it would be more exciting to collect
Gaudis.[8]

It is not surprising that Waugh should have wanted to collect Gaudis, as
unlikely as such a project would have been. Few experiences are so vividly
gratifying as those in which we find our suspicions confirmed by events
quite external to ourselves. In Gaudi's "two very distinct decorative methods," Waugh seems to have fastened onto an architectural equivalent of his
polarized world. This was just the kind of dichotomy that provoked his
imagination. It does not seem too much to say that Gaudi's buildings expressed for Waugh the disequilibrium fundamental to his vision in which
the extremes of impulse and reason are allowed to run wild. Their "amorphous," "evanescent" yearning echoes his portrayal of desire untempered
by thought. Their "minute and intricate" details suggest the impotent
workings of an intellect unable to achieve an overall formal integration
of the parts at its disposal. Above all, the aura of impermanence captivates him. As Waugh describes it, Gaudi seems to have celebrated in stone
moments of a purely subjective intensity unfettered by the constraints of
traditional convention. Despite his proclaimed classicism, Waugh finds
himself enthralled by these buildings and their willful disregard for the
forms and proportions appropriate to their materials. His comparisons are
telling: they are like "inarticulate fantasies"; rather than solid, habitable
buildings, they look like a "rough sea petrified," an "amorphous wave,"
and a "clumsily iced cake." Although these are institutional structures
meant for the centuries, they appear to be as ephemeral as the gimcrack
settings of a cheaply produced film. Nothing could better indicate how
contemporary assumptions about the nature and value of existence had
turned the artist away from his proper object. For traditionalists like
Waugh art was the one enterprise in which men had the opportunity to
transcend the accidents of time. Yet here was an artist of considerable talent who seemed to have ignored the essential, enduring forms of things in
order to pursue instead whatever stray, accidental impression had taken
his fancy.

Gaudi's buildings must have seemed to Waugh the architectural expression of the Bergsonian flux, which he was to parody a year later in *Vile
Bodies*. They literally concretized the élan vital. Their whimsical structures flouted any known architectural decorum, declaring each shape good

and just as important as every other, provided only that it be feelingly expressed. In Waugh's eyes this could only be viewed as a deliberately ahistorical art that celebrated the rapturous moment. Looking neither before nor after, it focused entirely on the climactic now of Bergsonian experience. Instead of memorializing the perdurable forms found in classical architecture, these buildings hallowed the perishable moment by taking their shapes from transitional intervals—waves about to break, cakes about to melt. For Waugh such works were at once deliciously grotesque and lamentably appropriate, exemplifying, as they did, the instability he thought endemic to the contemporary scene.

Gaudi seems to have engaged both the conservative and anarchist in Waugh. Accordingly, his response is an ironic amalgam of censure and delight. His classically trained mind might disapprove of architecture untempered by tradition and good taste, but his esthetic instinct responded to Gaudi's idiosyncratic energy. Standards may have been neglected, but, intentionally or not, Gaudi's amazing rule-breaking inventiveness did justice to a thoroughly indecorous age. With whatever mixture of irony, Waugh admired Gaudi's genius even as he deplored the vision it served. It is precisely this divided sensibility that he brought to his fiction.

Waugh returned to some of these issues inspired by Gaudi in 1956 when he wrote an essay explaining photography's harmful influence on painting, but he did so straightforwardly without the luxury of ironic appreciation. There is no ambivalence in "The Death of Painting," just a closely reasoned esthetic argument in which he comes closer than usual to making his case against modern art. The argument is especially revealing of Waugh's predispositions because of its implied philosophical grounds. It clearly relies on metaphysical assumptions similar to those that Lewis had enlisted in his dispute with Bergson. Speaking in his official voice, Waugh attributes the decline of representational art to the camera, which had done a "mortal injury to painters" that was "both technical and moral." By seeming to take over the province of pictorial verisimilitude, it had encouraged the artist to pursue either of two unsatisfactory alternatives.

One response was to allow photography to become "the ideological justification for sloth." The artist could forfeit representation to the camera altogether and abandon the traditional discipline of his craft. Why struggle to reproduce the standard "art-school clichés" of form and perspective when the camera can do as well without the effort? Instead of laboriously developing a technique, the artist can slothfully rely upon inspiration to imbue his nonrepresentational work with artistic merit. Slothfully, Waugh insists, because "verisimilitude was what took the time and trouble." In effect, the abstract painter was evading his responsibility to re-present the world and thereby invest it with his own interpretive order.

If the artist was not interested in abstraction, there was the other alternative. He could let the camera discover his subject for him. Since the snapshot had made it possible to arrest and analyze movement at any instant, including those instants that ordinarily elude the unaided eye, the painter could attempt to recreate the novel images so revealed. Although portrayal of this sort of representational truth might be as technically challenging in its way as the discipline of conventional verisimilitude, it begot paintings preoccupied with the transient ungainliness of the inessential moment, a result Waugh thought no less misguided than the abstractionist's product. "The 'slice of life,'" Waugh remarks, "became the principle of many compositions at the end of the nineteenth century" when "for a decade or more painting and photography were very close." The artist could now paint what had never been observable before: postures, grimaces, movement in stop-action, all manner of strained, off-balance subjects, animate or inanimate, that could never have been posed in a studio. All this and more the camera had made available.

> The simplest example is that of the galloping horse. Draughtsmen had achieved their own "truth" about the disposal of its legs. The camera revealed a new truth that was not only far less graceful but also far less in accordance with human experience. Similarly with the human figure. In posing a model a painter was at great pains to place her. His sense of composition, her sense of comfort, the feasibility of maintaining and resuming the pose, were important. . . . Then came the camera shutter to make permanent the most ungainly postures.

What was wrong with this ungainly truth of the camera? Didn't it provide the artist with novel attitudes? Waugh does not spell it out, but he seems to have in mind the same objections Lewis raised with regard to Futurist paintings that attempted to portray "temporal multiplicity" by spatially assembling stop-action moments of bodies in motion. Such art focused on the instantaneous fragment of time snatched from a rhythm that had yet to achieve its formal balance. Seemingly deprived of a unifying artistic force, these fragments spoke of life as though it were aimlessly indeterminate.[9]

Like Lewis, Waugh was convinced that the epistemological assumptions of twentieth-century art had deflected it from its proper course. Instead of the classic struggle to fit the mutable subject matter of this world to the perception of the timeless and essential, modern art either escaped into abstraction or occupied itself with the temporary and accidental. Rather than serving the human need for an abiding sense of continuity and permanence amidst daily uncertainty, it either turned its back on immediate experience or seized upon those aspects of it that exemplified its transient, perishable nature.

This, more or less, is Waugh's official line regarding modernist art. His jeremiads against it alternated between the sarcastic and the portentous and there is no doubt he meant his readers to take them seriously. But this did not prevent the subversive artist in him from appreciating the technical accomplishments of his unorthodox contemporaries.

Perhaps what is most important about Waugh's esthetic analyses is that they reveal at least as much about himself as they do about the art he discusses. His inclination is to polarize his subject matter into binary oppositions that ultimately derive from his initial cleavage of thought and desire. Here the polarity is expressed as form and formlessness, but it clearly parallels his other oppositions: order and energy, the pathetic and the drastic, Being and Becoming. As with everything else he confronted, he seizes upon what he takes to be the essential contradiction in the art he examines. In Gaudi's work he isolates the seemingly irreconcilable tension between the "evanescent and amorphous" on one side and the "minute and intricate" on the other. When he considers modern art in general, he divides it into two camps. There are those who lazily withdraw from life into abstraction and those who rush headlong to embrace the passing moment regardless of all proprieties. One response is fastidiously sterile, the other excessively mimetic.

This tendency to polarize his experience was so much a part of him that it became the basic structural unit of his work. Almost anything that came within his experience was liable to turn up in his fiction as part of a binary opposition, but modern art seems to have been a preferred candidate for this treatment. Perhaps this was so because, as the *Oxford Broom's* "Modern Credo" had suggested, the artistic imagination had a responsibility to resolve the conflict between "the cerebral [and] sensual irritations," between idea and experience, "the ultimate requisite [being] idealism incarnate."[10] To Waugh's mind the modern imagination had failed conspicuously in this enterprise and deserved to be reminded of its delinquency. At the same time its failure was instructive. The twentieth-century artist might not achieve the classic balance between mind and reality that had been his calling's traditional mission, but this shortcoming accurately portrayed the general failure of the modern temperament to sustain an incarnate ideal.

Waugh's first travel book, *Labels*, and his second novel, *Vile Bodies*, published in 1929 and 1930 respectively, offer a particularly vivid example of how he used the polarity he perceived in contemporary art to shape his fiction. To trace this process is to look into his mind and method. It begins in February 1929 in Paris, where he attended an art exhibit in the Rue Bonaparte entitled *Panorama de l'art contemporain*.[11] When he came to record his impressions a year later, two paintings that had been hung side by side remained particularly vivid in his memory. "It was very French," he wrote in *Labels:*

> [Francis] Picabia and [Max] Ernst hung cheek by jowl; these two abstract pic-
> tures, the one so defiant and chaotic, probing with such fierce intensity into
> every crevice and convolution of negation, the other so delicately poised, so
> impossibly tidy, discarding so austerely every accident, however agreeable,
> that could tempt disorder, seemed between them to typify the continual
> conflict of modern society.[12]

Although Waugh mentions many other works on display, it was these two paintings that particularly intrigued him. Clearly he seems to have discovered in their juxtaposition a perfect illustration of his central theme, as a closer examination of their contrast will bear out.

Waugh does not identify the paintings by title and the only extant review of the exhibition does not itemize individual canvases; still it is possible to deduce the style and character of the works he encountered. In the preceding decade Picabia and Ernst had developed styles unmistakably their own. We can be reasonably confident of the type of painting with which each would have been represented in a fashionable art show of 1929. Picabia had become known for his blend of Cubist abstraction and Futurist drollery; Ernst, for his seething surrealism. While we can only guess, Waugh probably neglected to name the paintings because he was more interested in the contradiction they suggested than in the individual merits of either. This would explain what seems to be an obvious discrepancy in the passage just quoted. Although Waugh mentions Picabia first, the sequence of his impressions does not follow this lead. His description of Ernst's "fierce intensity" comes before his assessment of Picabia's "delicately poised" order. Waugh may have arranged his comments negligently, but they are too much to the point to have been carelessly composed. Few sentences could have caught so simply the essential difference between these two painters. The sureness of his response suggests how fully their works engaged his imagination. And how could it have been otherwise? Put side by side as they were, they visually portrayed the antagonistic extremes with which he was always preoccupied. The "continual conflict" they suggested to his mind was, of course, as much a reflection of his divided self as it was a portrayal of the contradictions of modern society. They exemplified once again the incompatibility of rational order and willful energy to which he was always preternaturally alert. Each seems to have contributed to Waugh's portrait of an age in which mind often seems to be in retreat from refractory experience.

Picabia's paintings from this period resemble diagrammatic drawings of machines to which, perversely enough, he assigned human titles such as

The Infant Carburetor, Universal Prostitution, and *The Daughter Born without a Mother.*[13] Resembling the bright color-coded illustrations one might see in an issue of *Popular Mechanics,* these canvases display sanitized mechanisms which have never been sullied with oil or grease, as if to suggest the triumph of the technical over the biological. With whatever mixture of irony, Picabia's vision reveals a self-contained technological world sealed off from dirt and decay, a Futurist celebration in which speed and geometric shape liberate man from the messy unreliability of organic nature. Picabia seems to have taken ironic pleasure in announcing the new age of triumphant mechanism. In his *Daughter Born without a Mother* one machine brings another into existence out of its own internal workings as if to parody the twentieth century's claim to be self-created, self-sufficient, and therefore radically discontinuous with the centuries preceding it. Questions about origin and purpose have been put to rest. Picabia's purely technocratic vision renders such thinking merely quaint. In the world he portrays, efficiency is all. The metaphysician's why has been exchanged for the pragmatist's how.

Ernst's surrealism, on the other hand, presents a world entirely alien to Picabia's. Between 1925 and 1928 he created a series of hallucinatory wildernesses in such paintings as *Forest, The Grey Forest, The Great Forest,* and *Forest, Sun and Birds.*[14] These canvases are crowded with fierce vegetation. Through dense shadows, we glimpse writhing shapes that seem familiar enough at first but, upon closer examination, elude our attempts to identify them. The wild organic vitality of these paintings defeats the mind's inclination to name and categorize. It is a world that evades definition at every turn because it is blankly indifferent to civilized modes of order.

The juxtaposition of these two painters could not have been better suited to Waugh's satiric imagination. They portrayed for him the alternative types of dehumanization that result when men lose confidence in the ability of reason to discover some essential order underlying the chaos of experience. In Waugh's formulation, Picabia stands for an Apollonian retreat from the disorder of immediate experience into a kind of idealized geometric poise, while Ernst represents a mindless abandonment to the Dionysian ecstasy of pure unordered sensation. Given their emblematic importance for Waugh, it is not surprising to see him echo their paintings in *Vile Bodies,* which was published the year following his trip to Paris. Near the end of this novel, he places two contrasting scenes which, like the Picabia and Ernst canvases, are "hung cheek by jowl" without benefit of explanatory or transitional signals of any kind. Their debt to the paintings seems unmistakable. In the first, Nina Blount is physically sickened by the strange perspectives of her first airplane ride; in the second, Agatha Run-

cible drifts into hallucination as she lies in her hospital bed dying from in-
juries she has sustained in an automobile accident.

> Nina looked down and saw inclined at an odd angle a horizon of straggling
> red suburb; arterial roads dotted with little cars; factories, some of them
> working, others empty and decaying; a disused canal; some distant hills sown
> with bungalows; wireless masts and overhead power cables; men and women
> were indiscernible except as tiny spots; they were marrying and shopping
> and making money and having children. The scene lurched and tilted again
> as the aeroplane struck a current of air.
> "I think I'm going to be sick," said Nina.
> "Poor little girl," said Ginger. "That's what the paper bags are for."
>
> There was rarely more than a quarter of a mile of the black road to be seen
> at one time. It unrolled like a length of cinema film. At the edges was confu-
> sion; a fog spinning past; *"Faster, faster,"* they shouted above the roar of the
> engine. The road rose suddenly and the white car soared up the sharp ascent
> without slackening of speed. At the summit of the hill there was a corner.
> Two cars had crept up, one on each side, and were closing in. "Faster," cried
> Miss Runcible. "Faster."
> "Quietly, dear, quietly. You're disturbing everyone. You must lie quiet or
> you'll never get well. Everything's quite all right. There's nothing to worry
> about. Nothing at all."
> They were trying to make her lie down. How could one drive properly ly-
> ing down?
> Another frightful corner. The car leant over on two wheels, tugging out-
> wards; it was drawn across the road until it was within a few inches of the
> bank. One ought to brake down at the corners, but one couldn't see them
> coming lying flat on one's back like this. The back wheels wouldn't hold the
> road at this speed. Skidding all over the place.
> *"Faster. Faster."*
> The stab of a hypodermic needle.
> "There's nothing to worry about, dear . . . *nothing at all . . . nothing."*
> (The emphasis is Waugh's.) (pp. 284–85)

The descriptions of these two scenes are remarkably analogous to Waugh's
impressions of the Picabia and Ernst paintings. Nina's countryside is as
"impossibly tidy" as the geometries of a Picabia canvas; Agatha's hallucination has as much "fierce intensity" as any of Ernst's chaotic scenes.

In addition to the internal textual evidence that links these fictional
scenes with Waugh's comments on Picabia and Ernst, two nonliterary considerations support this reading. First, there is their closeness in time: the
comments in *Labels* must have been composed between 1929 and 1930,
the same period in which Waugh was working on *Vile Bodies.* Second, this
same travel book includes what must have been his source for Nina's dis-
tressing aerial vision. A few pages before he makes his comments on Pica-

bia and Ernst, he describes the flight that brought him to Paris for the exhibition. It was unpleasantly memorable.

> I was sick into the little brown bag provided for me. One does not feel nearly as ill being air-sick as sea-sick; it is very much more sudden and decisive, but I was acutely embarrassed about my bag. . . . if we had been over the channel it would have been different, but I could not bring myself to throw it out of the window over the countryside. In the end I put it down the little lavatory. As this opened directly into the void the effect was precisely the same, but my conscience was easier in the matter.
>
> The view was fascinating for the first few minutes we were in the air and after that very dull indeed. It was fun to see houses and motor cars looking so small and neat; everything had the air of having been made very recently, it was all so clean and bright. But after a very short time one tires of this aspect of scenery. I think it is significant that a tower or a high hill are all the eminence one needs for observing natural beauties. All one gains from this effortless ascent is a large scale map. Nature, on an elusive principle, seems usually to provide its own view-points where they are most desirable.[15]

Waugh's flight to Paris seems unquestionably the personal experience on which he drew for his description of Nina's plane ride in *Vile Bodies.* Granted this, it would be reasonable to expect that he incorporated some of his other travel experiences into his fiction. So it is not surprising that his comments on Picabia and Ernst a few pages later can be applied with equal justice to Nina's sickening prospect and Agatha's fatal hallucination.

In the first scene, Nina is presented with a picture of the twentieth century done in the Futurist mode. The unnatural perspective of flight has distorted the conventional countryside scene so that it reveals its distressingly modern condition. This is a world in which standard expectations have been turned thoroughly inside out. Even the usual distinction between the organic and inorganic can no longer be taken for granted. From Nina's plane people seem to be no more than the nearly indiscernible dots one might find on a statistician's graph. The inorganic structures, however, are invested with a vitality that dominates the scene: roads have become "arterial," bungalows are "sown," factories are "decaying." Compared with them, the faceless human beings have faded into their functions, "marrying and shopping and making money and having children" with mechanical regularity. The peculiar arrangement of this last clause reinforces Waugh's point. We would expect to hear that these people are marrying and raising families, earning and spending. By shuffling these activities and adding an extra coordinate conjunction so that first "marrying" and "shopping" are linked and then "making money" and "having children," Waugh suggests syntactically that there are no value distinctions among these activities. In the twentieth century people are reduced to the measurable functions of an economist's report which refuses to distinguish between love and material consumption. In the foreground of Nina's vision, "wireless masts and overhead power cables" form the technological grid under which the century takes its shape. This is a world in which things, especially mechanical things, are more alive than people. Like the geometric poise of a Picabia painting, the scene is "impossibly tidy" and thoroughly dehumanized.

If, in fact, Waugh deliberately connected modern abstract painting with the view of the earth to be had from a plane, then he was doing no more than providing an early demonstration of the point he would make eighteen years later when he asserted that no matter what the artist's personal preferences are he is always in the advance guard.[16] Indeed, Waugh seems to have been ahead of the official avant-garde in this instance. It was not until five years after he wrote of Nina's upsetting flight that Gertrude Stein had occasion to make the same association. Her first experience in a plane led her to record impressions strikingly similar to Waugh's.

> When I looked at the earth I saw all the lines of cubism made at a time when not any painter had ever gone up in an airplane. I saw there on the earth the mingling lines of Picasso, coming and going, developing and destroying themselves, I saw the simple solutions of Braque, I saw the wandering lines of Masson, yes I saw and once more I knew that a creator is contemporary . . . he is contemporary and as the twentieth century is a century which sees the earth as no one has ever seen it, the earth has a splendor that it never has had, and as everything destroys itself in the twentieth century and nothing continues, so then the twentieth century has a splendor which is its own and Picasso is of this century, he has that strange quality of an earth that one has never seen and of things destroyed as they have never been destroyed.[17]

As Waugh seems to have done implicitly, Stein explicitly associated her aerial view of the countryside with the vision of abstract painters. It would be interesting to know if Waugh ever read this passage. One thing seems certain: if he did, he would have agreed with Stein that modernism was aspiring to the discontinuity of a radically present-tense existence, but he would have deplored her congratulatory tone. He had little sympathy for Stein, judging her work to be "outside the world-order in which words have a precise and ascertainable meaning and sentences a logical structure." As for the modernist painters she admired, he thought the "message" of such artists "one of chaos and despair which is not the message of art."[18] Yet, as was evident in his response to Gaudi and other figures such as Gropius, Waugh was hardly insensitive to contemporary experimental art, however much he complained of its improprieties. Here, too, the modernism he officially deplored seems to have become a source of unofficial inspiration. Nina's view of the "impossibly tidy" countryside is quite at one with Stein's vision of a strange "earth that one has never seen" in which "nothing continues." The only difference is that the abstract "splendor" of this new world does not lead Nina to applaud but to vomit, as it also did her creator.

Turning from Nina's distress, Waugh's narrative abruptly enters Agatha Runcible's death-bed nightmare. There is no preparation, no warning. The reader is simply plunged into the chaos of Agatha's hallucination in which her consciousness has been reduced to the rush of black road over which her imagined race car speeds at an uncontrollable velocity. Having come to grief in what the narrator describes as one of the cars of Becoming, Agatha's world has become a blur, not unlike an Ernst painting, filled with shapes without recognizable forms, experience without defining categories. Her hallucination is a surreal parody of Becoming, or, to be more precise, of Wyndham Lewis's account of Becoming. There is no perspective, no past, no future, only the confused sensation of each new moment as she rushes into it. The experience is unquestionably vibrant, "probing," as Waugh had said of Ernst's work, "into every crevice and convolution of negation." It is also fatal. When Agatha's nurse repeatedly assures her "there's nothing to worry about . . . *nothing at all . . . nothing,*" she is correct in a way she does not intend. Nothingness is indeed worrisome. The suggestion is that Becoming leads to nihilism. Pursued to its limits, it literally leaves one with nothing. For Agatha, votary and victim of Becoming, the perspectives of place and destiny evaporate like the "fog spinning past" her. The flux of unordered sensation first knocks her on her back and then overwhelms whatever ability she once might have had for steering her car. As she speeds toward the final nothingness of death, she has no chance to make sense of her experience. There is only the exhilarating but mindless imperative to go *"faster, faster."*

These two scenes mark the course through which Waugh's fiction runs. Their juxtaposition constitutes a principle at once structural and thematic. At one extreme, static, inhuman order; at the other, the unmanageable flux.

Binary oppositions such as this appear throughout his work, forming units of isotonic tension upon which his satire is constructed. The pressure they exert against one another creates the energy characteristic of his narratives. Recurring in large and small ways, some of these polarities are so strikingly obvious that they halt the story, while others linger inconspicuously just beneath the narrative surface. Either way, polarity is always near to hand. It is Waugh's signature, an idiosyncratic expression of personality anterior to any particular writing. His stories are as hostage to his binary imagination as the abstract canvas is to the modern artist's preferred shapes. Waugh announced as much with his early story "The Balance," in which an art studio figures prominently. At one point the narrator stops to observe a "promising pupil" who constructs his life-class figure drawings on geometric principles. While the model takes her break, he continues "calculating the area of a rectangle" that he has abstracted from the shape of her body. Implicit in this scene is the balance of the story's title, a balance poised uneasily at the intersection of biology and artifice. The narrative concludes with its protagonist deciding against suicide and choosing instead to pursue his craft as he reflects that art is one with "the appetite to live—to preserve in the shape of things the personality whose dissolution you foresee inevitably."[19] Waugh approaches his subject matter in much the same way, extracting design from confusion with an almost geometric stylization. But to do satiric justice to the confusion, his designs do not resolve contradictory tensions but rather intensify them. By incorporating the extremes of Picabia and Ernst, he can both satirize and defeat them.

A number of Waugh's binary oppositions have been discussed already and there will be occasion to consider others in chapters to come, but it might be useful to pause here and sample a few more in order to suggest something of their frequency and variety.

Some of these oppositions are little more than throwaway lines. In *A Handful of Dust,* Mrs. Beaver, an interior decorator ever alert to business opportunities, assesses the effects of a fire with a ghoulish inversion of the expected sentiments. It "never properly reached the bedrooms, I am afraid," she laments, but then takes heart. "Still they are bound to need doing up, everything black with smoke and drenched in water and luckily they had that old-fashioned sort of extinguisher that ruins *everything*. One really cannot complain" (p. 3). Elsewhere in the novel, we are told that Tony and Brenda Last hold themselves to a diet "although they were both in good health and of unexceptional figure. . . . It gave interest to their meals and saved them from the two uncivilized extremes of which solitary diners are in danger—absorbing gluttony or an irregular regimen of scrambled eggs and raw beef sandwiches. Under their present system they denied themselves the combination of protein and starch at the same meal. . . . Most normal dishes seemed to be compact of both so that it was fun for Tony and Brenda to choose the menu" (p. 27). The word *normal* in this passage gives the game away. Even as they take precautions against uncivilized extremes, Tony and Brenda have slipped into a world of abnormal division.

In *Scoop,* William Boot, the most reluctant of foreign correspondents, sends his news-starved editor a cable from the African republic of Ishmaelia advising him on local conditions. It concludes, "LOVELY SPRING WEATHER BUBONIC PLAGUE RAGING" (p. 208). In another scene, the elegant Julia Stitch is discovered at the Duchess of Stayle's ball "in the Duke's dressing room, sitting on a bed, eating foie gras with an ivory shoehorn" (p. 101). In *The Loved One*, the sculpture of the colossally vulgar cemetery, Whispering Glades, includes pieces exhibiting grotesque misalliances of material to subject, such as "a toddler clutch[ing] to its stony bosom a marble Mickey Mouse" (p. 80). These comic disjunctions put the reader through verbal pratfalls. Set up to expect one thing, we trip over its opposite. Some are fun, others cleverly underwrite a theme. The bathetically sentimental statue of a toddler, for instance, has a bosom as stony as that belonging to the unctuously solicitous mortician-entrepreneur, Dr. Kenworthy.

These passing instances supply the background against which Waugh builds larger binary structures. In *Scoop* the oppositions dovetail into one another. Mr. Salter, Foreign Editor for the *Beast*, one of London's leading newspapers, recalls how he had been taken from the "ordered discrimination" of the humor page and "thrown into the ruthless, cut-throat, rough-and-tumble of the *Beast* Woman's Page. From there, crushed and bedraggled, he had been tossed into the editorial chair of the Imperial and Foreign News." His reminiscences are prompted by his present painful assignment. Under direct orders from Lord Copper, the *Beast's* owner, he must convince the retiring William Boot to leave his cloistered country home and hurl himself into the intrigue of an African civil war. *The Loved One* reveals the two faces of Dr. Kenworthy's Whispering Glades with a sudden contrast between its public and professional appearances as the narrator moves from the reception desk to the embalming laboratory.

> The pickled oak, the chintz, the spongey carpet and the Georgian staircase all ended sharply on the second floor. Above that lay a quarter where no layman penetrated. It was approached by elevator, an open functional cage eight feet square. On this top floor everything was tile and porcelain, linoleum and chromium. Here were the embalming rooms. (p. 65)

Below, the fake warmth of pseudo-traditional architecture and decoration, aged wood and soft carpeting; above, the chrome-cold intelligence that has contrived this travesty of funeral customs to profit from the public's exorbitant fear of death.

All of these juxtapositions echo Waugh's original polarity between the cloistered idea and boisterous experience, between what should be and what is. Confronted by modern reality, the intellect retires to its Picabia world of perfect, unsullied patterns, leaving the will to wander blindly through the Ernst forest.

V

SMASHING AND CRASHING
WAUGH ON THE MODERNIST ESTHETIC

If Waugh, in his official guise, was convinced that art and architecture had deserted the cause of sanity and civilization, he was no more sanguine about modernist literature. Sometimes his reactions were flat and specific. Proust was "mentally defective," "plain barmy"; he had "no plan" and the structure of his work was "raving."[1] Virginia Woolf's novels, he recorded in his diary, were no good.[2] Joyce could be detected going mad sentence by sentence in *Ulysses*.[3]

Generalizing from these specific instances, he decided that "the failure of modern novelists since and including James Joyce, is one of presumption and exorbitance. . . . They try to represent the whole human mind and soul and yet omit its determining character—that of being God's creature with a defined purpose."[4] No matter how technically accomplished, art that did not acknowledge, at least by implication, a purposeful reality beyond the sphere of human affairs was incomplete and incoherent. More particularly, the modernist author too often adopted an exorbitantly "subjective attitude to his material."[5] As Waugh implied in his portrayal of the madly self-obsessed worldlings who inhabit his novels, extreme subjectivity was a deranged willfulness that cut one off from the larger picture. It encouraged people to take themselves too seriously on psychological grounds but not seriously enough with respect to their place in mankind's common destiny. When Waugh, who always chose his words fastidiously, called the subjective tendency in modernism exorbitant, he meant just that. As far as he was concerned, it went beyond the bounds of reason.

Waugh neither argues nor illustrates his charge that the modern novel has become excessively subjective. As suggested earlier, his literary criticism generally consists of fragmentary observations. This is why his more carefully reasoned analyses of the visual arts are particularly useful. His remarks on Gaudi's architecture, for instance, serve very nicely to reveal what must have lain behind his criticism of contemporary experimental novels. It will be useful to recall them in relation to Virginia Woolf's explicit program for modernist narrative, especially since her work affronted Waugh's literary taste. In 1919, Woolf had urged novelists to leave behind the constraints of traditional narrative conventions and focus on subjective experience.

> Examine for a moment an ordinary mind on an ordinary day. The mind receives a myriad of impressions—trivial, fantastic, evanescent, or engraved with the sharpness of steel. From all sides they come, an incessant shower of innumerable atoms. . . . Life is not a series of gig-lamps symmetrically arranged; life is a luminous halo, a semi-transparent envelope surrounding us from the beginning of consciousness to the end. Is it not the task of the novelist to convey this varying, this unknown and uncircumscribed spirit, whatever aberration or complexity it may display, with as little mixture of the alien and external as possible? We are not pleading merely for courage and sincerity; we are suggesting that the proper stuff of fiction is a little other than custom would have us believe it.[6]

Woolf's commitment to the varying "uncircumscribed spirit" distinctly resembles the motive force Waugh discovered in Gaudi's shapeless architecture, which appeared to be guided by the whims of spontaneous emotion rather than the discipline of classic archetypes. Woolf's insistence that the artist find his subject in his daily impressions, whether "trivial, fantastic, evanescent, or engraved with the sharpness of steel," seems to anticipate Waugh's description of Gaudi's "two very distinct decorative methods . . . the one so evanescent and amorphous, the other so minute and intricate."[7] While it may be impossible to prove that Waugh was consciously paralleling Gaudi's sensibility with Woolf's, there is evidence that he had taken professional notice of her esthetic in the years just preceding his discovery of Gaudi on his trip to Barcelona in 1929. Certainly his description of "the romantic outlook" in his 1928 book on Dante Gabriel Rossetti recalls Woolf's celebration of life's "luminous halo."

> The romantic outlook sees life as a series of glowing and unrelated systems, in which the component parts are explicable and true only in terms of themselves; in which the stars are just as big and as near as they look, and *"rien n'est vrai que le pittoresque."* It is this insistence on the picturesque that divides, though rather uncertainly, the mystical from the romantic habit of mind.[8]

Whether or not Waugh was thinking about Woolf when writing about Rossetti and Gaudi, he would have recognized the "romantic habit of mind" in all three. A work such as *To the Lighthouse* would certainly have struck him as being as much a product of the impulsive self and as little tempered "by considerations of tradition or good taste" as one of Gaudi's buildings.[9] As modernists, Gaudi and Woolf shared an epistemology that sanctioned an ahistorical preoccupation with the momentary sensations of purely private experience. Their metaphysics logically led to a misconceived esthetic focused on the "uncircumscribed spirit" of subjective truth. Although Waugh's argument with modernism was less the polemic he sometimes suggested and more a struggle with an opponent some of whose tactics he could not help but admire, he was nevertheless adamantly opposed to what he took to be its goal of setting up the self as the final arbiter of whatever fragment of truth could be discovered in a world emptied of theological transcendence. In his judgment, this permitted every kind of vulgar excess in the name of personal fulfillment, including Gaudi's happenstance architecture and Woolf's uncircumscribed spirit. Instead of external standards established by tradition, modernism, at least the modernism advocated by Woolf, relied on the spontaneous judgment of the self to shape artistic expression, or so it seemed to Waugh. There was no more fallible guide in his estimate.

Of course, there are modernisms and modernisms. What Waugh found objectionable was the quasi-mystical phase of the modernist development that offered itself as a replacement for lost faith. Irving Howe has described this as a fusion of ideology and sensibility that

> strips man of his systems of belief and his ideal claims, and then proposes the one uniquely modern style of salvation: a salvation by, of, and for the self. In modernist culture, the object perceived seems always on the verge of being swallowed up by the perceiving agent, and the act of perception in danger of being exalted to the substance of reality. *I see, therefore I am.* Subjectivity becomes the typical condition of the modernist outlook. In its early stages, when it does not trouble to disguise its filial dependence on the romantic poets, modernism declares itself as an inflation of the self, a transcendental and orgiastic aggrandizement of matter and event in behalf of personality.[10]

Allied with Bergsonian metaphysics, this brand of modernism offered a particularly seductive view that experience was explicable without recourse to a transcendental religious principle. Given his temperament, Waugh was sure to think this dangerous enough to require his combative attention.

Waugh's narrative strategies seem frequently constructed with this modernist esthetic in mind, as if for satiric purposes he were devising a variant and, at times, parodic version of it. Again Woolf provides a convenient contrast. She and Waugh began in essential agreement: the nineteenth-century novel had died. There was no point to rewriting it now that contemporary experience belied its assumptions about the ultimate reasonableness of the world. Having arrived at this conclusion, they go their separate ways. Woolf moves inward on her characters, attempting to render their whole minds. Waugh stays outside, rarely giving us more than a glimpse of motivation.

Woolf was reacting against her predecessors' subordination of character to social and economic issues, and their related assumption that character was a function of material conditions which could be evoked by painfully elaborate exercises in verisimilitude. In her essay "Mr. Bennett and Mrs. Brown" (1924), she imagines Arnold Bennett's handling of a hypothetical Mrs. Brown, glimpsed in the corner of a train carriage. After quoting a long passage from one of Bennett's novels filled with minute description of a middle-class home with its frayed furniture, grimy windows, and prospect of a neighbor's garden, she concludes:

> Mr. Bennett . . . is trying to hypnotize us into the belief that, because he has made a house, there must be a person living there. With all his powers of observation, which are marvelous, with all his sympathy and humanity, which are great, Mr. Bennett has never once looked at Mrs. Brown in her corner. There she sits in the corner of the carriage—that carriage which is travelling, not from Richmond to Waterloo, but from one age of English literature to the next, for Mrs. Brown is eternal, Mrs. Brown is human nature, Mrs. Brown changes only on the surface, it is the novelists who get in and out—there she sits and not one of the Edwardian writers had so much as looked at her. . . . They have developed a technique of novel-writing which suits their purpose; they have made tools and established conventions which do their business. But those tools are not our tools, and that business is not our business.[11]

"For moderns," as Woolf wrote elsewhere, "the point of interest lies very likely in the dark places of psychology."[12] Their subject was to be the self, precisely at those moments when, whether by accident or design, it eludes the conventions of its society. In this undertaking, environment was interesting only as the occasion of the self's emotionally charged sensations, for "the task of the novelist (was) to convey this varying, this unknown and uncircumscribed spirit . . . with as little mixture of the alien and external as possible." To do this, Woolf proposed to discard the novel's conventional methods of representation. Like other modernists, she thought the commonly agreed-upon categories used to explain the world and human life in it were founded upon the unwarranted assumption that the mind had access to objective truth. The commonsense reality of public opinion, however, was better understood to be the product of society's consensual delusion that phenomena could be impartially assessed and made to yield an accurate report of things as they are in themselves. For Woolf, the world was unavoidably colored by subjective longing. There were no clear boundaries separating fact from opinion, certainty from desire. Like Bergson, she refused to satisfy the intellect's thirst for objective definitions. Instead she offered a romantic epistemology that sought reality in the fleeting impressions and intuitions experienced in those moments of unreflective communion that occur before the perceiving subject has the opportunity to distinguish itself from its perceived object. Uncontaminated by culturally acquired intellectual habits, these moments were largely inaccessible to discursive reason. They yielded the kind of unconditioned experience romantics like Wordsworth celebrated for its power to remove the blinders of routine that ordinarily limit our daily awareness of the world around us. But Woolf's romanticized experience differed from Wordsworth's in one important respect. Wordsworth had postulated, however vaguely, a unifying intelligence that imparted to these moments some ultimate purpose. Woolf accepted the epistemology but rejected the teleology. For her there was nothing that bound these experiences together, nothing that made any final sense of them other than the honesty of the artist at the moment of creation. This was what lay behind her ironic contention that human nature had changed in 1910.[13] On the eve of the Great War men were beginning to realize that they were living outside the conventional structures that had been provided in earlier eras by tradition and religion.

Now that artists had been deprived of the usual sources of order, she argued that they had no choice but to explore the self apart from society. The subject matter of art was to be the immediate data of consciousness, that amorphous, endlessly fascinating interpenetration of sensation and sensibility. Novelists must give up the conventions of realism that demanded detailed observation of the social world. Instead, they would depict the genuine self in its moment-by-moment awareness—fertile, chaotic, infinitely suggestive. The self, Woolf's Mrs. Brown, must be rescued from the worn-out furniture of realism.

> At whatever cost of life, limb and damage to valuable property Mrs. Brown must be rescued, expressed, and set in her high relations to the world . . . so the smashing and crashing began. Thus it is what we hear all round us, in poems and novels and biographies, even in newspaper articles and essays, the sound of breaking and falling, crashing and destruction.[14]

This "smashing and crashing" can be heard everywhere in Waugh's fiction, but his aims are quite different from Woolf's. Waugh applied a modernist technique without a modernist ideology. The conservative in him rejected the notion that subjective truth and "the dark places of psychology" were art's special province, but the artist in him welcomed experiment. As a novelist he set himself the task of developing narrative innovations that would reflect the confusion of his age. But he was determined to do this without succumbing to the self-indulgent vagaries which he considered the fundamental modernist mistake. He found his solution, eccentrically enough, in the works of Ronald Firbank.

In his 1929 essay praising Firbank as the novelist's novelist, Waugh announced what must have seemed, supposing anyone noticed, a contradictory appraisal of the twentieth-century novel. On the one hand, he saluted modern narrative innovations, such as authorial neutrality, temporal dislocation, associational psychology, and the suspension of the ordinary laws of logic; on the other, he rejected the modernist preoccupation with subjectivity. The true innovator, he claimed, was Firbank because, while experimental, his fiction remained objective.

Waugh found in Firbank's novels a way to avoid both the restrictive conventions of realism and the psychoanalytic excesses of modernism. His elliptically evanescent narratives provided an avant-garde strategy that never lapsed into self-absorbed solemnity. Firbank "emphasized the fact which his contemporaries were neglecting," Waugh wrote approvingly, "that the novel should be directed for entertainment." Unlike other novelists whose attempts to deal with the contemporary world had "forced [them] into a subjective attitude to [their] material, Firbank remained objective." He did so with a wit that Waugh described as "structural." Unintimidated by the realist tradition of the novel, Firbank was content to be elegantly artificial. This was extremely important for the young Waugh who was as determined as any of his contemporaries to escape the earnest humanism of the nineteenth-century novel. Although Waugh did not fault the Edwardian novelists as Woolf had done for their lack of psychological insight, he did object to their naive narrative logic that assumed the world was reasonable and human behavior intelligible.

> Nineteenth-century novelists achieved a balance of subject and form only by complete submission to the idea of the succession of events in an arbitrarily limited period of time. Just as in painting until the last generation the aesthetically significant activity of the artist had always to be occasioned by anecdote and representation, so the novelist was fettered by the chain of cause and effect. Almost all the important novels of this century have been experiments in making an art form out of this raw material of narration.[15]

This sounds like a passage from a modernist manifesto—and it is, in its own way. Waugh may not have set out to rival Proust and Joyce but he did experiment with narrative form and Firbank provided a useful point of departure.

Firbank's novels are constructed with a series of counterpointed scenes that flash on and off with disconcerting speed. The mainstays of the traditional narrative—descriptive detail, logical transitions, plausible characterization, orderly chronology—have all but disappeared. His plots do not progress in a linear fashion; rather, they strike a sequence of poses, each expressing its own fey attitude. Although the scenes change rapidly, his narrative seems static. The reader is presented with a series of tenuously connected tableaux reminiscent of a frieze; but, unlike conventional friezes in which the carved relief figures have been arranged to tell a story, Firbank's figures are juxtaposed in mute irony, leaving the reader to fill in the narrative connections. At the beginning of his career, Waugh was obviously impressed by this technique. Particularly pleased with Firbank's disregard for the usual marks of plausibility, Waugh continues in this essay:

> His later novels are almost wholly devoid of any attributions of cause to effect; there is the barest minimum of direct description; his compositions are built up, intricately and with a balanced alternation of the wildest extravagance and the most austere economy, with conversational *nuances*. They may be compared to cinema films in which the relation of caption and photograph is directly reversed; occasionally a brief, visual image flashes out to illumine and explain the flickering succession of spoken words. . . . In this way Firbank achieved a new art form primarily as a vehicle for bringing coherence to his own elusive humor. But in doing this he solved the problem which most vexes the novelist of the present time.[16]

What is the problem that "most vexes the novelist of the present time"? Waugh never quite says, but we can infer that it is the same one Virginia Woolf confronted when she wrote that contemporary writers had lost the sense of certainty that is "the condition which makes it possible to write." However rebellious or experimental earlier artists had been, they generally believed their world was intelligible, at least in theory. But with the decline of belief, twentieth-century artists could no longer feel certain that the world they were representing had any validity beyond their own immediate perceptions. It followed, paradoxically enough, that for all their esthetic groundbreaking, contemporary artists were not as free as, say, Walter Scott or Jane Austen, who were supported in their enterprise by the conviction that the world they inhabited and wrote about made sense not only personally but also publicly and even cosmically. As Woolf herself put it, "to believe that your impressions hold good for others is to be released from the cramp and confinement of personality."[17]

Waugh wanted a method that would allow him to reflect the contemporary lack of certainty without cramping him in the toils of personality. Firbank was his answer. The flickering counterpoint of briefly sketched scenes edited cinematically and held together by a narrative tone best described as dandyish mockery: this was Firbank's lesson and Waugh applied it enthusiastically, pursuing what he referred to as his "absorbing task, the attempt to reduce to order the anarchic raw materials of life."[18] Of course, he could have learned these techniques elsewhere, but Firbank's absurd subject matter, weightless characters, and elliptical wit—in sum, his gossamer inconsequence—were congenial to Waugh's satiric temperament. Here were the materials and methods with which he could construct his vision of man in the contemporary world, stripped of "his systems of belief and ideal claims." Waugh had learned to explode traditional literary conventions with great enthusiasm. Plot and character are laughed away with a surreal salute. Narratives splinter into as many as six or seven unrelated scenes within a few pages. Characters are drawn with paper-thin inconsequence, introduced with no more ado than that allotted Adam Fenwick-Symes in *Vile Bodies*, of whose appearance we learn nothing more than that "he looked exactly as young men like him do look" (p. 7). Verisimilitude dissolves completely when Waugh's narrators interrupt themselves to comment on the unreality of these figures.

That established notions of character in particular should be cast aside in Waugh's fiction stresses how his assumptions differ from those of both Bennett and Woolf. Bennett saw character as the product and instrument of large socioeconomic forces; Woolf saw it as the evanescent succession of momentary feelings and responses. Waugh, however, was convinced that men take their identity from the physical and spiritual structures they inhabit. He used architecture to make his point in *Brideshead Revisited*. This novel's narrator, Charles Ryder, whom Waugh elsewhere identified as his own spokesman in cultural matters, tells us that he "regarded men as something much less than the buildings they made and inhabited, as mere lodgers and short-term sub-lessees of small importance in the long, fruitful life of their homes."[19] As a corollary to this vision of architectural continuity, a man's sense of himself may be said to derive from the culture that preceded him and that, in normal times, he can expect to succeed him. By foregrounding scenes of architectural destruction in his novels, Waugh is able to suggest just how abnormally insignificant and transient he believed life had become in the twentieth century.

The "smashing and crashing" Woolf had urged as necessary to liberate Mrs. Brown resounds in Waugh's fiction as though he had taken Woolf's advice and applied it quite literally. As a result, ancestral homes fall right and left throughout his pages. *Decline and Fall* sets the pattern for Waugh's architectural motif when Margot Beste-Chetwynde replaces her sixteenth-century home with a "surprising creation in ferro concrete and aluminum" that has been designed to eliminate "the human element from the consideration of form" (p. 59). In novel after novel, ancestral homes are razed to make way for functional structures, usually apartment buildings comprised of one-room flats suited for an unsettled generation of self-obsessed transients. This is Waugh's image of a rootless modernity in which people are too preoccupied with themselves to consider anything more than the satisfactions of the present moment. The collapse of traditional structures does not lead, as Woolf had promised, to self-discovery; rather, it reveals the shallow inconsequence of characters who are left to lead absurdly pointless lives amidst the wreckage. Some, like Tony Last in *A Handful of Dust*, temporarily stave off these bleak consequences by repairing to fake replicas of an earlier and presumably healthier age. Others are quite content to exist in the bare functional buildings of modern architecture, blandly and uncritically acquiescing in the metaphysical despair Waugh read in such structures.

Charles Ryder in *Brideshead Revisited* seems particularly close to Waugh on this point. Ryder is an artist who makes his living by painting ancestral homes just before they are torn down, and his career becomes an elegiac mission to record the remains of a dying civilization lest it disappear without a trace. Waugh seems to have thought his fiction would perform a similar function. In 1946 he remarked portentously that he foresaw "in the dark age opening that the scribes [might] play the part of the monks after the first barbarian victories." The monks "were not satirists," he reminds us, but chroniclers of civilization's decline.[20] That would be his role also: a sardonic scribe recording the negligence with which the West was letting itself slip into ruin.

But Waugh did much more than record. Armed with Firbank's structural wit, he set out to create an alternative vision to that of Woolf and other modernist novelists who were pleased to pursue and indulge the self "at whatever cost to life . . . and valuable property." Waugh took modernist assumptions to what he reasoned were their logical conclusions. Consequently, in his satires Mrs. Brown, left unsupported by the common cultural props of personality, dissolves and fades like Paul Pennyfeather into "the kaleidoscope of dimly discerned faces" that constitutes the featureless society of the twentieth century.

VI

BECOMING CHARACTERS
THE SHAMELESS BLONDE AND THE
MYSTERIOUSLY DISAPPEARING SELF

The protagonist of *Vile Bodies* is as inconsequential as any to be found in Firbank. He is introduced as he is about to cross the Channel from France to England.

> A young man came on board carrying his bag. There was nothing particularly remarkable about his appearance. He looked exactly as young men like him do look; he was carrying his own bag, which was disagreeably heavy, because he had no money left in francs and very little left in anything else. He had been two months in Paris writing a book and was coming home because, in the course of his correspondence, he had got engaged to be married. His name was Adam Fenwick-Symes. (p. 7)

Although he is still in his twenties and painfully inexperienced, the book Adam has been writing is his autobiography. Upon his arrival, the English Customs Officers promptly confiscate his manuscript along with another confessional work he is carrying in his luggage, Dante's *Purgatorio*. Both, it seems, are examples of indecent literature. "I knows dirt when I sees it or I shouldn't be where I am today" (p. 25), as one of the officers puts it. After minimal protest, Adam gives up his appeal to reason and soon finds himself in London penniless and quite without prospects. He does nothing further to regain his manuscript and we never learn anything about its contents.

Stripped of his personal past and his cultural tradition—his autobiography and his copy of Dante—he drifts lost in the present moment without plans for the future. He appears without distinguishing marks, a passive victim thoroughly acquiescent to the whims of an arbitrary society. He is one of Waugh's interchangeable people. Bereft of an abiding identity, he shuttles haphazardly from one role to another—would-be author, gossip columnist, vacuum salesman, impromptu pimp, and, finally, a soldier lost in the uncharted landscape of "the biggest battlefield in the history of the world" (p. 314). All the while he remains as featureless as his original description implies. Not only are we left in the dark concerning his physical appearance, we never learn what he thinks and feels. He comes no closer to expressing genuine emotion about his predicament than to vaguely register his discontent with "things" in general: "I'd give anything in the world for something different" (p. 273). His complaints never become more specific. He does not seem to have the resolve to know what he wants. Whatever he was before, once Adam returns to England he is transformed into a creature of Becoming, living haphazardly from moment to moment.

As a character Adam cannot be classified. It would be tempting to think of him as a Candidean innocent but he does not fit the mold. He is quite capable of worldly and even low calculation. He is not above fabricating news to fill his gossip column in the *Daily Excess* and seems to have no compunction about "selling" his fiancée to a competing suitor in order to pay an overdue hotel bill.

There is something essentially undecipherable about him. Because he is deprived of a cultural context and a recognizable psychological interior, we can neither place him nor readily discern his satiric function. He is one of the novel's several unsolved mysteries. Others include a political conspiracy of unspecified intent and the unaccountable world war with which the novel abruptly closes. Like Adam these elements are put before us without apology or explanation.

Waugh deprived his early works of background exposition wherever he could do so without rendering them wholly unintelligible. One's first reading of these novels is something like trying to follow a detective story constructed by an author who has willfully neglected to include some of his plot's important clues and motives. Initially, there does not seem to be any definite solution to the mystery that is so cheerfully flaunted. Someone or something is missing but we are never told who or why. There are criminal forces abroad but no one has any definite charges to press. Shadowy characters flicker about in the middle distance. They find themselves implicated in acts of random cruelty. Mindless violence is liable to break in on them at any moment. And all this proceeds unremarked. Wandering dazed, without the resources to protest their plight, submitting to almost any outrage that happens to come their way, Waugh's characters leave us stranded. Instead of a clearly defined norm from which to gauge lapses in manners and morals, we encounter a disturbing emptiness. Something has been left out. Indeed, Waugh's novels are distinguished as much by what they omit as by what they include. Psychological exposition is especially conspicuous by its absence.

Waugh's fiction seems at first remarkably deficient when it comes to creating the illusion of depth. His characters are stubbornly superficial; they resist all attempts to sound their psychological interiors. Their actions seem to spring into the world without the ground of inward motivation. However appalling the accidents and treacheries that routinely beset them, they rarely express their feelings. In *Vile Bodies* a young couple repeatedly make and break their engagement through the course of their frequent telephone conversations, never raising their voices or forgetting to add a polite good-bye before hanging up. Though they are the novel's central characters, we never learn what they feel about their fluctuating romance. A child in *Decline and Fall* is accidentally shot in the foot, contracts gangrene, and finally dies. His slow decline is reported casually in a series of brief asides over the space of a hundred pages. The only lament is his mother's annoyance that people will think her refusal to attend a wedding a manifestation of her grief rather than the snub it's meant to be. In the same novel the protagonist Paul Pennyfeather discovers that his guardian has used the occasion of his undeserved dismissal from Scone College as a pretext to cheat him of his inheritance. When he diffidently inquires about his rights, he receives no comfort. "Have I no right to any money at all?" he asks. "'None whatsoever, my dear boy,' said his guardian quite cheerfully." So much for Paul's rights. He never raises the issue again and we never learn how he feels about being cheated. The narrator merely observes that "Paul's guardian's daughter had two new evening frocks [that spring], and, thus glorified, became engaged to a well conducted young man in the Office of Works" (p. 12). Not only are we left wondering what Paul Pennyfeather feels about his greedy uncle, we are also kept from all but his most routine responses to the rest of "the unusual series of events of which his shadow was witness" (p. 164).

One critic refers to Waugh's refusal to display his characters' interior development as the "blank silence" that thwarts the reader's understanding at every turn.[1] There is some justice in this charge. Waugh's characters rarely give voice to their feelings. They seem to have little to say about the moral and emotional implications of their experiences however urgent, painful, or startling. In *Black Mischief* Basil Seal inadvertently partakes of a cannibal feast in which the primary ingredient is comprised of his lover's remains. Atrocious as this episode is, neither Basil nor the narrator comments on it, unless one takes as moral commentary Basil's response, on returning to London, to inquiries about his future plans: "No plans; I think I've had enough of barbarism for a bit" (p. 305). And that is all. The same silence characterizes Brenda Last's adulterous affair with John Beaver in *A Handful of Dust*. Other than her vague boredom with married life, we never discover Brenda's motives for taking up with someone who she herself admits is a hopeless dullard.

As mentioned earlier, Waugh at the beginning of his career found Wyndham Lewis's fictional theories useful, especially his ideas about characterization. Lewis was committed to an esthetic of surfaces that were to be rendered by "the external approach" with "the wisdom of the eye." This was a strategy designed to hold direct psychological investigation to a minimum and put sentimental subjectivism under proscription. Character was to be discovered not in Virginia Woolf's "dark places of psychology," but rather in the glare of boldly drawn appearances.[2] Waugh seems to have taken Lewis's prescription and added a dash of Firbank's mockery for good measure. Whether farcical or poignant, Waugh's characters are presented to us deadpan. Their narrative existence is almost wholly external. Character and event are portrayed with the flat, evenhandedness of a craftsman apparently more interested in the style of his prose than the minds of his subjects. The deliberate, ironic counterpoint between Waugh's elegant prose and his inarticulate characters suggests the utter hopelessness of things: complaints would be quite beside the point. There are no remedies. There is nothing to be done but gracefully report the futility of human existence in the twentieth century. Such were Waugh's appetites and inclinations; his satiric vision required that he create a world of shallow little characters who have no consequence because they have blandly resigned themselves to live in a treacherous world without hope of recourse to any effective moral order. These figures have been made to race through a series of mishaps laughably referred to as their lives. In a pointless world there are no depths to be registered. Since purpose is unknowable, there are only appearances to be recorded. Deprived of tradition and order, Waugh's characters have been living in a state of alarm for so long that they have become morally and emotionally numb. There is no outrage they cannot pass over in blank silence.

In the early and some of the later novels, Waugh deprived himself of the conventional narrative techniques used to construct characters. There is little if any interior monologue or omniscient eavesdropping. Instead we listen to a dandyish narrator as he calmly reports the most ludicrous and outrageous behavior in a tone of mocking detachment. This is the narrative voice that can tell us there is "tradition behind the Bollinger" and illustrate the point by recalling that "at the last dinner, three years ago, a fox had been brought in in a cage and stoned to death with champagne bottles." His only comment on this marvelously efficient, if devolutionary, version of the upper order's penchant for riding to hounds is to remark, "What an evening that had been!" (p. 1). By excluding the interior dimension, Waugh developed a tone of bitter mockery that shut out conventional sentiment. Of course, satire typically requires a diminishment or distortion of its characters' psychology in order to prevent the reader from empathizing with its targets. But Waugh's novels exclude the interior dimension so relentlessly that they must be considered a special case. Even in those that moved away from farce toward realism, Waugh continued to use his external approach. There are, however, exceptions. The later works, notably *Work Suspended* and *Brideshead Revisited,* are novels in a much more traditional manner. And there is one quite revealing partial exception in one of the earlier novels, *A Handful of Dust.*

In an interesting way it is this early exception to his general rule of the external approach that best allows us to see what Waugh is doing. Tony Last in *A Handful of Dust,* unlike the characters who surround him, comes equipped with a cultural background and an interior psychology. As a character he is constructed according to the conventions of a traditional novel while the others are presented as surfaces without interiors. This difference in characterization makes Waugh's point about the quality of twentieth-century life. It is a contrast worth examining in some detail.

Tony's initial appearance signals his anomalous condition in Waugh's fictional world. "All over England people were waking up, queasy and despondent. Tony lay for ten minutes very happily planning the renovation of his ceiling." He is not yet queasy with the sickness of Waugh's version of the modern wasteland; he has yet to recognize fear in a handful of dust and still thinks of himself as an individual with purpose, one constructively involved with maintaining a viable tradition of which his ancestral estate, Hetton Abbey, is one of the more important emblems. He believes that he can live apart from his time as though he were a self-assured Christian gentleman of the Victorian period. Accordingly, Tony is still capable of an interior life worth reporting because he insists upon thinking of himself as part of a continuous heritage that extends from the past into the future. He naturally assumes responsibility for its maintenance and renovation. At the novel's opening he has not yet suffered Adam Fenwick-Syme's fate; his personal and cultural traditions have not yet been taken from him by the Customs Officers of modern England. His ancestral home, however spurious its Gothic pretension, is the outward sign of his inward allegiance to the historical sense and it is this sense of his place in history, flawed though it is, that provides him with personal depth.

In contrast, Tony's friends and family have lost this perspective. If they think of it at all, history is a subject filled with curious events and artifacts to be studied and classified rather than a tradition to be understood and lived. Tony's brother-in-law Reggie illustrates this perfectly. When he advises Tony to accept the inevitability of change, he does so with an example taken from his experience as an archaeologist. "Why, ten years ago I couldn't be interested in anything later than the Sumerian age and I assure you that now I find even the Christian era full of significance" (p. 203). Already dead and fossilized, the Western tradition has become a matter of archaeological interest which some may find fascinating but few think relevant to the present. It is this attitude, Waugh suggests, that has permitted the sordid capitulation to efficiency in twentieth-century life typified by the drably functional housing projects spreading throughout London like a seductive disease. Unlike Tony, people generally seem eager to abandon their tradition-laden homes for the chromium-plated apartments featured in these projects. These are the anonymous, streamlined dwellings that serve as Waugh's metaphor of the rootlessness of modern urban life among the affluent. Reggie urges Tony to give up his ancestral house as he has done. "It was a nasty wrench at the time of course, old association and everything like that, but I can tell you this, that when the sale was finally through I felt a different man, free to go where I liked. . . . Big houses are a thing of the past in England I'm afraid." Tony disagrees: "I don't happen to want to go anywhere else except Hetton" (p. 206). In the conflict between Tony's guileless nostalgia and his brother-in-law's ruthless practicality, the novel dramatizes the clash between the sentiment of tradition and the deracinated transience of the twentieth century.

Tony clings to his tradition, but this involves a serious problem. His idea of tradition is as childishly sentimental as his inability to remove his boyhood toys from his bedroom. It is because he does not really understand what he is paying allegiance to that he is unable to defend it when it is attacked by the representatives of modernity, one of whom is his wife.

As the novel opens, we discover that Brenda Last has been thoroughly infected with the twentieth century's peculiar disease. Her sequestered life at Hetton Abbey has not protected her against the virulence of the wasteland. The symptoms can be read in her restless boredom and mindless superficiality. Like Tony, Brenda makes her first appearance as she awakens, but the world she rises to is quite different from his.

> Brenda lay on the dais. She had insisted on a modern bed. Her tray was beside her and the quilt was littered with envelopes, letters and the daily papers. Her head was propped against a very small pillow; clean of makeup, her face was almost colourless, rose-pearl, scarcely deeper in tone than her arms and neck.
> "Well?" said Tony.
> "Kiss."
> He sat by the tray at the head of the bed; she leant forward to him (a nereid emerging from fathomless depths of clear water). She turned her lips away and rubbed against his cheek like a cat. It was a way she had. (pp. 16–17)

Brenda's insistence upon a modern bed sounds ominous within the context of Tony's ancestral home, his cherished Victorian replica of Gothic architecture. Then the litter of letters and papers abandoned across the quilt speaks of a less purposeful awakening than her husband's.

But it is Brenda's colorless face that most gives her away even while it, paradoxically enough, obscures her personality from us. Her nereid face appears to emerge from fathomless depths of clear water. At first this description of Brenda's approach to Tony is troubling. It does not seem to make visual sense. However clear water may be, it will not remain translucent indefinitely. Light can penetrate only so far and certainly does not reach to fathomless depths. At some point even the clearest water turns opaque to the searching eye. How, then, can those depths from which Brenda rises be clear and fathomless at once? Is this an invitation to look into her depths for ourselves? Or is it a signal that there is nothing to be found there? As we examine the passage more closely, we find the fathomless/clear opposition signals how thoroughly its terms are at odds with one another. To reinforce the apparent contradiction between vision and obscurity, the text joins images of shallowness and depth in puzzling tandem. Although Brenda appears to emerge from some fathomless ocean floor, her colorless face is "scarcely deeper in tone than her arms and neck." Waugh makes her a provocatively opaque figure. As a woman who leaves her husband for her lover the day after her son's funeral and then demands that he sell his cherished estate in order to support her new liaison, she behaves with such apparently willful malice that we come to expect the narrative at one point or another to divulge the deeply rooted motives that must account for it. Is Brenda emotionally unstable? Has she been irremediably wronged by Tony at some point prior to the time of the novel? Or is she simply without conscience? We are given no explanations. There is nothing to indicate what Brenda may be feeling beyond a vague boredom with Tony's world. Nor does she ever express any serious doubt or guilt about her behavior. In keeping with her initial appearance, Brenda remains an opaque nereid throughout the novel. She is at once fathomless and shallow, inexplicable and transparent. We are teased with suggestion of depths but each time we try to plumb them we find there is nothing behind her appearances. Brenda is a creature of surfaces that should have an interior explanation and we are puzzled as much as Tony when none is revealed to us.

Without psychological explanation Brenda's willfulness seems inexcusably monstrous. Yet so little information is given, we cannot be sure of our judgment. We know her acts but we never know her. This kind of character development might not be so troublesome in a novel like *Vile Bodies* or *The Loved One* in which Waugh's satire approaches farce. But *A Handful of Dust* is in a different key altogether. Brenda's betrayal of her husband and the pain it causes him are portrayed realistically and quite movingly. Yet when we look for Brenda's motives and thoughts, Waugh serves us with his usual blank silence.

But silence, even blank silence, can have its own eloquence. With regard to Brenda, it speaks quite persuasively. Brenda's lack of resonance suggests that something is missing in her makeup. An earlier age might have called it soul. Whatever is missing, it has left her less than human. Tony's inability to see what lies at the bottom of his wife's fathomless clarity is indicative of what happens when the traditional moral categories come face to face with the dull, unresponsive void of twentieth-century life.

Read this way, Waugh's decision not to dramatize the interior dimension helps to advance an aspect of his theme. He was convinced that this century's failure to sustain credible moral absolutes had diminished the possibilities for personal independence. Rather than making up their own minds according to their understanding of a few immutable principles, people were encouraged to drift along at the whim of the Zeitgeist, hapless automatons incapable of loyalty or commitment to anything other than contemporary fashion. Brenda's liaison is a case in point. The narrator makes it emphatically clear that her affair does not spring from love or even lust. Rather she seems motivated by an externally imposed need to keep up with her fashionable set. It is what her friends are doing—taking maisonettes and arranging assignations, divorcing and remarrying. A creature of her changing times, she simply does not want to be left behind. "The danger that faces so many people today," Waugh wrote in 1932, is "to have no considered opinions on any subject, to put up with what is wasteful and harmful with the excuse that there is 'good in everything,' which in most cases means an inability to distinguish between good and bad." In his opinion, it was clearly "better to be narrow-minded than to have no mind, to hold limited and rigid principles than none at all."[3] Submitting to the fashionable relativism that had permeated moral and philosophical discussion since the beginning of the century was the same as having no mind of one's own. Waugh would have agreed with Wyndham Lewis's argument that only settled principles could provide a fulcrum on which one could leverage the force of individuality. In this line of thought, relativism had the same consequences as Bergson's metaphysic. If the relativist is true to his vision, he must let go of all philosophical positions. Positions imply stability, which the relativist has forsworn. Instead he must allow himself to be swept along in the ceaseless flux of Becoming, never able to gain the footing necessary to stand up and assert his own identity. He is perforce a creature of time and fashion.

While this argument, in one form or another, appealed to Waugh, he was not one to let matters lie so simply disposed. He was ready to concede that relativists did not, like Brenda Last, necessarily lapse into faceless conformity with prevailing fashions. Some clearly had the character necessary to exert their individuality without the support of a communal ethos. But to do so required an endless effort of will which, in Waugh's portrayal, incurred an exorbitant human cost. Mrs. Rattery in *A Handful of Dust* supplies the example here. She is one of Waugh's supremely modern types, a line of characters he originated with Otto Silenus and Margot Metroland, née Beste-Chetwynde, in *Decline and Fall*. As a thoroughly modern creature casually negligent of the artifacts of tradition and without a recognizable emotional interior, she seems at first to be the very embodiment of all that Waugh despises in the contemporary world. Yet she is the novel's only character, other than Tony himself, who is capable of loyalty and her loyalty is completely disinterested at that.

Understanding Mrs. Rattery and the type she represents is crucial for appreciating Waugh's fiction. As distant as she is from the conservative Waugh, her cool, unaffected modernity is very much of a piece with the dandyish, avant-garde pose Waugh liked to adopt as an artist. Ruthlessly unsentimental, she has the Silenus touch that Waugh found a useful antidote to the insipid pieties of humanism.

At the invitation of Tony's friend, Jock Grant-Menzies, Mrs. Rattery visits the Last estate on the eve of the fox hunt in which Tony's son will be accidentally killed.

> Jock's blonde was called Mrs. Rattery. Tony had conceived an idea of her from what he overheard of Polly's gossip and from various fragments of information let fall by Jock. She was a little over thirty. Somewhere in the Cottesmore country there lived a long-legged, slightly discredited Major Rattery, to whom she had once been married. She was American by origin, now totally denationalized, rich without property or possessions, except those that would pack in five vast trunks. Jock had had his eye on her last summer at Biarritz and had fallen in with her again in London where she played big bridge, very ably, for six or seven hours a day and changed her hotel, on an average, once every three weeks. Periodically she was liable to bouts of morphine; then she gave up her bridge and remained for several days at a time alone in her hotel suite, refreshed at intervals with glasses of cold milk.
>
> She arrived by air on Monday afternoon. It was the first time that a guest had come in this fashion and the household was appreciably excited. Under Jock's direction the boiler man and one of the gardeners pegged out a dust sheet in the park to mark a landing for her and lit a bonfire of damp leaves to show the direction of the wind. The five trunks arrived in the ordinary way by train, with an elderly, irreproachable maid. She brought her own sheets with her in one of the trunks; they were neither silk nor coloured, without lace or ornament of any kind, except small, plain monograms.
>
> Tony, Jock and John went out to watch her land. She climbed out of the cockpit, stretched, unbuttoned the flaps of her leather helmet, and came to meet them. "Forty-two minutes," she said, "not at all bad with the wind against me."
>
> She was tall and erect, almost austere in helmet and overalls; not at all as Tony had imagined her. Vaguely, at the back of his mind he had secreted the slightly absurd expectation of a chorus girl, in silk shorts and brassière, pop-

ping out of an immense beribboned Easter Egg with a cry of "Whooppee, boys." Mrs. Rattery's greetings were deft and impersonal. (pp. 131–32)

Mrs. Rattery is the complete twentieth-century woman, a type that fascinated Waugh. She is without background, "totally denationalized, rich, without property or possessions." The insistence on her uprootedness is reinforced by what is left out of her presentation. But for the barest circumstantial details, we never learn what has driven her to achieve her remarkable presence in the world. She is simply there, changing her "hotel on an average, once every three weeks," periodically "liable to bouts of morphine." Rootless and bored, she is the ultimate twentieth-century transient. In her ceaseless search for sensation, she willfully dictates the rhythm of her life with the use of drugs. Like Margot Metroland in *Decline and Fall,* Julia Stitch in *Scoop,* and Virginia Crouchback in the *Sword of Honour* trilogy, Mrs. Rattery is one of Waugh's goddesses of modernity; her spirit presides over *A Handful of Dust* in much the same way these other goddesses preside over their respective narratives. Like one of George Orwell's streamlined people, she has dispatched the nostalgic accessories of the past and abandoned the needless bother of an interior life as if it were so much excess baggage. Asked her opinion of the ancestral Last estate, she replies that she never notices houses one way or the other. Houses, ancestral houses at least, establish a link from one generation to the next but Mrs. Rattery simply does not value the continuity they represent. She is supremely indifferent to the conventional concerns people have for their past and future. Tony is surprised to learn she has two sons; she offhandedly explains she does not see them often but she knows "they're at school somewhere" (p. 158). Mrs. Rattery's existence is radically present tense. With no background and no interior, she is ideally suited to modern life.

Mrs. Rattery is all cool efficiency, capable of meeting the contemporary world on its own terms. Because Tony Last lives in another world, he cannot understand her. As always happens in Waugh, the traditional categories no longer fit present experience. Before she arrives, Tony conceives of Mrs. Rattery as a "Shameless Blonde," popping out of an immense Easter Egg. In fact she is so far from being a frivolous chorus girl that she seems "almost austere." Her bed sheets gauge the distance between her world and Tony's. They are neither silk nor colored as Tony seems to have expected. Instead they are functional, without ornament except for the "small plain monograms" that mark them with her practical, straightforward, and very contemporary personality. The sexual import of the sheets is quite clear. Tony, living in his sentimental Victorian dream, thinks of unmarried sexual activity as colorfully wicked, silkenly decadent. Mrs. Rattery lives under a different dispensation altogether. Sex, like any other transaction, is to be managed efficiently and practically. She comes equipped with nothing but essentials. We are made to feel that despite her mysterious presence there is nothing hidden about Mrs. Rattery, no depths to be explored. She recalls Brenda's fathomless transparency; like Brenda, Mrs. Rattery seems at first a contradictory mixture of the apparently hidden and the shamelessly revealed. Even the fact that we never learn her first name promotes this sense of a mystery that has nothing to hide. She is as functional in a peremptory sort of way as the no-nonsense formality of her surname from which the frivolous adornment of a given name has been removed. She is in fact neither more nor less than the succession of her appearances.

Tony's "Shameless Blonde" epithet is correct in a way he did not intend. Mrs. Rattery is shameless in that everything about her is completely externalized. She has no reserve, no doubt, no apology. There is no inward self, no private interior distance between what she thinks and what she does. She is indivisibly at one with her visible behavior. In other words, she is not really human but rather an exotic mixture of machine efficiency and animal vitality. In *Decline and Fall* Professor Silenus, exasperated by all that is slovenly human, pays tribute to the perfectly inhuman extremes that Mrs. Rattery seems to bring together: "On one side the harmonious instincts and balanced responses of the animal, on the other the inflexible purpose of the engine, and between them man, equally alien from the *being* of Nature and the *doing* of the machine" (p. 160). As the novel's goddess of modernity, Mrs. Rattery cannot be touched by the usual human emotions.

She arrives at Hetton by plane; like the goddess she is meant to be, she descends from the sky bringing with her the twentieth-century restlessness that will permanently disturb Tony's Victorian dream. She lives the life Brenda dimly aspires to. While staying at Hetton, she discovers Brenda has arranged for an interior decorator to modernize the morning room. Having decided the Victorian molding and dado are depressingly antiquated, Brenda has ordered that the walls be covered with functional chromium plating. Mrs. Rattery cannot resist putting on her overalls and helping the workmen, she is that committed to smoothing away the inconveniences of traditional attachments.

Tony's whimsical dream cannot stand up to Mrs. Rattery's energetic reality. It seems grimly appropriate that her visit should coincide with the death of Tony's son, John Andrew. This misfortune signals the breakup of his nineteenth-century idyll, prompting, as it does, Brenda's departure and her subsequent attempt to have Hetton sold.

There is, however, an important complication concerning Mrs. Rattery. She is not simply an occasion for Waugh to revile the present and lament the loss of a more civilized past. Although Mrs. Rattery is made to represent the modern world's gratuitous destruction of traditional values, she is also the only character in the novel whose personal behavior is wholly admirable. After John Andrew's fatal accident, she stays on at Hetton to manage the affairs that Tony is too upset to handle. She keeps unwanted sympathizers away and provides Tony with the distraction of card games, the only solace that works for him in the absence of faith. Mrs. Rattery's aid is unsolicited and disinterested. She has nothing to gain. Having seen Tony through his ordeal, she flies away before he or anyone else can thank her, never to be seen again.

Mrs. Rattery's presence in the novel puts in question the object of Waugh's satire. Is he attacking modern transience measured against traditional stability? If so, why does he portray Mrs. Rattery, the transient *déracinée*, sympathetically as a worldly wise woman with a disinterested concern for others that she puts into action by coming to their aid so effectively? If Tony Last represents traditional values, the simple moral virtues of a good nineteenth-century gentleman, why is he shown to be so childishly helpless at moments of crisis and so culpably innocent with regard to his wayward wife? We may pity Tony but we are hardly invited to sympathize with him or with what he thinks he stands for. Mrs. Rattery, on the other hand, commands our respect. Here, as elsewhere, Waugh leaves us on our own. In the absence of either psychological explanation or moral evaluation within his narrative, this work, like his other early productions, does not lend itself to a simple explication.

Mrs. Rattery is one of those characters who reveal Waugh's ambivalence about his roles as artist and conservative. There seems to be little doubt that he invested more in Mrs. Rattery than was required of her narrative function. Like Otto Silenus in *Decline and Fall,* she incarnates the modern spirit without apology and Waugh has respected her integrity in doing so. If there is no transcendent principle that makes sense of existence, then her approach to life is indeed commendable. She accepts the nihilism implicit in the world of Becoming, the "perpetual flux" as Waugh had portrayed it in *Vile Bodies.* She is content to live each moment for all it is worth without sentimental nostalgia, making what sense she can of her limited time. We can see this in her addiction to cards, her one unflagging enthusiasm. They serve to relieve the general sense of life's pointlessness by supplying her with moments of order. She kindly urges Tony to take up their existential consolation as he sits numb and inarticulate with grief for his dead son. The modern world has nothing more to offer, Waugh suggests. Traditional rituals no longer make sense of life's accidents. As mentioned earlier, Tony is merely embarassed by his minister's futile attempt to console him. Religion, after all, is "the last thing one wants to talk about at a time like this" (p. 158).

But as well as making its thematic point within the novel, Mrs. Rattery's card playing echoes Waugh's esthetic practice. As cited earlier, he believed that "the artist's only service to the disintegrated society of today is to create little independent systems of order of his own,"[4] a statement analogous to this description:

> Mrs. Rattery sat intent over her game, moving little groups of cards adroitly backward and forwards about the table like shuttles across a loom; under her fingers order grew out of chaos; she established sequence and precedence; the symbols before her became coherent, interrelated . . . then [she] drew them towards her into a heap, haphazard once more and without meaning. (pp. 150–51)

In a "disintegrated society" lacking a commonly held belief structure, Mrs. Rattery creates her own "little independent systems of order," however ephemeral they may be, enjoying her game's fleeting consolations even as she resigns herself to its ultimate futility. This is an instance of her practical, managerial approach to life. Do what you can; accept the inevitable. She responds to the apparent absence of meaning with the kind of resilience Waugh looked for in an artist. As we have seen, Waugh believed that, whatever their private convictions, artists required a special sympathy for their times if they hoped to produce significant results. Like it or not, they were in the avant-garde.[5] If in the twentieth century this meant putting on an inhuman mask, it could only be said that in a soulless age the artist cannot afford conventional human sentiment. One thinks of Waugh's disengaged narrative voice calmly, even delightedly organizing spectacles of outrage that leave his characters hopelessly stricken and befuddled.

Without a trace of nostalgia, Mrs. Rattery is entirely at home in a world emptied of transcendental explanations. When she attempts to assuage Tony's anguish, she prescribes the stoical remedy of one who has jettisoned all illusions: "Stop thinking about things" (p. 152). Here and elsewhere, her determined superficiality appears unimpeachable because it proceeds from her accurate assessment of contemporary life. She accepts things as they are. Clearly Waugh found her response to present conditions more realistic than Tony's, which is founded upon a sentimental humanism that Waugh thought quite spineless since it assumed that one could retain a sense of purpose without the vulgar bother of grappling with metaphysical questions. Commenting on *A Handful of Dust*, he claimed that it "contained all I had to say about humanism" and, indeed, one cannot read this novel without becoming painfully aware that men like Tony Last—obviously decent, well-intentioned, given to inward reflection—often cannot stand up to the casual amorality of an age that largely ignores any claims on its ethical sensibility that extend further than the practical concerns of the here and now.[6] Although Waugh despised the world Mrs. Rattery represents, we cannot help but feel that he nevertheless admired her ability to prosper under the conditions of twentieth-century life. If she achieves nothing else, she at least develops a style that banishes sentimentality and false nostalgia. She does not pretend that nothing has changed since the nineteenth century. Under different guises, Waugh returned to Mrs. Rattery again and again, obviously fascinated if somewhat appalled by the apparent ease with which the various incarnations of her species could accommodate themselves to the moral vacuity of contemporary life.

Mrs. Rattery serves Waugh's satire well. She gives the lie to those who would use tradition to evade the difficulties of the present by enshrining themselves in some charming fantasy of a harmonious past. He takes a certain pleasure in exploding the delusions of his static characters who expect to achieve peace and stability without exertion. Until Mrs. Rattery's appearance in his life, Tony Last exemplifies this line in all its guileless simplicity.

Tony reveres the past but his traditionalism is more a childish dream than a commitment to cultural continuity. He lives in an ancestral home the rooms of which have been named after the figures of Arthurian legend. It is a boy's idea of the perfect house filled with the emblems of the heroic past. But for all his veneration of this tradition, Tony seems to be willfully unaware of some of its darker themes. Although his wife's room is named Guinevere, he is too dim to read the obvious signals of her infidelity until it is much too late to do anything about it. When she leaves him, he finds himself evicted from his Tennysonian reverie. His reaction is to dash off recklessly on a private pursuit for his personal version of the holy grail. This takes the shape of a mythical city, the supposed achievement of some extraordinary civilization hidden away in the jungles of Brazil. He imagines it will replace decadent London and restore the values he had thought present in his life before his wife's betrayal. Again Tony shows himself culpably ignorant of the tradition he claims to respect. Tennyson's Arthur had warned his knights against impractical expeditions after the shadowy grail, which, after all, might have no earthly existence. It was more important to tend to the immediate problems of the realm's daily affairs, however less glamorous they might be compared with such a quest. Like so many of Arthur's knights, Tony chooses to embark on the dreamy quest for an impossible ideal rather than keep up the pedestrian struggle to support civilized values at home. He may value his tradition, but he does not trouble himself to understand it. Like Waugh's other naïfs, he has not thought through its implications and is therefore incapable of applying its lessons to the contemporary scene.

Tony's decision illustrates one of Waugh's recurrent themes: the suicidal negligence of those whose vested interest it should be to preserve Western civilization. It was obvious to Waugh that what men called civilization was a fragile fortress recently carved from the wilderness and that the maintenance of its protective walls demanded unwavering vigilance against the savagery outside to say nothing of the savagery inside. Tony's behavior is one more instance of the widespread dereliction of civilized people throughout England and Europe. Now that "man had deserted his post," as Waugh put it elsewhere, "the jungle was creeping back to its old strongholds." Soon the "seeming-solid, patiently built, gorgeously ornamented structure of Western life was to melt overnight like an ice-castle, leaving only a puddle of mud."⁷

In one way or another almost all of Waugh's novels deal with desertion or eviction from Western life. The painfully unassuming protagonist of *Scott-King's Modern Europe*, however, is no deserter, so when he finds himself facing eviction, he suddenly discovers the resources necessary to resist. Having just returned from a tour of a modern totalitarian state to the school at which he has been teaching classics for twenty-one years, he has had a glimpse of what such eviction would mean and is not about to submit quietly when his headmaster informs him that his program may have to be phased from the curriculum.

> "What are we to do? Parents are not interested in producing the 'complete man' any more. They want to qualify their boys for jobs in the modern world. You can hardly blame them, can you?"
> "Oh yes," said Scott-King. "I can and do." (p. 88)

Considerate of his usually obedient employee, the headmaster offers Scott-King the opportunity to begin teaching other courses, such as economic history, against the day when there may be "no more classical boys at all," but he dismisses this kindness as if it were an unworthy temptation.

> "I will stay as I am here as long as any boy wants to read the classics. I think it would be very wicked indeed to do anything to fit a boy for the modern world."
> "It's a short-sighted view, Scott-King."
> "There, head master, with all respect, I differ from you profoundly. I think it the most long-sighted view it is possible to take." (p. 89)

The year before writing of Scott-King's commitment to this cultural holding action, Waugh sardonically described his own mission in similar terms. As remarked earlier, he saw himself as a contemporary "scribe," who, like the monks of the Dark Ages, would preserve Europe's ideals during its decline into a period of ignorance and disorder. One of these ideals was the "complete man."

In his function as scribe, Waugh was determined to remind his readers of what they were in danger of abandoning. To do this, he arranged to contrast the shriveled expectations of his wanton deserters and reluctant evacuees with the earlier ideal of the "complete man" that achieved its supreme expression in the Odyssean hero. In the Renaissance revival of classical education, this model of confident leadership was especially prized. He was a hero whose settled vision of the world was founded upon unquestioned ethical principles. The certainty of his vision enabled him to pursue his destiny with sure determination. Odysseus and Aeneas might stray from the path of obligation occasionally but they were always aware of their deviations and eventually corrected their courses. In fact, their lapses and recoveries were portrayed as just so many further instances of their heroism. It was the apparent neglect of this heroic ideal in his own society that exercised Waugh to satiric mockery. This is nowhere so evident as in his attacks on the age's unwillingness to commit itself to definite principles. It's hard to be heroic when you no longer know what you stand for.

In Waugh's view of the matter, philosophical relativism had so infected the twentieth-century mind that life for many had become an aimless journey filled with travail and tedium relieved only by moments of intense experience. Whatever spiritual dissatisfaction this may have caused, it was not without its economic usefulness for the capitalist state ready to supply the anodyne of periodic sensation delivered in doses of ever-changing products and amusements. Accordingly, Waugh's world often seems a ceaseless pursuit of excitement in plane rides, automobile races, chromium-plated flats, ridiculous movies, and an endless series of parties that are as expensive as they are foolishly elaborate. There is little room for the Odyssean hero determined to stand by his convictions in an economic system that relies for its prosperity on a ceaselss round of purchase and disposal of insubstantial goods and entertainments. His sort of constancy might retard profits. This is why those who prosper in Waugh's fictional world are precisely those who are most flagrantly inconstant. These are the characters who have surrendered themselves happily to the world of Becoming in which each moment constitutes a total break with the last. Like Lord Copper, the bullying press baron of *Scoop,* or Sir James Macrae, the stupendously forgetful film producer of "Excursion in Reality," they live completely in the present moment, unable to recall today what they said and did yesterday. The degree of their worldly triumph is in direct proportion to the ease with which they can shed earlier commitments. Far from a liability, their forgetfulness is a positive asset.

While Copper's and Sir James's forgetfulness may be farcical, Rex Mottram's in *Brideshead Revisited* is nothing less than strategic. Mottram's is a selective amnesia. In order to enter a politically advantageous marriage, he agrees to convert to Catholicism. His previous marriage and current affair do not deter him from his goal nor does he think himself at all insincere. He is genuinely amazed that his fiancée's family should take exception to his suit upon discovering his former and current ties. Rex's opportunism is a practical consequence of the metaphysics of Becoming. In a relativistic world there is simply no point in subscribing to anything more lasting than the stratagem of the day. Through his narrator, Charles Ryder, Waugh makes it clear that he detests Mottram's type, but he is honest enough to portray this careerist as a competent man of the world. On Waugh's grounds, Mottram may be a metaphysical imbecile, but he is, nevertheless, a skilled politician who knows all the right people and understands how his society works. Regardless of law and regulation, he gets things done. He may have to resort to a shrewdly cultivated contact, a strategically chosen lover, or a smoothly delivered bribe, but, after all, his experience in modern London has taught him that success comes to those who make it a point never to respect absolute standards any further than they can serve immediate ends. By ordinary measurements Rex appears to be an accomplished man of the world, but his achievement has come at a cost. Committed only to his self-advancement, he fails to meet the requirements of Scott-King's "complete man." He is the result of an education designed to fit him for life in the modern world, and so he is something less than he seems. As the Jesuit who undertakes to assist him through his nominal conversion puts it, "The trouble with modern education is you never know how ignorant people are. With anyone over fifty you can be fairly confident what's been taught and what's been left out. But these young people have such an intelligent, knowledgeable surface, and then the crust suddenly breaks and you look down into depths of confusion you didn't know existed" (p. 193). Mottram's disillusioned wife puts it far more forcefully.

> He simply wasn't all there. He wasn't a complete human being at all. He was a tiny bit of one, unnaturally developed; something in a bottle, an organ kept alive in a laboratory. I thought he was a primitive savage, but he was something absolutely modern and up-to-date that only this ghastly age could produce. A tiny bit of a man pretending he was the whole. (p. 200)

It is precisely Rex Mottram's lack of wholeness that enables him to be infinitely adaptable to the ends of contemporary politics and commerce. In contrast, the classically trained find themselves ill-equipped to meet the

demands of the modern world. As Paul Pennyfeather and Tony Last belatedly discover, gentlemanly attributes provide little defense against the unprincipled barbarism of the twentieth century.

The concept of the complete man hovers like a mocking reproach in the
background of Waugh's fiction. It was against this classical standard that he
measured the world. Parody was his chosen gauge.

Classical parody is an essential ingredient in many of Waugh's works.
Decline and Fall sets the pattern by mimicking the epic journey. Once we
think of the novel this way, its episodic anarchy begins to make sense. Paul
Pennyfeather's adventures are not the rambling, haphazard hijinks they at
first appear to be. Instead, they have been specially contrived to mark him
as an inversion of the classical hero. Waugh signals his intention when he
has his narrator interrupt the story line, such as it is, with a peremptory
flourish to address the reader directly in a manner at once avant-grade and
dandyish. He cooly reports that the character we have been reading about
for more than 160 pages is only a

> shadow that has flitted about this narrative under the name of Paul Penny-
> feather. . . . In fact, the whole of this book is really an account of the myste-
> rious disappearance of Paul Pennyfeather, so that readers must not complain
> if the shadow which took his name does not amply fill the important part of
> hero for which he was originally cast. (pp. 162–63)

If Paul is at all representative of the results of contemporary education
then it is clear that, for the twentieth century, classical values have become
little more than shadowy memories of a more civilized age.

Pursuing theological studies at Oxford, Paul thought he was on his way
to becoming Scott-King's complete man, but once he is expelled and
forced to enter the twentieth century outside his college's walls, he
quickly becomes a two-dimensional figure of ridicule. Then, for a brief interval, the narrator allows him to materialize "into the solid figure of an intelligent, well-educated, well-conducted young man . . . . who had been
developing in the placid years which preceded this story" (pp. 162–63).

As quickly as he has solidified, however, Paul disappears again because,
as the narrator airily observes, he "would never have made a hero, and the
only interest about him arises from the unusual series of events of which his
shadow was witness" (p. 164). Here, as elsewhere in Waugh, the classical
tradition is mocked. Whereas the epic hero descends into the underworld
to meet the shades of the dead who impart to him the knowledge he needs
to prevail in his mission, it is as a shade himself that Paul descends into the
underworld of the twentieth century where he meets figures who are vi-
brantly, if grotesquely, alive. Rather than instilling competence, these encounters only serve to weaken further Paul's already enfeebled will.

Paul's classical Oxford education might have prepared him to deal with "all the emergencies of civilized life," but it has not equipped him for a hero's role in the barbarous conditions of the contemporary world. In a novel comprised of running gags, one of the more persistent and revealing is Paul's squeamish reluctance to play Aeneas or Dante to the fools, rogues, and madmen he meets on his mock-epic journey through the bizarre climate of the century. As in the conventional epic, each new character feels compelled to recite his life story to Paul upon their first meeting. "I expect you wonder how it is that I come to be here?" (p. 63) "I don't know why I'm telling you all this; nobody else knows. I somehow feel you'll understand" (p. 36). They will make their confession whether Paul wants to hear it or not. At first Paul politely resigns himself to his undesired role. Soon he tries to resist.

> "No," said Paul firmly, "nothing of the kind. I don't in the least want to know anything about you; d'you hear?"
> "I'll tell you," said Philbrick; "it was like this—"
> "I don't want to hear your loathsome confessions; can't you understand?" (p. 63)

But they don't understand; they continue to confide in him in spite of his protests. As the epic traveler, however unwilling, Paul has no choice but to listen. But listening is not learning. Paul is all too easily overwhelmed by the rogues and shameless opportunists whom he meets outside the precincts of his classical retreat. Hired to teach in a criminally negligent school in Wales, he readily complies with the headmaster's advice that "schoolmasters must temper discretion with deceit" (p. 24). Taken up by Margot Beste-Chetwynde, a Circe of modernity who collects men as one might stamps, he becomes her willing tool. When she sends him abroad to assist some young women in her employ with their travel arrangements, she neglects to explain that her business is comprised of a chain of South American brothels and the girls he is to help are in the profession. Naive and inexperienced, Paul so hopelessly lacks the resources of the wily Odysseus that he is taken in completely by this Siren. When he goes to prison, accepting the punishment that should be hers, we see that this is one Circe who need not worry about meeting her match in a masterful Odysseus.

In the novel's conclusion, Margot arranges for Paul to be smuggled out of prison and returned to his studies at Scone College. To protect him, she has arranged matters so that the authorities will be convinced Paul Pennyfeather has died and the person who has taken his place at Scone is his cousin. This parody of death and resurrection allows Paul to resume his theological studies grimly determined to avoid any further contact with the contemporary world. And so the novel turns back upon itself, an inverted epic journey that leaves Paul where he began.[8] Odysseus also came full circle, but when he returned to his home in disguise, he did so only to reveal himself and take charge of his kingdom once more. Paul, however, returns in order to hide himself and avoid contact with the issues of contemporary life. We last see him reading about ancient heresies and delighting in the punishment meted out to those who strayed from the fold.

> There was a bishop in Bithynia, Paul learned, who had denied the Divinity of Christ, the immortality of the soul, the existence of good, the legality of marriage, and the validity of the Sacrament of Extreme Unction. How right they had been to condemn him! . . . So the ascetic Ebionites used to turn towards Jerusalem when they prayed. Paul made a note of it. Quite right to suppress them. Then he turned out the light and went into his bedroom to sleep. (pp. 288, 293)

Whereas Odysseus had been determined to impose his values on the world around him, Paul has forsaken the struggle to shape experience according to either the classical or Christian vision. Instead he is reduced to taking what consolation he can in the spectacle of other ages in which ideas were taken seriously indeed. Having done so, he can shut his eyes and sleep through his own.

As many another twentieth-century artist, Waugh frequently took the measure of contemporary man by comparing him unflatteringly with the traditional hero. Along with Paul, the protagonists of *Vile Bodies*, *A Handful of Dust*, *Scott-King's Modern Europe*, and *Sword of Honour* all suffer the fate of T. S. Eliot's Prufrock. Each has heard "the voices dying with a dying fall beneath the music from a farther room" and been powerless to renew his song. They constitute an antithesis to the classical hero whose place in the world was established by his carefully memorialized ancestry, his personal reputation, and his determination to achieve his destiny. As we have seen, Adam Fenwick-Symes allows himself to be stripped of his personal and cultural past when England's Customs Office confiscates his autobiography and copy of Dante. Tony Last's Arthurian quest proves as futile as it is misguided. Scott-King manages to put up a holding action against modern encroachments on his classical program for developing the complete man, but the prospects are not encouraging. Even in the more hopeful, at least personally hopeful, *Sword of Honour* trilogy which features a protagonist who does not fade into insubstantial shadowiness, heroism seems only fleetingly attainable and then only with gravely mixed results. When he decides to become something of a gentleman warrior at the outbreak of the Second World War, Guy Crouchback looks to the medieval crusader, Sir Roger of Waybroke, as his model. He envisions himself battling a league of new barbarians who have signaled unmistakably their animus to

Western civilization with the Hitler-Stalin nonaggression treaty of 1939. "The enemy was at last in plain view, huge and hateful, all disguise cast off. It was the Modern Age in Arms. Whatever the outcome there was a place for him in that battle" (MAA, pp. 7–8). Only after some painfully humiliating lessons administered by the political realities of war does Guy belatedly realize that matters are not nearly so clear-cut. His commitment to the values of the Christian Knight will not enable him to achieve the unqualified success he had hoped for when first volunteering for military service. Like Paul Pennyfeather and Tony Last before him, he discovers that the virtues of courage, honor, and fidelity are thought to be childishly naive by those who have accommodated themselves to the workings of the modern world. But worse than this, he must learn that pursuing his ideal of Christian militancy has led him seriously astray. Acting courageously and with the best intentions, he unwittingly becomes instrumental in destroying those he seeks to save. When he attempts to help a group of Jewish refugees escape their Yugoslavian captors, his efforts only succeed in removing them to another form of imprisonment and, worse, lead to the execution of the two leaders he had befriended. It seems that revering the civilized values of the past can be as delusive as the unquestioning acceptance of the progressive ideology of the present.

Waugh's decent characters are people who have misconstrued the significance of their cultural heritage. They have been encouraged to entertain a childishly idealized portrait of Western civilization that leaves them feeling completely disaffected from the present age. In some instances, their respect for the past, however intense, has about it the curator's instinct to fix objects and events, each in its proper display case. Conservators of antique charm, they cherish their cultural past but neglect what was for Waugh its essential ingredient: the faith that he was convinced had made this civilization vital and productive. Tony Last in *A Handful of Dust* wouldn't dream of missing church on Sunday. It is a weekly routine that helps him maintain his sense of familial and national history. But, sitting in his family's ancestral pew week after week, he does not hear much less believe anything his pastor has to deliver from the pulpit. His religious observance is no more than a trifling ornament to his role as country squire. It has nothing to offer him at times of crisis such as his son's death. But Tony's lack of faith does not merely deprive him of consolation, it leaves him without the strength of conviction to stand by his chosen way of life when it comes under assault by modernity.

Mr. Samgrass in *Brideshead Revisited* provides a more extreme instance of Waugh's criticism of traditionalists who have lost sight of the faith he thought tradition's only justification. *Brideshead's* narrator, Charles Ryder, describes Samgrass as an encyclopedically informed scholar whose

knowledge of history and culture is indisputably exhaustive, buts finds his
learning nonetheless spurious.

> Mr. Samgrass was a genealogist and a legitimist; he loved dispossessed roy-
> alty and knew the exact validity of the rival claims of the pretenders to many
> thrones; he was not a man of religious habit, but he knew more than most
> Catholics about their Church; he had friends in the Vatican and could talk at
> length of policy and appointments, saying which contemporary ecclesiastics
> were in good favour, which in bad, what recent theological hypothesis was
> suspect, and how this or that Jesuit or Dominican had skated on thin ice or
> sailed near the wind in his Lenten discourses; he had everything except the
> Faith, and later liked to attend benediction in the chapel at Brideshead and
> see the ladies of the family with their necks arched in devotion under their
> black lace mantillas; he loved forgotten scandals in high life and was an ex-
> pert on putative parentage; he *claimed* to love the past, but I always felt that
> he thought all the splendid company, living or dead, with whom he associ-
> ated, slightly absurd; it was Mr. Samgrass who was real, the rest were an in-
> substantial pageant. He was the Victorian tourist, solid and patronizing, for
> whose amusement these foreign things were paraded. (p. 110)

For Mr. Samgrass all of Western civilization is a glorious waxworks museum, a source of constant amusement for which he feels no responsibility.
The other characters treat him with the contempt that they do, one suspects, because they intuitively recognize his fundamental insincerity. He
becomes Sammy, the slightly repulsive little man who makes his way in the
world by toadying to the whims of his aristocratic patrons. For all his eru-
dition, he is no more than a soulless flunky, at best an object of scorn, at
worst an interfering nuisance.

If the complete man provides a positive model, Mr. Samgrass provides a
negative one. To the degree a character, even an essentially decent one,
subscribes to Mr. Samgrass's sterile knowingness, he falls just that much
further from grace, as an example also taken from *Brideshead Revisited* will
illustrate. When Charles Ryder tries to jolly Julia Flyte out of the spiritual
crisis she suffers because of her adulterous affair with him, he insensitively
resorts to an unfortunate irony, describing Julia's distress as though she
were acting a part in a play. She asks whether the play is a comedy and he
replies, "Drama. Tragedy. Farce. What you will. This is the reconciliation
scene. . . . Estrangement and misunderstanding in Act Two." Not amused,
Julia angrily retorts, "Oh, don't talk in that damned bounderish way. Why
must you see everything secondhand? Why must this be a play? Why must
my conscience be a Pre-Raphaelite picture?" (p. 291).

Indeed, Charles does see everything secondhand as in a play. Without
belief in any absolutes, the only order he can construct for himself is that
supplied by a taxonomy of the past. Present experience must always be a

belated rendition of the forms established by a cultural canon which has no essential validity beyond a genteel compact among civilized people that it should serve to arrange their lives with a sense of decorum. But grounded as it is on nothing more than a sort of gentlemen's agreement without the support of a transcendental authority, this order cannot hold. Charles Ryder's profitable painting career bears witness to its doomed fragility. As mentioned earlier, he achieves his greatest commercial success painting portraits of the great English country homes, each redolent of centuries of tradition, just before they are to be torn down and replaced by some purely functional modern structure. Like Mr. Samgrass, he knows and delights in the achievements of the past but is powerless to preserve them as anything more than occasions for "an insubstantial pageant" of pretty memories.

For Waugh, Scott-King's "complete man" was not just a matter of classical education, but a state of being achieved through theological commitment. Without belief in some absolute principle, he argued, men are not fulfilled. He made his conviction explicit in 1946, writing about his purpose as a novelist. In subsequent novels he planned to pursue two goals: "a preoccupation with style and the attempt to represent man more fully, which to me, means only one thing, man in his relation to God." "I believe that you can only leave God out by making your characters pure abstractions."[9] When Waugh wrote this, he had just published *Brideshead Revisited* in which, for the first time, he had introduced the question of God and attempted to represent people more fully than he had ever before. The results were mixed as he himself would come to think. He would try these themes again in *Helena, The Ordeal of Gilbert Pinfold* and *Sword of Honour,* but in his other fiction, excepting his unfinished *Work Suspended,* he avoided treating religious issues directly and, accordingly, drew his characters as abstractions. In *Work Suspended* his protagonist, John Plant, a successful detective novelist with no metaphysical or theological pretensions, describes just this approach to characterization.

> The algebra of fiction must reduce its problems to symbols if they are to be soluble at all. I am shy of a book commended to me on the grounds that the "characters are alive." There is no place in literature for a live man, solid and active. At best the author may maintain a kind a Dickensian menagerie, where his characters live behind bars, in darkness, to be liberated twice nightly for a brief gambol under the arc lamps; in they come to the whip crack, dazzled, deafened, and doped, tumble through their tricks and scamper out again, to the cages behind which the real business of life, eating and mating, is carried on out of sight of the audience. "Are the lions really alive?" "Yes, lovey." "Will they eat us up?" "No, lovey, the man won't let them"— that is all the reviewers mean as a rule when they talk of "life." The alterna-

tive, classical expedient is to take the whole man and reduce him to a manageable abstraction. Set up your picture plain, fix your point vision, make your figure twenty foot high or the size of a thumb-nail, he will be life-size on your canvas; hang your picture in the darkest corner, your heaven will still be its one source of light. Beyond these limits lie only the real trouser buttons and the *crêpe* hair with which the futurists used to adorn their painting.[10]

Waugh wrote this in a novel in which he was himself about to attempt a portrayal of "the whole human mind and soul" by including "its determining character—that of being God's creature with a defined purpose."[11] But until this work his practice had been to use the "classical expedient," reducing the whole man to "a manageable abstraction." This is why Firbank was so useful to Waugh. Firbank's weightlessly insubstantial characters, often little more than waggish voices hung on wonderfully implausible names like Miss Miami Mouth and Dr. Cuncliffe Babcock, were perfectly suited to Waugh's intention, which was to satirize the aimless shallowness of people living without "defined purpose."

Of course, Waugh's "algebra of fiction" did not stop with characterization. He endeavored to organize entire novels with an abstractionist's delight in mathematical poise, using stylized recurrences and juxtapositions to create his own "little independent systems of order." To do so he drew on a variety of contemporary art forms. As we have seen, he frequently put the conventions of modern architecture and avant-garde painting to satiric ends. But it was film, the uniquely twentieth-century art, that became his most abiding inspiration. Admittedly, this seems at first an unlikely proposition. Waugh frequently mocked the movie industry and seems to have given little effort to his brief tenure as a scriptwriter.[12] There is, however, abundant evidence that he entertained a lifelong fascination for the esthetic potential of film despite his continuing disappointment with most of its commerical productions. From his earliest stories he consciously constructed his narratives according to cinematic principles. Both in theory and practice, film had just what he needed to shape his antic vision of our century.

It is to this interest and strategy we now turn.

VII

FILM
THE GLARING LENS OF SATIRE

Although Waugh had little respect for the film industry and its products, he frequently expressed himself in terms of cinematic strategy. In 1921, responding to a friend whose story he had read in manuscript, he advised him to

> try and bring home thoughts by actions and incidents. Don't make every-thing said. This is the inestimable value of the Cinema to novelists (don't scoff at this as a cheap epigram it is really very true.) Make things happen. . . . Don't bring characters on simply to draw their characters and make them talk. Fit them into a design. . . . It [the story] is a damn good idea. Don't spoil it out of slackness or perversity. . . . Have a murder in every chapter if you like but do do something. GO TO THE CINEMA and risk the headache.[1]

Thirty-five years later, when a struggling writer asked him for some professional advice on how to proceed with a biography that was giving him trouble, Waugh suggested he think of his material cinematically.

> Could you not conceive of Maria Pasqua's life as a film? I don't mean— Heaven forbid—that it should be filmed, or that you should attempt to give it any of the character of a Hollywood script. I mean in the *mechanics* of the *imagination.* Instead of seeing it as an historical document, imagine yourself watching a film—each incident as precise and authentic as in the present version, but with the *continuity* (in the technical cinematographical sense) and selective dramatic emphasis and scenery of a film. And then write as though describing the experience. (The emphasis is Waugh's)[2]

This advice may or may not have helped his correspondents, but it certainly aids our understanding of Waugh and the mechanics of his imagination. As a satirist who frequently played the role of farceur in order to mock the decline of Western culture, he necessarily ran the risk of allowing his fiction to lapse into the shapeless slapstick his esthetic temperament abhorred. But there was to be nothing carelessly slack or perverse in his

work. Even at its most knockabout, his fiction always exhibits the craftsman's attention to design. He learned a good deal of his craftsmanship from
cinema, which supplied him with the mechanics to build underlying patterns into his narratives, no matter how helter-skelter their surfaces might
seem to the casual reader.

At least as early as his days writing undergraduate film criticism, Waugh
liked to draw upon the cinematographer's art for his illustrations. It was,
for instance, the filmmaker's mobile camera that became a key element in
his self-portrait. In his one avowedly autobiographical novel, *The Ordeal of
Gilbert Pinfold*, published in 1957, he described himself as a "combination
of eccentric don and testy colonel" (p. 13), a role he devised to keep the
unwelcome at bay. Writing about himself in the third person, he added
that "he offered the world a front of pomposity mitigated by indiscretion,
that was as hard, bright, and antiquated as a cuirass" (p. 13). From behind
this character armour

> he looked at the world *sub specie aeternitatis* and he found it flat as a map; ex-
> cept when, rather often, personal annoyance intruded. Then he would come
> tumbling from his exalted point of observation. Shocked by a bad bottle of
> wine, an impertinent stranger, or a fault in syntax, his mind like a cinema
> camera trucked furiously forward to confront the offending object close-up
> with glaring lens. (p. 12)

The contrasting similes used to illustrate mind and character in this passage are more revealing than their casual deployment would suggest. To
describe his mind, Waugh uses a cinema camera that alternates between
coolly detached long-shots of a remote world and extremely vivid close-
ups of its various outrages. As Pinfold-Waugh's camera-mind darts about
the twentieth century, however, his sensibility remains encased in its
cuirass of tradition. These images may be incongruous, but they are not
careless. The juxtaposition of cuirass and camera aptly expresses his contradictory nature, gauging as it does the tension between his public pose
and private sensibility. On one hand he is the hardened old-guard reactionary encased by views so unalterably settled that he has "never voted in a
parliamentary election, maintaining an idiosyncratic toryism which was
quite unrepresented in the political parties of his time" (p. 6); on the other,
he is the ever-alert satirist enthusiastically, if furiously, rushing out to seize
the provocation of the moment with whatever techniques his age has provided him.

Waugh the reactionary may have sought safe seclusion behind the
armament of tradition, but Waugh the artist liked nothing better than to
zoom in for close-ups of the world's scandals. As he put it himself, his tastes

might have been "formally antique" but he was nonetheless esthetically in the "advance guard."

The cuirass/camera juxtaposition is another instance of the split between the static and dynamic we have already detected in Waugh. The camera seems to have been an especially appropriate figure for him. Other than its contrast with the cuirass, the film medium, or at least its theoretical potential, touched something essential in his ambivalent nature. This is perhaps due to film's special balance of the passive and the active. As an instrument, the camera both records and shapes events; it is simultaneously detached and engaged, incorporating the worst traits of the retiring Paul Pennyfeather and the interfering Basil Seal. In part, this may explain Waugh's lifelong involvement with its possibilities. Film was an ideal tool for a satirist who was both repelled and fascinated by his subject matter.

No one familiar with the sequence of Waugh's work can be surprised by his choice of a cinematic analogy to describe the workings of his own mind. Film always played a prominent part in his life and writing. Some thirty-odd years before *The Ordeal of Gilbert Pinfold* the twenty-one-year-old Waugh helped produce and acted in an amateur film entitled *The Scarlet Woman.* Distinguished by Elsa Lanchester's screen debut, this work had a bizarre plot that included the Pope's attempt to blackmail first the Prince of Wales and then the rest of the royal family into the Roman Church.[3] Two years later he published his first piece of fiction after leaving Oxford, a short story entitled "The Balance." This experimental narrative is arranged, awkwardly at times, to resemble a silent film in progress complete with scene directions and block-lettered captions. There are even italicized remarks made by a viewing audience that is supposed to be "attending" the story with the reader.[4] His first novel, *Decline and Fall,* has for its strange spokesman Silenus, the architect who has gained his unlikely eminence in the world by designing film sets. *Vile Bodies* includes a parody of filmmaking that is as central as anything else in its relentlessly eccentric narrative, which is itself edited much like an elliptical avant-garde film devoted to individual scenes while sublimely negligent of coherent plot development. In "Excursion in Reality," a short story from 1934, and *The Loved One* from 1949 he drew upon his experience as a would-be writer-consultant for the film industry.[5]

Since the metaphorical suggestiveness and organizational strategies of film suffuse Waugh's work, it is not surprising to learn that he was convinced this medium had the potential to become "the one vital art of the century."[6] True, he did not expect it to realize this potential, given the economic constraints of producing and marketing films for a mass audience. He knew artistic considerations would be invariably the first discounted on a balance sheet tallied to accord with the priorities of a commercial film budget. Still, he insisted that film had "taught a new habit of narrative" to novelists. This might be "the only contribution the cinema [was] destined to make to the arts," but for Waugh, one surmises, this was enough to justify serious attention to its craft.[7] His early adoption of Ronald Firbank as a model, for instance, had much to do with the cinematic techniques he detected in Firbank's novels. Firbank, according to Waugh, had abandoned the linear plot in favor of a contrapuntal structure similar to montage. As we have seen, Waugh compared the effect of this practice with that of silent films "in which the relation of caption and photograph is directly reversed; occasionally a brief, visual image flashes out to illumine and explain the flickering succession of spoken words."[8] In his own novels Waugh borrowed Firbank's method in order to construct a narrative equivalent of a film edited in staccato montage. Disparate scenes, unexpectedly spliced together, rush by at a reckless pace contributing to his theme of headlong irresponsibility.

His friend Graham Greene was another filmic novelist whose craft Waugh admired. Reviewing one of his novels in 1948, he praised Greene for approaching his material as would a film director arranging his narrative so as to do away with the need for "an observer through whom the events are recorded and emotions transmitted."

> It is as though out of an infinite length of film, sequences had been cut which, assembled, comprise an experience which is the reader's alone, without any correspondence to the experience of the protagonists. The writer has become director and producer.[9]

Whether or not this fairly describes Greene's practice, it certainly explains Waugh's.

But Waugh's interest in film was more than purely technical. His attraction was at least as theoretical as it was practical. The medium's peculiar perceptual qualities seemed to express just those unquestioned assumptions of his age that he most wanted to satirize. Of course, when we come to discuss his cinematic borrowings, we will find that matters are not so neatly separable. Theory and technique, as we would expect, blend in the finished work. So before going on to review Waugh's application of cinematic strategies, it will be useful to pause for a moment and set forth in a general way how film affected his thinking and practice.

Film was the perfect analogue for Waugh's vision of a world that had forfeited the consoling stability of Being for the impassioned tumult of Becoming. He had counseled other writers to imagine themselves watching a film when attempting to organize their subject matter. He followed his

own advice, but with this difference: he used cinematic strategies to organize his vision of disorder. The resulting portrait displays a world that has
lost its head and with it any sense of purpose larger than personal aggran-
dizement. As Wyndham Lewis, Arnold Hauser, Marshall McLuhan, and
other theorists have argued, film's esthetic experience is one that dissolves
the conventional perspectives of time and space, presenting in their stead
a dreamlike amalgam of disparate sensations held together by an associational rather than strictly sequential logic. It is a medium that can link the
most unlikely images, deploy multiple perspectives as easily as changing a
camera angle, and celebrate motion with an immediacy unavailable to any
other art form.[10] As such, it was ideal for insulting the classical, literate
mind conditioned to expect continuity and logical progression in works of
art, and Waugh delighted in using it this way.

If film's formal characteristics suited Waugh's satiric ends, so did its
manner of presentation. A typical film audience rarely has the opportunity
or inclination to achieve that state of detached contemplation which had
been the ideal of classical art. Film encourages a sensuous immersion in the
flow of its images. Its appeal is primarily emotional, even visceral, and only
secondarily intellectual. This is true both because of its extraordinary formal features and the way they are experienced. Unlike other arts, film
traps its audience during its unreeling and leaves scant opportunity for
critical reflection. The viewer in his theater seat cannot review a difficult
passage at will. He cannot indulge his intellectual curiosity to reconsider
individual scenes from new perspectives. At least not until he attends another screening. This temporal aspect of film most resembles music. But
even music permits the kind of reviewing necessary to intellectual analysis
when it is translated into a score or, in our age, recorded so that the listener
can repeat passages as he wishes. Of all arts, film has proven most resistant
to critical analysis because it has been generally experienced in theaters
which do not permit the viewer any control over its presentation. With literature and art one can return to the works under consideration to sift and
weigh impressions, correcting and amplifying them as renewed experience
indicates. Until the recent introduction of inexpensive home viewing
equipment, this was a luxury few of the general film audience enjoyed.
Furthermore, unlike drama scripts, only a tiny percentage of screenplays
are published for general consumption. As a result, viewers have not had a
permanent document to refer to and have been hard pressed to formulate
fully developed responses to films, let alone interpretations adequately
tested by reexamination of the primary evidence. Of course this is changing now that it has become an easy matter to view a film privately with the
means to control the speed and direction of its images. When Waugh was

writing, however, film watching was done passively in a theater and as such
it provided him with an apt metaphor of the traditionally formed mind confronted by experience over which it was powerless to exert an interpretive
order. He only had to exaggerate film's formal characteristics, constructing
his narratives as though he were a director sublimely indifferent to the excesses of his mobile camera and montage editing.

On the evidence of his fiction, this was film's basic appeal for Waugh. It
allowed him to achieve his goals as satirist and esthete simultaneously. If
the nature of cinema's structure and reception helped him evoke a society
out of control, it also provided him with the means to stand aside from the
confusion he portrayed and manage it. The distinction here is between ex-
periencing film and making it. His typical early novel might be a whirligig
of futility, but it is, nevertheless, assembled with the purposeful deliberation of a director standing apart from the complex operation of filmmaking
so that he can make the decisions necessary to bring together its many
components. The results may be a cacaphonous farce, but the reader is
rarely in doubt that there is a cool, detached intelligence orchestrating the
noise. This is nowhere more evident than in the discrepancy between the
apparent shapelessness of Waugh's frenetic novels and the superbly man-
nered voice that narrates them. Waugh was drawn to the paradoxical nature of filmmaking because it was a medium that perfectly expressed the
headlong nature of contemporary life, but did so only at the bidding of a serene, calculating intelligence. (Was Waugh parodying himself in *Decline
and Fall* in the character of the sublimely disinterested Otto Silenus, architect and film-set designer, sitting at the still center of life's spinning
wheel?) Although there is every reason to believe Waugh's art sprang as
much from his emotions and intuitions as from his intellect, he seems to
have been pleased to think of himself as a purely intellectual craftsman
building an esthetic structure that at once expressed and contained his satiric energy.[11] His obvious enthusiasm for conceiving of himself as an un-
emotional, disinterested craftsman shows up in his praise of those writers
like Firbank and Greene whose relation to their works is that of "director
and producer." By adopting this directorial role, the novelist can deal with
extremity and absurdity without seeming to be affected by them. This is, of
course, another version of the split between reason and passion that marks
every aspect of Waugh's work. Here it is expressed structurally.

The esthetically committed but intellectually disinterested artist is one
of the recurring phenomena of our century. In "The Film Age" chapter of
his *Social History of Art* Arnold Hauser argues that the twentieth-century
artist sets out with "the intention . . . to write, paint and compose from the
intellect, not from the emotions" as though any given artistic project were
an intricate problem demanding reasoned solutions rather than subjective

convictions. Hauser goes on to say that the writer has found one of these solutions in cinema. Specifically, the novelist has learned from the film editor the device of montage which so successfully represents

> the new concept of time, whose basic element is simultaneity and whose nature consists in the spatialization of the temporal element, . . . expressed in no other genre so impressively as in this youngest art, which dates from the same period as Bergson's philosophy.

Paradoxically enough, however, the intellectual artist employs cinematic logic to render the confusion and randomness of twentieth-century experience.

> The Bergsonian concept of time undergoes a new interpretation, an intensification and a deflection. The accent is now on the simultaneity of the contents of consciousness, the immanence of the past in the present, the constant flowing together of the different periods of time, the amorphous fluidity of inner experience, the boundlessness of the stream of time by which the soul is borne along, the relativity of space and time. . . . In this new conception of time almost all the strands . . . of modern art converge: the abandonment of plot, the elimination of the hero, the relinquishing of psychology, . . . and, above all, the montage technique and the intermingling of temporal and spatial forms of the film.[12]

This seems to explain film's structural value for Waugh. Here was a medium that was at once poised yet perfectly suited to represent the teeming mindlessness of contemporary society. It provided him with a method that allowed for the stillness of artistic control even as it portrayed hopeless confusion. It is no wonder that he adapted cinematic form to do justice to his vision of a divided world.

Hauser relates the technical appeal of film to the philosophical influence exerted by Henri Bergson in the opening decades of this century. There is little question of the general validity of this connection and, I think, it is one that applies specifically to Waugh. This can be detected in the manner with which both philosopher and novelist turned to cinematic analogies to express themselves.

In scenes meant to suggest the breakdown of psychic and social order, Waugh frequently employed cinematic strategies which, as often as not, were explicitly labeled as such. But film was more than a technical resource. As adapted by Waugh, it also implied an epistemology that seems to derive from his knowledge of Bergson's work. Bergson had found it useful to speak analogically of the intellect as though its processes were parallel to those of a cinematograph. This is a figure that appears in Waugh's writing repeatedly. As we have seen, in *The Ordeal of Gilbert Pinfold* he explicitly describes the workings of his own mind with a cinematic met-

aphor. When we recall that Waugh's first two novels contain central episodes devoted to parodying Bergson's concept of Becoming, the line of
influence seems unquestionable.

In *Creative Evolution* Bergson illustrates the intellect's estrangement
from reality by comparing its operation to that of cinematography. "The
cinematographical instinct of our thought," he states, prevents us from
fully understanding "universal becoming," the essential reality. The filmic
metaphor suits his argument. Bergson wants to demonstrate that the analytical mode of thinking characteristic of Western man depends upon an
artificial separation between subject and object. Film offers the perfect
model. Bergson argues that we have been trained to assume that we can
only come into possession of real knowledge by intellectually standing
apart from the object of our interest in order to bring it into focus much as
a camera must be positioned at the proper distance from what it is to film.
Instead of intuiting reality from the inside, the intellect looks on, as does
Pinfold's camera-eye, from the outside. By doing so, it puts itself outside its
natural place in the universal becoming. Adopting the fiction of an external
vantage point, it can manage Becoming by dividing it conceptually into a
series of "snapshots taken at intervals of its flowing," as Bergson puts it.
Like a cinema camera, the abstracting intellect reduces experience to a sequence of static representations or frames. This is why Western thinkers
had never accounted for change in a convincing way. Examined by the intellect alone, change always seems an illusion. No matter how diligently it
tries to account for Becoming, the intellect cannot reconstitute it. Bergson
explains this in terms of "the contrivance of the cinematograph."

> Instead of attaching ourselves to the inner becoming of things, we place our-
> selves outside them in order to recompose their becoming artifically. . . .
> Whether we would think becoming or express it, or even perceive it, we
> hardly do anything else than set going a kind of cinematograph inside us. . . .
> The application of the cinematographical method . . . leads to a perpetual
> recommencement, during which the mind, never able to satisfy itself and
> never finding where to rest, persuades itself, no doubt, that it imitates by its
> instability the very movement of the real. But though, by straining itself to
> the point of giddiness, it may end by giving itself the illusion of mobility, its
> operation has not advanced it a step, since it remains as far as ever from its
> goal. In order to advance with the moving reality, you must replace yourself
> within it. Install yourself within change, and you will grasp at once both
> change itself and the successive states in which it might at any instant be im-
> mobilized. But with these successive states, perceived from without as real
> and no longer as potential immobilities, you will never reconsititute move-
> ment.

Reality becomes an abstraction when we, the perceiving subjects, are differentiated from the perceived object, inevitably prompting a sense of alienation from the world outside ourselves. Bergson recommends intuitive knowing as an antidote. Only this approach to experience produces the lively awareness of the irreducibly real necessary to foster the emotional and imaginative harmony with the world for which we long.[13]

So runs Bergson's argument. Many early twentieth-century novelists found its logic and its use of cinematic analogy pertinent to their own concerns. On the evidence of his fictional conceits, so did Waugh.

When in *The Ordeal of Gilbert Pinfold* Waugh described the workings of his own mind with a cinematic metaphor that recalled Bergson's, he was doing no more than following a personal tradition he had established many years before. Time and again, he adapted, consciously or not, Bergson's cinematographical intellect to his own very unbergsonian purposes. How else explain that in novel after novel we discover a traditionally formed, literate mind desperately "straining itself to the point of giddiness" in an attempt to assemble and interpret its cinematic experience of the world? It is as though Waugh had been literally working out the implication of Bergson's metaphor of the cinematographical intellect confronted by the unmanageable flow of Becoming. We have considered one example of this already in *Vile Bodies,* the scene in which Agatha Runcible, suffering hallucinations and strapped to her hospital bed, imagines herself trying to steer a car racing at impossible speeds over a course that offers severely limited visibility. From Agatha's prone position "there was rarely more than a quarter of a mile of the black road to be seen at one time. It unrolled like a length of cinema film. At the edges was confusion; a fog spinning past" (p. 284). This hallucinatory passage I take to be Waugh's parody of Bergson, an image of the cinematographical intellect helpless before the helter-skelter rush of Becoming. With or without explicit reference to film, it recurs throughout Waugh's fiction. Before examining its implications, I want to quote two other versions of it. Like the first, they also acknowledge their debt to film. Considered together, all three strongly argue that Waugh had quite deliberately appropriated Bergson's cinematographical intellect and bent it to his own ends.

The second example occurs in the cinematically structured story, "The Balance" (1925), when Adam Doure is shown recovering from a drunken suicide attempt. It is particularly pertinent for the way in which it distinguishes between his initial befuddlement and his dawning awareness of his surroundings. His mental confusion manifests itself as a two-dimensional cinematic experience he must endure passively until he can regain his sense of order. Once he does, the world returns in all its purposeful, three-dimensional solidity.

He still wore the clothes in which he had slept. But in his intellectual dishevelment he had little concern for his appearance. All about him the shadows were beginning to dissipate and give place to clearer images. He had breakfasted in a world of phantoms, in a great room full of uncomprehending eyes, protruding grotesquely from monstrous heads that lolled over steaming porridge; marionette waiters had pirouetted about him with uncouth gestures. All around him a macabre dance of shadows had reeled and flickered, and in and out of it Adam had picked his way, conscious only of one insistent need, percolating through to him from the world outside, of immediate escape from the scene upon which the bodiless harlequinade was played, into a third dimension beyond it. And at length, as he walked by the river, the shapes of the design began to advance and recede, and the pattern about him and the shadows of the night before became planes and masses and arranged themselves into a perspective, and like the child in the nursery Adam began feeling his bruises.[14]

The third scene comes from the 1937 novel, *Scoop*, and recalls Agatha Runcible's death-bed hallucinations. Lord Copper, the autocratic publisher of London's leading newspaper, the *Beast,* finds himself about to address a banquet with a speech grossly inappropriate to the ostensible guest of honor. Written to dignify a man in his twenties, the address must now serve for a rather disreputable looking codger of questionable sanity who has been unaccountably installed on the dais. Seeing "the words 'young in years' looming up at him, [Lord Copper] swerve[s]." As he glances "grimly through the pages ahead of him," the speech takes on the high-speed characteristics of Agatha Runcible's filmic hallucination.

For some time now his newspapers had been advocating a new form of driving test, by which the applicant for a license sat in a stationary car while a cinema film unfolded before his eyes a nightmare drive down a road full of obstacles. Lord Copper had personally inspected a device of the kind and it was thus that his speech now appeared to him. (pp. 317–18)

Waugh returns to the cinematic imagery of these three scenes again and again. Obviously, it was a comparison that resonated with special significance for him as closer examination reveals. In each a helpless character finds himself plunged into an inexorable flow of experience that flickers, reels, and "unroll[s] like a length of cinema film" over and around him. In each an unmanageable rush of sensation overwhelms a mind powerless to resist. In Waugh, reason is always about to be submerged by experience; his characters find themselves pushed into a two-dimensional filmlike world in which the usual distinctions between background and foreground, essential and incidental, evaporate like the "fog spinning past" the helpless Agatha Runcible. There is no chance to direct one's life toward a purposeful end; there is only the all-consuming now of immediate sensation. Daily experience resembles a badly composed film in which everything has a flattened, foreshortened quality. Peripheral details shove themselves into the foreground, short-circuiting depth perception. The resulting scene visually portrays a world deprived of the classical perspective that had once enabled people to steer their lives along a course of rational and moral distinctions. Now, like Agatha, they find themselves flat on their backs, unsupported by a coherent ethos. Abandoned to a brutally foreshortened perspective, they are nevertheless expected to steer for themselves as best they can.

Although Waugh's characters seem only dimly aware of it, the possibility of fitting contemporary experience into an intelligible pattern has long since passed. Forswearing absolutes, the twentieth century has allowed the objective world to slip through its fingers. What it calls reality is so fluidly elusive that nothing so feeble as an idea can restrain its mercurial course. With neither an objective, stable reality nor an epistemology that allows one to behold it from a civilized distance, the individual, like Paul Pennyfeather, disappears, merging with the "kaleidoscope of dimly discernible faces" of the undifferentiated masses.

Bergson's image of the cinematographical intellect turns up in Waugh's fiction with a vengeance. It becomes his metaphor of the civilized mind's loss of conviction in its ability to impose order on what is otherwise a senseless onslaught of daily experience. Typically, his characters must suffer one of two possible fates. There are the thoughtless, who, having embraced Bergsonian Becoming, are left to swim with the flux of a relativistic world in which the value of existence is gauged by the intensity of the moment rather than its proximity to an ideal. These are the characters who have lost any sense of commitment to a design that might transcend their immediate experience. Then there are the reflective types, who must stand on the bank and watch the flailing swimmers breast the stream as well as its shifting currents will allow. Without faith in the ordering power of ideas, they have no counsel or aid to offer their floundering opposites. They can do little more than watch experience unreel like "an infinite length of film" full of spectacle but devoid of purpose.

VIII

THE SATIRIST OF
THE FILM WORLD

Film unquestionably provided Waugh with some of his most characteristic strategies and metaphors. In this chapter I will examine the most prominent of them. For the sake of clarity and convenience, I have arranged them under five headings: incoherence and the subversive detail, the narrator as director, discontinuity, leveling, and primitivism. I do not mean to suggest that this list is immutable. Its divisions are not sealed off from one another. A strategy or metaphor examined under one heading may at times serve as well to exemplify another. My only purpose in making these admittedly artificial distinctions is to organize what I have to say about Waugh's application of film to his fiction.

Incoherence and the Subversive Detail

In his analysis of Graham Greene's narrative technique, Waugh noted that "the affinity to the film is everywhere apparent" and then illustrated his point with Greene's use of "significant detail," the writer's equivalent of film's close-up images. With a cinematic metaphor, he compares the narrator to a "camera's eye which moves from the hotel balcony to the street below, picks out the policeman, follows him to his office, moves about the room from the handcuffs on the wall to the broken rosary in the drawer, recording significant detail. It is the modern way of telling a story."[1]

Waugh does not elaborate further, but one must suppose he was thinking not only of film but the course of the modern novel since Flaubert. The modernity of this technique resides in its seeming absolution of authorial responsibility. The reader is left to discover meaning for himself. With respect to the novel before him, he finds himself in much the same position he is in when confronting a universe deprived of the intervention of a divine intelligence. He must pick his way among the details and come to his own conclusions. Of course, this is modern fiction's fiction. As Waugh

110

points out, the writer is stage-managing the details from behind the scenes all along, imbuing them with significance that will lead the alert reader to the "correct" conclusion. An experimental work comprised of a plotless gathering of apparently random observations will turn out on closer examination to cohere around an authorial attitude. Even in the case of a writer who sets out to prove that life has no purpose the resulting work will necessarily bear the impress of his artistic purpose. This may be no more than his negative demonstration, but it will nevertheless provide his work with a coherence he professes to find absent in the world around him.

As Martin Price reminds us, novelistic details are often "pulled between the demands of structure and the consistent texture of a plausible fictional world." He goes on to observe that "their nature is not unlike those of our own lives that are jointly to be explained by outward circumstance and inward motive."[2] In *Fiction and the Camera Eye* Alan Spiegel analyzes this use of detail in cinematic terms reminiscent of Waugh's discussion of significant detail. Using what at first appears to be the neutrality of a camera eye, the modern writer, according to Spiegel, presents the narrative equivalent of a film close-up. He chooses a seemingly unimportant detail from the story's realistic background and then makes it contribute to the story's "undercurrent of interior resonance beneath the narrative surface." As Spiegel sees it, this is a strategy that attempts "to resolve the dramatic incompatibility between an object's adventitious appearance as part of a chaotic and senseless material flux and its meaningful depths."[3] In other words, a writer will avail himself of the metaphoric and symbolic possibilities inherent in his setting's realistic details in order to reinforce his theme and unify his work. To take an obvious example, the snowfall that concludes James Joyce's *The Dead*, covering and joining both the natural and man-made environment, is at once real snow and an image of common mortality.

Although Waugh complained that many modern novelists were presumptuous and exorbitant in their attempts to "represent the whole human mind and soul" without reference to any ultimate design, he could admire the technical dexterity with which a Joyce deployed his "significant details" so as to invest his work with artistic if not theological unity.[4] Waugh adapted this strategy for his own works, but he did so with an important difference. He gave it an ironic twist so that it served to mock rather than affirm the longing for coherence among people who had forsaken, knowingly or not, their belief in a providential order.

Waugh, of course, made no secret of his belief that existence was purposeful. Yet he frequently arranged his details so that they signified the opposite, as if to give his readers a sardonic glimpse of a world without any meaning. This is so true of some of the early novels that there are those who have assumed the fiction is as disorderly and slapdash as the world it portrays. What Waugh called the "significant detail" in other works turned subversive in his own. In effect, he played against his reader's expectations. The modern novel has trained us to look for signals of coherence in the details an author selects for prominent display. Waugh's satiric strategy was to give close-up treatment to details that disrupt this expectation. In effect, he provides an ironically negative demonstration of Price's and Spiegel's case. The "undercurrent" of his details speaks of an incoherent world. In the early novels, it is disorder itself that paradoxically serves as the organizing principle around which character and incident revolve. His significant details typically contribute to the "chaotic and senseless material flux." Within the story they are generally placed so as to subvert any pretension to purposeful order that may be entertained by an unusually thoughtful character. These are the details that Waugh treats in merciless close-up. They are almost always of a kind with the bad bottle of wine, the impertinent stranger, and the syntactical lapse that shocked Gilbert Pinfold's mind into reacting like a cinema camera. As such, they impinge on two levels of the reader's awareness. Viewed from without, these details form part of the overall construction. But viewed from within, the same details belie the fiction of civility with which people hide from themselves those indecorous questions about life's purpose. They organize the story with their metaphorical suggestiveness, as Waugh argued Greene's significant details did, but they have been meticulously orchestrated to signify metaphysical confusion rather than coherence. Of course, this is not surprising in satire. As Alvin Kernan has demonstrated, this is a genre that often makes its point by accumulating a riot of particulars that defeat the mind's longing for order. Certainly Waugh provides enough examples to confirm Kernan's thesis. One thinks of the bewildering catalogue of parties in *Vile Bodies.*

> . . . Masked parties, savage parties, Victorian parties, Greek parties, Wild
> West parties, Russian parties, Circus parties, parties where one had to dress
> as somebody else, almost naked parties in St. John's Wood, parties in flats
> and studios and houses and ships and hotels and night clubs, in windmills and
> swimming baths, tea parties at school where one ate muffins and meringues
> and tinned crab, parties at Oxford where one drank brown sherry and
> smoked Turkish cigarettes, dull dances in London and comic dances in Scot-
> land and disgusting dances in Paris—all that succession and repetition of
> massed humanity. . . . Those vile bodies. . . . (pp. 170–71)

What is the purpose of itemizing this endless proliferation but to extinguish rational assessment?

Then there is the overheard political conversation of *Brideshead Revisited*. The year is 1936 and people are talking about the problems of Edward VIII and the hostilities that will lead to World War II.

"Of course, he can marry her and make her queen tomorrow."

"We had our chance in October. Why didn't we send the Italian Fleet to the bottom of the Mare Nostrum? Why didn't we blow Spezia to blazes? Why didn't we land on Pantelleria?"

"Franco's simply a German agent. They tried to put him in to prepare air bases to bomb France. That bluff has been called, anyway."

"It would make the monarchy stronger than it's been since Tudor times. The people are with him."

"The press are with him."

"I'm with him."

"Who cares about divorce now except a few old maids who aren't married, anyway?"

"If he has a showdown with the old gang, they'll just disappear like, like . . . "

"Why didn't we close the Canal? Why didn't we bomb Rome?"

"It wouldn't have been necessary. One firm note . . . "

"One firm speech."

"One showdown."

"Anyway, Franco will soon be skipping back to Morocco. Chap I saw today just come from Barcelona . . . "

" . . . Chap just come from Fort Belvedere . . . "

" . . . Chap just come from Palazzo Venezia . . . "

"All we want is a showdown."

"A showdown with Baldwin."

"A showdown with Hitler."

"A showdown with the Old Gang."

" . . . That I should live to see my country, the land of Clive and Nelson . . . "

" . . . *My* country of Hawkins and Drake."

" . . . *My* country of Palmerston . . . "

"Would you very much mind not doing that?" said Grizel to the columnist, who had been attempting in a maudlin manner to twist her wrist. "I don't happen to enjoy it." (pp. 275–76)

The self-delusion and pointlessness of such talk speaks for itself. As different as they are, the catalogue of parties and the snippets of conversation are alike in that neither receives the benefit of narrative mediation. In both passages detail and dialogue are heaped on the reader without the usual filtering mechanisms of earlier fiction. There is no context to speak of, the principle of arrangement is obscure, and the narrator's voice is either ironic or enigmatic. The effect is to create a sense of aimless futility. But Waugh did not rely exclusively on these relatively simple means to portray the incoherence of his world. Another strategy he liked to use re-

quired that he first contrive a scene redolent of cultivated taste and imbued with the stability of long tradition. Having done so, he would then
subvert it. To do this he would select an apparently incidental detail from
the background and treat it with cinematic logic, as a scene from *Vile
Bodies* illustrates quite clearly. Lord Metroland has just returned home
from a conversation with the mysterious Jesuit, Father Rothschild, and the
current prime minister, Walter Outrage. Rothschild has tried to make Metroland aware of the "radical instability" that besets the modern world.

> By ill-fortune he [Metroland] arrived on the doorstep to find Peter Past-
> master fumbling with the lock, and they entered together. Lord Metroland
> noticed a tall hat on the table by the door. "Young Trumpington's, I sup-
> pose," he thought. His stepson did not once look at him, but made straight
> for the stairs, walking unsteadily, his hat on the back of his head, his um-
> brella still in his hand.
> "Good night, Peter," said Lord Metroland.
> "Oh, go to hell," said his stepson thickly, then turning on the stairs, he
> added, "I'm going abroad tomorrow for a few weeks. Will you tell my
> mother?"
> "Have a good time," said Lord Metroland. "You'll find it just as cold every-
> where, I'm afraid. Would you care to take the yacht? No one's using it."
> "Oh, go to hell."
> Lord Metroland went into the study to finish his cigar. It would be awk-
> ward if he met young Trumpington on the stairs. He sat down in a very com-
> fortable chair. . . . A radical instability, Rothschild had said, radical
> instability. . . . He looked round his study and saw shelves of books—the
> *Dictionary of National Biography,* the *Encyclopaedia Britannica* in an early
> and very bulky edition, *Who's Who*, Debrett, Burke, Whitaker, several vol-
> umes of Hansard, some Blue Books and Atlases—a safe in the corner painted
> green with a brass handle, his writing-table, his secretary's table, some very
> comfortable chairs and some very businesslike chairs, a tray with decanters
> and a plate of sandwiches, his evening mail laid out on the table . . . radical
> instability, indeed. How like poor old Outrage to let himself be taken in by
> that charlatan of a Jesuit.
> He heard the front door open and shut behind Alastair Trumpington.
> Then he rose and went quietly upstairs, leaving his cigar smouldering in
> the ash-tray, filling the study with fragrant smoke. (pp. 186–87)

After dramatizing the general breakdown of authority with this particular
comic instance of a drunken youth's hostility for his fawningly solicitous
stepfather, the scene progresses by means of visual close-ups selected from
its background. Convinced the world is cold everywhere and having been
advised by his stepson to go to hell, Metroland is in no mood to meet young
Trumpington, owner of the tall hat, who is visiting his wife upstairs. Instead, he follows his stepson's advice and does go to hell, an unacknowl-
edged hell of his own devising in which he can lapse into a complacency

that resembles nothing so much as despair. Pathetically stubborn in his need to believe all is right with his world, Metroland retreats to his study where he reassures himself that there is an ordered continuity to his existence by selectively reviewing his bookshelves. There he finds the *Dictionary of National Biography*, *Who's Who*, the *Encyclopaedia Britannica*, official publications of parliamentary proceedings, listings of the peerage and socially prominent, and maps of the world. Although there must be many other titles and objects in this room, we never hear of them. Metroland's eyes fall unfailingly on just what he wants to see: the works that establish one's place in the world by recording order and precedence and providing rational categories with which to organize experience. In his study Metroland can convince himself that he is at the center of a coherent, eminently manageable world, but young Trumpington's hat in the outer hall and the smoldering cigar left behind in the ashtray tell a very different story. Waugh deploys his "significant details" in a manner that invites a filmic reading of this scene. In doing so, he subverts Metroland's pretension to an ordered existence. Trumpington's potently tall hat has cowed Metroland into retreat. He would rather surround himself with the comforting illusion of order than confront his wife's infidelity. When Trumpington departs, leaving the field clear once again, Metroland approaches his wife disarmed, his masculine cigar left behind to burn itself out impotently among the bankrupt mementos of a once orderly society. Waugh's narrator operates as would a skillful film director marshaling the background of the scene to serve his intention. All the forces of order and tradition are no match for that incidental hat and cigar. The center cannot hold against the merely peripheral.

This suspension of the expected relationship between the central and peripheral is also apparent in *A Handful of Dust* in a scene that is less obviously cinematic but is conceived in much the same way. This is the scene in which Tony Last struggles to maintain the appearances of gentlemanly behavior in the absence of the principles upon which such behavior presumably rests. In order to expedite the divorce his wife desires, he must escort a prostitute to a seaside resort where detectives retained for the purpose will obligingly take evidence of his "infidelity." This episode shatters what remains of Tony's sense of the proprieties not only because his overprotected sensibility is offended by having to play this charade of intimacy, but also because he is forced to realize that his hired woman has more genuine concern for her child than his wife ever displayed for theirs. Knowing Tony's intentions are directed at the appearance of vice and not the deed, the woman avails herself of this opportunity to bring her daughter to a resort. She does so over the detectives' disapproval that it "sets a nasty, respectable note bringing a kid into it" (p. 185). (Of course, in

Waugh's inverted world, the respectable naturally provokes dismay.) In contrast, before their son's death, Tony's wife had spent a good deal of effort to keep the boy at a distance so that he would pose no unseemly obstacle to her adulterous adventures.

It is during this mockery of vice at the resort that Tony realizes how far he has fallen from his dream of a principled life. Bred to a world in which virtue and propriety were unfailingly honored if not always practiced, he finds himself adrift in a society that no longer subscribes to the categories of traditional morality. Nevertheless, as he prepares to take his guest to dinner, he recalls the duties of a host.

> Tony . . . reminded himself that phantasmagoric, and even gruesome as the situation might seem to him, he was nevertheless a host, so that he knocked at the communicating door and passed with a calm manner into his guest's room; for a month now he had lived in a world suddenly bereft of order; it was as though the whole reasonable and decent constitution of things, the sum of all he had experienced or learned to expect, were an inconspicuous, inconsiderable object mislaid somewhere on the dressing table; no outrageous circumstance in which he found himself, no new mad thing brought to his notice could add a jot to the all-encompassing chaos that shrieked about his ears. (p. 189)

While not explicitly cinematic, this scene turns on an extended simile that has much in common with the strategies of the more obviously filmic passages. Like them, it plays with the distinction between the central and the peripheral. Here Tony's reasonable world, all he has been trained to expect, has become nothing more than an "inconsiderable object," a cuff link perhaps, carelessly mislaid on a littered dressing table. Everything that had been central in his life has been submerged in a chaotic clutter of detail. Having misplaced the organizing power of his central vision, Tony can do no more than passively observe the random details that now haphazardly clamor for his attention. Here again we encounter a disruption of the expected relation between the essential and incidental. It is as though Tony were watching a film that failed to distinguish between foreground and background. With neither spatial nor rational distinctions, every sensation is as important and as unimportant as every other. The resulting experience resembles a nightmare in which Tony becomes a passive center encompassed by shrieking chaos.

In Waugh's fiction the traditional mind shaped by a culture of literacy finds its linear view of the world knocked askew by events that resemble a poorly edited film in which detail, proportion, and sequence defy its rational expectations. Paul Pennyfeather was able to handle the idea of drunkenness but completely unprepared to face the drunkard. Even the far more formidable Gilbert Pinfold cannot manage his experience of the modern world. His relationship with reality is a matter of momentary confrontations. He prefers to view the world *sub specie aeternitatis* from a sequestered distance. It is only the more provocative of personal annoyances that bring him "tumbling from his exalted point of observation" (p. 12) and even then there is every evidence that he is no match for these disturbances of his cultivated poise. After all, he does not stride forth to meet them. Instead, they set him tumbling. He has little chance of winning the battle on their terrain. His mind may be like "a cinema camera truck[ing] furiously forward to confront the offending object close-up with glaring lens," but his eyes are those of "a drill sergeant inspecting an awkward squad, bulging with wrath that was half-facetious, and half-simulated incredulity" (p. 12). This is hardly the portrait of one genuinely in command. With his half-facetious, half-simulated parody of a drill sergeant, Pinfold can hardly expect to quell the subversive details of a disorderly world. Having confronted them, the best he can hope to do is escape them once more by retreating to his "exalted point of observation."

There are other characters who, when faced with the cinematic disorder of contemporary experience, are quite sure they can manage it without fuss. Their confidence, however, almost always proves unfounded. In *Scoop* we find Julia Stitch doing her best but even her masterful hand cannot sustain its grip for long. When she first appears, she is

> still in bed although it was past eleven o'clock. Her normally mobile face was encased in clay, rigid and menacing as an Aztec mask. But she was not resting. Her secretary, Miss Holloway, sat at her side with account books, bills and correspondence. With one hand Mrs. Stitch was signing cheques; with the other she held the telephone to which, at the moment, she was dictating details of the costumes for a charity ballet. An elegant young man at the top of a stepladder was painting ruined castles on the ceiling. Josephine, the eight-year-old Stitch prodigy, sat on the foot of the bed construing her day's passage of Virgil. Mrs. Stitch's maid, Brittling, was reading her the clues of the morning crossword. She has been hard at it since half-past seven. (p. 5)

With its welter of disparate detail and action, few passages better illustrate Kernan's turbulent scene of satire. The reader is kept off balance by its hodgepodge of opposites (rigidity and mobility, art and business, work and play) and its odd juxtapositions of the high and low (translating Virgil and filling in a crossword puzzle) as well as the refined and decayed (the "elegant young man . . . painting ruined castles on the ceiling") Above all, there is the indecorous tendency of these elements to spill over into one another's precinct so that they cease to be clearly distinguishable. When Julia's friend, the novelist John Boot, enters her room a few lines later, she congratulates him on his latest book. But her admiration becomes entangled with her praise for the painter who has just executed, so to speak, a headless abbot on her ceiling.

> "I absolutely loved *Waste of Time.* We read it aloud at Blakewell. The headless abbot is grand."
> "Headless abbot?"
> "Not in Wasters. On Arthur's ceiling. I put it in the Prime Minister's bedroom." (pp. 6–7)

This headless inability to maintain distinctions serves as both the spring for the novel's primary action and a wry comment on the writer as illusionist.

The comic muddle of this scene prefigures the farce to follow. Julia so mismanages events that the reclusive William Boot will be mistaken for the worldly John Boot and get packed off as a correspondent to cover an African civil war, an assignment for which he has absolutely no qualifications and even less inclination. But beyond its foreshadowing function, the confusion in this scene calls attention to the fragile nature of art in an age uncertain of itself.

When John Boot misunderstands Julia, the lapse has more to do with literary than conversational conventions. After all, the speech he cannot follow would be perfectly clear in a real conversation. Just consider Julia's puzzling words once again: "I absolutely loved *Waste of Time.* We read it aloud at Blakewell. The headless abbot is grand." In an actual conversation a listener would have little difficulty distinguishing the references of these three sentences. Routine aural and visual clues—a pause, a change in tone or volume, a glance, a turning head—any one or several would unmistakably separate the last sentence from the first two so that the listener would have no doubt it applied to the painting rather than the book. It is only when the sentences are strung together on the page without aid of graphic or narrative signals that confusion arises. From what we know of Waugh's interests and methods, I think it likely that this is in part a joke at the expense of an art that has become overly self-conscious and scrupulous about its conventions. Especially at question is what the novelist must do to achieve mimesis in a world that no longer seems knowable. What meaning can language achieve when the objects of its reference have become suppositional at best? A reading of the passage that raises these questions accords with Waugh's conviction that modern art had been deprived of its representational credibility because of its pernicious and, to his mind, unwarranted assumption that there is no abiding pattern to be discovered beneath the play of experience. It is on this question that all else stands or falls. Existence either has a purposeful order or not. If not, then no degree of managerial skill, whether in life or art, will ever be sufficient to make sense of things in any essential way.

By dismissing the possibility of a metaphysical order, the artist subverts his own order-making ability. Reasoning analogically, it works something like this: if the external world has been divested of its conventional intelligibility, if its details and events can no longer be read as material and temporal signs of transcendent purpose, then the honest artist also must abandon the conventional signals that had once constituted his interpretive contract with his audience. Julia's words are strung together without benefit of paragraphing or other written devices that would signal a change in reference. The novelist's craft has been divested of the tools with which it might refer intelligibly to the external world. The confusion that follows is the only accurate mimesis of a society that has lost its conviction in the metaphysics that had once been the basis for its conventional belief in its collective destiny. Such mimesis is also Waugh's parody of the state of the arts in the twentieth century.

Julia Stitch is just one in a series of characters who play variations on Waugh's recurring portrayal of the would-be managerial mind defeated by intractable confusion. These are the characters who behave as though they were still able to impose order on the world disintegrating about them. Otto Silenus in *Decline and Fall* begins the series. His fondest wish is to find the still center of modern life's spinning wheel. Residing there would be accomplishment enough for him. But he is perpetually vexed by "the problem of all art." He cannot entirely eliminate the unpredictable "human element from the consideration of form" (p. 159). In *Vile Bodies* it is the ubiquitous, all-knowing Father Rothschild whose "happy knack" it is "to remember everything that could possibly be learned about everyone who could possibly be of any importance." But, for all his knowingness, Rothschild is remarkably ineffectual. Though he urges the soundest of counsel on those in power, they neither understand nor believe him. His Cassandra role is signaled at his first appearance. Looking down from the rail of a channel steamer, he resembles one of "the gargoyles of Notre Dame" while "high above his head swung Mrs. Melrose Ape's travel-worn Packard car, bearing the dust of three continents, against the darkening sky" (p. 2). The juxtaposition of Rothschild's gargoyle resemblance with Mrs. Melrose Ape's Packard visually prefigures the intellect's hopeless struggle with the will. Father Rothschild may be supported by the finely articulated tradition of his Judeo-Christian heritage, but he is no match for Mrs. Ape, the evangelist of enthusiasm and feel-good piety whose own beliefs are ambiguously compromised by her eagerness to turn a dollar. She is a weird mixture of primitive emotionalism and modern technology, singing her

famous hymn, "There ain't no flies on the Lamb of God," as she tours the
world in her Packard. But, weird as it is, this alliance of the primitive and
modern overshadows Rothschild as does the hoisted Packard, harbinger of
a darkening sky that will obscure whatever light of reason he might have to
offer. *A Handful of Dust* also has its still center in the austerely aloof Mrs.
Rattery. But even her superb competence cannot establish an abiding
sense of purpose. Under her card-playing fingers "order [grows] out of
chaos," but only for brief intervals between shufflings. Her game of pa-
tience provides little more than a pale memory of a more substantial order.

All of these figures blandly assume they can direct their circumstances
from their privileged positions at the centers of their respective worlds.
But, in truth, they are all equally subject to the same unruly currents that
overwhelm characters like Paul Pennyfeather and Tony Last.

The Narrator as Director

Whether it is Otto Silenus at the hub of his spinning wheel, Julia Stitch
behind her "rigid and menacing" cosmetic mask, or Gilbert Pinfold girded
with his bright cuirass of pomposity, Waugh typically includes a scene in
which he has placed one character at the center of his narrative turbulence
as a still consciousness trying to impose order on a senseless whirl of detail.
It might be a string of peremptory commands or a darting camera eye, but
each exhibits a self-assured directorial style. The joke is that their style,
however confident, never succeeds in imposing any but the most ephemeral meaning on their unsettling circumstances. Julia sends the wrong man
to Africa and drives her sports car with so little control that she inadvertently runs it into an underground public lavatory. Pinfold tries to maintain
his "exalted point of observation" behind his elaborate character armor,
but guilt-driven hallucinations eventually penetrate his fortifications and
take over his mind. The world is always too much for Waugh's characters.
They can retreat to seemingly safe vantage points, but, until the later novels, they are invariably impotent when confronted by the clamoring din of
daily life.

For all their incompetence, however, these would-be directors serve as
a gloss on Waugh's narrative strategy. Julia Stitch in her bed resembles
Waugh's typically unflustered narrators at the center of hectic and apparently aimless scenes; and, like Pinfold, Waugh's narrators cannot resist the
spectacle of outrage to which they pay the tribute of closeup attention. But
unlike Julia and Pinfold, Waugh's narrators seem content to forgo the discovery of any coherent pattern in the events they report with such sublime
detachment. They know a hopeless case when they see one.

These narrators, at least in the early satires, remain above the uncontrollable fray. They do so by adopting a disinterested directorial stance with regard to the spectacle they report, never leaving the vantage point of their detachment to empathize with their subjects. It is not that they are indifferent. Far from it. They speak enthusiastically, frankly relishing the wanton vulgarity, stupidity, and criminality of their stories. But theirs is a voice that has forsworn sympathy. They typically remain unmoved by their characters' tribulations. Nor do they invite the reader to become involved. Their object is entertainment, and everything is brought off lightly by virtue of a showman's instinct. They know how to pace and stylize even the grisliest episode to bring out its humor, however lunatic.

Waugh had commended Ronald Firbank for emphasizing "the fact which his contemporaries were neglecting that the novel should be directed for entertainment."[5] Waugh's use of the word "directed" in this passage is revealing, especially in light of the praise he subsequently paid Graham Greene for developing a narrative method in which "the writer has become director and producer."[6] The idea of the writer as director calmly orchestrating action at a distance must have had a strong appeal for Waugh. What better model could he have had for the cool, intellectual detachment needed to face an unpleasant reality without being overcome by it? At will a director and his editor can quicken or retard events, cut them into instantaneous fragments, or protract them indefinitely. They can shuffle incidents into any order or apparent disorder they choose and all the while remain disinterested craftsmen intent upon reducing "to order the anarchic raw materials of life."[7] It was an approach that provided for the kind of rational management of events that Waugh desired so much and yet, paradoxically, allowed him to emphasize just how thoroughly the world of experience was beyond the intellect's control and understanding.

Waugh projected himself as director of his fictions in a number of ways. We have already considered his use of close-up and shortly will examine his approximation of cinematic montage. But it was his invention of the directorial narrator that imparted to his satires their most distinctive feature: their sustained distance between tone and incident. This distinction between voice and event parallels his fascination for the contrast between the paintings of Picabia and Ernst which had spoken to him of "the continual conflict of modern society." Waugh created a narrative voice that has all the "delicately poised," "impossibly tidy" virtues he saw in Picabia and then used it to calmly report the "defiant and chaotic" outrage of an Ernst canvas.[8] The result can be illustrated with the following representative passage taken from *Scoop* which deals with the reception accorded Europeans by a small African nation.

Various courageous Europeans, in the seventies of the last century, came to

Ishmaelia, or near it, furnished with suitable equipment of cuckoo clocks, phonographs, opera hats, draft-treaties and flags of the nations which they had been obliged to leave. They came as missionaries, ambassadors, tradesmen, prospectors, natural scientists. None returned. They were eaten, every one of them; some raw, others stewed and seasoned—according to local usage and the calendar (for the better sort of Ishmaelites have been Christian for many centuries and will not publicly eat human flesh, uncooked, in Lent, without special and costly dispensation from their bishop). Punitive expeditions suffered more harm than they inflicted and in the nineties humane counsels prevailed. The European powers independently decided that they did not want that profitless piece of territory; that the one thing less desirable than seeing a neighbor established there, was the trouble of taking it themselves. Accordingly, by general consent, it was ruled off the maps and its immunity guaranteed. (pp. 105–6)

This exquisitely misanthropic excerpt pays homage to Swift's "A Modest Proposal" and proceeds in much the same way. Its satire lurks in the interval between its tone and its subject, between the poised narrator and the hideous events he reports. With unruffled reasonableness, the narrator calmly reviews the finely graded limits within which Christian cannibalism is permissible—the Ishmaelites "will not publicly eat human flesh, uncooked, in Lent, without special and costly dispensation from their bisop." The effect is outlandishly funny just because of the Ishmaelites' attempts to introduce restraints into their cannibalistic practices. And here is the focus of Waugh's satire: the absurd disjunction between man's pretension to order and his actual behavior. Waugh's characters, whether savage or civilized, are always observing polite forms as they indulge in the most atrocious excesses. He manages this type of scene with his seemingly detached narrator, who assembles the props and background as though he were only responsible for moving the show along quickly and efficiently. We are made to feel that any pause to evaluate the behavior being reported would be as pointless as it would be tactless.

"Incident in Azania" uses the same discrepancy between narrative tone and subject matter to mock the British tradition of never letting emotion interfere with good form. Set in an African nation modeled on Abyssinia of the 1930s, its subplot concerns terrorist attacks on European and American settlers. When natives bent on extortion kidnap a missionary and send his "right ear loosely done up in newspaper and string" (CRSD, p. 103) to the consulate, the British colonists display a capacity for restraint no less impressive than does the narrator. After some initial concern, "the life of the town began to resume its normal aspect—administration, athletics, gossip; the American missionary's second ear arrived and attracted little notice, except from Mr. Youkoumian [a local merchant], who produced an ear trumpet which he attempted to sell to the mission headquarters" (p. 106).

Nothing more is heard of the unfortunate missionary until the story's close when we learn in an aside that his "now memberless trunk . . . [had] been found at the gates of the Baptist compound" (p. 115). Faced with this news, the British commanding officer is quick to respond. "It's one of the problems we shall have to tackle; a case for action; I am going to make a report of the entire matter"(p. 115). It would be difficult to imagine a scene in which voice and subject were more wildly at odds with one another.

Using directorial distance, Waugh was able to create narrators who remain untouched by the squalor and turmoil they portray. The narrative voice that speaks to us in a typical Waugh novel is at once ironic and fastidious. It is the voice of one who finds it amusing to watch others flail about in a hopeless muddle but takes care never to get too close lest he risk falling in himself. Empathy is one temptation he can resist. He knows sentiment would compromise his style and he is too much the dandy to allow that. Brian Wicker makes this point very nicely in his *Story Shaped World.*

> Waugh's contribution to the literature of dandyism consists in his development, not of the dandyish character, but of the dandyish narrator. It comes out in the special tone of the early novels, and particularly in the narrator's studied neutrality towards actions and attitudes which by ordinary decent standards, cry out to be judged. This refusal to judge, coming as it does from a recognition that the only standards available from the bourgeois world, by which to make a judgement, are themselves irredeemably corrupt, gives the early novels their scandalous and outrageous, but also their valuably invigorating character.[9]

By looking on his scene with a probing but detached camera eye, this "dandyish narrator" can delight in its outrage and excess and yet keep his distance even as he records it. He may be fascinated, but he is not involved. There is never anything remotely censorious or approving in his voice. His amused disinterestedness suspends all judgment. With his unvarying tone of sophisticated tolerance, he never expresses an emotion stronger than mild wonderment. When Margot Beste-Chetwynde in *Decline and Fall* razes her sixteenth-century home, Waugh's narrator brightly announces the "surprising creation of ferro concrete and aluminum" (p. 159) with which she replaces it. Under his imperturbable gaze, the Bright Young People in *Vile Bodies* become a "litter of pigs . . . popping all together out of someone's electric brougham" and "squealing up the steps" (p. 125). He is pleased to report in *A Handful of Dust* that an African nation's birth control campaign is so misconstrued by its proposed beneficiaries that they are convinced the strange devices supplied them by their forward-looking government will confer an eagerly anticipated increase in their already abundant fertility. In his account of an acquisitive interior decorator prowling for new business, he finds nothing untoward in her complaint that a house fire "never properly reached the bedrooms" (p. 3). This is a narrator whose voice is unfailingly calm and reasonable regardless of its subject. He speaks as one who has passed through despair. Conditions may be quite hopeless, but, looked at from the right angle, nothing is so serious that it cannot be turned to laughter. Clearly, matters have gotten thoroughly out of hand, but there is some consolation to be had in the spectacle of a world slipping so clownishly to its perdition.

Supremely detached, thoroughly shockproof, Waugh's dandyish narrator is perfectly suited to report on people grown so accustomed to the absence of honor that they have quite forgotten it was once thought essential to human life. There is no warning, no chiding in this voice, just frank amusement. What better way to imply that there is nothing unusual about the grotesque buffoonery of those who have sacrificed their souls to modernity? This, apparently, is a fate so common there is no point in ringing any alarms. Consider, for example, Simon Balcairn's suicide in *Vile Bodies.* Lord Balcairn, a young aristocrat of an ancient and richly decorated family, desperately wants to further his career as a gossip columnist on the *Daily Excess*, but when an influential society hostess bars him from her parties in perpetuity, he realizes his quest is doomed. There is nothing left to do but file one last column, an incontestably libelous attack on the smart set that has so callously driven him from its glittering precincts. His effort to sully this group's reputation will prove futile, however. Nothing can do more to diminish their integrity than their own shameless behavior. But this is the only redress the redoubtable Balcairn can think of. As though acknowledging that it will afford meager solace, he does not bother to wait for publication, but proceeds immediately to make an expedient exit by sticking his head in his oven.

> Then he turned on the gas. It came surprisingly with a loud roar; the wind of it stirred his hair and the remaining particles of his beard. At first he held his breath. Then he thought that was silly and gave a sniff. The sniff made him cough, and coughing made him breathe, and breathing made him feel very ill; but soon he fell into a coma and presently died.
> So the last Earl of Balcairn went, as they say, to his fathers (who had fallen in many lands and for many causes, as the eccentricities of British Foreign Policy and their own wandering natures had directed them; at Acre and Agincourt and Killiecrankie, in Egypt and America. One had been picked white by fishes as the tides rolled him among the tree-tops of a submarine forest; some had grown black and unfit for consideration under tropical suns; while many of them lay in marble tombs of extravagant design). (p. 146)

Even by the standards of satire, the distance between the narrator's tone and what happens in this scene is quite remarkable. After unemotionally reviewing Balcairn's respiratory progression from sniffing to coughing to breathing to feeling very ill, the narrator concludes with the purest mockery: "but soon he fell into a coma and died." That "but" condescendingly absolves Balcairn of his unseemly sniffing and coughing as if to say that at least in dying he has displayed a vestigial sign of the good breeding that had led his ancestors to their more glorious if equally futile ends.

Of course, Waugh provided himself the luxury of such cold indifference to individual fate by never letting his readers feel his early novels were about real people in any but the most superficially schematic manner. Dehumanizing detachment from his characters has always been the satirists's privilege. Waugh simply availed himself of the tradition. But few satirists have been so relentlessly committed to populating their works with two-dimensionally abstract figures. Under Pinfold's camera-gaze, the world is indeed "flat as a map."

The use of the directorial narrator imparted to Waugh's fiction an abstract artificiality that appealed to him both esthetically and practically. Esthetically it enabled him to suggest that experience had exceeded the ·bounds of plausible representation and so no longer seemed "real." Practically, it enabled him to take a welter of pointless activity and reduce it to a manageable circus of charlatans, clowns, and fools.

Discontinuity

If Waugh approached his fiction as a director, he did so as one with a strong predilection for radical montage. This is evident throughout his work both structurally and metaphorically. His scenes are commonly spliced together with associational rather that linear logic, and direct references to cinematic editing frequently appear among his favorite tropes of modern life. In both ways, he used film to project his sense of the fragmentary, discontinuous nature of twentieth-century experience.

Black Mischief supplies an obvious example of film editing's possibilities. Early in the narrative we are presented with a foreshortening of the process by which political crises flare into public view for a moment only to be as quickly extinguished by collective indifference. By means of some adroit scene-hopping, Waugh has captured the fabricated frenzy of the daily press and its predictable effect on a busy public. The London newspapers, in their competitive struggle to attract an ever greater number of readers, jump from one alarming event to the next with unrelieved urgency and thereby only succeed in desensitizing their readers to real human suffering. The occasion of their latest exercise in futile hysteria is the plight of Azania, an African nation torn by a civil war promoted by outside interests.

It seems a number of European nations have determined that their economic positions will be improved considerably once Seth, the Oxford-
educated heir to the throne, begins his reign. Accordingly, they have
encouraged this young progressive to follow the way of European enlightenment and hasten the end of his father's tenure.

> Two days later news of the battle of Ukaka was published in Europe. It made
> very little impression on the million or so Londoners who glanced down the
> columns of their papers that evening.
>   "Any news in the paper tonight, dear?"
>   "No, dear, nothing of interest."
>
>   "Azania? That's part of Africa, ain't it?"
>   "Ask Lil, she was at school last."
>   "Lil, where's Azania?"
>   "I don't know, father." . . .
>
>   "Only niggers."
>
>   "It came in a crossword quite lately. *Independent native principality.* You
> would have it it was Turkey."
>   "Azania? It sounds like a Cunarder to me."
>   "But, my dear, surely you remember that *madly* attractive blackamoor at
> Balliol."
>
>   "Run up and see if you can find the atlas, deary . . . Yes where it always is,
> behind the stand in father's study."
>
>   "Things look quieter in East Africa. That Azanian business cleared up at
> last."
>
>   "Care to see the evening paper? There's nothing in it."
>
>   In Fleet Street, in the offices of the daily papers: "Randall, there might be
> a story in the Azanian cable. The new bloke was at Oxford. See what there
> is to it."
>   Mr. Randall typed: *His Majesty B.A. . . . ex-undergrad among the can-
> nibals . . . scholar emperor's desperate bid for throne . . . barbaric splendor
> . . . conquering hordes . . . ivory . . . elephants . . . east meets west . . .*
>
>   "Sanders. Kill that Azanian story in the London edition."
>
>   "Anything in the paper this morning?"
>   "No, dear, nothing of interest." (pp. 86–87)

Not only an example of cinematic editing, this passage also seems to be a
parody of a film convention popular in the thirties that visualized the passage of time or the development of issues as a sequence of newspaper headlines each of which flies into focus on the screen for a moment and then
disappears to make way for the next. Here, however, we do not see the
headlines themselves but rather surmise what they must be as they are re-
fracted in the conversation of a number of anonymous readers and journal-

ists. This, Waugh implies, is the history of human concern in our journalistic age—a heap of undeveloped impressions based on a whirling mill of poorly reported, disconnected news stories.

Beyond its structural implications for modern narrative, film also has served as a potent metaphor of this century's metaphysical disorientation and its anxiety about purposeful continuity. Many writers have used film is this way. In *Justine* one of Lawrence Durrell's characters wonders, "Are people continuously themselves or simply over and over again so fast that they give the illusion of continuous features—the temporal flicker of the old silent film?" Aldous Huxley had already answered this question in *Eyeless in Gaza* by having his protagonist flip through a series of old photographs of himself, his family and friends as though they were so many still frames from a film of his life. Instead of continuity, these pictures comprise a series of moments tenuously held together by the fiction of personal identity.

Waugh also turned to film when he wanted to express his sense of the modern world's discontinuity and unreality. Without conviction in any ultimate purpose to existence, the self and its experience become fragmented, arbitrary. As in Bergson's parody of Becoming, life unreels as a series of discrete sensations placed side by side like individual frames in a film, their continuity cranked up mechanically from the outside. There is little sense of inner growth toward a natural fruition when life becomes a series of random episodes. Under these conditions success goes to those comfortable with living in the moment without regard to the past or future. These are the economically prosperous characters such as Colonel Blount and Lottie Crump in *Vile Bodies*, Lord Copper in *Scoop*, Sir James Macrae in "Excursion in Reality," and Rex Mottram in *Brideshead Revisited*. They all succeed where others fail because they have come to terms with the world as it is. Their secret is that they forget what they are doing from one moment to the next. They prosper because they live within the instantaneous amnesia of the truly functional. They move with the flow of pure Becoming, never looking beyond the climactic now of the present moment. This serves them well, especially in business. After all, to meet the mercantile demands of the moment, one cannot always afford the cost of prior allegiances. This is the lesson Simon Lent, the protagonist of "Excursion in Reality," learns rather painfully.

Simon's celebrity as a fashionable young novelist has brought him the attention of a movie mogul looking for marketable writers. Soon Simon finds himself assigned to work on a screenplay with a continuity editor named Miss Grits. He is surprised but not displeased to discover it is Miss Grits's policy to enter into a sexual liaison with whomever she happens to be working at the moment. So he accepts her offer to become his full-time

production associate and part-time lover. By mixing pleasure with business, Miss Grits meets her human needs without any undue sacrifice of the
time and energy her career demands of her. It is a matter of indifference
who her lovers are. They come and go, as Simon discovers to his dismay.
Only her commitment to her career as a continuity editor endures. The
studio no sooner relieves him of his duties as a screenwriter than Miss Grits
excuses him from his more intimate labors. Obviously, Miss Grits's profession serves as an ironic comment on a personal life that seems cinematically
edited, comprised as it is of discontinuous episodes spliced together to
achieve an illusion of continuity. In fact, the one thing missing from her life
is any sense of a sustained purpose beyond what she contributes to the production of entertainments that are as ephemeral as they are vulgar.

   The Loved One makes a similar point by contrasting two Englishmen who
have gone to Hollywood to make their fortunes. One fails, the other succeeds. Their respective fates derive from their very different personalities,
especially as manifested in their opposed views of past and present. Sir
Francis Hinsley, the failure, is given to reminiscences that "strayed back a
quarter of a century and more to foggy London streets lately set free for all
eternity from fear of the Zeppelin; to Harold Monroe reading aloud at the
Poetry Bookshop; Blunden's latest in the London Mercury; . . . tea with
Gosse in Hanover Terrace" (p. 10). In contrast Sir Ambrose Abercrombie,
an indisputable success among the English colony in Hollywood, "had a
more adventurous past but he lived existentially. He thought of himself as
he was at that moment, brooded fondly on each several excellence and re-
joiced" (p. 10). Sir Ambrose proudly and fatuously announces that

> I've always had two principles throughout all my life in motion-pictures:
> never do before the camera what you would not do at home and never do at
> home what you would not do before the camera. (p. 9)

Ambrose succeeds where Francis fails because he has been able to discard
all sense of individual continuity and historical perspective in order to become a functioning part of the unwinding film of the present moment.

   Perhaps it is the ordeal of Hinsley and his actress protégée in *The Loved
One* that best displays Waugh's satire of what it means to live without an
abiding sense of personal and cultural tradition. It seems no accident that
filmmaking serves as the context in which he chose to make his point. Juanita del Pablo is a Hollywood film actress known for her protean capacity
to be put through one identity change after another in order to adapt her
image to the fluctuations of public taste. Upon first arriving in Hollywood,
she had been turned over to Sir Francis, who equipped her with an appropriate biography.

> *I* named her. *I* made her an anti-Facist refugee. *I* said she hated men because
> of her treatment by Franco's Moors. That was a new angle then. It caught on.
> And she was really quite good in her way, you know—with a truly horrifying
> natural scowl. Her legs were never *photogénique* but we kept her in long
> skirts and used an understudy for the lower half in scenes of violence. I was
> proud of her and she was good for another ten years' work at least. (p. 8)

But now that the studios have decided to make only "healthy films this year
to please the Catholic League of Decency," Juanita's image has become a
liability.

> So poor Juanita has to start at the beginning again as an Irish colleen.
> They've bleached her hair and dyed it vermillion. . . . She's working ten
> hours a day learning the brogue and to make it harder for the poor girl
> they've pulled all her teeth out. She never had to smile before and her own
> set was good enough for a snarl. Now she'll have to laugh roguishly all the
> time. That means dentures. (pp. 8–9)

What identity, what integrity can one have in a land where laughing rogu-
ishly all the time means dentures? This is classic Waugh: the sour juxtaposition of false exuberance with the dreary subterfuge that supports it.

But the dreariness has gotten to Sir Francis Hinsley. Profoundly disenchanted with the Hollywood ethos and what it has done to him, he can no
longer execute his assignments with enthusiasm and dispatch. He procras-
tinates until finally

> Juanita's agent was pressing the metaphysical point; did his client exist?
> Could you legally bind her to annihilate herself? Could you come to any
> agreement with her before she had acquired the ordinary marks of identity?
> (p. 25)

Juanita's case is not unique; the metaphysical point is always pressed in
Waugh. This was his way of satirizing the ready compliance with which
people connive at their own dehumanization. In a society that only values
power and wealth, it is not difficult to rationalize the commodification of
human beings. The combined forces of Juanita's studio, her agent, and her
own ambition have turned her into a product that can be parceled and re-
designed to meet market demands. Her career crisis does indeed raise
philosophical questions. Is it possible to preserve a coherent sense of identity when one's ethical vision extends no further than the material opportunity of the moment? Is personal integrity possible without a general belief
in the unique destiny of one's culture? For Francis Hinsley the answer is
no. Unable to keep pace with the studio's mindless policy of ceaseless
transformation, he finds that he himself has ceased to exist in its corporate

eyes. Returning to work one day he discovers his name and belongings
have been unceremoniously stripped from his office. There has been no
warning, no formal discharge; he is simply treated as a nonperson, which—
pressing the metaphysical point—is what he has become by accommodat-
ing himself, however reluctantly, to an enterprise that is, to use Waugh's
assessment of Hollywood's film industry in the 1940s, "empty-headed and
without any purpose at all."[10] Without commitment beyond the opportunity of the moment there can be no sustenance for the civilized self. And so
Hinsley hangs himself.

Leveling

Waugh associated film with what he considered the leveling or egalitarian tendencies of the twentieth century. This was for two closely allied
reasons, one esthetic, the other economic. The esthetic factor has been discussed already. This is film's natural penchant for sensationalism. By virtue
of its formal characteristics, film is a medium that readily encourages an
unreflective, emotional response to itself. This is its special appeal and one
that perfectly suits the economics of filmmaking. It is precisely the kind of
basic, visceral experience film creates so easily that draws the largest possible audience, and it is this mass audience that typical filmmakers have in
mind when devising their entertainments. After all, with immense production costs to meet, it is hardly likely that they would be unswervingly dedicated to producing works of art for the discriminating few.

Like Virginia Woolf and James Joyce, Waugh was drawn to the esthetic
possibilities of film form. At the same time, he was quite aware that its production expenses would rarely allow film to achieve its full potential. He
shared Woolf's opinion that filmmakers, despite their seemingly limitless
technical resources, had only succeeded in producing crude, primitive entertainments.[11] In a 1947 essay, "Why Hollywood Is a Term of Disparagement," Waugh made this jaundiced observation concerning the economic
obstacles set in the way of film's ever achieving artistic distinction:

> A film costs about $2,000,000. It must please 20,000,000 people. The film
> industry has accepted the great fallacy of the century of the Common Man
> . . . that a thing can have no value for anyone which is not valued by all. The
> economics of this desperate situation illustrate the steps by which the Com-
> mon Man is consolidating his victory.[12]

Waugh's disparagement of the Common Man should be addressed before
saying anything else about this passage. Although perfectly capable of in-
dulging elitist attitudes, Waugh did not intend this pejorative reference to

the century of the Common Man as an occasion to flaunt his snobbery. In another context he had given this term a specific application that had little to do with class distinctions ordinarily understood. The Common Man, he had argued, does not exist. He is an abstraction coined by "economists and politicians and advertisers and other professional bores of our period."[13] Common Man becomes Waugh's rubric for all those forces that militate against the individual and his ability to think for himself. The point is not that Hollywood has subversive intentions with regard to the classical world view of the cultivated gentleman, but rather that, like the rest of the technologically organized world, it is dominated by the economics of large numbers. Commercial filmmakers turn out a dehumanized product because they direct their energy to serve the most inhuman of all abstractions—the statistically average consumer. Waugh's own experiences in Hollywood convinced him that film producers had no purpose other than profit. It followed logically that "anyone interested in ideas is inevitably shocked by Hollywood according to his prejudices."[14]

But Waugh did not have to travel to California to reach this conclusion. He used filmmaking as a metaphor of contemporary society's leveling tendencies seventeen years before his trip to Hollywood. In *Vile Bodies*, Colonel Blount rents his house and estate to The Wonderfilm Company of Great Britain at reduced rates so that he can play a small role in the "all-talkie super-religious film" (p. 202) of John Wesley's life. Putting himself under the authority of the film's director-producer, Colonel Blount manages to reduce himself to playing the part of a yokel on his own ancestral estate. Begging the director for a larger part among the film's rustic characters, he presents a particularly ludicrous spectacle. Here is a man of some distinction who has sacrificed the dignity of his social position in order to become part of the film world he thinks so glamorous. Yet, having done so, he cannot erase his longing for individual recognition. Assigned a role among the faceless crowd, he nevertheless wants special treatment. It's no surprise that he takes to signing his checks "Charlie Chaplin," the screen's epitome of the little man as a star.

Waugh's most sustained treatment of filmmaking as the *locus classicus* of the leveling process of the twentieth century is his 1934 short story, "Excursion in Reality," in which Simon Lent suddenly finds himself hired by phone call to write a film script for Sir James Macrae, the elusive and sleepless producer. Whisked away at any hour of day or night by chauffeur-driven cars to attend production and writing conferences that rarely materialize, Simon belatedly discovers that Macrae has employed him to work on a production of a film version of *Hamlet*. Simon's "name naturally suggested itself," Macrae remarks, because "many of the most high-class critics have commended Mr. Lent's dialogue" (CRSD, p. 153).

When Simon points out that in the case of *Hamlet* "there's quite a lot of dialogue there already," Macrae patiently explains that "it's angle that counts in the film world" and he intends to produce *Hamlet* "from an entirely new angle" (CRSD, p. 152).

> There have been plenty of productions of Shakespeare in modern dress. We are going to produce him in modern speech. How can you expect the public to enjoy Shakespeare when they can't make head or tail of the dialogue. D'you know I began reading a copy the other day and blessed if *I* could understand it. At once I said, "What the public wants is Shakespeare with all his beauty of thought and character translated into the language of everyday life." (CRSD, pp. 152–53)

Macrae is right, of course. Film is the natural medium for such a project. Of all the arts, it makes the fewest demands on its audience. The exaggerated realism of its representation endows it with a visceral immediacy that can easily narrow its focus to the foreshortened perspective of the intensely emotional moment. From a commerical point of view, there is good reason to use common, transparent language. Elevated or poetic language would only call attention to itself and thereby disrupt the audience's unreflective enjoyment of the pleasant oneiric state film can so readily produce. While such disruption might make for a more challenging esthetic experience, it would not be nearly so inviting, nor would the resulting loss of patronage make it nearly so profitable. Economic interest dictates that film's language be that of the Common Man, as simple as possible. Soon Simon takes up the enterprise's egalitarian, collectivizing spirit himself. It will be art for the masses whatever the expense to the individual. When his girl friend complains that he has changed, Simon cheerfully agrees.

> "Yes!" said Simon, with great complacency. "Yes, I think I have. You see, for the first time in my life I have come into contact with Real Life. I'm going to give up writing novels. It was a mug's game anyway. The written word is dead—first the papyrus, then the printed book, now the film. The artist must no longer work alone. He is part of the age in which he lives; he must share—only of course, my dear Sylvia, in very different proportions—the weekly wage of the proletarian. Vital art implies a corresponding set of social relationships. Co-operation . . . co-ordination . . . the hive endeavour of the community directed to a single end . . . "
> Simon continued in this strain at some length, eating meantime a luncheon of Dickensian dimensions. (CRSD, p. 156)

Typically, this scene concludes with yet another example of Waugh's delight in ironic contradictions. Here the Dickensian luncheon mocks Simon's pretense to advanced socioeconomic theory. It is a touch that speaks for itself without need of any critical elucidation other than to point out once again that Waugh works as would a film director, juxtaposing conflicting elements to good effect.

In his haste to become successfully modern, Simon is quite ready to sacrifice individuality. He has no qualms about leveling his artistic expression to a packageable commodity that will sell to the public. He can go along with it all, or so he thinks. But then he discovers that "the hive endeavour of the community" is not without its competitive friction. As he turns in one "treatment" of the play after another, Macrae's board of experts—"production, direction, casting, continuity, cutting and costing managers, bright eyes, eager to attract the great man's attention with some apt intrusion"—insist that the original story elements require additions and substitutions to ensure mass-audience appeal.

> "Well," Sir James would say, "I think we can O.K. that. Any suggestions, gentlemen?"
> There would be a pause, until one by one the experts began to deliver their contributions . . . "I've been thinking, sir, that it won't do to have the scene laid in Denmark. The public won't stand for travel stuff. How about setting it in Scotland—then we could have some kilts and clan gathering scenes?"
> "Yes, that's a very sensible suggestion. Make a note of that, Lent . . . "
> "I was thinking we'd better drop this character of the Queen. She'd much better be dead before the action starts. She hangs up the action. The public won't stand for him abusing his mother."
> "Yes, make a note of that, Lent."
> "How would it be, sir, to make the ghost the Queen instead of the King . . . "
> "Yes, make a note of that, Lent."
> "Don't you think, sir, it would be better if Ophelia were Horatio's sister. More poignant, if you see what I mean."
> "Yes, make a note that . . . "
> "I think we are losing sight of the essence of the story in the last sequence. After all, it is first and foremost a ghost story, isn't it? . . . "
> And so from simple beginnings the story spread majestically. (CRSD, pp. 159–60)

Of course, the play becomes unrecognizable. Pieces from *Macbeth* are worked in, and it is renamed *The White Lady of Dunsinane*, but Macrae's board remains unsatisfied. Finally, Macrae calls a halt to the original project altogether: "No, it won't do. We must scrap the whole thing. We've got much too far from the original story. I can't think why you need introduce Julius Caesar and King Arthur at all" (CRSD, p. 161). Reminded that he had ordered these additions himself, Sir James is undeterred. His feeling now is that "what the public wants is Shakespeare, the whole Shakespeare and nothing but Shakespeare" (CRSD, p. 161). And so he makes plans to

film *Hamlet* in the original. Macrae is another in Waugh's gallery of emi-
nent characters who succeed precisely because they have the happy faculty of forgetting what they have said or done from one moment to the
next. Their instantaneous amnesia meshes perfectly with the fragmentary,
ahistorical reality film represents so well.

The ludicrous mixture of historical periods in Simon's film script suggests the general absence of perspective in the twentieth-century filmlike
world. As the story's title, "Excursion in Reality," suggests, this is contemporary reality: a ceaseless shifting of points of view that results in the
breakdown of all traditional distinctions. There is no authoritative perspective from which to pull the past and present into a continuous pattern.
As Macrae says, it is only "angle that counts in the film world" and one angle is as valid as another, the only question being which will make more
money. As Arnold Hauser and Alan Spiegel point out, film is ideally suited
to a relativistic epistemology. It is capable of suggesting the fluid, shifting
perspectives of a world without any fixed principles beyond profit, the
great leveler of all other value distinctions.[15]

Primitivism

The next chapter treats at length Waugh's fascination with primitivism
and his belief that modern technocracy unwittingly promotes reversion to
a barbarous sensibility that is so caught up with the claims of the here and
now as to be incapable of civilized thought and historical perspective. At
this point, I merely want to indicate that one of the ways Waugh associated
the barbarous with the modern was to link film with primitivism. Whenever the twentieth century's technological art form appears in his novels,
the jungle is likely to be nearby. In "The Balance" Adam Doure's contemplation of suicide is accompanied by a film montage that represents his
state of mind: "fragmentary scenes interspersed among hundreds of feet of
confusion" which include the recurring images of "a native village in Africa
on the edge of the jungle" and a naked man dragging himself into this jungle to die alone.[16] In "Excursion in Reality" Simon Lent is brought by high-
speed car to a film producer's house that is located on an estate as "black
and deep as a jungle in the darkness" (CRSD, pp. 145–46). *The Loved One*
opens with this description:

> All day the heat had been barely supportable but at evening a breeze
> arose in the West, blowing from the heart of the setting sun and from the
> ocean, which lay unseen, unheard behind the scrubby foothills. It shook the
> rusty fringes of palm-leaf and swelled the dry sounds of summer, the frog-

voices, the grating cicadas, and the ever present pulse of music from the neighboring native huts.

In that kindly light the stained and blistered paint of the bungalow and the plot of weeds between the veranda and the dry water-hole lost their extreme shabbiness, and the two Englishmen, each in his rocking-chair, each with his whisky and soda and his outdated magazine, the counterparts of numberless fellowcountrymen exiled in the barbarous regions of the world, shared in the brief illusory rehabilitation. (pp. 3–4)

The neighboring huts in these "barbarous regions" comprise the British colony of actors and screen writers who have settled in Hollywood's aggressively modern ambiance.

Why did Waugh associate film with primitivism? To answer this, we must remember that he began his career at a time when film was still new enough to shock the literate mind's sense of decorum. Waugh was not alone. Virginia Woolf and Wyndham Lewis, among others, made the same association.[17] Many artists and theorists have found film both a fascinating and disturbing medium because of the way its mode of representation subverts the assumptions of the classically formed mind. With its ability to faithfully recreate the visible world even as it suspends the logical coordinates of time and space, it offers a paradoxical esthetic that frustrates civilized expectations. Although intensely realistic, it floats on the shifting currents of dream consciousness. Under its gaze the most ordinary objects and events can loom into enormous significance while the essential elements of life get lost in its vibrant spectacle. It is no surprise that surrealists such as Luis Bunuel and Jean Cocteau experimented with film. This is a medium that lends itself to the surrealist project of bypassing the polite conventions which ordinarily serve as a comforting filter between consciousness and reality, sifting, whenever possible, the disquieting elements from daily experience. Despite the pedestrian uses to which it has been put by commercial producers, film has formal properties that seem almost capable of putting us in touch with experience unmediated by the standard preconceptions that have been instilled in us by our society.

I think it may have been this aspect of film that especially attracted Waugh. It was not that he wanted to join the surrealists in celebrating a victory over acculturation. Far from it. Instead he used what he learned from film to defamiliarize the world and thereby portray what life would be like without the ordering assumptions that give it shape and direction. For Waugh, it was precisely our shared cultural preconceptions that save us from regressing to a state of primitive consciousness, which he conceived as being lost in the moment's sensation without recourse to the detachment and perspective necessary for civilized life.

IX

CHROMIUM PLATING AND NATURAL SHEEPSKIN

THE NEW BARBARIANS

In *A Handful of Dust* it is Mrs. Beaver's devotion to the very latest in home remodeling that introduces what is to be both the novel's theme and its principle of organization. A ruthlessly efficient landlord, she is dedicated to converting traditional homes into warrens of one-room flats-to-let decorated in her chosen style, which favors chromium-plated walls and natural sheepskin rugs. This unsettling juxtaposition of the modern and primitive visually expresses the narrative's major preoccupation: the return of the barbarian in contemporary guise.

Mrs. Beaver is a promoter of the profitably modern for whom a home is a functional convenience no more personally significant than a hotel room. She is convinced that what modern people really want in living quarters is nothing more than a place "to dress and telephone" and describes herself as one who is simply meeting "a long felt need" (pp. 52–53). When Brenda Last brings this apostle of rootless transience to Hetton Abbey, her husband Tony's ancestral estate, she feels no compunction about criticizing her host's residence. Shown the morning room, she declares it "appalling" and sets about planning its renovation in spite of the difficulties posed by its Gothic structure.

> I know exactly what Brenda wants. . . . I don't think it will be impossible. I must think about it. . . . The structure does rather limit one . . . you know I think the only thing to do would be disregard it altogether and find some treatment so definite that it *carried* the room if you see what I mean . . . supposing we covered the walls with white chromium plating and had natural sheepskin carpet . . . I wonder if that would be running you in for more than you meant to spend. (p. 106)

Part of the joke in this passage is Mrs. Beaver's pause to consider how best to resolve the problem of structure. In fact, chromium plating and natural sheepskin comprise her uniform prescription for all interiors regardless of architectural style. And all England seems to be taking her medicine. Everywhere one looks in Waugh's fiction traditional buildings are being razed or renovated to make way for functional flats suited to the "base love," as Tony Last puts it, of a restless generation who have not the least inclination to consider the tradition and historical development architectural style implies. The space of their lives has contracted to whatever can take place in an austerely functional bed-sitting-room. Like the decorative dado and molding of an earlier age, their personal and family loyalties are treated as the remnants of a nostalgic but inconvenient interior design better covered and put out of sight with the impersonal smoothness of a chromium-plated life-style. Marinetti would have approved of this unsentimental, streamlined renovation and its purely functional ethos. Tony Last, however, finds it insupportable. He flees England in hopes of discovering a civilized city as yet untouched by Mrs. Beaver's special brand of technological barbarism. But, as he stumbles through uncharted Brazilian jungles, he comes to realize the futility of his quest in an hallucinatory insight: "I will tell you what I have learned in the forest, where time is different. There is no City. Mrs. Beaver has covered it with chromium plating and converted it into flats" (p. 288). Chromium-plated rooms carpeted with natural sheepskin—this unlikely juxtaposition is central to the vision of *A Handful of Dust* and all of Waugh's fiction. It serves as an emblematic condensation in which his technique and theme are fused.

We have already seen how Waugh linked film with primitivism so that wherever filmmaking enters his narrative we can expect some reference will be made to the jungle. But beyond this simple coupling, he also brought savagery and civilization together with cinematic montage, frequently employing the film editor's rapid crosscutting technique. In one paragraph a character is stranded in a Brazilian jungle, his Indian guides having left him to hunt wild pigs; in the next, an M.P. argues before parliament for a new pork import policy. Waugh used this type of juxtapositional contrast quite flexibly. Here it snaps shut as though insignificant the gap between savagery and civilization. At other times, juxtaposition yields to a counterpointing technique that moves with a slower, subtler rhythm. Two examples will serve to illustrate what I mean, one from *Black Mischief*, the other from *A Handful of Dust.*

In *Black Mischief*, the small, impoverished African nation of Azania must suffer many ignominies, but none are so trying as its new leader's attempts to bring it forcibly into the twentieth century. Dazzled by the enlightenment he received at Oxford, Seth, disputed heir to the throne, returns to his homeland boldly determined to modernize his backward people. His persistent struggle to transform Azania into Europe provides the novel with its running gag. Predictably, his efforts only result in a zanier version of contemporary European lunacies. A born reformer, he wants to make Esperanto compulsory and holds a Soviet-inspired "pageant of contraception" (p. 132) in which his uncomprehending people carry banners "emblazoned in letters of appliquéd silk with the motto: WOMEN OF TOMORROW DEMAND AN EMPTY CRADLE" (p. 189). Fearing his tank-equipped but barefoot soldiers will fail to win respect among the international community, he commands boots be issued and worn under penalty of hanging. Not nearly as worried about world opinion, his undernourished troops gratefully make a supper of them. But it is Waugh's charateristic use of counterpoint that makes his case most forcefully.

The absurdity of Seth's modernizing schemes is nowhere more apparent than in the implied parallel drawn between two households—one Azanian, the other English—with which the novel is framed. In the progress of the story, the narrator pauses briefly to observe an Azanian family living in a broken-down car that has been abandoned in the middle of what is supposed to be one of the country's primary thoroughfares. Evidently knowing an opportunity when they see it, these people have taken over the car and ingeniously "set up house in the back, enclosing the space between the wheels with an intricate structure of rags, tin, mud and grass" (p. 122). The accommodations may be limited, but they are happy to share them with their two goats. These people have nothing to do with the plot action and nothing more is said of them until in the closing pages we learn that for all Seth's efforts to make Azania conform to his vision of the European twentieth century, these resourceful and imperturbable homesteaders continue to block the road with their deteriorating car-house. Unable to budge them, the regime that has taken over since the collapse of Seth's utopian misrule has devised a more realistic solution. It plans to build a new road that will go around them. The situation presents a perfect image of the futility of grafting so-called progressive ideas onto a culture unprepared for such change. But there is more to it than this. True to the pun in their nation's name, the Azanian squatters turn out to be a slightly zanier version of another household in London. Before the novel's agent provacateur, Basil Seal, leaves England for Africa, he visits his friends Sonia and Alastair Trumpington, only to find them crapulous and still in bed at dinner time. Like their Azanian counterparts, they also share their quarters with lower life forms, although they do so with noticeably less equanimity.

> [Basil] drove to Montagu Square and was shown up to their room. They lay in a vast, low bed, with a backgammon board between them. Each had a separate telephone, on the tables at the side, and by the telephone a goblet of "black velvet." A bull terrier and chow flirted on their feet. There were other people in the room: one playing the gramophone, one reading, one

trying Sonia's face things at the dressing-table. Sonia said, "It's such a waste not going out after dark. We have to stay in all day because of duns."

Alastair said, "We can't have dinner with these infernal dogs all over the place."

Sonia: "You're a cheerful chap to be in bed with, aren't you?" and to the dog, "Was oo called infernal woggie by owid man? Oh God, he's made a mess again." (pp. 102–3)

Basil remarks "how dirty the bed is," and Sonia replies, "I know. It's Alastair's dog. Anyway, you're a nice one to talk about dirt" (p. 103). Then, having their dinner delivered, they proceed to dine together on the bed accompanied by the dogs and the mess. Many months later when Basil returns from his African adventures, the Trumpingtons are still lounging about their apartment hung over from yet another night-before. Vaguely aware that there has been a revolution in Azania and an economic crisis in England, they protest they do not want to hear any more about either. "Keep a stopper on the far-flung stuff" (p. 305), Alastair advises. The Trumpingtons and their dogs are as squalidly immovable, as impervious to external influence as the Azanian family in their abandoned car. Living amidst their own filth and litter, both families are happily oblivious to political and economic events around them. They represent the intransigent slovenliness of human physical life stripped of all ideological pretensions. As usual in Waugh the difference between primitive and civilized is made to seem negligible.

There are many instances in which Waugh used juxtaposition and counterpoint to subvert the distinction between savagery and civilization, but the most ingenious is in *A Handful of Dust*. An even more extreme example of attenuated counterpoint, it is prepared for early in the text but does not find its completion until the narrative is nearly over. Soon after the novel begins, we meet Brenda Last, the bored and restless young woman who will leave her husband for her lover just days after her son's death in a riding accident. She appears at her dressing table holding an interview with her son's governess while she makes up her face. At one point the narrator observes that "Brenda spat in the eye black" (p. 24). While the act of spitting in one's mascara may not be unusual in itself, as a narrative detail singled out for close attention in the behavior of a woman of Brenda's type, the act is at least mildly startling, especially so since she does it in the governess's presence. Why does the narrator select this detail rather than, say, Brenda's application of perfume, powder, or rouge? Of course, this is another instance of what Waugh called the "significant detail." Once we have read the novel through, it becomes clear that Brenda's spitting appears where and when it does as one element in a network of signals to the reader. Considered in light of her subsequent behavior, her spitting fits together with her initial appearance in bed, her "quilt . . . littered with envelopes, letters and the daily papers" (p. 16). Despite her refined personal appearance, Brenda is a woman who litters, spits, and seduces shamelessly in plain view of others. There is about her an essential vulgarity that allows her to become a careless, utterly self-centered seductress calmly betraying her husband to take up with a man who possesses no other interest for her than his availability at the moment she desires some excitement outside her marriage.

Having selected this spitting incident for brief but special attention, the narrator moves on with the story. But then, some 150 pages later, the spitting episode finds its primitive parallel and, in so doing, expands to its full meaning. At the end of the novel, Tony Last, driven from England by what he considers the unspeakably barbarous demands of Brenda's divorce suit, searches for an ideal city in Brazil. During his travels he learns about "Cassiri . . . the local drink make of fermented cassava." Tony's guide explains that "it is made in an interesting way. The women chew the root up and spit it into a hollow tree-trunk" (p. 240). This reference to Indian women spitting both echoes and mocks the earlier scene with Brenda. Whereas the civilized woman had used her saliva merely as an aid to her vanity, the Indian women put theirs to practical use. This is one possible reading of the counterpoint. Another might suggest that Brenda's made-up appearance, like the Indian women's cassiri, is an intoxicant vulgarly contrived to befuddle good judgment. Taken either or both ways, these two scenes form one strand in an elaborate network of juxtapositions, correspondences, and parallels with which the novel collapses the distinctions between the civilized and the savage in much the same way Joseph Conrad had done in *Heart of Darkness* by arranging his images of Brussels and the Congo so that they mirrored one another in their common rapacity and corruption. As in Conrad, so in Waugh, such comparisons belie Europe's pretense to civilization.

In Waugh's historical novel, *Helena,* Constantius, father of Constantine the Great, rhapsodizes about the Roman Wall that separates order from anarchy.

> I'm not a sentimental man, but I love the wall. Think of it, mile upon mile, from snow to desert, a single great girdle round the civilized world; inside, peace, decency, the law, the altars of the gods, industry, the arts, order; outside, wild beasts and savages, forest and swamp, bloody mumbo-jumbo, men like wolf-packs; and along the wall the armed might of the Empire, sleepless, holding the line. Doesn't it make you see what The City means?[1]

Taking his cue from this passage, Alvin Kernan has argued that Waugh's fiction portrays a world constantly under siege. The wilderness always threatens to invade the defensive walls of civilization and reassert its priority.[2] One can go a step further and say that Waugh took perverse enjoyment in making this wall his preferred vantage point. As we have seen, it was what he described as the "borderlands of conflicting cultures" that provided him with his keenest satiric inspiration. With its relentless juxtaposition of the modern and primitive, Waugh's fiction constantly calls us back to the fragile partition that separates the savage from the civilized not only in the world at large but also within ourselves. Whether his novels are dealing with the arrogant lunacy of applying European political categories to mercenary squabbles in Africa or the futility of trying to order impulse in a world devoid of moral consensus, they regularly return to this borderland experience. It is here that he can most effectively indict the civilized West for its negligence in allowing the barbarians to overrun the city once more.

Gathering his travel writing for republication in 1946, Waugh quotes Charles Ryder, the protagonist of *Brideshead Revisited*, as his spokesman. Like his creation, Waugh decided as a young man to explore the wilderness, leaving the sedate territories of Western Europe for a later day.

> "Europe could wait. There would be time for Europe," I thought; "all too soon the days would come when I needed a man at my side to put up my easel and carry my paints; when I could not venture more than an hour's journey from a good hotel; when I needed soft breezes and mellow sunshine all day long; then I would take my old eyes to Germany and Italy. Now, while I had the strength, I would go to the wild lands where man had deserted his post and the jungle was creeping back to its old strongholds." Thus "Charles Ryder"; thus myself. These were the years when Mr. Peter Fleming went to the Gobi Desert; Mr. Graham Greene to the Liberian hinterland; Robert Byron—vital today, as of old, in our memories; all his exuberant zest in the opportunities of our time now, alas! tragically and untimely quenched—to the ruins of Persia. We turned our backs on civilization. Had we known, we might have lingered with "Palinurus" [Cyril Connolly's pseudonym]; had we known that all that seeming-solid, patiently built, gorgeously ornamented structure of Western life was to melt overnight like an ice-castle, leaving only a puddle of mud; had we known man was even then leaving his post. Instead, we set off on our various stern roads; I to the Tropics and the Arctic, with the belief that barbarism was a dodo to be stalked with a pinch of salt.[3]

This jaundiced and, perhaps, half-facetious vision of civilization's collapse finds increasingly bitter expression in Waugh's diaries where he writes in 1962:

> *Abjuring the Realm*. To make an interior act of renunciation and to become

a stranger in the world; to watch one's fellow countrymen, as one used to watch foreigners, curious of their habits, patient of their absurdities, indifferent to their animosities—that is the secret of happiness in this century of the common man.[4]

The way to deal with the contemporary decline into barbarism is to remain imperturbably aloof, amused but detached like the unflappable narrative director of the early novels, who creatively reassembles the materials of the primitive and modern in subversively entertaining montages. But in 1963 he is less sanguine.

It was fun thirty-five years ago to travel far and in great discomfort to meet people whose entire conception of life and manner of expression were alien. Now one has only to leave one's gates.[5]

While there may be some irony in the first of these three passages, there is little evidence of it in two diary entries. In any event, taken together they seem to express his embitterment with a world that had divested itself of the marks of civilization. Yet this is odd. Despite the cheerless poignancy of these late entries, the evidence of his early fiction, much of it quite cheerful indeed, suggests Waugh was as convinced at twenty-five as he was at sixty that his society had forfeited its claims to civility. A crude, alien sensibility had elbowed its way onto the scene. What else do Captain Grimes, the Speed Kings, Lord Copper, Mrs. Rattery, and Rex Mottram, to name just a few, represent if not various hues in the spectrum of barbarity coloring the age? The only thing new about his later remarks is that Waugh had lost his youthful resilience. His subject had not changed, but in his sixties he was no longer as ready to be amused by its outrageous spectacle.

He always dwelled upon the juncture at which civilizing reason confronts barbarous impulse, a conflict as much internal as external. As Jeffrey Heath puts it, Waugh "never ceased to regard himself as a battleground between savagery and civilization."[6] If in his last years he sometimes thought the struggle unavailing, this did not detract from the point of his works, which was that men were to find their purpose in the dialectic of will and reason. His fear was that, between his age's complacency and its self-doubt, reason would surrender the field to the vagaries of the will. Paul Johnson has written of the conservative mind's apprehension when it confronts the intellectual history of the century, which often reads as though it were a chronicle of reason's retreat into self-absorbed systems of thought unconnected in any way with real events. He cites as his evidence modern philosophy's preoccupation with the technical problems of linguistics and semiotics to exclusion of anything remotely like metaphysical speculation.[7] As we have seen, Waugh detected similar danger signals. There are many is his writing: Paul Pennyfeather savoring the chastisement meted out to the heretics of the early church while just outside his window contemporary heretics work their destruction unchecked; the abstract artist's refusal to engage the world, preferring instead the "impossibly tidy" constructs of his own self-enclosed intellectual systems; extremely detached spectators such as Mr. Samgrass in *Brideshead Revisited*, who looks upon the world with the eye of an irresponsible solipsist seeing nothing but an "insubstantial pageant" arranged for his private amusement.

One way or another, the civilized mind in Waugh is always being seduced from its proper task, which is to grapple with the "savage at home." The temptation is to retreat from a bad world as, indeed, Waugh often did, isolating himself at his reclusive country home near Taunton. But, as he demonstrated in the autobiographical *Ordeal of Gilbert Pinfold*, as a strategy this was finally unavailing. The world is always with us; ignore it and, like Pinfold's demon-haunted hallucinations, it comes back at you all the more grotesquely.

When Waugh refers to the "savage at home," he does not have in mind an Anthony Burgess nightmare of hooligan hordes rampaging through London streets. His new barbarians are far more dangerous. Some have frankly dedicated themselves to razing the structures of Western tradition wherever they still stand. But almost worse are those who sentimentalize this tradition, whether motivated by uninformed nostalgia or simple greed. The architectural frauds that populate the novels serve as monuments to this decadent sentimentality. Tony Last's Hetton Abbey, for example, turns out to be a nineteenth-century counterfeit of the Gothic style and, as such, marks him as culturally shallow, however personally decent. It is ironically fitting that his estate should be turned into a commercial operation when his cousins take it over upon his presumed demise. Their decision to breed and sell silver foxes for hunting mocks the tradition Tony had blindly revered. Both Tony and his cousins exploit nostalgic images of the past. Tony's use of these memories is no less a travesty for being sentimental rather than mercenary. It is Dr. Kenworthy, the enterprising mortician in *The Loved One*, who takes this trend to its logical and grotesque extreme.

Waugh's fascination for the borderlands of savagery and civilization found its peculiarly appropriate climax in *The Loved One*. Opening with the conceit that California in the 1940s is one of "the barbarous regions of the world" (p. 4), the narrative quickly proceeds to demonstrate the justice of this claim. Like an inexperienced pioneer, the protagonist, Dennis Barlow, is both alarmed and curious when he encounters the outrageous banality of Whispering Glades. This is Waugh's version of Hollywood's prestigious burial grounds, Forest Lawn, where the dead go not to their rest but, according to the institution's prescribed euphemism, their slumber. Dennis finds the place exerts a strange influence that arrests his imagination.

> Whispering Glades held him in thrall. In a zone of insecurity in the mind where none but the artist dare trespass, the tribes were mustering. Dennis, the frontier-man, could read the signs. . . . The graves were barely visible, marked only by little bronze plaques, many of them as green as the surrounding turf. Water played everywhere from a buried network of pipes, making a glittering rain-belt waist-high, out of which rose a host of bronze and Carrara statuary, allegorical, infantile or erotic. Here a bearded magician sought the future in the obscure depths of what seemed to be a plaster football. There a toddler clutched to its stony bosom a marble Mickey Mouse. A turn in the path disclosed Andromeda, naked and fettered in ribbons, gazing down her polished arm at a marble butterfly which had settled there. And all the while his literary sense was alert, like a hunting hound. There was something in Whispering Glades that was necessary to him, that only he could find. (pp. 79–81)

This necessary something has to do with Whispering Glades being the ultimate meeting place of the barbarous and the modern. Here American enterprise and technology have managed to trash all of Western culture by trivializing it. Here people who obviously know little if anything about Shakespeare quote *Hamlet* as though its hero had written a play on the wisdom of calmly resigning oneself to death's inevitability. The Lake Isle of Innisfree is reproduced as an exotic improvement on lover's lane. "It's named after a very fancy poem" (p. 82), Dennis is informed by one of the many helpful attendants. It even includes the sound of humming bees thoughtfully provided by recording. No one need fear being stung at Whispering Glades. The groundskeepers have scientifically eliminated all insect life. To complete the improved, sanitized pastoral setting there is a family burial plot with a plaque designed to immortalize an enterpreneurial fruiterer famous for having bred the stoneless peach. Nothing disturbs this idyllic scene. There are none of the grim reminders of human travail so prominent in other less enlightened cemeteries. With his superbly developed marketing instincts, Dr. Kenworthy could do no less than take the wise precaution of banning all crosses and wreaths from his premises. In this wonderland of the stingless bee, stoneless peach, and crossless grave, the troubling contradictions of life have been replaced by uniformly pleasant sensations. The difficulties inherent in sustaining civilization, the tragic limitations of human life, the appalling mystery of death, all of this and more has been ignored, simply wished away in the guided-tour rhetoric of the cemetery that refers to death as a passage into "the greatest success story of all time" (p. 78). Not without reason is Dr. Kenworthy known as the Dreamer.

Dennis, the "frontier-man," can read the signs: the barbarians are already within the walls toying with the artifacts of a tradition alien to their sensibility and impenetrable to their untutored understanding. In their hands, the art and thought of the West have been reduced to decorative culture, adornments for a moment's pleasurable distraction from the real business of life. Whispering Glades is the culmination of this tendency. It offers the image of total deracination. Far worse than ignoring the cultural past, the technological barbarians have converted it into a Disneyland theme park.

Dr. Kenworthy is intent upon reproducing the art and architecture of high culture with none of its inconveniences. He scours Europe, "that treasure house of Art," for items "worthy of Whispering Glades" (p. 78). When he comes to the Church of St. Peter-without-the-walls, he is taken with its venerable Norman style but finds it "dark" and "full of conventional and depressing memorials" (pp. 78–79). Seizing the opportunity suggested by an apt misunderstanding of its name, he builds a replica literally without walls, putting glass in their stead. It is "a building-again of what those old craftsmen sought to do with their rude implements of by-gone ages. Time has worked its mischief on the beautiful original" (p. 78). But in Whispering Glades the replica is to be seen "as the first builders dreamed of it long ago . . . full of God's sunshine and fresh air, birdsong and flowers" (pp. 78–79). Dr. Kenworthy's enterprise is barbarously innocent of any sense of history or culture. Art is art as far as he is concerned. He assembles his replicas purely for decorative effect without regard to period, purpose, or influence. Art is simply what one produces to add that patina of dignity and solemnity so necessary to convince potential customers of one's earnest reliability. His vision subverts the linear sense of progressive time characteristic of the West. History does not matter. Even the past can be collapsed into the eternal now of immediate experience. Wandering among his updated and improved monuments of previous ages, twentieth-century man becomes something like an alien set down on a planet he finds interesting but quite unintelligible. His imagination lacks the necessary referential coordinates necessary to put his experience into a coherent perspective.

Because he is an artist, Dennis Barlow recognizes in a "moment of vision for which a lifetime is often too short" (p. 164) the basic alignment of the modern and primitive in this century. It is this recognition that he carries with him when he leaves Los Angeles. It is "a great, shapeless chunk of experience, the artist's load" that he bears "home to his ancient and comfortless shore, to work on it hard and long, for God knew how long" (pp.

163–64). The importance of this vision for Waugh cannot be overesti-
mated. It is a variant of his central thesis. The emergence of the primitive
sensibility in a supposedly civilized context is another version of the will
escaping the bounds of reason.

Waugh wrote a good deal about what he took to be the primitive sensibility. He was obviously intrigued by the topic and frequently drew upon
his travel experiences to assist him in portraying the uncivilized point of
view. But it must be said that he made no pretense to being an anthropolo-
gist. His depiction of the primitive mind has much more to do with his own
preoccupations than it does with his highly unsystematic observations of
Africans and South Americans. That is to say, he constructed a primitive
mind according to what he imagined it would be like to live with neither a
meaningful tradition nor the Western conception of time. That other cultures might have their own traditions and temporal schemes was not relevant to him. Waugh was entirely unembarrassed by what the sociologists
might call his ethnocentricity.[8] Western life was not one culture among
many. It was the "seeming-solid, patiently built, gorgeously ornamented
structure" of the only civilization worth talking about. It follows then that
his portraits of other cultures only have meaning with reference to his own.
He was not trying to capture the savage mind but rather to dramatize what
it would be like to live beyond the walls of Western culture. This said, I
want to consider Waugh's concept of the primitive sensibility which he
thought was overtaking the West in our century.

In *Work Suspended* Waugh's autobiographical character, John Plant, distinguishes between the savage and the civilized mind and the respective
worlds they create for themselves as he reflects on their very different experiences of mourning.

> For the civilized man there are none of those swift transitions of joy and pain
> which possess the savage; words form slowly like pus about his hurts; there
> are no clean wounds for him; first a numbness, then a long festering, then a
> scar ever ready to re-open. Not until they have assumed the livery of the de-
> fence can his emotions pass through the lines; sometimes they come massed
> in a wooden horse, sometimes as single spies, but there is always a Fifth Col-
> umn among the garrison to receive them. Sabotage behind the lines, a blind
> raised and lowered at a lighted window, a wire cut, a bolt loosened, a file
> disordered—that is how the civilized man is undone.[9]

This passage turns on an axis comprised of spontaneous emotion in one
direction and thoughtful deliberation in the other. Waugh's point is not
that one is inherently superior to the other but rather that a person is more
or less civilized according to how closely he or she manages to reside at
their juncture. He conceives of the savage mind as one that lives possessed

by the moment, thoughtlessly carried away with every passion. The civilized, in contrast, fortifies itself against emotional excess by deliberately filtering its feelings through a repertoire of linguistic and symbolic conventions. It is not that emotions should be inadmissible, but rather, in accord with British good breeding, that they should not be allowed unmonitored admittance. In Waugh's military metaphor, they must take on the appearance of rational discourse before being able to penetrate the defensive lines of the self. They must be given a recognizable and communicable form before they have a chance to overpower reason as, no doubt, they should when their provocation is sufficiently extreme. The savage's feelings may be intense, but they are also fleeting because they lack the formal articulation, "the livery of defense," which would allow a certain interval of detachment necessary for intellectual appreciation. Without an intellectual component, feelings cannot be connected meaningfully with the past and future. The savage may suffer no scars, but neither does he endure with a sense of history. Thus Waugh conceived of the primitive mind, which from all indications he thought of as living in an external now of Bergsonian Becoming. Possessed by the moment and self-absorbed, the primitive in Waugh's view is totally involved in his immediate sensations to the exclusion of any larger perspective that might give direction to his life. In *A Handful of Dust* Tony asks his Indian guides when they will finish the boats they are building. The answer is always "just now" regardless of how many more days the work requires. They live, Waugh implies, as they speak, in the present tense.

If this were anthropology, it would be at the very least seriously flawed. But Waugh's primitivism is purely mythical. It is meant to be used as a gauge of European behavior. As we have seen already, many of Waugh's supposedly civilized characters are just as limited. Several examples come to mind: Captain Grimes, whose only principle is to live in the moment unchecked by social conventions; Colonel Blount, whose life comes to resemble a series of film frames each entirely self-contained as he drifts forgetfully from one moment to the next; the corporate excutives like Sir James Macrae and Lord Copper, whose success depends upon their easy ability to forget today what they had decided yesterday; Mrs. Rattery, whose vagueness about her past and the location of her sons seems more a matter of pathological negligence than cool sophistication; and, more explicitly, Ambrose Abercrombie, who "live[s] existentially" never thinking of himself as anything but what "he was at that moment" (LO, p. 10).

As reflected in Waugh's writing, primitivism is not a matter of a particular time or place. It exists wherever and whenever mind allows itself to acquiesce in the "confused roaring" of immediate sensation and surrenders the resources of literacy and reason that enable it to transcend the sensate moment. He was not anthropologically concerned with the primitive in Africa or Brazil; he was, however, philosophically preoccupied with what he took to be the growth of primitivism at home. Primitivism meant abandoning the classical perspective based on a metaphysic of fixed essences in favor of engaging the fluid experience of Becoming. Waugh thought this alternative epistemology dangerously decadent.

This response seems to have been something more than the reactionary paranoia of an anxious conservative. The first decades of the twentieth century did in fact hear some sophisticated arguments favoring what Waugh considered a program for cultural regression. The metaphysical speculations of Bergson and other vitalist philosophers appealed to those looking for an animistic relation to the world to satisfy their longing for a sense of the mystical wholeness that had gone out of their lives along with their traditional faith. Others, more cold-blooded, searched for some purely secular substitute for theological certitude. John Maynard Keynes offers a revealing glimpse of what was nothing short of a search for a new ethic that would provide all the comforting security of the old orthodoxy with none of its inconvenient strictures. Writing in 1938, Keynes recalled how he and his friends among the Bloomsbury set came under the influence of G.E. Moore's *Principia Ethica,* which, as they understood it, taught that

> nothing mattered except states of mind, our own and other people's of course, but chiefly our own. These states of mind were not associated with action or achievement or with consequences. They consisted in timeless, passionate states of contemplation and communion, largely unattached to "before" and "after." Their value depended, in accordance with the principle of organic unity, on the state of affairs as a whole which could not be usefully analysed into parts. For example, the value of the state of mind of being in love did not depend merely on the nature of one's own emotions; but also on the worth of their object and on the reciprocity and nature of the object's emotions; but it did not depend, if I remember rightly, or did not depend much, on what happened, or how one felt about it, a year later. . . . How did we know what states of mind were good? This was a matter of direct inspection, of direct unanalysable intuition about which it was useless and impossible to argue.

With ironic humor Keynes goes on to say that he and the others conveniently disregarded the chapters of Moore's work that discussed practical morality. Although these Bloomsburians were surely unlike Waugh's rascal, Captain Grimes, in every other respect, they shared with him the desire to go their own way "careless of consequence."

> We were living in the specious present, nor had begun to play the game of

consequences. . . . We entirely repudiated a personal liability on us to obey general rules. We claimed the right to judge every individual case on its merits, and the wisdom, experience and self-control to do so successfully. This was a very important part of our faith, violently and aggressively held, and for the outer world it was our most obvious and dangerous characteristic. We repudiated entirely customary morals, conventions and traditional wisdom. We were, that is to say, in the strict sense of the term, immoralists. . . . In short, we repudiated all versions of the doctrine of original sin, of there being insane and irrational springs of wickedness in most men. We were not aware that civilization was a thin and precarious crust erected by the personality and the will of a very few, and only maintained by rules and conventions skillfully put across and guilefully preserved. We had no respect for traditional wisdom or the restraints of custom. We lacked reverence, as [D.H.] Lawrence observed—and as Ludwig [Wittgenstein] also used to say—for everything and everyone. It did not occur to us to respect the extraordinary accomplishment of our predecessors in the ordering of life (as it now seems to me to have been) or the elaborate framework which they had devised to protect this order.[10]

In contrast to Keynes and his friends, Waugh seems always to have been keenly aware of civilization's precarious state. One suspects this alertness had quite a lot to do with his own reckless enjoyment of the passionate moment to which the Bloomsburians theoretically aspired. Certainly Waugh was no stranger to impulsive behavior, as anyone who has read his biography and diaries knows. Whether it was carousing with friends or insulting celebrated acquaintances, Waugh was not one to exercise undue self-restraint. While an Oxford undergraduate, he sought to squelch charges of homosexuality leveled against his club by assuring those appointed to investigate it that on sight of an attractive woman in the street his colleagues unfailingly had a "complete orgasm."[11] Presumably exaggerated, this claim nevertheless testifies to Waugh's readiness to celebrate the passion of the moment, especially when such behavior served to put puritans to rout. On assignment in Yugoslavia during the Second World War, a man in his forties with a wife and children at home, he nevertheless, to Randolph Churchill's angry dismay, defiantly disdained shelter and walked about in the open while bombing raids were in progress.[12] There is no question that Waugh had a lively taste for living in the moment. If we did not have these anecdotes as evidence, there would be his unaffected fondness for those of his characters who regularly abandon themselves to impulse. Whatever his neurotic problems, Waugh was wise enough to understand *la nostalgie pour la boue*, the periodic need to throw off the trammels of civilized decorum. What he objected to was the modern disposition to justify impulsive behavior on grounds of principle.

There is, after all, little to choose between devotion to "states of mind" in "the specious present" and Captain Grimes going his way "careless of consequence." Delightful as such spontaneity may be when embraced as a fundamental principle of conduct, it can be expected to further the work of civilization just about as far as Grimes does, which is to say not at all. Exclusive preoccupation with private satisfaction leaves little room to develop a sense of responsibility to others; nor does it encourage a serious regard for historical continuity.

Waugh addressed this defection from civilized responsibility when he read *The Unquiet Grave*, a collection of *pensées* and aphorisms much in the Bloomsbury mode by his friend Cyril Connolly writing pseudonymously as Palinurus. Waugh registered his disapproval in the margins of his personal copy. At one point Connolly pays tribute to the intense moment as the means by which we can experience the nonrational oneness beyond intellectual distinctions: "Underneath the rational and voluntary world is the involuntary, impulsive, integrated world, the world of relation in which everything is one; where sympathy and antipathy are engrossed in their selective tug-of-war." Next to this passage, Waugh has inscribed in his firm, precise hand, "Not understood by Waugh or Palinurus." Elsewhere Connolly's mystical meliorism prompts Waugh to echo Keynes's judgment concerning those who are willfully optimistic about human self-improvement. "Ignorance of the doctrine of the Fall of Man" is Waugh's diagnosis and then, not at all like Keynes, he prescribes a dose of orthodoxy: "Almost all Cyril's problems are fully and simply explained in the catechism."[13] For Waugh neither "passionate states of contemplation" nor "the world of relation in which everything is one" offered any permanent solution to man's state. To be human was to be fallen, that is, self-conscious, self-absorbed, and irremediably alienated from the natural world. Despite the modern religion of self-fulfillment, there was for him no remedy, no return to prelapsarian wholeness.

Brenda Last in *A Handful of Dust* is one of Waugh's clearest examples of the consequences of trying to live in what Keynes called "the specious present" as if one could return to a state of innocence in which one's behavior had no untoward consequences. While hardly a Bloomsbury intellectual, she is portrayed as one who has inherited the self-absorbed attitude described by Keynes, and we are made to feel that she is savagely determined to let nothing get in the way of her desire for intense experience, not even the death of her son. Like the primitive in John Plant's description, she allows herself to be possessed by the whim of the moment.

A bit bored with her marriage, she acquires a lover in much the same way she might choose a new dress, not for its distinctive design but its ready serviceableness. Having done so, she then cajoles her culpably innocent husband into letting her rent one of Mrs. Beaver's chromium-plated bed-sitting rooms in the city on the pretext of needing a place to stay while taking a course in economics. The flat enables her to conduct her liaison with relative ease and it soon becomes the center of her life. During one of her extended visits to London, her son, John Andrew, suffers his fatal riding accident. Brenda takes this occasion to break with Tony. She correctly anticipates that without offspring their marriage is pointless and it is this pointlessness that Brenda chooses eagerly, decisively. Pointlessness suits Brenda; it justifies her behavior. In a world without purpose, pursuit of the intense moment, the vivid "state of mind," is not merely permissible, it is almost a moral obligation owed to the only authority that can possibly count: the self and its immediate desires.

When Brenda first makes veiled reference to her intended departure, Tony tries to replenish her hope in the future by naively suggesting that though their loss is tragic they can look forward to children yet to come: "We're both young. Of course we can never forget John. He'll always be our eldest son but . . . " (p. 169). Brenda, however, will not hear of a future of any kind especially one with more children: "Don't go on, Tony, please don't go on" (p. 170). She will have nothing to do with going on. To go on means to live responsibly, sustaining the continuity of past, present, and future. But Brenda has elected to live in the shameless now of her immediate feelings unburdened by the dreary weight of befores and afters. It is her emotions that count, nothing else. With its anonymous, cool efficiency, her one-room flat houses the careless transience of the life to which she aspires. She is so obsessed with "the specious present" of her emotional life that she cannot even respond to her son's death. When Tony's friend, Jock, first tells her of John Andrew's accident, she confuses her son's given name with her lover's, John Beaver. After Jock explains further, she realizes her mistake.

> She frowned, not at once taking in what he was saying. "John . . . John Andrew . . . I . . . Oh thank God . . . " Then she burst into tears.
>   She wept helplessly, turning round in the chair and pressing her forehead against its gilt back. (p. 162)

Typical of Waugh, he closes this scene with a visual detail that carries its weight on two counts. First, the gilded chair-back echoes Brenda's feeble attempt to cover up the enormity of her unspeakable gratitude, founded, as it is, upon the emotional betrayal of her son. Second, it indicates the superficial nature of the life she has chosen to lead in which personal loyalties need be no deeper than convenience dictates. She need not mourn John Andrew unduly. He belonged to Tony's world; he was the offspring who was to carry the family tradition from the past into the future. Wanting none of this, Brenda leaves Tony the evening following their son's funeral to attend a party with her lover. She cannot wait to declare her newly intensified feeling for him although to do so means she must figuratively step on her son's grave. "Until Wednesday, when I thought something had happened to you, I had no idea that I loved you" (p. 171). Wednesday was the day Brenda was told of her son's death. Pursuing the illusory satisfactions of a cheap story-book romance, she casually discards both her past and her future and expects Tony to do likewise. In their divorce negotiations, she does not think it untoward to demand that Tony sell his ancestral estate so that he can support her new life with Beaver. The shabbiness of her dereliction is captured in the exchange that follows her perfervid declaration of love to Beaver. By way of reply, he can think of nothing better than, "Well, you've said it often enough" (p. 171). But this does not deter Brenda. " 'I'm going to make you understand,' said Brenda. 'You clod' " (p. 171). They are both little better than clods; they have slipped into the amorphous mud of their emotional whims where they are content to abandon the moral burdens of a civilized consciousness and drift aimlessly in the immediacy of the passing moment.

Worst of all, they haven't even the excuse of a grand passion, theirs being the most remarkably tepid of affairs. If neither infatuation nor lust motivates them, what does? Beaver's interest is at least comprehensible, if more than a little tawdry. He wants Brenda's money. What Brenda wants we are left to guess. She easily admits Beaver has little to offer. He is neither attractive nor charming and is decidedly without either financial or social assets. Her only motivation seems to be a need to keep up with her enlightened friends, all of whom are determined to be as modern as possible, which means, among so much else, an open flouting of sexual conventions. Beaver has nothing to recommend him but his availability. Because no one else wants him, he is there when she needs someone with whom to prove herself liberated from traditional restraints. The irony, of course, is that in seeking to escape one orthodoxy, she has only succeeded in succumbing to another. She has bought the modern prescription of self-indulgence, which in Waugh's view is in its way no less compulsory than Tony's Victorian code of manners.

In its closing, A Handful of Dust uses a more explicit juxtaposition of the savage and civilized to portray the twentieth century's abdication of historical responsibility. This abdication results in the expulsion of the novel's characters from what Keynes referred to as "the game of consequences" into a form of primitive timelessness in which the mind surrenders itself to the oblivion of the present moment. Lost and delirious, Tony wanders through the Brazilian jungle tormented by hallucinatory visions in which England and the wilderness fuse indistinguishably. A vision of Brenda appears wearing a soiled cotton gown, the typical dress of the local Indian women, and reminds him that he must attend the regular Wednesday County Council meeting at Hetton. When Tony objects that it is not Wednesday, Brenda assures him repeatedly that "time is different in Brazil" (p. 279). It is revealing that Tony's objection has to do with time. England and the jungle have become so identified in his mind that he does not even consider the obstacle of distance. Further, he has not yet grasped that the re-emergence of a primitive sensibility has undermined the conventional Western sense of ordered time and replaced it with an all-consuming now that makes schedules irrelevant. Mr. Todd will help him understand.

Tony's fate is to be evicted from time. When we last see him, he has just awakened from two days of drugged sleep to discover his watch has been stolen and he has missed a party of Englishmen who have been beating the Amazon jungles to locate him. It seems his host and captor, a backwater village tyrant named Mr. Todd, knowing in advance of the search party's approach, has prevented his rescue by giving him a powerful sleeping potion under the guise of a ceremonial Indian drink. He has taken his prisoner's watch and handed it over to the searchers as proof that Tony had come to his village and subsequently died. There is even the burial site of a previous captive to add color to his story. So the search party returns to England with the watch and the false report, and Mr. Todd keeps his Englishman whom he has appointed to read and re-read to him the complete works of Dickens. With his official death accomplished, Tony wakes to the realization that he is trapped in one of the barbarous borderlands of the twentieth century where the past and present, primitive and modern confront one another in a timeless stalemate. On one side there is the murderous illiterate who indulges a sentimental attachment to Dickens ("There are passages . . . I can never hear without the temptation to weep" [p. 302], Mr. Todd informs Tony); on the other, a young woman who insulates herself from her maternal feelings and responsibilities with the impenetrable armor of a chromium-plated life-style.

With Tony's fate established, the scene shifts abruptly to Hetton Abbey in England where we learn

> everything was early that year for it had been a mild winter. High overhead among its gargoyles and crockets the clock chimed for the hour and solemnly struck fourteen. It was half past eight. The clock had been irregular lately. (p. 303)

The irregular clock at Hetton is of a piece with Tony's missing watch and the hallucinatory refrain that had assaulted him in the wilderness, "time is different in Brazil." Time is different everywhere. Tony and what he represents have been expelled from historical time just as decisively as the would-be modern characters who have deliberately chosen to turn their

backs on history. He and Hetton Abbey exist only as badly weathered artifacts of an earlier age that had believed in its mission, its consequence, and
its destiny. As noted earlier, Tony's brother-in-law, an amateur archaeologist, had settled the matter when he remarked that he once "couldn't be interested in anything later than the Sumerian age" but now finds "even the
Christian era full of significance" (p. 203). From the modernist point of
view, which Waugh implicitly satirizes, Western Europe is just one more
culture; its fate is no more important than that of any other. It does not
have a unique destiny but rather moves through the expected cyclical pattern of rise and fall. Like any other culture that has completed its cycle,
Western civilization offers the archaeologist an interesting dig but tells
him little more about man than that his aspirations are finally futile.

And so Tony is deprived of his illusion that he has ever exerted temporal
consequence. He discovers he had been living in a dream of historical destiny. There is no history for him any longer. His life will not form a link in
the continuous development of a purposeful future; he will have neither
heirs nor an estate to bequeath to the future. Doomed to the Sisyphean
task of reading the entire works of Dickens over and over again to his Brazilian captor, Tony exemplifies all those decent, well-meaning people who
avoid taking a real stand vis-à-vis the modern world. Tony had affected the
forms of the Victorian gentleman without troubling himself to examine the
assumptions upon which these forms were based. When Mr. Todd asks him
if he believes in God, Tony replies, "I suppose so. I've never really thought
about it much" (p. 291). Indeed, while at Hetton he attended church regularly but only as a matter of form. The point here is not so much whether
he believed or not, but rather that he did not come to terms with the issue
of belief that underpinned the code of ethics to which he subscribed.

Having attempted to escape the present moment by retreating to a comforting illusion of what nineteenth-century life was supposed to be, Tony
finds himself lifted out of history. His grimly appropriate fate is to be
trapped in a repetitive cycle of Dickensian grotesquery that mocks the
make-believe world he had tried to establish for himself at Hetton Abbey.

X

THE WISDOM OF THE EYE

Waugh generally associated barbarism with noise and civilization with vision. This was a natural corollary of his dialectic of Dionysus and Apollo, the gods of music and light respectively. So it is not surprising to discover that much of his organizational strategy springs from an inherent tension between ear and eye. Examples are virtually everywhere in the novels, but it is *A Handful of Dust* that offers the most telling. In its closing episode one of the younger inheritors of Tony Last's estate has carelessly left her two-stroke motorcycle in front of the entrance to Hetton Abbey. This detail seems innocent enough until we recall the circumstances of the accident in which Tony's son, John Andrew, met his death. It was the explosive report of a motorcycle's backfire that set the tragic event in motion. Far from innocent, the image of the motorcycle is placed where it is as an emblem of everything that has gone wrong with the world in which Tony finds himself. As a closer examination of John Andrew's accident will demonstrate, it is the explosive noise of the motorcycle that fatally signals a culture's passing.

Tony's world comes to an end the day his son joins the neighbors in a traditional fox hunt. Having learned to handle his new pony with a fair degree of competence, John Andrew is to be allowed to ride with the adults for the first part of the day's course. Among the members of the hunting party there is a Miss Ripon who, at her father's insistence, has mounted an unruly horse she does not feel confident of controlling. Her father wants to sell the horse and thinks the fox hunt a good opportunity to display the animal. But, as the villagers observe, it is "a beast of a horse to ride" and "Miss Ripon had no business out on *any* horse" (p. 139). When another member of the party decides to come out on her two-stroke motorcycle, the stage is set for disaster. As several of the riders proceed along the road, they encounter a country bus. Miss Ripon's horse begins to shy but she keeps it under control until the motor bike, running in neutral gear to let her pass, suddenly backfires with a sharp detonation. The sound thoroughly panics Miss Ripon's horse. In its scramble to get away from the motorized vehicles, the frantic animal knocks John from his own mount and kicks him in the head. The boy dies instantly. In the aftermath everyone agrees that "it was nobody's fault; it just happened" (p. 145). Repeated four times in as many pages, these words soon sound hollow, as though spoken by those in desperate search of an absolving formula. The hectic defensiveness with which everyone uses the same expression cannot but arouse the reader's suspicion. In one way, of course, the ritual-like utterance is just the simple truth: indeed, no one intended John Andrew's death. In another, however, we are made to feel that those who have resorted to this formula have entered into an unwitting complicity with forces they are either unable or unwilling to recognize.

What are these forces? They are implied by the circumstances of the accident itself which, in effect, becomes their lethal intersection. John Andrew, the heir who was to carry on the tradition Tony valued so highly, is cut down by what has so often proved a perilous fusion: commercial interest (Mr. Ripon's insistence that his horse be displayed as a salable commodity regardless of the danger it poses) and modern technology (the motorcycle and the bus). The combined forces of the twentieth century abruptly and irrevocably deprive Tony of his Victorian idyll. Mechanized speed and the manipulation of goods purely for profit—neither is conducive to a code of gentlemanly values. Tony, the last gentleman as his surname suggests, fails to realize that he lives in a society that not only tolerates but encourages an ethos of immediate gratification, which in practical terms translates as economic ruthlessness exacerbated by a carelessly managed technology.

The novel's conclusion is unmistakable on this point. With Tony thought dead in Brazil, his ancestral estate has been taken over by the formerly impoverished branch of the Last family, who have turned matters to account by scientifically breeding silver foxes in wire cages in preparation for market. So much for fox hunting, so much for tradition. Waugh had already used this conceit to satirize the decay of tradition in *Decline and Fall*. A caged fox plays an integral role in one of the more bumptious excesses of the Bollinger Club. "There is tradition behind the Bollinger; it numbers reigning kings among its past members. At the last dinner, three years ago, a fox had been brought in a cage and stoned to death with champagne bottles" (p. 1). The twentieth century expresses itself with backfiring motorcycles and caged foxes, explosive technology and exploitative commerce. These are the forces that destroy ancestral houses in order to make room for blocks of characterless one and two-room flats. The results are at once absolutely modern and perfectly primitive. In *Brideshead Revisited* Charles Ryder is informed that Anchorage House will be taken down to be replaced by a building with "shops underneath and two-roomed flats above." Having just returned from his expedition in the Brazilian wilderness, he sees the demolition of traditional architecture in favor of contemporary efficiency housing as "just another jungle moving in" (p. 232).

In order to emphasize its dual nature as a talisman of careless savagery and reckless modernity, Waugh anticipates the closing image of the motorcycle in *A Handful of Dust* with another one that is set in the jungles of Brazil. At one point in his fevered wanderings through the wilderness, Tony comes to believe he is in the midst of a group of bicyclists wheeling around him. This scene recalls all those others in which a befuddled consciousness finds itself in the midst of swirling confusion. There seems to be only one component missing to complete its reprise of the format: noise. At this point in his life, Tony is too well acquainted with modernity not to notice its absence. He has become used to associating meaningless din with the breakdown of the social and moral order; earlier in London, he had perceived the sense of futility closing in on him as an "all-encompassing chaos that shrieked about his ears" (p. 189). Conditioned as he is, he cannot resist advising the imaginary cyclists to get motor bikes because, as he explains, they are "much faster and noisier" (p. 287).

For Waugh's purposes the motorcycle was an especially apt metaphor because it combined the acoustic primitivism of *Decline and Fall's* "confused roaring" with the technological speed of Silenus's pointlessly spinning wheel. As with the race cars in *Vile Bodies*, its barbarously vulgar noise is unredeemed by any sense of civilized gain. The would-be motorcyclists of Tony's hallucination wheel about him, describing as they do an image of circular futility. This is what it is like to live without historical vision lost in the delirium of immediate experience. Instead of the poised perspective of a linear tradition unfolding from an intelligible past into a purposeful future, contemporary life has devolved into a repetitive and meaningless circuit of feverish sensations, a circuit that carries a message no more articulate than a roaring engine.

Clearly, Waugh thought that this immersion in the present moment at the expense of the historical imagination was regressive. It could only foster an increasingly primitive imagination. His characters are routinely enveloped by hubbub and tumult. This is why such a cacophony of "confused roaring" stalks his pages. As we have seen, *Decline and Fall* opens and closes with the "confused roaring" of "English county families baying for broken glass" (p. 2). The whining racing cars of *Vile Bodies* drown all possibility of intelligible speech. As if to enforce the disastrous nature of this failure to communicate rationally, the novel's final sentence closes the acoustic circuit common to the world of Waugh's satire with the image of a mechanized war loudly waged with pointless savagery: "And presently, like a circling typhoon, the sounds of battle began to return" (p. 321). The climax of *Black Mischief* occurs against the background of an African feast filled with tribal sounds: "round and round circled the dancers . . . tireless hands drumming out the rhythm; glistening backs heaving and shivering in the shadows" (p. 302). It is at this moment, immersed in the aboriginal pulse beat, that Basil Seal discovers he has inadvertently taken part in a cannibal feast in which the remains of his lover were a primary ingredient. When the eponymous hero of *The Ordeal of Gilbert Pinfold* succumbs to paranoid delusions, they manifest themselves as the encircling voices of unseen conspirators whose plots he believes he is overhearing by chance. The hallucinations that hound him to and over the precipice of madness are exclusively aural. Their lack of any visual dimension is precisely why he finds it so difficult to quell them. Guy Crouchback in the *Sword of Honour* trilogy finds the loud popular music played on the wireless by the enlisted men as an unwarranted assault on his peace of mind. But it is Tony Last's entrapment at the close of *A Handful of Dust* that best expresses the hostility between ear and eye that recurs throughout Waugh's work.

When Waugh imagined his most ghastly nightmare, it turned out to be one in which the eye is held hostage, literally hostage to the ear. In *A Handful of Dust* a civilized man finds himself trapped in a tribal setting precisely because he is literate and can read Dickens to his barbarous captor. Tony Last's fate was for Waugh a model of what he feared was happening to the contemporary world in which the fine discriminations of a literate, visual culture seemed to be in the process of being submerged by the featureless sensate life of a semiliterate, even illiterate, aural culture filled with the confused roaring of a technologically dependent people heedless of their origins in the generations that had preceded them.

Waugh's treatment of auditory space was more than a fictional conceit. His portrayal of noise as a personal and cultural affront speaks of a man who fundamentally distrusted the world of the ear. His disdain for the sense of hearing was so exaggerated that in his diaries he wrote of deafness as a blessing.

> The Church, in our last agony, anoints the organs of sense, sealing the ears against the assaults of sound. But nature, in God's Providence, does this long before. One has heard all the world has to say, and wants no more of it.[1]

Of all the senses hearing is most disconcerting to those like Waugh who are determined to keep the world at a distance. One can avert the eyes from what one does not want to see. To a limited degree, touch, taste, and smell can be kept from undesired contact. But the ear can neither be closed nor averted. It is the most passive of the senses. Least able to exert control over its circumstances, it is entirely vulnerable to its aural surrounding. Whatever defensive measures one puts up, the world can always penetrate the self's fortress through the unguarded portals of the ears. Unless, of course, one suffers a loss of hearing.

This is why Waugh did not merely celebrate his deafness, but also used it as a weapon. Claud Cockburn records a particularly apt anecdote in this regard. It concerns Waugh's mischievous use of the outsized ear trumpet he affected in his later years and is worth repeating at length.

> His ostentatious, self-dramatizing rejection of reality required, in middle life, an equally ostentatious symbol. He found it in the form of an enormous ear trumpet. He must, I suppose, have had it specially custom-built. For although in shape and general design it resembled the ear trumpets depicted in Victorian cartoons . . . it seemed larger than any ear trumpet anyone had ever used before. . . . The function of the ear trumpet was not simply to assist hearing. On the contrary, it was to emphasize and portray, in an unmistakable physical manner, the laborious difficulty its owner had in understanding any communication the modern world might be seeking to make to him.
>
> It was both an advertisement of his personal attitude, a form of rebuke, and a weapon. I once saw it thus used, inflicting terrible wounds. . . .
>
> He had come to London to attend some very high-toned literary lunch or dinner. The guest of honor and principal speaker was some pompous statesman, a member, I think, of the Cabinet, with unjustified pretensions as a scholar and writer. It was understood that he was going to use this feast as the vehicle or sounding board for a major pronouncement on the future of civilization or something of that kind. . . .
>
> The chairman spoke briefly, and the trumpet seemed to be devouring his words. Then the guest of honor rose to speak, with all the confidence of a man who had won much acclaim for wit, wisdom, and polished oratory. The receiving end of the trumpet was trained upon him. He had been speaking for perhaps a minute when Evelyn was seen to be unscrewing the thing from his head. He removed it from his ear, placed its great bulk on the tablecloth in front of him, and sat gazing intently at his plate. The guest of honor could have dealt easily with some rude heckler. But the gesture with the trumpet utterly dismayed and discomfited him. He stared at the contraption with incredulity. He paused and slightly stammered. Probably for the first time in decades of public speaking, he lost the thread of his discourse. His pronouncement to the nation rambled almost incoherently. The reporters present stopped taking notes. He sat down after speaking for less than half the time allotted to him. As he did so, Evelyn picked up the trumpet and began adjusting it once more to the listening position.[2]

And so, after a fashion, Waugh was able to triumph over the confused roaring in his later years.

Even as a young man he had little use for the world of the ear. Both Harold Acton and Christopher Sykes make this a special point of their respective accounts of him. Each recalls that for all his absorption in the esthetics of the eye, Waugh had no parallel appreciation of music. For Acton this was the only source of serious difference he had with Waugh. "There is only one rift in our lute," he wrote in 1948; Waugh "has no ear for music and can barely tell one tune from another."[3]

The tension between ear and eye was fundamental to Waugh's sense of a world divided between savagery and civilization. In his fiction, savagery always manifests itself aurally. It is typically represented as a juncture of noise and illiteracy. Civilization, on the other hand, makes itself known visually. This is especially true of all those tranquilly described scenes in which his more fortunate characters have an opportunity to contemplate the architecture of ancestral homes, if only, like Charles Ryder, in the brief interval before their razing. With this sustained argument between hearing and seeing, Waugh's novels frequently seem to be early demonstrations of the differences between aural and visual cultures that Marshall McLuhan would be diagnosing more than a quarter of a century later. In fact, in both his life and his works Waugh seems fit to be a textbook case for the media theorist, and one is surprised to discover that he is not a featured exhibit in McLuhan's work. Here was an artist who unmistakably stood at the borderland between traditional Western civilization and what McLuhan described as the technological re-tribalization of modern man. He could not have been better situated to illustrate McLuhan's theories. After all, what else is Tony Last's fate but an anticipatory parody of McLuhan's central thesis that the primitive culture of the ear has returned to dislodge the dominance of the literate culture of the eye?

I want to pursue this connection further for what it reveals of Waugh's characteristic asumptions. Before I do, however, I should say that I am not making a case for McLuhan's theories. McLuhan has been widely criticized for being overly reductive and there seems to be justice in the charge.[4] He often makes extraordinarily inflated claims for the explanatory power of ideas that seem more provocative metaphors than closely reasoned, fully supported arguments. In fact, McLuhan himself liked to hedge his bets by calling his more ingenious speculations "probes" as if to suggest their tentative nature and perhaps to allow himself some room to maneuver should they fall flat under the prodding of critical examination. However this may be, when his ideas are applied to Waugh, they make a surprising fit. To see this, it will be useful to outline McLuhan's major themes and consider how Waugh anticipated them.

In *The Gutenberg Galaxy* and *Understanding Media*, McLuhan distinguished between literate and preliterate man by examining the differences in their characteristic modes of perceiving the world and themselves. His findings led him to construct a theory of media-induced epistemologies. These, he claimed, had the power to shape minds and through them the world at large. According to McLuhan's argument, the literate man tends to be visual, individualistic, and detached, while the preliterate is aural, communal, and involved. The reasons for these differences stem from their respective means of disseminating information. Literate man in his typographical environment is above all a visual creature. He takes in the information he needs to live through his eyes, reading silently and alone. This naturally encourages the development of self-sufficient individualism. The manner in which print presents itself also plays a part in creating the characteristic Western sense of the world. As McLuhan's phrase has it, the medium is the message. The printed page with its linear arrangement of a typographically uniform phonetic alphabet exerts subliminal influences of far-reaching consequences. The phonetic alphabet alone, McLuhan contends, is largely responsible for cultivating the attitudes necessary to develop the advanced technology for which the West is at once famous and infamous. Because the phonetic alphabet is an easily manipulated code founded upon a system of signs arbitrarily attached to their referents, it has encouraged a habit of mind by which symbols are used not only to represent the external world, but also to direct it.

To demonstrate his point, McLuhan compares Western with other cultures and finds that historically the push for technological innovation has been nowhere so insistent as it has been in the West. Until this century, it did not exist with anything like a similar intensity in cultures whose literacy originated in ideographical, hieroglyphic, or pictographic writing. It was not that other peoples were without the knowledge and materials. In some instances, such as the Chinese, it could be argued that they were far more sophisticated than Occidentals. They did not have the Western way of looking at the world, however, a habit of mind first nurtured by the phonetic alphabet and later intensified by movable type. In cultures using pictographic writing, signs originate as visual approximations of their referents. The symbol is shaped to fit what it represents. Accordingly, the culture produced by this form of literacy moves people to adapt themselves, as they do their signs, to the natural world about them. Western civilization, on the other hand, has grown up with a phonetic alphabet in which individual characters do not represent anything other than a neutral sound that bears no necessary relation to anything outside itself. Unlike pictographic writing, phonetic characters were never married to particular external referents. They were always ready to be combined, disassembled, and recombined into signs whose reference to the external world is generally a function of collective usage over time. Once this maneuverability was enhanced by the advent of movable type, the resulting pattern of the printed page became the organizing grid through which the West viewed the world. The linear uniformity of mechanical typography with which Europeans began to devise written models of the world in the Renaissance led them to think of their external environment in linear terms. Space became a continuously extended field in which every effect could be understood to follow logically from an antecedent cause. The world opened as a series of perspectives that could be controlled as one could control the printed page. The characteristics of Western man's information media, McLuhan argues, have imbued him with a view of the world that is essentially technological. Under the regime of phonetic literacy and movable type, he has been disposed to think that the material objects of his environment can be as readily taken apart and reassembled as the manipulable code with which he signifies them. The world presents itself to him as an object decidedly external to himself to be perceived, evaluated, and altered under his detached, directorial eye. Bergson had traced the cause of the split between subject and object to the intellect's natural tendency to abstract from immediate experience. McLuhan argues the phonetic alphabet was a critical factor. Whatever the cause, both emphasize that this fissure between self and world stimulates a strong sense of individuality that expresses itself as the will to master material existence. But such a pronounced sense of self carries with it a liability. Stretched too far, the distance between subject and object produces feelings of alienation and impotence. This is especially true when the world frustrates typographically conditioned expectations and stubbornly resists human designs. If it is this latter experience on which Waugh's fiction dwells, this is because the world he portrays has lost its metaphysical confidence that there is any necessary congruence between mind and matter. Gilbert Pinfold looks upon the world *sub specie aeternitatis*, but cannot really manage it. Other characters assume their ideas will make sense of reality only to find reality does not share their assumption. The more sensitive retreat to unworldly sanctuaries. The thicker-skinned by virtue of their invincible ignorance stay in the game but are no more successful at imposing order on a world grown refractory in the absence of any transcendental authority.

In contrast to the literate sensibility, McLuhan's preliterate lives in a world of the ear. Under wilderness conditions in which danger is more likely to be heard before it is seen, hearing will often be more important than seeing. Consequently, a primitive's aural sensitivity will be far more acute than that of people living in a domesticated environment. He does not perceive his surroundings as a civilized person does. Space does not open into a series of indefinitely extensible perspectives ready to be arranged to his liking. Instead it is alive, vibrant, constantly surrounding and absorbing him with a ceaseless pulse of aural messages. He approaches it more in the hope of placating than mastering it. Neither able to interrupt nor direct his aural world, the preliterate experiences his surroundings and himself as a field of interpenetration. Nor does he make the sharp distinction between subject and object common to literate, visual cultures. Because he must listen to his tribal community not only to learn his tradition, but also for the information he needs to survive, he tends to have a less highly developed sense of individuality. He finds his identity in the tribal group. Further, McLuhan argues, the preliterate is not prepared to develop the technological habit of mind. With neither a phonetic nor pictographic system of writing, his symbols have limiting abstracting ability; they are not sharply distinquished from the concrete particulars they are meant to represent. He is conditioned to adapt himself to the natural world by various homoeopathic and totemic strategies. Relying on his ear for his identity and safety, preliterate man is necessarily submerged in his tribal community and immediate experience to a degree that severely limits his capacity for the Western style detachment and analytical reasoning that comprise the foundation of technology.

McLuhan makes this comparison of aural and visual cultures in order to clarify what he takes to be a basic change in contemporary consciousness. His point is that in superseding the mechanical technology of the industrial world, twentieth-century electronic technology has reorganized our sensorium. It has brought into existence an all-encompassing information environment that resembles more closely the preliterate's predominantly aural apprehension of reality than it does the literate's visual experience of it. The proliferation of information sources—many of them transmitted aurally—encircles contemporary man in an elaborate web that interconnects him with everyone else in what McLuhan calls the global village. McLuhan does not purport to evaluate this situation; he claims merely to describe it and tries to interpret what it means for man's sense of himself.[5]

The validity of McLuhan's speculations is not at question here. What is important is that the shift in cultural sensibility he describes is the same one Waugh portrayed in his fiction long before either *The Gutenberg Galaxy* or *Understanding Media.* Unlike McLuhan, however, Waugh did evaluate the change. His fiction portrays what McLuhan would later describe as the return to the auditory space of primitive consciousness. As we have seen, Waugh dramatized this as a way of apprehending the world that encouraged a kind of surrender to immediate experience. The consequence of such surrender could only lead to a sense of futility. Without the detachment necessary to rise above the sensate moment, one is deprived of the leverage necessary to put experience into any kind of manageable perspective. Or so Waugh thought. This is why so many of his novels rework the standard Candide plot. His naïfs are forever being evicted from a sequestered life into the roa·ing confusion of the present moment. From *Decline and Fall* onward, he portrayed the age's problem in terms of a fall from a tranquil perspective into the blare of disordered sensation. The possibility of a purposeful vision depends upon having the will to detach, to abstract oneself from the immediate moment. This cannot be accomplished in the world of the ear where the borders between the self and its surroundings are indistinct. It is only in the world of the eye that the individual can maintain the distance between subject and object necessary to a focused perspective.

It was Waugh's visual predisposition that led to his appreciation of what Wyndham Lewis called the Great Without, "the method of external approach . . . the wisdom of the eye, rather than that of the ear."[6] Like Lewis, he was unwilling to surrender metaphysical clarity. He assumed the self to be a rational spectator of a world that answers to the dimensions of human understanding, however much it may exceed them. Waugh's fierce determination to believe that existence made sense was his way of confronting the fear his fiction dramatized obsessively, the fear that the contemporary world had abandoned the achievement of the traditional essentialist epistemology in favor of the confused roaring of acoustic primitivism in which the individual dissolves into the communal mass. His work is one long report of what he seems to have thought was a collective lapse into an amorphous state of diminished consciousness.

Waugh is often called a reactionary and, indeed, he was, but not merely in the pejorative political sense. He was in reaction against the trend established by his immediate modernist predecessors, such writers as Proust, Woolf, and Joyce, and continued by many of his contemporaries. This was the strain of modernism that sought a new species of redemptive experience to be achieved by closing the distance between subject and object. These modernists were attempting to recreate—if only momentarily within the boundaries of their art—the prelapsarian harmony between self and world that Bergson had celebrated as the way to restore metaphysical health to a culture grown spiritually sterile. For Waugh, however, the world was irretrievably fallen. There is no redemptive sustenance to be drawn from a rapprochement of subject and object. In fact, his blessed moments, when they occur, are almost always characterized by silent detachment. Paul Pennyfeather's experience is typical. He finds the four weeks of solitary confinement he spends at Blackstone Gaol "among the happiest of his life" (p. 229). Then there are all the recluses who achieve what little peace of mind they can by living apart from others. Theirs is a negative, limiting sort of achievement that generally proves to be a remedy worse than the disease it would cure. There are, however, other more positive examples of isolation's rewards. Three instances are especially telling in this regard. The first comes from "The Balance," the second from *The Ordeal of Gilbert Pinfold*, and the third from *Unconditional Surrender* (published in America as *The End of the Battle*), the final volume of his Second World War trilogy, *Sword of Honour.*

Adam Doure, the protagonist of the 1926 story "The Balance," recalls an incident from his seventh year in which he climbed to the top of some precariously balanced nursery furniture only to have it collapse beneath him, precipitating a startling and painful fall to the floor. Looking back on it, he finds it to have been the first time he fully recognized himself to be distinct from the world about him. The experience has remained with him as his first intimation of the rewards of detachment.

> Adam had been too well brought up to remember very much of his life in the days before he went to his private school, but this incident survived in his memory with a clearness, which increased as he became farther removed from it, as the first occasion on which he became conscious of ill as a subjective entity. His life up till this time had been so much bounded with warnings of danger that it seemed for a moment inconceivable that he could so easily have broken through into the realm of positive bodily harm. Indeed, so incompatible did it seem with all previous experience that it was some appreciable time before he could convince himself of the continuity of this existence; but for the wealth of Hebraic and mediaeval imagery with which the idea of life outside the body had become symbolized, he could in that moment easily have believed in his own bodily extinction and the unreality of all the sensible objects about him. Later he learned to regard these periods between his fall and the dismayed advent of help from below, as the first promptings towards [the] struggle for detachment.[7]

The next two passages describe a very different sort of fall. Both are based on a single incident from Waugh's life which, despite its painful conclusion, also served to reveal the rewards of detachment. During his mottled career as an officer in the Second World War, he briefly undertook some parachute training. Although he seriously injured his knee on his first and last jump, he found the experience thoroughly exhilarating. "For one who values privacy there is no keener pleasure than the feeling of isolation as you float down, but it is all too short-lived, the ground is very hard and the doctors decided—as I could have told them—that I was too old to hope for many such pleasures."[8] It is this episode that turns up prominently in *The Ordeal of Gilbert Pinfold*, published in 1957.

> Once during the war [Pinfold] had gone on a parachute course which had ended ignominiously with his breaking a leg in his first drop, but he treasured as the most serene and exalted experience of his life the moment of liberation when he regained consciousness after the shock of the slipstream. A quarter of a minute before he had crouched over the open manhole in the floor of the machine, in dusk and deafening noise, trussed in harness,

crowded by apprehensive fellow-tyros. Then the despatching officer had
signalled; down he had plunged into a moment of night, to come to himself
in a silent, sunlit heaven, gently supported by what had seemed irksome
bonds, absolutely isolated. There were other parachutes all round him holding other swaying bodies; there was an instructor on the ground bawling advice through a loudspeaker; but Mr. Pinfold felt himself free of all human
communication, the sole inhabitant of a private, delicious universe. The rapture was brief. Almost at once he knew he was not floating but falling; the
field leaped up at him; a few seconds later he was lying on grass, entangled
in cords, being shouted at, breathless, bruised, with a sharp pain in the shin.
But in that moment of solitude prosaic, earthbound Mr. Pinfold had been
one with hashish-eaters and Corybantes and Californian gurus, high on the
back-stairs of mysticism. (pp. 208–9)

In 1961, the material that had gone into the making of Gilbert Pinfold's experience reappears in *The End of the Battle* when Guy Crouchback makes
his first and last parachute jump:

The harness was more uncomfortable than it had seemed on the ground.
They sat bowed and cramped, in twilight, noise, and the smell of petrol. At
length the despatching officer and his sergeant opened the man-hole. "Coming into the target area," he warned. "First pair ready." . . .
   Guy jumped. For a second, as the rush of air hit him, he lost consciousness.
Then he came to himself, his senses purged of the noise and smell and throb
of the machine. The hazy November sun enveloped him in golden light. His
solitude was absolute.
   He experienced rapture, something as near as his earthbound soul could
reach to a foretaste of paradise, *locum refrigerii, lucis et pacis*. The aeroplane
seemed as far distant as will, at the moment of death, the spinning earth. As
though he had cast the constraining bonds of flesh and muscle and nerve, he
found himself floating free; the harness that had so irked him in the narrow,
dusky, resounding carriage now almost imperceptibly supported him. He
was a free spirit in an element as fresh as on the day of its creation.
   All too soon the moment of ecstasy ceased. (pp. 129–30)

Allowing for their obvious circumstantial differences, there is a pattern
common to these passages. In each a character suffers a fall that thoroughly
unsettles his conventional habit of mind so that he is forced to recognize
his estrangement from the world of his ordinary perception. Curiously,
this sharpened awareness of his fundamental alienation does not instill the
metaphysical unease that, say, a Jean-Paul Sartre might have derived from
it. Instead Waugh's protagonists savor these experiences as moments that
foretell some future transfiguration which will render their present confusion and suffering intelligible. Between his fall and the realization of his injury, Adam Doure recognizes himself for the first time as fully distinct from
his surroundings. His experience reflects the traditional breach between

mind and matter in Western thought. While his familiarity with "the wealth of Hebraic and mediaeval imagery" sustains his sense of his own continuing identity, he doubts the reality of "all sensible objects about him," including his own body. Although the incident is painful, it does not seem to be negative. As the years go by, he recalls it with increasing clarity as one of his "first promptings towards that struggle for detachment" which is to shape the rest of his life.

Waugh's parachute training took place some seventeen years after he wrote "The Balance," and these passages in which he dealt with it imaginatively were not written for another fourteen and sixteen years respectively. Despite these intervals, when he came to write of his free-fall, it prompted reflections remarkably similar to those occasioned by the boyhood spill of his early story, but expressed in terms that unmistakably call attention to the antinomy of the loudly embattled ear and the serenely detached eye. In both parachute passages, the protagonist takes an unsettling fall through space. First, he passes out. Then, having "regained consciousness," he experiences a "moment of liberation" from the "crowded" world of "deafening noise" filled with the "smell and throb of the machine." In this moment, "his senses purged," he enters "a private, delicious universe" in which he is "absolutely isolated" in a "silent sunlit heaven" that "envelops him in a golden light." Then the moment passes; the sensible world rushes in upon him once more as he feels the pain of returning to earth.

Waugh makes sure that his readers recognize the importance of these passages and the wartime incident that gave rise to them. Without any trace of irony, the autobiographical Pinfold is said to treasure the episode "as the most serene and exalted experience of his life." The experience is, in fact, replete with religious significance for Waugh, its metaphysical implications unmistakable. It is presented as a foretaste of Elysium and Waugh even quotes from the Latin mass to describe it as a version of the "place of comfort, light and peace" *(locum refrigerii, lucis et pacis)* to which the deceased are commended by the living. This is a Platonist's model of salvation: free-fall as an intimation of one's final release from the complexities of the sensible world into the uncluttered, changeless realm of the mind, finally delivered from the gravity and noise of material existence. To be really free one must escape the enveloping treachery of the physical world. Short of that, the pain, the din, the confusion always return.

In accord with the extreme dualism of his vision, Waugh insisted upon detachment not only as the way to salvation, but also as the prudent course to take in one's daily dealings with the world. "The secret of happiness," he had written, was "to make an interior act of renunciation and to become a stranger in the world."[9] Like Pinfold, he frequently and extravagantly defied his own counsel, but he seems to have believed in its wisdom nevertheless. This put him seriously at odds with early twentieth-century modernism whose leading champions looked for deliverance from what they considered the artificial strictures of Western culture with its narrow emphasis on the detached analytical intelligence as the only way to truth. By the time Waugh had begun to publish, literary and artistic fashion had turned to a romantic existentialism that sought fulfillment by means of an ecstatic union of subject and object, self and world, a sort of secular mysticism frequently founded upon a rediscovery of an animistic interpretation of experience closer to primitive than to modern Western consciousness. The important goal was to get rid of the cultural assumptions that had been blocking one's unmediated intuition of reality. Against this movement, Waugh stood squarely and unashamedly for the Western essentialist tradition that distinguished between the unreliable world of the senses and the incorruptible region of pure ideas, between sensation and perception, between the random flow of material existence and the purposefully organizing power of mind, between the confused roaring and the wisdom of the eye.

FANATICAL EXISTENCE VS. AESTHETIC EDUCATION

This study began by asserting that Waugh resisted what he thought to be the fashionable relativism that characterized the literature and philosophy of his day. To do this, he devised an alternative to mainstream modernist fiction. As we have seen, he achieved his aim by borrowing the strategies of contemporary art and film in order to parody what had become the standard themes of modernism in the first decades of the twentieth century. The point of his early novels was to illustrate the bankruptcy of a world view divested of absolutes, and dependent upon subjective sincerity and emotional conviction for its sense of values. For all their humor, these works invariably return to the sense of overriding futility that Waugh felt to be the inescapable condition of a society that had abandoned the fixed coordinates of its essentialist tradition. In his later fiction, however, Waugh attempted to break this circle of futility with realistic novels that offered plausible responses to what he considered the bleak assumptions of the modern world.

These works—the unfinished *Work Suspended*, *Brideshead Revisited*, *Helena*, and *Sword of Honour*—are, of course, quite different from his satires, yet they share with these the same philosophical premises. In their own way they continue Waugh's resistance to conventional modernist pieties concerning the nature and function of art. To illustrate this point, we need only compare a representative passage from a writer like Virginia Woolf with one from Waugh. I have chosen the particular passages presented below for two reasons: they seem to me to typify each writer's manner, and they display these respective manners as applied to similar subjects—each excerpt describes the interior of a house. The first passage appears in Woolf's *The Waves*.

> The sun fell in sharp wedges inside the room. Whatever the light touched became dowered with a fanatical existence. A plate was like a white lake. A knife looked like a dagger of ice. Suddenly tumblers revealed themselves upheld by streaks of light. Tables and chairs rose to the surface as if they had

been sunk under water and rose, filmed with red, orange, purple like the bloom on the skin of ripe fruit. The veins of the glaze of the china, the grain of the wood, the fibres of the matting became more and more finely engraved. Everything was without shadow. A jar was so green that the eye seemed sucked up through a funnel by its intensity and stuck to it like a limpet.[1]

The second passage appears in *Brideshead Revisited.*

It was an aesthetic education to live within those walls, to wander from room to room, from the Soanesque library to the Chinese drawing-room, adazzle with gilt pagodas and nodding mandarins, painted paper and Chippendale fret-work, from the Pompeian parlour to the great tapestry-hung hall which stood unchanged, as it had been designed two hundred fifty years before; to sit, hour after hour, in the pillared shade looking out on the terrace. (p. 80)

The passage taken from *The Waves* exemplifies conventional modernism's attempt to raise ordinary experience to an occasion of extraordinary revelation. Woolf clearly wants us to see this room stripped of any preconceptions, as though dinnerware, chairs, and tables had never existed before. Her language seeks to defamiliarize the setting. To do so, it deliberately undermines our conventional mode of perceiving light and objects. She has attempted to create a moment of pure, unconditioned sensation in which the naive eye—as though untutored by previous experience of the physical world—perceives light that is as tangible as it is visual. Sunlight has the solidity of wedges and its reflection forms columnar streaks that support glass tumblers where they stand. We do not merely see this light, we *feel* the "fanatical existence" it radiates on everything it touches in this particular moment. This is all that seems to matter. There are no references either to the style or the period of the furniture, no attempts to place this room in its historical context. In fact, the language enforces the sense of a world without duration at all. The tables and chairs have just risen to the surface as if from under water and now shimmer iridescently, newborn, in the sunlight. Everything has just arrived and continues to pulse with the process of its birth; the sun has just fallen into the room; the tumblers "suddenly" reveal themselves; the wood grain and matting fibres are becoming "more and more finely engraved." What this room was before and what it will be afterward are for this moment irrelevant questions. There is only the all-consuming immediacy of the room itself.

As discussed in chapter IX, John Maynard Keynes wrote about such experiences in his essay on G.E. Moore's influence on the Bloomsbury circle. They constituted for his friends what really mattered in life. These were the occasions for cultivating "timeless, passionate states of contemplation and communion, largely unattached to 'before' and 'after.'"[2] In order to recreate this passionate state of mind, Woolf strives to fill the void between the perceiving self and the external world, reconnect mind with matter, and, in short, return to the edenic harmony between the individual and his environment. The result should ideally be a condition that precedes linguistic conceptualization and historical categories. As the eye, captivated by the jar's intense green, becomes "stuck to it like a limpet," so subject and object become sealed in a timeless moment of blissful union. This is what Bergson meant by *durée*, the unreflective experience in which one feels oneself indisputably engaged with the very life of things and overcomes the alienation that exists intellectually between perceiver and perceived. The experience is intuitive rather than cognitive. One *feels* the truth of existence in the eternal now of Becoming. It cannot be intellectually conceptualized and linguistically packaged for ready verbal communication to others, at least not with conventional discourse. Artists, however, wielding the defamiliarizing strategies of poetic language, can sometimes recreate the conditions in which such an experience becomes available, even though they cannot rationally explain it. Obviously, neither the analytical nor the historical imagination is of any use here. Accordingly, neither enters into Woolf's description.

In contrast to Woolf's timeless room, Waugh's is thoroughly historical. He *places* each part, each object according to its style and period: the Soanesque library, the Chinese drawing room, the Chippendale fret-work, the Pompeian parlor. We are meant to see this suite of rooms through the categories of the historical imagination. However charming its immediate dazzle, it is, as Charles Ryder says of architecture elsewhere in the novel, more important in its duration beyond the moment of his perception. Its significance is in its continuity, which we are invited to contemplate as Ryder has done "hour after hour, in the pillared shade looking out on the terrace." This is no occasion for metaphysical transcendence of the interval that separates the perceiver from the perceived. Instead the beholder is led to meditate on the tradition the building represents. He is asked to reflect on the significance of its structure, designed 250 years earlier so that it would provide him views of the surrounding parklands as they appear in their present fullness. On these terms, architecture is an "aesthetic education" in the original sense of the word: it leads one out of the darkness of self-absorption and subjectivity into the awareness of the external world one shares with others, a world which requires a clear understanding of the division between subject and object. With this awareness, the individual can achieve a proportionate sense of his worth and limits. For Waugh there was no salvation to be had in this world through art or any other secular means. The modern return to a type of animistic union between mind and matter was, of course, anathema to him. This is why he insisted upon keeping clear the distinction between subject and object.

Waugh's resistance to the modern attempt to make art a substitute for religion is nowhere more apparent than in *Brideshead Revisited*. This resistance is not only evident in the novel's themes but also in its style. While his earlier fiction uses figurative language sparingly, *Brideshead Revisited* is remarkable for its persistent, almost obsessive use of simile. The frequency and elaborate nature of these similes have led a number of critics to complain of the novel's ornate style and express their disappointment that Waugh had given up the spare, direct prose that had suited his ironic vision so well. But there is another way to look at this departure from the earlier style: in *Brideshead Revisited* the simile becomes the device with which Waugh opposes the assumptions that underlie conventional modernist writing. To illustrate, I have chosen five of these similes using no principle of selection other than to list them in the order they appear in the novel.

> There is no candour in a story of early manhood which leaves out of account the home-sickness for nursery morality, the regrets and resolutions of amendment, the black hours which, like zero on the roulette table, turn up with roughly calculable regularity. (p. 62)

> I knew him well in that mood of alertness and suspicion, like a deer suddenly lifting his head at the far notes of the hunt. (p. 127)

> The subject was everywhere in the house like a fire deep in the hold of a ship, below the water-line, black and red in the darkness, coming to light in acrid wisps of smoke that curled up the ladders, crept between decks, oozed under hatches, hung in wreaths on the flats, billowed suddenly from the scuttles and air pipes. (p. 163)

> Up, down and round the argument circled and swooped like a gull, now out to sea, out of sight, cloud-bound, among irrelevancies and repetitions, now right on the patch where the offal floated. (pp. 196–97)

> The indiscriminate chatter of praise all that crowded day had worked on me like a succession of advertisement hoardings on a long road, kilometre after kilometre between the poplars, commanding one to stay at some new hotel, so that when at the end of the drive, stiff and dusty, one arrives at the destination, it seems inevitable to turn into the yard under the name that had first bored, then angered one, and finally become an inseparable part of one's fatigue. (p. 270)

These selections constitute only a small sampling of the similes that appear throughout the novel. Allowing for individual variations, these figures tend to become more elaborate and extended as the narrative progresses. Two questions arise: first, why does Waugh return to the simile as his favored trope throughout this novel, and second, why does he seem to be intent upon calling our attention to this esthetic decision by making these similes so strikingly complex? The answer to both questions lies, I think, in his reaction to the modernism of his immediate predecessors.

To illustrate, let us compare Waugh's similes to Woolf's. In *The Waves* Woolf's figurative language does not point outward to the external world but rather inward to the subjective experience the external environment occasions. This I take to be what she meant when she wrote of the "luminous halo," the "semitransparent envelope surrounding us from the beginning of consciousness to the end." It was "the task of the novelist to convey" this inward experience "with as little mixture of the alien and the external as possible."[3] Accordingly, in these figures, the first terms, the objects that provoke comparisons, are not nearly as important as the second terms—the wedges of sunlight, the white lake, the dagger of ice. As we have seen, the point of this language is to appropriate externals in an ecstatic embrace of the imagination that cancels the distinction between the image and what it represents, between mind and object.

Waugh's similes have the opposite effect. They never lead to any confusion between subject and object, nor is there ever any doubt that the second term in these comparisons is subordinate to the first. However elaborately developed, the second term's purpose is always clearly illustrative. We are never in danger of fusing the two sides of the comparison in an instant of imaginative transcendence. Rather than transforming a familiar concrete object into some new and arresting sensation, the second term in these comparisons usually visualizes either a particular idea or the sequence of a character's reflections. They are not meant to defamiliarize the first term of the comparison, but rather simply to clarify it. Just as we could never mistake a statue of a blindfolded, scale-carrying woman for Justice itself, so, in the fifth simile above, we would never mistake the image of successive roadside advertising hoardings for the indiscriminate chatter of superficial praise that exhausts Charles Ryder. Waugh's similes are in the classic tradition; their second terms make public and accessible what is essentially private and unique. They are openly artificial, their function only to elucidate and elaborate.

But Waugh's use of figurative language has more than an illustrative function; it testifies to his conviction that this is an irremediably fallen world and that the only way to make it bearable is to participate in the civilized endeavor to impose order on the "anarchic raw materials of life." He thought of this endeavor as the ongoing cumulative effort of generations, the results of which could be best discerned in art which endures beyond the individual even as it shapes his life with the historical perspective it uniquely affords. This is why his similes have been constructed with Homeric elaboration, beginning with a simple comparison and then driving it through one permutation after another. They are thoroughly traditional, taking up the classical attempt to make sense of things in a way that will be communicable not only to one's contemporaries but also to future generations. Typically Waugh's simile suggests the deliberation of architecture, his favored art; it holds the two poles of its comparison in plain view, clearly separated from one another, and invites detached contemplation of its poised artifice. Their verbal construction allows for the silent space between object and figure necessary for intellectual rather than intuitive apprehension. Beyond their illustrative and decorative functions, these similes speak of Waugh's belief in the civilizing power of the word that discovers rational order in the confused roaring of our experience.

NOTES

Introduction

1. Critics representative of those who think Waugh's work lacks a consistent rationale are Donat O'Donnell (Conor Cruise O'Brien), *Maria Cross: Imaginative Patterns in a Group of Modern Catholic Writers;* Sean O'Faolain, *The Vanishing Hero: Studies in Novelists of the Twenties;* Frederick J. Stopp, *Evelyn Waugh: Portrait of an Artist;* Malcolm Bradbury, *Evelyn Waugh;* and David Lodge, *Evelyn Waugh.* With varying degrees of success, moral interpretations have been provided by Stephen Jay Greenblatt, *Three Modern Satirists: Waugh, Orwell, and Huxley,* and William J. Cook, *Masks, Modes, and Morals: The Art of Evelyn Waugh.* While all these commentators have provided important insights, it seems to me that those who have addressed both Waugh's metaphysical concerns and his personal contradictions have come closest to what makes him relevant today. Alvin B. Kernan, *The Plot of Satire,* and James F. Carens, *The Satiric Art of Evelyn Waugh,* have revealed the subtlety and complexity of Waugh's enterprise. More recently, Jeffrey M. Heath, *The Picturesque Prison: Evelyn Waugh and His Writing,* has given us an especially sensitive appraisal of how Waugh projected his personal conflicts into his fiction.

2. "Fan-Fare," *Life,* 8 April 1946, collected in *The Essays, Articles, and Reviews of Evelyn Waugh,* p. 304. In subsequent references this collection will be identified as *Essays.*

3. "The War and the Younger Generation," *Essays,* p. 62.

4. "Tolerance," *Essays,* p. 128.

5. *Decline and Fall,* pp. 1–2. Subsequent references to the Little, Brown republication edition of Waugh's works will appear parenthetically in the text.

6. Waugh subtitled this novel a conversation piece and explained in a prefatory note that Pinfold was modeled on himself.

7. O'Faolain, pp. 68–69.

8. *Labels: A Mediterranean Journal,* pp. 11–12.

9. Christopher Sykes, *Evelyn Waugh: A Biography,* p. 308. See *Evelyn Waugh and His World,* ed. David Pryce-Jones (London: Weidenfeld & Nicolson, 1973), p. 209, for a photograph of Eurich's painting.

10. "Felix Culpa," *Commonweal,* 16 July 1948, *Essays,* p. 360.

11. "Felix Culpa," p. 360.

12. "The War and the Younger Generation," *Essays,* p. 62.

I. Confused Roaring

1. This confrontation between the barbarous aristocracy and the temperate middle class seems much indebted to Matthew Arnold's *Culture and Anarchy,* from which Waugh may have also taken the title of his second novel. In discussing middle-class philistinism, Arnold declares himself "a sort of *corpus vile* to serve for illustration."

2. See Kernan, *Plot of Satire,* pp. 152–55, for a persuasive demonstration that satire naturally tends toward a circular plot because the satirist generally portrays a futile world in which progress and change are impossible.

3. Friedrich Nietzsche, *The Birth of Tragedy and The Genealogy of Morals,* trans. Francis Golffing (New York: Doubleday, 1956), pp. 34–35.

4. See Evelyn Waugh, "Come Inside," in *The Road to Damascus*, ed. John A. O'Brien (New York: Doubleday, 1949), and now collected in *Essays*, p. 367, in which Waugh recalls undertaking "an unguided and half-comprehended study of metaphysics" while at Lancing. *The Diaries of Evelyn Waugh*, include a number of brief references to his philosophical interests; the entry of 26 August 1925, p. 218, mentions he was "reading a little Bergson."

5. *Birth of Tragedy*, pp. 97, 108–9. Here and elsewhere, Nietzsche argues that the individuating categories of the intellect impose an Apollonian illusion of order and stability on the flux of existence.

6. *Birth of Tragedy*, pp. 101–2.

7. "Converted to Rome: Why It Has Happened to Me," *Essays*, p. 104.

8. *Birth of Tragedy*, p. 81.

9. Edmund Wilson, "'Never Apologize, Never Explain': The Art of Evelyn Waugh," *Classics and Commercials*, p. 146.

10. Carens, *Satiric Art*, p. 73.

11. *Labels*, p. 11.

12. Oswald Spengler, *The Decline of the West: Form and Actuality*, pp. 382, 377–428.

13. "Fan-Fare," *Essays*, p. 304.

II. Desire, Doubt, and the Superb Mean

1. "The Balance," *Georgian Stories 1926*, pp. 253–91.

2. Harold Acton, *Memoirs of an Aesthete*, p. 126.

3. Kernan, *Plot of Satire*, p. 167, considers this point but does not arrive at a definite conclusion.

4. Ronald Knox, *God and the Atom*, p. 93.

5. "The War and the Younger Generation," *Essays*, p. 62.

6. *When the Going Was Good* (Middlesex: Penguin, 1951, 1946), pp. 8, 187. In the first quotation Waugh refers to his character Charles Ryder of *Brideshead Revisited*, concluding, "Thus 'Charles Ryder'; thus myself."

7. "Half in Love with Easeful Death: An Examination of Californian Burial Customs," *Essays*, p. 336.

8. "Come Inside," *Essays*, p. 368.

9. Sykes, p. 287.

10. Sykes, p. 334.

11. "The War and the Younger Generation," *Essays*, p. 62.

12. *Diaries*, pp. 437, 443.

13. Waugh's Preface to Ronald Knox, *A Spiritual Aeneid*, p. vi.

14. "Fan-Fare," *Essays*, p. 304.

15. "Conservative Manifesto," *Essays*, pp. 161–62.

16. Martin C. D'Arcy, *The Nature of Belief* (St. Louis: Herder, 1958, 1931), pp. 65–66.

17. *Labels*, pp. 8–12; "Converted to Rome," *Essays*, pp. 103–5; and "Come Inside," *Essays*, pp. 366–68, are notable examples.

III. An Unguided and Half-Comprehended Study of Metaphysics

1. "A Modern Credo," *Oxford Broom*, 1923, I, unpaginated. A copy is held by the Humanities Research Center, University of Texas at Austin.

2. "Come Inside," *Essays*, p. 367.

3. "Come Inside," *Essays*, p. 367.

4. *Diaries*, p. 218.

5. Filippo Tommaso Marinetti, "The New Religion-Morality of Speed," *Marinetti: Selected Writing*, p. 96.

6. "Satire and Fiction," *Essays*, p. 102.

7. *The Letters of Evelyn Waugh*, ed. Mark Amory, p. 30. This is an undated note to Waugh's agent, A.D. Peters. Amory places it between October 1928 and February 1929.

8. Wyndham Lewis, "Winn and Waugh," *The Doom of Youth*, pp. 99, 106–7.

9. Wyndham Lewis, *Satire and Fiction*, p. 51.

10. "Satire and Fiction," *Essays*, p. 102. Fredric Jameson, *Fables of Aggression: Wyndham Lewis, the Modernist as Fascist*, p. 2, suggests that Lewis is read today as "a more scandalous and explosive Waugh." Put this way, Jameson's remark seems to slight Waugh for not being as ideologically extreme as Lewis. Aside from its implied devaluation, however, the assessment is a fair one. Waugh had a good deal in common with Lewis. They were especially alike in their ambivalent response to modernism. Jameson argues that Lewis fashioned his esthetic in reaction to mainstream modernism. As I argue in this and the next two chapters, Waugh also wrote in reaction to modernist fashions. He was never as systematically rigorous as Lewis, but this does not preclude the very likely possibility that Lewis served him as a model. Certainly his review of *Satire and Fiction* suggests this.

11. Henri Bergson, *Creative Evolution*, pp. 330–87.

12. Norman Mailer, "The White Negro," *Advertisements for Myself* (London: Andre Deutsch, 1961, 1957), p. 298.

13. Lewis argues throughout *Time and Western Man* against Bergson's tenets but considers his thought most closely in Book II, "An Analysis of the Philosophy of Time," pp. 131–463, which also includes discussions of Samuel Alexander, Alfred North Whitehead, and Oswald Spengler among other "time-philosophers," as Lewis called them.

14. *Satire and Fiction*, pp. 51–53.

15. *Time and Western Man*, pp. 162–259.

16. Marinetti, "The New Religion-Morality of Speed," *Marinetti: Selected Writings*, p. 96.

17. Marinetti, "The Founding and Manifesto of Futurism," *Marinetti: Selected Writings*, p. 41.

18. "Fan-Fare," p. 302.

19. Marinetti, "The Birth of a Futurist Aesthetic," *Marinetti: Selected Writings*, p. 81.

IV. A Pure Aesthete

1. Reported in Martin Stannard's review of Waugh's diaries, *New Review*, December 1976, collected in Stannard's *Evelyn Waugh: The Critical Heritage*, p. 493. The interview was conducted by John Freeman on *Face to Face*, a BBC program.

2. *Work Suspended*, in *Tactical Exercise*, p. 140.

3. "A Call to Orders," *Essays*, p. 216.

4. "The Death of Painting," *Essays*, pp. 504–5.

5. "In Defense of Cubism," *Essays*, p. 8.

6. "A Neglected Masterpiece," *Essays*, p. 82.

7. "Felix Culpa," *Essays*, p. 360.

8. *Labels*, pp. 173–82.

9. "The Death of Painting," *Essays*, pp. 503–7.

10. "A Modern Credo," I, unpaginated.

11. The exhibit was reviewed by Charensol, "Les Expositions," *L'Art Vivant*, February 1929, with some general comments about the artists included.

12. *Labels*, p. 20.

13. See reproductions in William Camfield's *Francis Picabia* (Milan: Galleria Schwarz, 1972), unpaginated.

14. See reproductions in Pamela Pritzker, *Ernst* (New York: Leon Amiel, 1975), unpaginated.

15. *Labels*, p. 14.

16. "Felix Culpa," *Essays*, p. 360.

17. Gertrude Stein, *Picasso* (London, 1939), as quoted in Wylie Sypher, *Rococo to Cubism in Art and Literature* (New York: Macmillan, 1960), pp. 310–11.

18. *Letters*, p. 215.

19. "The Balance," p. 262.

V. Smashing and Crashing: Waugh on the Modernist Esthetic

1. *Letters*, p. 270.

2. *Diaries*, p. 29.

3. *Letters*, p. 622.

4. "Fan-Fare," *Essays*, p. 302.

5. "Ronald Firbank," *Essays*, p. 59.

6. Virginia Woolf, "Modern Fiction," *Collected Essays* (New York: Harcourt, 1967), II, p. 106.

7. *Labels*, p. 181.

8. *Rossetti: His Life and Works* (New York: Dodd, Mead, 1928), p. 52.

9. *Labels*, pp. 181–82.

10. Irving Howe, *The Idea of the Modern in Literature and the Arts*, p. 14.

11. Woolf, "Mr. Bennett and Mrs. Brown," *Collected Essays*, I, p. 330.

12. Woolf, "Modern Fiction," p. 108.

13. Woolf, "Mr. Bennett and Mrs. Brown," p. 321.

14. Woolf, "Mr. Bennett and Mrs. Brown," pp. 333–34.

15. "Ronald Firbank," *Essays*, p. 57.

16. "Ronald Firbank," pp. 57–59.

17. Woolf, "How It Strikes a Contemporary," *Collected Essays*, II, p. 159.

18. "Fan-Fare," *Essays*, p. 303.

19. *When the Going Was Good*, p. 8. In the preface to this collection of his travel writings, Waugh quotes Charles Ryder at some length and then explicitly identifies Ryder's point of view with his own.

20. "Fan-Fare," p. 304.

VI. Becoming Characters: The Shameless Blonde and the Mysteriously Disappearing Self

1. Graham Martin, "Novelists of Three Decades: Evelyn Waugh, Graham Greene, C. P. Snow," in *The Modern Age*, VII of *The Pelican Guide to English Literature*, ed. Boris Ford (Middlesex: Penguin, 1961), p. 400.

2. See Waugh's review, "Satire and Fiction," p. 102.

3. "Tolerance," *Essays*, p. 128.

4. "Fan-Fare," p. 304.

5. "Felix Culpa," p. 360.

6. "Fan-Fare," p. 304.

7. *When the Going Was Good*, p. 8.

8. Kernan, *Plot of Satire*, pp. 90–103, 152–55.

9. "Fan-Fare," p. 302.

10. *Work Suspended*, as quoted by Christopher Hollis, *Evelyn Waugh*, p. 8. Hollis used the unrevised text published by Chapman & Hall, London, in 1942 in a limited edition of 500 copies. Martin Stannard, "*Work Suspended*: Waugh's Climacteric," pp. 312–13, compares the original 1942 text with the 1949 version and

finds that a good deal has been eliminated in revision, including the passage Hollis quotes.

11. "Fan-Fare," p. 302.

12. In *Diaries*, pp. 413, 418, Waugh describes the film plot he is supposed to be working on as "vulgar" and the film he watches as "appalling"; also see "Why Hollywood Is a Term of Disparagement," *Essays*, pp. 325–31.

VII. Film: The Glaring Lens of Satire

1. *Letters*, p. 2.

2. *Letters*, p. 464.

3. Sykes, pp. 55–56; *Diaries*, p. 169; The Humanities Research Center, University of Texas at Austin, kindly allowed me to screen their print.

4. "The Balance," pp. 253–91.

5. "Excursion in Reality," *Tactical Exercise*, pp. 53–69; Sykes, p. 171, discusses Waugh's work for Alexander Korda, the film producer.

6. *Labels*, p. 11.

7. "Felix Culpa," p. 360.

8. "Ronald Firbank," p. 58.

9. "Felix Culpa," pp. 362–63.

10. See Arnold Hauser, "The Film Age," in *The Idea of the Modern in Literature and the Arts*, pp. 225–35; Marshall McLuhan, *Understanding Media*, pp. 284–96.

11. "Fan-Fare," p. 303.

12. Hauser, pp. 226–34.

13. Bergson, pp. 330–35.

14. "The Balance," p. 287.

VIII. The Satirist of the Film World

1. "Felix Culpa," p. 362.

2. Martin Price, "The Irrelevant Detail and the Emergence of Form," in *Aspects of Narrative: Selected Papers from the English Institute*, ed. J. Hillis Miller (New York: Columbia University Press, 1971), p. 81.

3. Alan Spiegel, *Fiction and the Camera Eye*, pp. 92–93.

4. "Fan-Fare," p. 302; "Felix Culpa," p. 362.

5. "Ronald Firbank," p. 59.

6. "Felix Culpa," p. 362.

7. "Fan-Fare," p. 303.

8. *Labels*, p. 20.

9. Brian Wicker, "Waugh and the Narrator as Dandy," *The Story Shaped World*, pp. 155–58.

10. "Why Hollywood Is a Term of Disparagement," p. 328.

11. Virginia Woolf, "The Cinema," *Collected Essays*, II, pp. 268–72.

12. "Why Hollywood Is a Term of Disparagement," p. 329.

13. "Fan-Fare," p. 302.

14. "Why Hollywood Is a Term of Disparagement," p. 328.

15. Hauser, pp. 233–35; Spiegel, p. 32.

16. "The Balance," p. 278.

17. Woolf, "The Cinema," pp. 268–72.

IX. Chromium Plating and Natural Sheepskin: The New Barbarians

1. *Helena*, p. 47. This 1950 novel has not been republished with the others,

which is unfortunate. Whatever one makes of its apologetics, it is an entertaining historical romance with a good deal of colorful legend thrown in.

2. Alvin B. Kernan, "The Wall and the Jungle," pp. 199–202.

3. *When the Going Was Good*, p. 8.

4. *Diaries*, p. 787.

5. *Diaries*, p. 791.

6. Heath, *Picturesque Prison*, p. 381.

7. Paul Johnson, *Modern Times: The World from the Twenties to the Eighties* (New York: Harper, 1983), pp. 1–12, 697–98.

8. Claud Cockburn, "Evelyn Waugh's Lost Rabbit," p. 57, recalls that Waugh's xenophobia was so pronounced that he could not believe that Cockburn, who was his second cousin, had Hungarian relatives.

9. *Work Suspended*, in *Tactical Exercise*, pp. 157–58.

10. John Maynard Keynes, "My Early Beliefs," in *Two Memoirs* (New York: Augustus M. Kelley, 1949), pp. 83–84, 95–100.

11. Cockburn, p. 57.

12. Sykes, p. 267.

13. Cyril Connolly, *The Unquiet Grave: A Word Cycle by Palinurus* (London: Horizon, 1944), pp. 19, 49. Waugh's copy with his marginalia is in the collection of the Humanities Research Center, University of Texas at Austin.

X. The Wisdom of the Eye

1. *Diaries*, p. 788.

2. Cockburn, p. 59.

3. Sykes, p. 106; Acton, p. 127.

4. Paul Johnson, *Enemies of Society* (New York: Atheneum, 1977), pp. 149–50, argues the case against McLuhan forcefully. Like many others, however, he mistakes the media theorist's purpose. McLuhan did not intend to approve the technologically induced return to aural space; he only meant to describe it.

5. McLuhan, pp. 22–55, 77–88.

6. Lewis, *Satire and Fiction*, p. 53. Certainly Waugh's review of Lewis's book ("Satire and Fiction," *Essays*, p. 102) displays an enthusiastically admiring tone uncharacteristic of the urbane pose his other pieces cultivate.

7. "The Balance," p. 287.

8. *Letters*, p. 181.

9. *Diaries*, p. 787.

XI. Fanatical Existence vs. Aesthetic Education

1. Virginia Woolf, *The Waves* (1931; rpt. New York: Harcourt, 1959), pp. 109–10.

2. Keynes, p. 83.

3. Woolf, "Modern Fiction," p. 106.

SELECTED BIBLIOGRAPHY

Novels by Evelyn Waugh

The following works by Evelyn Waugh were republished by Little, Brown & Co., Boston, between 1977 and 1982. Each title appears with the date of its original publication.

Decline and Fall, 1928.
Vile Bodies, 1930.
Black Mischief, 1932.
A Handful of Dust, 1934.
Scoop, 1938.
Put Out More Flags, 1942.
Brideshead Revisited, 1945.
The Loved One, 1948.
Men at Arms, 1952.
Officers and Gentlemen, 1955.
The Ordeal of Gilbert Pinfold, 1957.
The End of the Battle (Unconditional Surrender), 1961.
Charles Ryder's Schooldays and Other Stories, 1982.

Other Works by Waugh

"The Balance." In *Georgian Stories 1926*. Volume 4. Ed. Alec Waugh. London: Chapman & Hall, 1926, pp. 253–91.

The Diaries of Evelyn Waugh. Ed. Michael Davies. London: Weidenfeld & Nicolson, 1976.

Edmund Campion. New York: Doubleday, 1946, 1956.

The Essays, Articles, and Reviews of Evelyn Waugh. Ed. Donat Gallagher. Boston: Little, Brown, 1983.

Helena. Boston: Little, Brown, 1951, 1950.

Labels: A Mediterranean Journal. London: Duckworth, 1930.

The Letters of Evelyn Waugh. Ed. Mark Amory. New York: Ticknor & Fields, 1980.

A Little Learning: An Autobiography. Boston: Little, Brown, 1964.

A Little Order. Ed. Donat Gallagher. London: Eyre Methuen, 1977.

Mr. Loveday's Little Outing and Other Sad Stories. London: Chapman & Hall, 1936.

Monsignor Ronald Knox. Boston: Little, Brown, 1959.

Ninety-Two Days. New York: Farrar & Rinehart, 1934.

Preface to Ronald Knox. *A Spiritual Aeneid*. 1948. Rpt. London: Burns, Oates, 1958.

Remote People. London: Duckworth, 1931.

Robbery under the Law: The Mexican Object-Lesson. London: Chapman & Hall, 1939.

"Ronald Firbank." In *Life and Letters*. Volume 2. March 1929, pp. 192–94.

Rossetti: His Life and Works. London: Duckworth, 1930.

Scott-King's Modern Europe. Boston: Little, Brown, 1949.

Sword of Honour. One-volume edition. London: Chapman & Hall, 1965.

Tactical Exercise. Boston: Little, Brown, 1954. (Includes *Work Suspended*.)

Tourist in Africa. Boston: Little, Brown, 1960.

Waugh in Abyssinia. London: Longmans, Green, 1936.

When the Going Was Good. London: Duckworth, 1946

Secondary Sources

Acton, Harold. *Memoirs of an Aesthete*. London: Methuen, 1948.

Bergonzi, Bernard. "Evelyn Waugh's Gentlemen." *Critical Quarterly* 5 (1963), pp. 23–36.

Bergson, Henri. *Creative Evolution*. Trans. Arthur Mitchell. New York: Random House, 1944, 1911.

Blazac, Alain. "Technique and Meaning in *Scoop*: Is *Scoop* a Modern Fairy-Tale?" *Evelyn Waugh Newsletter* 6 (1972), pp. 1–8.

Bradbury, Malcolm. *Evelyn Waugh*. Edinburgh and London: Oliver & Boyd, 1964.

Burgess, Anthony. *The Novel Now: A Guide to Contemporary Fiction*. New York: Norton, 1967.

Carens, James F. *The Satiric Art of Evelyn Waugh*. Seattle: University of Washington Press, 1966.

Cevasco, George A. "Huysmans and Waugh." *Evelyn Waugh Newsletter* 17 (1983), pp. 5–7.

Churchill, Thomas. "The Trouble with *Brideshead Revisited*." *Modern Language Quarterly* 28 (1967), pp. 213–28.

Cockburn, Claud. "Evelyn Waugh's Lost Rabbit." *Atlantic* 232 (December 1973), pp. 53–59.

Cook, William J. *Masks, Modes, and Morals: The Art of Evelyn Waugh*. Rutherford: Fairleigh Dickinson University Press, 1971.

Coxe, Louis O. "The Protracted Sneer." *New Republic* 8 (November 1954), pp. 20–21.

Davis, Robert M. *Evelyn Waugh*. St. Louis: Herder, 1969.

———. "Evelyn Waugh on the Art of Fiction." *Papers on Language and Literature* 2 (1966), pp. 243–52.

———. *Evelyn Waugh, Writer*. Norman: Pilgrim Books, 1981.

———. "*Harper's Bazaar* and *A Handful of Dust*." *Philological Quarterly* 48 (1969), pp. 508–16.

———. "The Mind and Art of Evelyn Waugh." *Papers on Language and Literature* 3 (1967), pp. 270–87.

———. "Notes towards Waugh's Aesthetic." *Evelyn Waugh Newsletter* 18 (1984), pp. 1–2.

———. "Title and Theme in *A Handful of Dust*." *Evelyn Waugh Newsletter* 6 (1972), p. 1.

Delbaere-Farant, J. "'Who Shall Inherit England?': A Comparison between *Howards End*, *Parade's End*, and *Unconditional Surrender*." *English Studies* 50 (1969), pp. 101–5.

Dennis, Nigel. "Evelyn Waugh: The Pillar of Anchorage House." *Partisan Review* 10 (July-August 1943), pp. 350–61.

DeVitis, A.A. *Roman Holiday: The Catholic Novels of Evelyn Waugh*. New York: Bookman, 1956.

Dooley, D.J. "Waugh and Black Humor." *Evelyn Waugh Newsletter* 2 (1968), pp. 1–3.

Doyle, Paul A. *Evelyn Waugh: A Critical Essay*. Grand Rapids: Eerdmans, 1969.

———. "Waugh's *Brideshead Revisited*." *Explicator* 24 (1966), Item 57.

Dyson, A.E. "Evelyn Waugh and the Mysteriously Disappearing Hero." *Critical Quarterly* 2 (1960), pp. 72–79.

Eagleton, Terry. *Exiles and Emigres*. New York: Schocken, 1970.

Farr, D. Paul. "Evelyn Waugh: Tradition and a Modern Talent." *South Atlantic Quarterly* 68 (1969), pp. 506–19.

———. "Waugh's Conservative Stance: Defending 'The Standards of Civilization'." *Philological Quarterly* 51 (1972), pp. 471–84.

Frank, Joseph. "Spatial Form in Modern Literature: and "The Dehumanization of Art." In *The Widening Gyre: Crisis and Mastery in Modern Literature.* New Brunswick: Rutgers University Press, 1963.

Frye, Northrop. *Anatomy of Criticism.* Princeton: Princeton University Press, 1973, 1957.

Fussell, Paul. "Evelyn Waugh's Moral Entertainments." In *Abroad.* New York: Oxford University Press, 1980.

Gill, Richard. *Happy Rural Seat: The English Country House and the Literary Imagination.* New Haven: Yale University Press, 1972.

Greenblatt, Stephen Jay. *Three Modern Satirists: Waugh, Orwell, and Huxley.* New Haven: Yale University Press, 1965.

Greene, Donald. "Evelyn Waugh's Hollywood." *Evelyn Waugh Newsletter* 16 (1982), pp. 1–4.

Hauser, Arnold. "The Film Age." In *The Social History of Art.* Collected in *The Idea of the Modern in Literature and the Arts.* Ed. Irving Howe. New York: Horizon, 1967, pp. 225–35.

Heath, Jeffrey M. *The Picturesque Prison: Evelyn Waugh and His Writing.* Montreal: McGill-Queen's University Press, 1982.

Hollis, Christopher. *Evelyn Waugh.* London: Longmans, Green, 1954.

Howarth, Herbert. "Quelling the Riot: Evelyn Waugh's Progress." In *The Shapeless God: Essays of Modern Fiction.* Ed. Harry J. Mooney and Thomas F. Staley. Pittsburgh: University of Pittsburgh Press, 1968, pp. 67–69.

Howe, Irving. *The Idea of the Modern in Literature and the Arts.* New York: Horizon, 1967.

Hynes, Joseph. "Varieties of Death Wish: Evelyn Waugh's Central Theme." *Criticism* 14 (1972), pp. 65–77.

Hynes, Samuel. *The Auden Generation: Literature and Politics in the 1930s.* New York: Viking, 1977.

Jameson, Fredric. *Fables of Aggression: Wyndham Lewis, the Modernist as Fascist.* Berkeley: University of California Press, 1979.

Jebb, Julian. "Evelyn Waugh: An Interview." *Paris Review* 8 (1963), pp. 73–85.

Jervis, Steven A. "Evelyn Waugh, *Vile Bodies,* and the Younger Generation." *South Atlantic Quarterly* 66 (1967), pp. 440–48.

Kaplan, Stanley R. "Circularity and Futility in *Black Mischief.*" *Evelyn Waugh Newsletter* 15 (1981) pp. 1–4.

Kenner, Hugh. *The Pound Era.* Berkeley: University of California Press, 1971.

Kermode, Frank. "Mr. Waugh's Cities." In *Puzzles and Epiphanies.* London: Routledge & Kegan Paul, 1962, pp. 164–75.

Kernan, Alvin B. *The Plot of Satire.* New Haven: Yale University Press, 1965.

———. "A Theory of Satire." In *The Cankered Muse: Satire of the English Renaissance.* New Haven: Yale University Press, 1962, 1959, pp. 1–36, 192—246.

———. "The Wall and the Jungle." *Yale Review* 53 (Winter 1963), pp. 199–220.

Knox, Ronald. *God and the Atom.* London: Sheed & Ward, 1945.

Kosok, Heinz. "The Film World of *Vile Bodies.*" *Evelyn Waugh Newsletter* 4 (1970), pp. 1–2.

Lane, Calvin W. *Evelyn Waugh.* Boston: Twayne, 1981.

———. "Waugh Incunabula." *Evelyn Waugh Newsletter* 17 (1983), p. 4.

Lewis, Wyndham. *Satire and Fiction.* London: Arthur Press, 1930.

———. *Time and Western Man.* 1927. Rpt. Boston: Beacon, 1957.

———. "The Vorticist." *Vogue* (September 1956). Collected in *Wyndham Lewis on Art: Collected Writings 1913–1956.* Ed. Walter Michel and C.J. Fix. New York: Funk & Wagnalls, 1969.

———. "Vortices and Notes." In *Wyndham Lewis on Art: Collected Writings 1913–1956.*

————. "Winn and Waugh." In *The Doom of Youth*. New York: Robert McBride, 1932.

Linck, Charles E., Jr., and Robert M. Davis. "The Bright Young People in *Vile Bodies*." *Papers on Language and Literature* 5 (1969), pp. 80–90.

————. "Waugh-Greenidge Film—*The Scarlet Woman*." *Evelyn Waugh Newsletter* 3 (1969), pp. 1–7.

Linklater, Eric. "Evelyn Waugh." In *The Art of Adventure*. London: Macmillan, 1948, pp. 44–58.

Littlewood, Ian. *The Writings of Evelyn Waugh*. Oxford: Basil Blackwell, 1983.

Lodge, David. *Evelyn Waugh*. New York: Columbia University Press, 1971.

Marcus, Steven. "Evelyn Waugh and the Art of Entertainment." *Partisan Review* 23 (Summer 1956), pp. 348–57.

Marinetti, Filippo Tommaso. *Marinetti: Selected Writings*. Ed. R.W. Flint. Trans. R.W. Flint and Arthur A. Coppotelli. New York: Farrar, Straus, 1971.

McCaffrey, Donald W. "*The Loved One*: An Irreverent, Invective, Dark Film Comedy." *Literature/Film Quarterly* 11 (1983) pp. 83–87.

McLuhan, Marshall, *Understanding Media: The Extensions of Man*. New York: McGraw-Hill, 1964.

Mikes, George. "Evelyn Waugh." In *Eight Humorists*. London: Wingate, 1954, pp. 131–46.

Nichols, James W. "Romantic and Realistic: The Tone of Evelyn Waugh's Early Novels." *College English* (October 1962), pp. 45–56.

O'Donnell, Donat (Conor Cruise O'Brien). *Maria Cross: Imaginative Patterns in a Group of Modern Catholic Writers*. London: Oxford University Press, 1952.

O'Faolain, Sean. *The Vanishing Hero: Studies in Novelists of the Twenties*. London: Eyre & Spottiswoode, 1956.

Phillips, Gene D. *Evelyn Waugh's Officers, Gentlemen and Rogues*. Chicago: Nelson-Hall, 1975.

Pritchett, V.S. "Cleverest English Novelist Alive." *New Statesman and Nation* (May 7, 1949), p. 473.

Pryce-Jones, David, ed. *Evelyn Waugh and His World*. Boston: Little, Brown, 1973.

Slater, Ann Pasternak. "Waugh's *A Handful of Dust*: Right Things in Wrong Places." *Essays in Criticism* 32 (1982), pp. 48–68.

Spengler, Oswald. *The Decline of the West: Form and Actuality*. New York: Knopf 1976, 1926.

Spiegel, Alan. *Fiction and the Camera Eye: Visual Consciousness in Film and the Modern Novel*. Charlottesville: University Press of Virginia, 1976.

Stannard, Martin. "Debunking the Jungle: The Context of Evelyn Waugh's Travel Books." *Prose Studies* 5 (1982), pp. 101–26.

————. *Evelyn Waugh: The Critical Heritage*. London: Routledge & Kegan Paul, 1984.

————. "*Work Suspended*: Waugh's Climacteric." *Essays in Criticism* 28 (October 1978), pp. 312–26.

Stopp, Frederick J. *Evelyn Waugh: Portrait of an Artist*. Boston: Little, Brown, 1958.

Sykes, Christopher. *Evelyn Waugh: A Biography*. Boston: Little Brown, 1975.

Ulanov, Barry. "The Ordeal of Evelyn Waugh." In *The Vision Obscured: Perceptions of Some Twentieth-Century Catholic Novelists*. Ed. Melvin J. Friedman. New York: Fordham University Press, 1970, pp. 79–93.

Wasson, Richard. "*A Handful of Dust*: Critique of Victorianism." *Modern Fiction Studies* 7 (1961–62), pp. 327–37.

Waugh, Alec. *My Brother Evelyn and Other Profiles*. London: Cassell, 1967.

Wicker, Brian. "Waugh and the Narrator as Dandy." In *The Story Shaped World.* Notre Dame: University of Notre Dame Press, 1975.

Wilson, Edmund. "'Never Apologize, Never Explain': The Art of Evelyn Waugh" and "Splendors and Miseries of Evelyn Waugh." In *Classics and Commercials.* New York: Farrar, Straus, 1950, pp. 140–46, 298–305.

Woolf, Virginia. "The Movies and Reality." *New Republic* (4 August 1926).

Worcester, David. *The Art of Satire.* New York: Russell & Russell, 1960, 1940.

INDEX

Absolutes, 2, 17, 35, 36; lack of, 82, 91, 96–97, 109, 169
Abstract art, 48, 55–58, 62, 143
Acton, Harold, 21, 29, 36, 159–60
Adultery (infidelity): in *Brideshead Revisited*, 96; in *Handful of Dust*, 77, 82, 88, 115–16, 140; in *Vile Bodies*, 115
Aeneas, 90
Alphabet: role in literacy, 161–63
Anarchy, 7, 21, 27, 29, 55
Anaxagoras: Nietzsche on, 15
Ancestral (country) homes, 73–74, 160; in *Brideshead Revisited*, 74, 97, 156–57; in *Decline and Fall*, 4, 73; in *Handful of Dust*, 14, 74, 79–81, 84, 88, 136–37, 156
Apollonian, the, 13–14, 18, 155, 176n.5; need for the Dionysian, 28; seen in Pacabia, 59
Architecture, 51, 52, 53–55, 66–68, 160; role in Waugh's fiction, 73–74, 136–37, 145, 171. See also *Ancestral homes*
Arnold, Matthew: *Culture and Anarchy*, 175n.1
Art, 32, 48, 51–63, 87, 169, 171; Bergson's influence on, 45; criticism of, 66–67, 103; film as, 101–102; and narrative style, 40; role in *The Loved One*, 143
Artificiality, 71, 125
Audience, film, 103, 130–31, 132
Authority, 11, 24–25, 114, 162
Automobiles. *See* Cars
Automobilism, 47, 48
Avant-garde, 49–50, 51–52, 62, 71, 87, 101

"Balance, The," 21, 48, 63–64, 134; cinematic structure in, 101, 107–108; portrayal of detachment in, 164–65, 166–67
Barbarism (primitivism; savagery), 29, 34, 136–54, 157; associated with sound, 155, 157–58, 160, 162–63, 164; and Becoming, 43, 44; in *Black Mischief*, 77; in *Decline and Fall*, 9, 10–11; and film, 134–35, 137; in *Vile Bodies*, 25
Bauhaus movement, 6–7, 12
Becoming, 38–39, 46, 48, 57, 86, 109; Bergson on, 39, 41–43, 46, 49, 106–107; and characterization, 90–91; film as portrayer of, 102, 106–107; Lewis on, 40, 43–44; parodies of, 106; portrayal of, in *Decline and Fall*, 16, 23, 40–41; portrayal of, in *Vile Bodies*, 38, 40, 46–47, 48, 63, 76; and the primitive mind, 147, 148; as reality, 13–14; and relativism, 82
Being, 13–14, 38–39, 57, 102; Bergson on,

39, 41–43; Lewis on, 43–45; portrayal of, in *Vile Bodies*, 38, 46, 48
Bennett, Arnold, 69, 73
Bergson, Henri, 37–49, 54–55, 105–107, 109, 162, 164, 171
Binary oppositions. *See* Polarities
Birth of Tragedy, The (Nietzsche), 13–14
Black Mischief, 21, 25, 77, 137–39; cinematic editing in, 125–27; role of sound in, 157–58
Blast, 39
Bloomsburianism, 148–49, 170–71
Brideshead Revisited, 30, 32, 35, 169, 170, 171–73; characterization in, 79, 91, 95–97; cinematic techniques in, 113, 127; portrayal of detachment in, 143; role of architecture in, 73, 74, 156–57
Butler, Samuel, 39

Camera, 55–56; as metaphor, 100–101, 105–106, 117; narrator compared to, 110–11, 120, 123
Cannibalism, 122, 158
Carens, James F., 16–17, 175 n.1
Cars (automobiles), 60, 63, 157, 158; as metaphors, 38, 39, 43, 46–48
Catholicism. *See* Roman Catholicism
Cemeteries, 29, 143–45
Chaos, 15, 49, 62, 116
Characterization, 69, 73–74, 75–98
Cinematic technique, 110–35, 137; Bergson on, 106–107; use by Firbank, 72, 102; use by Waugh, 99–101, 103, 105. *See also* Film
Circular plot, 11, 175 n.2
Civilization, 2, 19, 41, 43, 89, 95–96; associated with vision, 155, 160–63; juxtaposed with barbarism, 29, 137–54; portrayal of, in *Decline and Fall*, 10–11, 15
Classical education, 89–90, 92–93, 97
Classicism, 13, 18–19, 92, 98, 103; and romantic energy, 27, 29; Waugh's support of, 51, 54–55
Close-ups: use in fiction, 110–12, 114–15
Cockburn, Claud: on Waugh's use of ear trumpet, 159
Commitment, 97, 109
Common Man, age (century) of the, 47, 130–31, 132
Complete (whole) man, 89–90, 91–92, 96, 97, 98
Connolly, Cyril (Palinurus), 150
Conrad, Joseph, 34, 140
Consciousness, 105, 120, 135, 163

186

Consciousness, primitive, 43, 44, 163
Conservatism, 21, 40, 55, 70–71, 142, 148
Contradictions, 29–30, 51; in art, 57, 58; in "Excursion in Reality," 132–33
Counterpoint, 21, 71–72, 78, 137–40
Country homes. *See* Ancestral homes
Creative Evolution (Bergson), 43, 47, 106
Cubism, 52, 58, 62
Culture and Anarchy (Arnold), 175 n.1

Dandyism, 123–24
D'Arcy, Martin, 34–35
Daughter Born without a Mother, The (Picabia), 59
Dead, The (Joyce), 111
Deafness, 158–59
Death, 14, 63, 85–86, 93, 156; view of, in *The Loved One*, 25, 144–45
"Death of Painting, The," 55
Decency, 14–15, 34, 156
Decline and Fall, 3, 6, 8–17, 19, 101, 156; acoustic primitivism in, 157; characterization in, 77, 78, 84, 95; cinematic technique in, 119, 120, 123; detachment in, 143, 164; disguises in, 49; as parody, 92–94, 104; polarities in, 21–25, 33–34, 39; role of architecture in, 4, 73; role of Becoming in, 40–41, 48
Decline and Fall of the Roman Empire (Gibbon), 17
Decline of the West, The (Spengler), 17–19
Dehumanization, 59, 125, 129, 131
Desire, 12, 54, 57
Despair, 37, 62, 114–15, 124
Detachment, 78, 121–25, 142, 143, 147, 163–67
Detail: use of, 110–21, 139–40
Dickensian, 132, 154
Dionysian, the, 13–14, 16, 18, 23, 28, 59
Dionysus, 13, 155
Director: narrator as, 120–25
Discontinuity, 125–30
Disguise: Waugh's use of, 49
Disorder, 9, 30, 112, 117; film as portrayer of, 102–103, 105. *See also* Order
Dr. Jekyll and Mr. Hyde (Stevenson), 32–34
Doubles, 21
Drastic, 31, 57
Durée, 42, 44, 48, 171
Durrell, Lawrence, 127
Dynamic, 12–13, 31, 48, 101

Ear trumpet: use by Waugh, 159
Economics, 90–91, 130–31, 156
Education, 89–90, 91, 92–93, 97
Egalitarianism, 130–34
Elan vital, 46, 54
Electronic technology, 163
Emotions, 41, 104, 146–47, 151
Empathy, 123
End of the Battle, The (Unconditional Surrender), 19–20, 164, 166. *See also Sword of Honour*
Energy, 22, 23; in opposition to order, 8, 21, 57, 58
Entertainment, 71, 121, 130
Epic journey, parody of, 92–94
Epistemology, 17, 56, 105, 109, 148, 164; Bergson on, 41–42, 44–45; McLuhan on, 160–63; in modernism, 68, 70, 72; relativistic, 134; Spengler on, 18
Ernst, Max, 58–61, 63, 65, 121
Essay on Man (Pope), 37
Essence, 38–39, 44–45
Essentialism, 38–39, 41, 46, 49, 164, 168
Esthetics, 28, 49–50, 51–65, 87, 99; and film, 103, 104, 130–31; Lewis on, 45, 78; Marinetti on, 47–48; of modernism, 66–74; and use of similes, 173; Woolf on, 67–68
Ethnocentricity, 146
Eurich, Nicholas, 5
"Excursion in Reality," 90–91, 101; cinematic techniques in, 127–28, 134; portrayal of filmmaking in, 131–34
Existence, 38–39, 44–45, 46, 54, 164; Bergson on, 42, 43; Lewis on, 44
Existentialism, 38–39, 45, 48, 49, 168
Experience, 49, 59, 115, 125, 163, 170–71; Bergson on, 41–43; Lewis on, 44; and modern art, 56; relationship to ideas, 12, 18; relationship to reason, 108–109, 121; role in modernist epistemology, 68, 70
Eyeless in Gaza (Huxley), 127

Faith, 35, 37, 45, 86–87, 95
Fanaticism, 24–25
Farce, 99, 104, 118
Fiction and the Camera Eye (Spiegel), 111
Figurative language, 172–74. *See also* Metaphors; Similes
Film, 98, 99–109, 137, 179 n.12; "The Balance" viewed as, 21, 101; Waugh's application to fiction, 110–35. *See also* Cinematic technique
Firbank, Ronald, 71–73, 74, 78, 98, 121; use of cinematic techniques, 102, 104
Flight (flying), 4–5, 59–62, 83
Flux, 46, 49, 54–55, 63
Forgetting, 90–91, 134
Form, 43–44, 57
Formlessness, 57
Forms, Platonic, 18, 31, 44–45
Free-fall, 166–67
Free will, 33
Freud, 28
Futurism, 7, 39, 47–48, 49, 61, 98; Lewis on, 43, 56; in painting, 58–59
Futurist Manifesto (Marinetti), 39, 47

Gaudi i Cornet, Antonio, 53–55, 57, 66–68
Generational division: satirized, 21

Gibbon: *Decline and Fall of the Roman Empire*, 17
Global village, 163
Great War (World War I): effects of, 28, 37
Greene, Graham, 102, 104, 110, 121
Gulliver's Travels (Swift), 33
Gutenberg Galaxy, The (McLuhan), 160
Hallucinations: role in *Handful of Dust*, 152–53, 157; role in *Ordeal of Gilbert Pinfold*, 120; role in *Vile Bodies*, 60, 63, 107, 108–109
Handful of Dust, A, 14–15, 64, 74, 155–56, 157–58; barbarism juxtaposed with civilization in, 136–37, 139–40, 143, 147, 150–54; characterization in, 77, 79–89, 94, 95; cinematic techniques in, 115–16, 120, 123–24
Hauser, Arnold, 103, 104–105, 134
Hearing, 158–60, 164, 167; as world of the preliterate, 162–63. *See also* Noise
Heart of Darkness (Conrad), 140
Heath, Jeffrey, 142, 175 n.1
Helena, 97, 140, 169, 179–80 n.1
Heroism, 14, 19, 90, 92–95
History, 79, 145, 147, 153–54, 157
Hitler-Stalin nonaggression treaty (1939), 30–31, 95
Hollis, Christopher, 178–79 n.10
Honor, 124; code of, 16–17, 19
Howe, Irving, 68
Humanism, 71, 83, 87
Human nature, 18, 33–35, 36, 40–41, 70
Humor, 21, 38, 121, 124, 169
Huxley, Aldous, 127

Identity, 38, 73, 75, 127, 129, 163
Illiteracy, 160–63
Illusion, 13–14, 176 n.5
Imagery: in film, 103, 108–109
Imagination, 57, 99, 145, 157
Impulse, 20, 27, 28, 54, 142; relationship to reason, 12, 21–27, 30, 32; role in Waugh's behavior, 149. *See also* Will
"Incident in Azania," 122–23
Incivility (rudeness): as characteristic of Waugh, 30
Incoherence, 110–20
Individualism, 43, 44, 161
Individuality, 82, 133, 162–63
Infidelity. *See* Adultery
Intellect, 20, 41–42, 54, 104, 121; Bergson on, 105–107; Lewis on, 40, 43–44; Nietzsche on, 176 n.5; Woolf on, 70. *See also* Reason
Intelligence, unifying, 70
Intelligibility, 38, 72
Intuition, 41–43, 46, 104, 106–107
Irony, 27, 40, 55, 78, 111, 123, 142; in *Brideshead Revisited*, 96; in *Decline and Fall*, 17; in "Excursion in Reality," 128, 132–33; in Firbank's works, 71; in *Hand-*

ful of Dust, 152; in *Sword of Honour*, 30
Isolation: rewards of, 164–67

Jameson, Fredric, 177 n.10
Johnson, Paul, 142
Joyce, James, 34, 45, 111, 130; Waugh on, 52, 66
Justine (Durrell), 127
Juxtaposition, 137–54

Kernan, Alvin B., 112, 140–41, 175 n.1
Keynes, John Maynard, 148–49, 150, 152, 170–71
Knowledge. *See* Epistemology
Knox, Ronald, 27–28, 31

Labels, 4–5, 57–59, 60–61
Language, 41, 132
Lawrence, D. H., 6, 34
Leveling, 130–34
Lewis, Wyndham, 39–41, 43–47, 51, 56, 81, 177 n.10; on characterization, 77–78; on film, 103, 135
Light: Woolf's perception of, 169–70
Literacy: McLuhan on, 160–63
Literature, 103; Waugh on, 32, 51, 66–74
Loved One, The, 25, 65, 134–35, 143–46; background for, 29, 101; characterization in, 81; cinematic techniques in, 128–30

McLuhan, Marshall, 103, 160–63, 180 n.4
Mailer, Norman, 42
Mann, Thomas, 34
Marinetti, Filippo Tommaso, 39, 47–48, 49, 137
Metaphors, 46, 101, 109, 110–11, 146–47; camera as, 106, 107; film as, 127, 131; McLuhan's theories as, 160; use in *Decline and Fall*, 24, 48; use in *Ordeal of Gilbert Pinfold*, 100–101, 105–106, 107
Metaphysics, 14, 36–50, 119, 148, 167; and art, 53, 55; of modernism, 68, 162; and morality, 2–3, 4, 14–15
Mimesis, 57, 118–19
Mind: camera as metaphor for, 100–101, 105–106, 107, 117
Mockery, 32, 78, 90, 111, 116
Modern art, 6, 48, 51–53, 56–57, 63
"Modern Credo, A," 36, 57
Modernism, 5–7, 62, 154, 164, 168; Lewis on, 45, 177 n.10; in literature, 66–74; Waugh's alternative to, 169–74
Modernity, 3, 5, 31, 110; portrayal of, in *Handful of Dust*, 136–37; portrayal of, in *Vile Bodies*, 21, 25; and primitivism, 144, 156–57; women as representatives of, 18–19, 25, 80, 83–86, 93
"Modest Proposal, A" (Swift), 122
Montage, 102, 105, 125, 134, 137, 142
Moore, G. E., 148, 170–71
Morality, 2–3, 4, 16, 19, 28, 116; Blooms-

burians on, 148–49; Lewis on, 44; and principles, 14–15, 17, 32, 82; relativism in, 29, 33, 82; and satire, 2, 16–17; and sin, 20, 33
Motivation, 77, 81
Motor cars. *See* Cars
Motorcycles, 155–56, 157
Music, 103, 159–60

Narrative technique, 40, 52, 70–71, 78, 120–25; use of details, 110–20; used by Greene, 121; Woolf on, 67
Narrator: compared to camera's eye, 110; as director, 120–25
Nature of Belief, The (D'Arcy), 34–35
Nietzsche, 13–14, 15, 18, 176 n.5
Nihilism, 63, 86
Noise, 155, 157–58, 160, 164. *See also* Hearing
Nothingness, 63
Notoriety: Waugh's courting of, 39

Object: as distinct from subject, 43, 106, 162–63, 164, 172, 173
Odysseus, 90, 93–94
Ontology. *See* Being
Opposites. *See* Polarities
Ordeal of Gilbert Pinfold, The, 3, 97, 158; camera as simile in, 100–101, 105–106, 107; cinematic technique in, 117, 120; detachment in, 143, 164, 165–66, 167
Order, 21, 27, 29, 59, 111–12, 162; creation of, 87, 98, 118–20; in existence, 118–19; narrator as imposer of, 120–21; Nietzsche on, 15, 176 n.5; in opposition to energy, 57, 58; in opposition to flux, 63; role in *Decline and Fall*, 8, 9–11, 15, 17; use of cinematic techniques to portray, 115, 116; and Waugh's characterizations, 78, 98. *See also* Disorder
Ortega y Gasset, 6
Oxford Broom, 36, 57

Palinurus (Cyril Connolly), 150
Panorama de l'art contemporain, 57–58
Parachute jumping, 4; sense of detachment during, 165–66, 167
Parody, 13–14, 19, 92, 104, 106, 169; in *Black Mischief*, 126–27; mimesis as, 119; in *Ordeal of Gilbert Pinfold*, 117; Picabia's paintings as, 59; in *Vile Bodies*, 45–47, 63
Passivity, 27, 43–44
Pathetic, 31, 57
Perception, 42, 72, 171
Philosophy, 13, 37, 40. *See also* Metaphysics
Phonetic alphabet: role in literacy, 161–63
Photography: and painting, 55–56. *See also* Camera
Picabia, Francis, 58–61, 62, 65, 121
Picasso: Stein on, 62
Pictographic writing, 161

Plato, 36, 38
Platonic forms, 18, 31, 44–45
Polarities (binary oppositions), 19, 21–35, 57, 63–65, 117–18
Politeness, 122
Politics: Waugh's stands on, 30–31
Pope: *Essay on Man*, 37
Preliterate man: McLuhan on, 160, 162–63
Price, Martin, 111, 112
Primitive consciousness, 43, 44, 163
Primitive sensibility, 146, 153
Primitivism. *See* Barbarism
Principia Ethica (Moore), 148
Principles, 3, 29, 32, 37, 82, 97; and law, 16; and heroism, 90; Lewis on, 45
Proprieties, 8, 115–16
Proust, 66
Psychology, 40, 69, 71; role in characterizations, 76, 78–79, 80
Purpose, 111, 118–19, 142; lack of, 66, 78, 127

Race cars, 60, 63, 157, 158; as metaphors, 38, 39, 47–48
Reactionism, 100, 148, 164
Realism: in film, 132, 135; in modernism, 70, 71; in Waugh's late fiction, 169
Reality, 13–14, 66, 70, 109; Bergson on, 41–42, 106–107; experience of, 162, 163; Lewis on, 44–45, 46; as represented in film, 134, 135; Waugh on, 15, 45, 46, 117
Reason, 20, 54, 59, 108; abdication of, 6; and emotions, 147; Lewis on, 43, 45; relationship to will, 12, 14–15, 17, 21–27, 30, 32, 34–35, 142, 146; role in *Dr. Jekyll and Mr. Hyde*, 33; role in *Gulliver's Travels*, 33. *See also* Intellect
Rebirth: in *Decline and Fall*, 14
Referents: role in literacy, 161
Relativism, 45, 46, 82, 90–91, 169; in film, 134; moral, 29, 33, 82
Religion, 97–98, 167; role in *Brideshead Revisited*, 95–96, 97; role in *Decline and Fall*, 24; role in *Handful of Dust*, 15, 87, 95. *See also* Roman Catholicism
Representation, 42; in film, 69, 135
Representational art, 55–56
Repression, 27–28, 33
Resurrection: parody of, 93
Roman Catholicism, 31–32; role in *Brideshead Revisited*, 91, 96; Waugh's conversion to, 15, 30, 37
Romanticism, 42, 67–68, 70; and classicism, 18–19, 27, 29
Rudeness (incivility): as characteristic of Waugh, 30
Russia: Waugh's views on, 30–31
Salvation, 68, 167–68, 171–72
Satire, 2, 4, 20, 40, 43, 78; on abdication of authority, 24–25; on barbarism juxtaposed with civilization, 141; in *Handful of*

Dust, 86, 88; on modernism, 154; and morality, 16–17, 33–34; polarities in, 27, 29–30, 32, 59, 63–64; use of cinematic techniques, 99, 101, 102, 104, 112, 117–19, 121–22, 124–25, 128–29; use of circular plot, 175 n.2; use of mockery, 90; use of modernist esthetic, 68, 74; in *Vile Bodies*, 21, 157

Satire and Fiction (Lewis), 40

Savagery. *See* Barbarism

Scarlet Woman, The (film), 101

Scoop, 64–65, 84, 90–91; cinematic techniques in, 108, 117–19, 120, 121–22, 127

Scott-King's Modern Europe, 89, 94

Self, 85, 127, 162, 164; role in modernism, 68, 69–70, 74

Sensation, 6, 41, 127, 163, 170, 173; role in film experience, 103, 108–109; role in modernist epistemology, 68

Sensationalism, 130

Sensibility, 55, 100, 115, 146, 153

Sentimentality, 21, 40, 123, 143

Shadow: protagonist as, in *Decline and Fall*, 14, 92

Shame: produced by satire, 2, 20

Significant detail, 110–12, 115, 139–40

Signs: role in literacy, 161

Silent film, 21, 101, 102, 127

Silenus (in mythology), 13

Similes, 100, 116, 172–74

Sin, 20, 33

Slice of life, 56

Snobbery, 131

Social History of Art (Hauser), 104

Society, 19, 69–70, 118–19

Space, 103, 162

Speed, 47, 49, 60, 63, 156, 157

Speed kings, 48

Spengler, Oswald: *Decline of the West*, 17–19

Spiegel, Alan, 111, 112, 134

Spiritual Aeneid, A (Knox): Waugh's introduction to, 31

Spitting: significance in *Handful of Dust*, 139–40

Spontaneity, 149–50

Stability, 13–14, 82, 86, 102, 176 n.5; relationship to Being, 38, 46

States of mind, 148, 149–50, 151

Static, 12–13, 31, 49, 101

Stein, Gertrude, 45, 62

Stevenson, Robert Louis: *Dr. Jekyll and Mr. Hyde*, 32–34

Story Shaped World (Wicker), 123

Stream of consciousness, 49

Stunt flying, 4–5

Subject: as distinct from object, 43, 106, 162–63, 164, 172, 173

Subjectivism, 45, 78, 173

Subjectivity, 66–67, 68, 69, 71

Subversive detail, 112–20

Suicide, 21–22, 29, 124–25, 130; role in "The Balance," 64, 107, 134

Superb mean, 25–27, 51

Superficiality, 40, 76, 87

Surrealism, 49, 63, 73, 135; in painting, 58, 59

Swift, Jonathan: *Gulliver's Travels*, 33–34; "A Modest Proposal," 122

Sword of Honour, 36, 97, 158, 169; characterization in, 84, 94–95; detachment in, 164, 166; polarities in, 21, 27

Sykes, Christopher, 5, 159

Symbols, 41; and literacy, 161–63

Sympathy, 121, 123

Technology, 156, 161–63

Thing-in-itself, 42, 46

Thomism, 34–35

Thought, 12, 14, 54, 57

Time, 56; as aspect of film, 103–104, 105; Bergson on, 42–43, 105; role in civilization/primitivism dialectic, 146, 152–54

Time and Western Man (Lewis), 39, 40, 43–46

To the Lighthouse (Woolf), 67

Tradition, 4, 6, 19, 29, 34, 100; in architecture, 137; and art, 54; and conservatism, 27; loss of, 78, 128, 156, 157; role in *Brideshead Revisited*, 95, 171; role in civilization/savagery dialectic, 143, 145, 146; role in *Decline and Fall*, 17, 19; role in *Handful of Dust*, 79–80, 85–86, 88–89; role in *Vile Bodies*, 37, 114; in tribal communities, 163

Transcendance, 68, 87, 97, 173

Transiency, 84, 86

Typography, 161–62

Ulysses (Joyce), 66

Unconditional Surrender (The End of the Battle), 19–20, 164, 166. *See also Sword of Honour*

Understanding Media (McLuhan), 160–63

Unquiet Grave, The (Connolly), 150

Unreality, 127

Vile Bodies, 25, 36–37, 39, 49, 59–63, 157; characterization in, 75–76, 77, 81, 94; cinematic techniques in, 112, 114–15, 119–20, 123, 124–25, 127; parody of filmmaking in, 101, 107, 108–109, 131; polarities in, 21, 25–27, 57, 59–63; role of cars in, 38, 46–48, 60, 63

Vision, 155–68

Vortex, 46, 49

Waves, The (Woolf), 169–71, 173

Whitehead, Alfred North, 39, 44

Whole man. *See* Complete man

"Why Hollywood Is a Term of Disparagement," 130–31

Wicker, Brian, 123

Will, 14, 18, 20, 32; Lewis on, 40, 44; relationship to reason, 12, 14, 21–24, 30, 34–35, 142, 146. *See also* Impulse

Wilson, Edmund, 15

Woolf, Virginia, 34, 66–70, 72, 73–74, 169–71, 173; on film, 130, 135; Lewis on, 45

Wordsworth, 70

Work Suspended, 21, 97–98, 146–47, 169, 178–79 n.10; characterization in, 79; on modern art, 51–52

World War I (Great War): effects of, 28, 37

Writing, types of: and literacy, 161–63

Xenophobia, 180 n.8

Yeats, 34

Zeitgeist, 6, 51, 82

GEORGE McCARTNEY teaches English and film courses in St. Vincent's College at St. John's University. His articles have appeared in several publications, including *National Review* and *The American Spectator*.